Emma Hornby is the author of *A Shilling for a Wife*, *Manchester Moll*, *The Orphans of Ardwick* and *A Mother's Dilemma*. Before pursuing a writing career, she had a variety of jobs, from care assistant for the elderly to working in a Blackpool rock factory.

She was inspired to write because of her lifelong love of sagas and after researching her family history; like the characters in her books, many generations of her family eked out life amidst the squalor and poverty of Lancashire's slums.

Emma lives on a tight-knit working-class estate in Bolton with her family.

You can follow her on
🐦 Twitter @EmmaHornbyBooks
f Facebook at www.facebook.com/
emmahornbyauthor
www.emmahornby.com

www.penguin.co.uk

Also by Emma Hornby

**A SHILLING FOR A WIFE
MANCHESTER MOLL
THE ORPHANS OF ARDWICK
A MOTHER'S DILEMMA**

and published by Corgi Books

A DAUGHTER'S PRICE

Emma Hornby

CORGI BOOKS

TRANSWORLD PUBLISHERS
61–63 Uxbridge Road, London W5 5SA
www.penguin.co.uk

Transworld is part of the Penguin Random House group of companies
whose addresses can be found at global.penguinrandomhouse.com

Penguin
Random House
UK

First published in Great Britain in 2020 by Bantam Press
an imprint of Transworld Publishers
Corgi edition published 2020

A CIP catalogue record for this book
is available from the British Library.

ISBN 9780552175760

Typeset in 11/13.25pt ITC New Baskerville by Jouve (UK), Milton Keynes.
Printed and bound in Great Britain by Clays Ltd, Elcograf S.p.A.

Penguin Random House is committed to a sustainable
future for our business, our readers and our planet. This book
is made from Forest Stewardship Council® certified paper.

1 3 5 7 9 10 8 6 4 2

For my mum, with love and thanks. Keep on dreaming! And my ABC, always x

God bless these poor folk that are strivin'
By means that are honest an' true,
For some'at to keep 'em alive in
This world that we're scramblin' through . . .

Edwin Waugh, Lancashire poet

Chapter 1

LAURA CANNOCK WRAPPED a scrap of cloth around the handle of the black-bottomed kettle and lifted it from the belly of the fire. The soft hiss as she poured hot water into the teapot, scalding the dark leaves within, whispered through the dimly lit kitchen, mingling with her sigh as she glanced once more at the clock.

How will I tell him? she asked of herself again, her sorrow mounting. *Yet more worry, more disappointment to be heaped upon that good man's shoulders. I should have listened, should have heeded his warning* ... 'But I didn't,' she added out loud. 'I thought I knew best. And now we're paying the price.' *Why, why did I come back here?*

Eyes burning with unshed tears, she brought down two plates from a wooden rack and dished out their evening meal of potatoes and back bacon – his favourite. She'd prepared it specially; some small token to make up for the nightmare telling to come. Of course, it was ridiculous. As though a bit of grub could compensate for what she'd brought about! But what else was there? How in God's name else *could* she portray how heartsore she was about this? Shaking her head, she set to cutting the small loaf.

A flurry of noise from below told her that their landlady, Mrs Hanover, was preparing to close shop – hasty farewells to the last stragglers, the jingle of the bell atop the door as she shut out the final customer of the day – and Laura's stomach dropped further. For all too soon the familiar clop of hooves would sound below the window, heralding her father's impending return, and the words she'd have done anything to bite back for ever more would have to be given life. God help her . . .

All was as it should be, as it was each night, when Amos Todd finally entered their small rooms. Dragging her eyes up to greet him, Laura could manage but a half-smile.

'Hello, Father.'

'Lass.' He dipped his chin in weary acknowledgement.

'You look fit to drop. Come, sit by the fire, rest awhile, whilst I finish dishing up. A sup of tea first, though, I think.' She inclined her head to his well-worn chair then returned her attention to the teapot, grateful for the distraction.

After adjusting the sacking that protected the seat's cushion from the dirt of his trade, Amos eased his large frame into it with a gruff groan. He accepted the steaming mug, wrapping it in his shovel-like hands and closing his eyes, as though to soak up the heat and thus new life into himself.

As far back as Laura could remember, he'd always be stripped of his work clothes, and his coal-dust-ingrained body scrubbed in the tin bath, before taking the weight off at the day's end. Lately, however, he couldn't seem to garner the energy to complete his ablutions without a brief rest upon his return. When this change had taken place, she couldn't rightly say. Certainly, in the few weeks she'd been back beneath his roof, she'd noticed the shift in routine.

Was the hard graft that came with life as a coalman becoming too much for him of late? she wondered again now. It was true to say he wasn't getting any younger, after all. Not that he'd ever admit to it. Not her father, never. His pride, she knew, wouldn't allow it. *I should be looking after you, now, Father, at your time of life, as you've allus done for me. And yet . . . yet . . .* Just what make of daughter was she? She didn't deserve him. She *didn't.*

For several minutes, the flames' soft crackles and Amos's steady breathing were the only sounds. Any other evening, she'd have welcomed this with blessed thankfulness. Since her return, she'd relished this time of day. Her father home from a day's toil, their meal together and light chatter. Afterwards, the companionable silence as they sat facing one another by the good fire, she busy with her darning, he smoking his pipe, the pewter world beyond their window shut out, leaving it just the two of them, just as she wanted, for no one else was needed. Content. Safe. Now, the quiet felt ominous. The clock's ticking appeared louder, her heartbeat the same. Now it was ruined, changed for ever.

For her father's sake, she must leave here once more. Only this time, she must never, ever come back.

Amos placed his empty mug on the hearth and crossed to his bedroom. Laura heard him fill the wash bowl with fresh warm water from the pitcher, followed by soft splashes as he rinsed his hands and face. He returned to the kitchen and took a seat at the table, and she rose to serve him his meal. All the while, it took every inch of her will to stop her eyes straying to his kind, weathered face. Let him eat first. Leave him in his ignorance just a little while longer. *Just a little longer, before I must shatter his heart for a second time . . .*

'Eeh.' Behind his drooping white moustache, his lips shifted in a smile as she placed his dish in front of him.

'Your favourite, Father.'

'Aye.'

'Eat up afore it grows cold,' she instructed softly, lifting her own fork from the table, despite doubting she'd ever get a morsel past the lump in her throat.

Throughout the meal, Amos paused to study her once or twice; she'd felt his stare boring into her bowed head. It was only when he'd retired back to the fireside, his clothes now changed and the body beneath them clean, and sat filling his pipe that he spoke.

'Is tha for telling me what's afoot, then?'

His quiet voice brought instant tears to her eyes. Quickly, she blinked them away. Keeping her back to him, she continued returning the washed dishes to the cupboard. *Please, don't make me say it . . .*

'Laura?'

Letting her hands fall to her sides, she dropped her head to her chest. 'Father . . .'

'Look at me.'

She turned. Her fingers plucked at her apron as her gaze travelled up to meet his.

Amos's voice was barely above a whisper: 'Tell me.'

'They . . . They've been here.' She watched him close his eyes for the briefest moment then blow a steady plume of blue smoke towards the ceiling. 'Father. I . . . must . . .'

'They saw thee? They were here at the house?'

'Nay, nay.' God above, that that even needed asking. She'd not be here this minute – not breathing at any rate – were that the case. 'Mrs Hanover downstairs came up to see me earlier. She described them down to a T. Dark-haired, the pair were. Had an uncanny way about them, she said, amongst the rest. It were them, Father, it was, it *had* to be—'

'Come. Sit thee down. Now, from the beginning,' her father instructed when she'd dropped, gulping back sobs, into her chair. 'What exactly did Mrs Hanover say?'

'There were two men. Seems they were calling at every premises they passed . . . They were in the shop below asking questions.'

'What questions?'

'They asked whether she knew of anyone by the name of Laura Cannock.'

Releasing air slowly, Amos rubbed at the whiskers on his chin.

'Glory be to God, Mrs Hanover didn't much trust the look of them so said that she never.'

Again, Amos breathed deeply. 'When was this?'

'Shortly before noon.' She reached for his hand and stroked it softly. 'Father. It's time. I must—'

'You'll do nowt of the sort.'

'But Father—'

'Nowt of the sort,' he repeated in a fierce whisper, fingers tightening around hers.

After a long silence, she lifted her chin. Dry-eyed, voice firm, she shook her head. 'I'll not see thee hurt.'

'Nor I thee. So. We must plan what we're to do.'

'We . . . ? Nay.' Her head swung again in horror-filled refusal. 'This is my mess and mine alone. I must leave, *must*. I'll not see you dragged into—'

'I'm your father.'

'Oh, Father.' The last of Laura's resolve broke. 'Why didn't I listen to thee? You had Adam Cannock marked right from the start, yet I was blinded by infatuation, couldn't see it . . . How has it come to this?'

'Past is the past. It's ahead to which we must look, now. You're my lass. I'm with thee on this, on owt, now and forever. You hear?'

5

This from him, a man of so few words, uttered in his own calm tone, fed her veins with strength – and pulverised her spirit with the pain of it all in equal measures. She knew he spoke the truth; never in her life had Amos Todd let her down. *But the risk, the danger . . .*

'I loathe what I'm doing to thee. Please let me go.' Though she knew a last-ditch attempt to spare him would fall on deaf ears, she had to try. 'Adam's brothers . . . they'll not rest till they find me, Father. Should you stand beside me in this, it's your blood they'll be baying for, an' all. Please . . . *Please.*'

'You're my lass,' he repeated huskily, enveloping her in his bear-like embrace, and she allowed further protest to die on her lips. For as much as she hated herself that he'd become embroiled in the nightmare that was now her life, the relief of his alliance, his attempt at protection, was impossible to shake.

'Together,' she heard herself murmur. And her father's steady response, without hesitation:

'They don't stand a bloody chance.'

'My mind's made up, Laura. We leave for Manchester first thing.'

Manchester. A city that lay some ten miles away but might as well have been the other side of the world, for all she knew of it. Leave here? This smoggy, cotton-mill-choked town that was Bolton – all she knew and loved – for ever? More importantly, all her father knew and loved? A lifetime of memories, his dear wife, her mother, sleeping the eternal sleep beneath the earth at nearby St Peter's this past year? He'd never bear it. *I'll never bear it!*

'Our Ambrose shall see us right, fret not.'

Uncle Ambrose, her father's brother. A man whom

she'd met no more than a handful of times in her twenty-three years. *Oh, this was madness.*

'Been mithering me since your mam passed, he has, to up sticks and join him in his business. And ay, I'd sooner be lining his pockets than someone else's. Aye. Happen now's as good a time as any, is the kick I needed.'

He was being overly optimistic to salve her guilt, she knew. Truth was, the upheaval would shatter his heart. And yet . . . What choice was there? He'd never see her face this alone, and remaining here was an impossibility now *they* were on the prowl. The Cannock brothers. The devil's own sons, rotten to the marrow, *merciless* in their dealings . . . Mrs Hanover downstairs might not have given them what they wanted to know – what if others in the vicinity did? Father, as usual, was right. They had to leave this place completely, get right away from here, away from the accusations. And the sooner the better, for both their sakes.

'Kenneth will be up to the journey?' Laura asked now. Her father's bay-coloured shire was much more than just a working horse; he was a firm member of the family. She'd hate for him to overexert himself on the long trek.

'Aye. He's a tough 'un.'

She nodded. The sacks of coal, several tons in weight, that he hauled around the town each day on the cart was testament to that. However, like her father, the gentle giant wasn't growing any younger. In their time of life, the pair should have been taking things easier. Would Uncle Ambrose prove a fair master? She certainly prayed so. Hopefully, the new direction they were set to embark upon would prove more satisfactory to their health than their present situation. As they said, after all: a change was as good as a rest.

'Not much to pack up, anyroad,' Amos stated.

Looking around at their meagre possessions, Laura nodded. They shouldn't have any trouble getting the few sticks of furniture they owned on to the cart.

She made for a battered chest in the bedroom and returned with a large sheet. 'I'll bundle up our bits and pieces in this.' She nodded to the material, which she'd spread out on the table. 'Meantime, Father, go on through and get some shut-eye. Rest,' she pressed him when he made to protest. 'Else you'll be fit for nowt come the morrow.'

When he'd gone she paused and looked around. A lifetime of remembrance swirled around her like a whispery hug, making her want to weep again.

'How did it come to this?' she asked of the emptiness.

The answer flitted forth in the shape of another memory, only this was one she battled her every waking hour to keep at bay. She swallowed hard.

Her husband of four years, dead. An upturned clog on the middle stair, lost during the fall. Clear green eyes she'd first fallen in love with, which she'd never have believed in the beginning but was later to discover could hold such fearsome rage, staring unseeing at the ceiling. Long limbs twisted beneath him at unnatural angles. The spread of dark red beneath his head on the hall flagstones . . .

'Not my fault,' she mouthed, squeezing her eyes tight. 'Whatever his brothers believe, Adam Cannock *didn't* lose his life at my hands.'

With effort, she banished the image from her thoughts and returned to the task at hand.

Hints of gold and cream were smudging the navy sky, heralding dawn's approach, when Laura went to rouse her father. She hadn't slept a wink herself, the impending journey heavy on her mind, and was saddened to see that Amos didn't appear to have snatched much either. The shadows beneath his grey eyes and the strain within them tore at her. Had he been fretting away the twilight hours, too? Was all this proving too much for him, his state of health? Lord how she detested herself for putting him through this! Murmuring that she'd brewed a fresh pot of tea and that she'd pour him a sup whilst he dressed, she escaped back to the kitchen.

Joining her minutes later, Amos stopped dead in his tracks. Slowly, his gaze took in the bare room. The few pictures and cheap ornaments that had been her mother's pride and joy, the rag rug from in front of the fire, along with the curtains and few pots and pans, were safely packed in the bedsheet, now standing in readiness by the door atop their stacked bits of furniture. For a long moment he stood, taking in every inch, as though to engrave the place in his mind for ever. Then he nodded once and crossed to the table for his mug of tea.

'I could collect Kenneth and the cart from Mr Johnson's, Father, let you rest a while longer afore we leave?' Laura offered, sounding brighter – for his sake – than she felt. But Amos shook his head.

'Nay, it has to be me. I must explain to him our leaving, thank him face to face for his kindness these past years in letting me keep the horse at his. Anyroad, I'm rested well and good, no need to fuss.'

This last statement from him she didn't believe, but she nodded nonetheless. However, he was right about one thing: Mr Johnson did deserve a proper goodbye from his long-time friend. As her father said, without him allowing them to house Kenneth in his yard on nearby Bradshawgate for a few pence a week – their landlady hadn't the room on her premises – they would have been at a loss. The men would miss each other, she knew, the knowledge of which served only to stab her conscience further.

'I'll call by the coal yard on t' way, leave a message with one of the lads for the boss that I've terminated my employment.'

A good thing he was going to Uncle Ambrose and need not worry about a character reference, and no mistake. His master would have likely spat in his eye had he asked for one, she reckoned, what with Father leaving like this without giving notice. *Oh, please let everything work out well in Manchester . . .*

'Be ready to leave on my return,' Amos continued quietly as he donned his rough jacket and cap. 'Meantime, bolt yon door and don't open it to no one. I'll not be long.'

Laura did as he bid her and passed the time alone by wandering from room to room, rechecking all was prepared and that they were not leaving anything behind. Finally, her father's voice sounded from the landing; she unlocked the door and let him in. Searching his face, she raised her eyebrows. 'All set?'

'Kenneth's waiting outside.'

'I'll go on down with this, shall I?' she asked, lifting the bedsheet.

'Aye. Wait for me on t' cart.'

Despite what she'd said, she made no attempt to leave. The bundle clutched to her chest, she gazed at the man in front of her. When the tears came, she let them run down her face, and her eyes told him of her heartbreak and crippling guilt, and of her love. With a calloused palm, he wiped her cheeks dry. Then he lifted his chin in resolution and guided her around by the shoulders towards the door. Doing her best to match his strength, she gulped back her emotion and descended the stairs.

Within minutes, their worldly possessions were piled on the cart. Joining Laura on the narrow seat behind the horse's rump, Amos lifted the reins. A final glance towards their dwelling, then he commanded Kenneth: 'Move on, lad!' and they were off.

'I feel terrible that we're leaving Mrs Hanover's without saying goodbye,' Laura said, refusing to look back as they trundled through Ashburner Street.

'I left a message for her with Mrs Blake next door; she promised to pass it on.'

Eyes widening, she turned to him. 'You didn't make mention of Manchester, Father . . . Did you?'

'Fret not, I were vague. Our true and honest thanks, along with regret we had to go, were the top and bottom of it; no more, no less.'

No one would track them down, Laura told herself, breathing a little easier. She might have mentioned her uncle in passing many moons ago to Adam, but doubted he'd relayed the information to his brothers. Glory be to God, they would soon be safe.

'It'll shortly be over, lass.' This from Amos, as though he'd read her thoughts, swelled her heart further for this man she loved with everything that she was.

'They believe me a murderess, but they're wrong, Father,' she whispered.

'Aye.'

Was he completely certain of her innocence? she wondered, not for the first time, shooting him a sidelong look. Would it have made a difference either way? The black hatred he'd held for her brutish husband was

11

no secret – did he much care about the circumstances surrounding Adam's demise so long as he was gone from here and could no longer hurt her? She hadn't the answers. Nor was she sure that it mattered. His loyalty and support told her all she needed to know and more.

They drew to a halt as they approached her mother's resting place. Gazing out across the age-beaten gravestones, they spoke silently to her what was in their hearts and said their goodbyes. Once again, they set off.

By now, a little more light touched the sky. Wisps of milky blue traced thin fingers through the darkness, whilst the arc of white moon added its own dying shimmer.

Laura knew she shouldn't, knew it would make the loss harder to bear, but the pull was too strong; biting her lip, she stole a final look at her home over her shoulder – and a scream caught in her throat.

Above the huddle of buildings they had just left behind, a cloud of thick black smoke and orange flames raged towards the heavens. The inferno that was Mrs Hanover's shop was a sight straight from hell.

They would never stop until they found her. She'd been a fool to hope otherwise.

The Cannock brothers' reign of revenge had only just begun.

Chapter 2

'BROTHER. IT'S GOOD to see thee.'

'Amos, lad? By! Are my eyes deceiving me?'

Figuring he'd find Ambrose here, Amos had directed the horse straight to his place of business in the heart of the bustling city.

Like her father, Ambrose Todd was a mountain of a man. White-haired, with thick mutton-chop whiskers of the same shade and the same pale grey eyes, he cut a striking figure. The only marked differences were her uncle's demeanour – what Amos lacked in outgoingness, the lively Ambrose made up for, for the pair of them – and his sharp apparel. No mucky working man's clothes for him but a proper suit in smart dark brown. A coal merchant with his own yard, Ambrose employed others to toil for him, hadn't the need to sully his hands. Like Amos, he, too, had started out delivering the precious fuel that this country's very survival depended upon. Be it through good fortune or sheer determination, that he'd progressed further up the ladder of success than his brother was plain to see.

Laura climbed down from the cart; tired, aching and emotionally wrung dry.

Snapping from the hypnotic sight of devastation, they had urged Kenneth onwards and fled Bolton

13

without another backward glance. Over the hours and miles to get here, bitter tears and recriminations had been in constant supply – *damn* those Cannocks to all hell's horrors! As she'd dreaded might happen, a local must have inadvertently informed them where she dwelled during their probing of her whereabouts. Poor, dear Mrs Hanover: all she'd worked for, gone in the blink of an eye. For what? Had their wreaking destruction been merely a message, a warning, of what they were capable of, what horrors awaited her, should they find her? Or, as she secretly feared, had they thought her present? Had they meant for her to perish in that fire?

If she and her father hadn't left when they did . . . had they dallied just a matter of minutes longer . . . To dwell upon the consequences turned her stomach inside out with bilious terror. And just what would they concoct once they realised their plan of evil had failed, that she lived and breathed still? God help her.

Scattering the plague of worries from her mind and returning her attention to the here and now, she hung back as the men shook hands. That they were pleased to see one another was clear; despite everything, the corners of her mouth lifted at the gladsome greeting.

'And who's this, then?' Ambrose teased, catching sight of his niece. 'Eeh, tha gets bonnier each time I see thee.' Leaning in, he pressed his lips to her cheek. 'No husband with thee, lass?'

She and Amos exchanged a look. It was the latter who answered: 'Well, you see, our Laura's been a widow this month past.'

'Ay, lass. It's sorry I am to hear that. It don't seem two minutes since the wedding.'

'Thank you, Uncle Ambrose.' Forcing a sniff, she bowed

her head. She and her father had agreed on the journey here to keep the truth of things between themselves. The fewer who knew how matters stood, the better.

'Adam, he . . . he died in an accident,' Amos added. 'At work.'

The older man clicked his tongue several times sympathetically. 'And so young. Mind, it's thankful you, lass, must try to be that no babbies resulted from your time together, eh? I imagine it's a damned hard struggle providing for a family alone.'

'Aye.' However much she wanted children one day, she, too, had mused more than once on this being a blessing in disguise.

'So.' Ambrose looked from one to the other. 'You're well, the pair of youse?'

Amos nodded. 'Aye, and thee?'

'Oh, gradely, aye.' Curiosity lurked behind his smile. Finally, he threw his arms in the air, bursting out, 'Well, don't leave me in suspense, then, lad! To what do I owe the pleasure this fine day?'

'Well, I'm here to stay if you're for having me. Having us, I mean,' Amos amended with a nod to Laura and the horse.

Lifting his hat and scratching his head, Ambrose blew out air slowly. 'By. It's took thee long enough, eh?'

'Aye, well. I'm here now.'

'That you are.'

In the ensuing silence Laura glanced from one man to the other, and dread rolled through her. This wasn't quite the reaction to the news she'd pinned her hopes upon. Had her uncle changed his mind about her father relocating here? Was it the fact Amos wasn't alone that was the problem? Had her presence ruined the one option open to them?

15

'There's life in t' owd lad yet,' Amos stated, patting Kenneth's long neck. 'Same goes with me.'

Ambrose nodded, and Laura held her breath. Then her heart pounded with relief as, a slow smile spreading into a grin, her uncle laughed and clapped his brother on the back. 'It's happy I am to hear it, an' all. Eeh, come here.' He pulled Amos into a firm embrace. 'Welcome to Manchester. 'Ere, and thee, lass,' he added with a wink, giving her hand a squeeze.

Laura and her father exchanged a small, discreet smile. *Thank you, Lord.*

'You could do with a sup of summat warm inside you, I'll bet.' Ambrose turned and beckoned a man across. 'Clough, unharness my brother's horse, here, and see he gets a good feed and rub down.'

The whites of his eyes standing out starkly from a face lost beneath a thick layer of black dust, his employee nodded. 'And the cart, sir?'

'Erm . . . wheel it over to the corner of the yard for now. It don't look like we're due rain; its cargo shall be safe enough. Well, go on, then, get on with it.'

After flashing Laura a cheeky smile – for which he received a swift kick up the backside from his boss – he took Kenneth's bridle and, grinning, led him off to a row of stable-like constructions.

'Impertinent swine, that Nathan Clough,' Ambrose said as he watched him go. 'Doesn't know his place, that one, nay. It's a different kind of boot he'll be getting if he carries on the way he is – right through the bloody gates.'

Though Laura accepted her uncle's apologetic smile for what he deemed his worker's caddish behaviour, she had to bite her lip to suppress a chuckle. Nathan had only smiled at her, after all; hardly a criminal offence.

16

And yet a warmness settled inside her for this relative who clearly also had her best interests at heart. With him *and* her father to protect her, she wouldn't go far wrong.

'Now then.' Jerking his head, Ambrose strode away, adding over his shoulder, 'Come along to the office.'

They passed beneath a wide archway displaying a black sign in bold green lettering – A.T. Coal Merchants – and into a good-sized yard. This was a hive of activity. Men and boys, some occupied in shovelling coal from huge mounds that dotted the ground, others heaving the filled sacks on to their shoulders to take to waiting carts, attached to which patient horses stood at the ready, barely gave them a glance. Laura, on the other hand, soaked up everything in sight with interest. The strength of these muscle-bound men – even the youths, set to be as powerfully built with time – amazed her, and gave her a new-found respect for her father.

He'd been a coalman all her life and, though she knew he laboured hard, she hadn't really wondered nor appreciated just how much until now. His job was his job – he never complained, even when the exhaustion screamed from him – he'd simply got on with it to put food in his family's bellies and a roof over their heads. The question was, for how much longer could he endure the physical demands?

Already he was showing signs of slowing down – hadn't she seen it with her two eyes? And what of Ambrose when the strain proved too much for her father? Brother or no, there was no onus on him – he surely wouldn't be prepared to tolerate an encumbrance amongst his workforce? Nor would they remain here on his charity.

Her chest tightened with worry. No matter what, she wouldn't see him work himself into an early grave – nay, never. There were no two ways about it: she, too, must find employment, help share the financial burden, and fast.

They continued towards a small brick building at the edge of the yard. Inside, Ambrose poured them tea from a grubby-looking pot – in fact, and unsurprisingly given the trade, everything seemed to hold a dark-dust sheen – and motioned to some chairs. He sat facing them across his messy desk and beamed. 'By, a grand sight.'

Her father frowned. 'What is?'

'Eeh, our Amos, quick-witted as ever . . . Youse, sitting there, you daft bugger, yer!'

His normally sober face stretched in a grin as Ambrose threw back his head and laughed. 'Oh aye, yeah. The same, lad, the same.'

'Ay, I have missed thee, Amos, lad.'

'And me thee.'

'You'll stop on with me, aye, till youse get yourself a place to dwell?'

Amos nodded. 'If that's all right?'

'Say now. I'd be offended if you didn't.'

'Eeh, ta, Uncle Ambrose.' On impulse, Laura reached across and pressed his hand, which was resting on a mound of papers on the desktop. She felt tears not too far away and had to blink several times to quell them. They really had struck solid gold in coming to this kind-hearted giant. What on earth would they have done without him?

Eyes deepening, he returned the pressure on her hand then rose suddenly, saying, 'Right, then. The horse will stay here; the lads'll take sound care of him. Youse take youselfs along to the house and get settled – tha remembers the address, Amos?' Then at his brother's confirmation: 'Good, good. I'll arrange for your belongings from t' cart to follow. Go on, I'll see you both later.'

Outside again in the mild September air, Laura couldn't hide her quiet pleasure. She sighed to Amos, who returned it, and they headed back across the yard with a lighter step.

Reaching the iron gates, she spied the employee Nathan from earlier, busy humping loaded sacks on to a cart. He looked up and his teeth flashed white in a smile, and she returned it. Then her eye caught a movement by the office and it slipped from her face to see her uncle, lips tight in anger, watching them from the doorway.

Lowering her head with a slight frown, she hurried to catch up with her father.

Chapter 3

THERE HAD NEVER been a *Mrs* Ambrose Todd.

Why, Laura couldn't say, nor had she really given it thought. Her father didn't appear to have questioned it either. Ambrose was, to all intents and purposes, married to his work, and it seemed he was happy to keep it that way.

Though money couldn't buy love, it did pay for a live-in maid to undertake most of what a wife's duties entailed, and his needs were catered to by a local Irishwoman named Bridget Figg.

Of average height and build, with an average shade of mousy hair and average looks, she was the epitome of ordinary. However, she was keen-eyed with a ready smile, and Laura took to her instantly.

'Well, now, I need no introduction as to who you are, sir!' she exclaimed to Amos with a gap-toothed grin, welcoming them inside the modest but well-kept home off Great Ancoats Street, a few minutes' walk from the coal yard. 'It's like looking at Mr Ambrose hisself, so it is.'

After Amos had given their names and explained why they were here, he and Laura were ushered into the kitchen and, within moments, a large black teapot and platter of bread and ham had appeared on the long, light-wood table. Nimble as a girl, the maid flitted off again, returning with butter and a small jar of pickle chutney. She motioned to the chairs. 'Sit yourselves down whilst I pour.'

Amos removed his hat and Laura her shawl, passing them to the woman waiting with outstretched hands to hang them up.

'Would you look at that, now. A rare beauty, to be sure.'

Realising the compliment was meant for her, and having never been one to receive them easily, Laura flushed, mumbling, 'Nay, nay.'

'Aye, *aye*.' Bridget nodded emphatically. 'Such hair! Sure, I'd give my left arm and half of the right for locks like that.'

As her father smiled on with quiet pride, Laura's hand strayed to the light blonde mass, bound in a loose knot at her nape. Adam had loved her hair. *She didn't want to think about that – him*. 'Ta, thanks, Bridget.'

A look of horror chased the smile from the maid's face. ''Ere, no, colleen. You mustn't address me so. 'Tis plain old Figg to you and your father here.'

'Oh. Well, I don't much mind about protocol and the like—'

'Aye, but your uncle does, so we must stick to the rules,' Bridget insisted, straightening her frilled white cap. 'Now, then. I'll get back to my duties, leave you to your tea and grub. Shout when you're done and I'll show youse to your rooms.'

Alone, Laura and her father shared a look.

'I never had Uncle Ambrose down as a snob.'

Amos pursed his mouth in agreement.

''Ere but I shouldn't speak so,' she added contritely, biting her lip. 'He's been kindness itself insisting we stay on here.'

21

'Aye.'

'Sorry, Father.'

He nodded, and the two of them partook of the refreshments in silence.

A little after six o'clock men from the yard arrived with their belongings and, shortly afterwards, Ambrose returned home. True to her word, Bridget had directed them to where they were to sleep – a scrupulously clean and spacious room each, situated either end of the short landing, which she'd aired out as they ate and supplied with fresh bedding – and father and daughter were resting when the front door rattled, heralding the homeowner's return.

Hearing the maid's welcome from the hallway below, Laura rose from her bed and, after tidying her hair in the small mirror, made for Amos's bedroom. He lay on his back, arms folded across his barrelled chest, his cap over his face, snoring softly. She reached out to touch his shoulder then changed her mind. Better to leave him be. He'd had a taxing day, in mind as well as body; the sleep would do him good. Instead, she closed the door quietly behind her and headed downstairs alone.

Her uncle was seated at the kitchen table when she entered. Upon seeing her, a big smile spread across his face, and she reciprocated with not a little relief that his earlier displeasure regarding her and Nathan was seemingly forgotten.

'Well! You've settled in, I hope, lass?'

'Aye yes, ta. Father's resting. I didn't want to waken him.'

Ambrose nodded. 'No matter. He can have his grub later; Figg shall leave it to warm by the fire.' He patted the seat closest to his. 'Come. Sit and eat.'

Laura did as he bid. Whilst Bridget scurried about

22

getting the evening meal together, uncle and niece made small talk. Yet as the minutes wore on the silences between their bouts of chatter grew longer and an awkwardness set in, for Laura at least. Her flesh-and-blood family this man might be but, truth be told, he was little more than a stranger.

The last time they had met was at her and Adam's wedding; even then, Ambrose had only stuck around for the ceremony, insisting he'd have to give the small tea party Amos had laid on a miss if he was to be back in Manchester in time for closing at the coal yard. They had seen nothing of him since, not even for her mother's funeral, for which he'd sent word offering his condolence, along with apologies that he couldn't be there due to work commitments. Other than the odd brief visits as a child, she'd barely set eyes on him throughout her life, and it showed. She shifted uncomfortably in her seat as yet another thick silence filled the air between them, wishing she'd roused her father after all.

''Ere youse are, then.' Smiling, Bridget put slices of roast beef before them, and Laura could have kissed her for the distraction it afforded. 'Help yourselves to potatoes and vegetables,' she added, motioning to the silver dishes she'd placed in the centre of the table.

'Thank you,' said Laura when her uncle merely acknowledged the maid with a stiff nod. 'This looks delicious.'

'Ay, thank ye, miss.' Her eyes creased in pleasure then flicked once more to her employer. 'Mr Amos's grub's all dished up and waiting, sir, as you asked.'

'Thank you,' Laura said again after some moments – and with increasing embarrassment – forced to answer for him when, yet again, he completely ignored the Irishwoman.

Finally, Ambrose met her stare. 'That will be all, Figg.' He dismissed her with a flap of his hand and began to eat.

'Aye, sir. Very good, sir.'

When the door shut quietly behind the maid, Laura, avoiding her uncle's eye, lifted her fork. To say she had no experience of servants and masters, the rights and wrongs of how these business relationships were conducted, was true. But surely there was no need for such blatant rudeness? Arrogance, even, she'd have called it. First Nathan, now Bridget – both exchanges had been uncomfortable to witness.

Was her uncle always like this with people? Or did he save this priggish side for those he deemed beneath him – his staff, both here and at the yard? Whatever the answer, she didn't like it. Nor, she was certain, would Amos. She could never in a month of Sundays imagine her father treating *anyone* as poorly as his brother just had.

And yet, how kind Ambrose had been to them since they arrived ... His personality seemed at odds with itself and, now, her feelings were conflicted. Perhaps he was simply having a trying day? Everyone was entitled to one now and then. Aye yes, that's what it'll be, she told herself, and her uneasiness abated. Flashing him a small smile, she turned her attention to her meal.

They were almost finished when Amos entered. 'Kenneth?' he enquired immediately upon seeing his brother.

Ambrose brushed aside his concerns. 'The horse is settled and well, don't fret none. Come, lad. Sit and eat.'

Bridget, hovering nearby, needed no telling; she'd collected Amos's meal and placed it on the table before his buttocks had met the chair. ''Ere ye are, Mr Amos, sir.'

'Ta, wench.' He smiled and began to eat. 'Summat

24

wrong?' he added to his brother through a mouthful of carrots, catching him staring at him.

Chin resting on his steepled hands, Ambrose shook his head. Then: 'Well, as a matter of fact . . .'

'Aye?'

Ambrose threw his eyes in Bridget's direction. 'The maid, there. Beneath this roof, she's addressed as Figg.'

'I did explain to the sir and miss earlier, Mr Ambrose—'

He held up a hand, cutting off Bridget's babbled speech, though his gaze remained fixed on the other man. 'It ain't the done thing to get overfamiliar with servants. They forget their place, else. You see?'

Holding his stare, Amos chewed and swallowed. Then he nodded once. 'As you wish, brother. Your home, your rules, after all.'

'That's right. But ay, let's forget about all that,' Ambrose added brightly, clapping Amos on the shoulder. 'My baby brother's here – that calls forra celebration, I reckon. What say me and thee head to the Soho Tavern forra jar of porter or two, eh?'

'You go, Father,' Laura intervened when she saw he was about to refuse. Anything to be free of her uncle's company. She'd been right all along – he was a down-and-out snob and she had no desire whatsoever to converse with him a moment longer this night. Besides, once the ale had mellowed him, maybe Amos would be able to talk some sense into him. He disapproved as much as she, it was plain.

Minutes later, the brothers had set off into the cool, clear night. After helping the maid – despite her protestations – to clear the table, Laura retraced her steps to her room. Inside was stiflingly warm; Ambrose had instructed Bridget earlier to feed well the bedroom fires. The whole house, in fact, felt like it was baking under a blazing sun. That its owner had access to an ever-ready supply of fuel was acutely apparent – wiping an arm across her clammy forehead, she went to open the window.

She undressed and slipped between the sheets. Hugging her pillow, she watched the fire's yellow flames playing over the coals through half-open eyes. The sight soon evoked visions of Mrs Hanover's engulfed shop and she heaved a painful sigh. Just how many more innocent folk would be dragged into this awful situation before those maniacs were through?

How did it come to this, Adam? was her last thought before the heat, coupled with the emotionally draining day, took their toll and a fitful sleep claimed her.

Of the men's return later that night she heard not a thing. What did reach through the adjoining wall just before dawn break and into her subconsciousness were the dull squeaks of her uncle's bedsprings, intermingled with Bridget's muffled cries. Laura's dislike – now mixed with disgust – of him settled deeper within her.

He'd had the front to pour out disapproval to her father concerning overfamiliarity with servants? The hypocrisy of it. Of that, he was clearly an experienced master.

Had they really done the right thing in coming here, to Manchester? she found herself wondering again, covering her head with her pillow to block out the carnal sounds. More to the point, had they been right to seek out Ambrose Todd?

Chapter 4

'YOUR HAT, FATHER.'

Amos turned back inside the house and a weak smile lifted his mouth as he took it from Laura. 'What am I doing? I could have sworn I had it on.'

'Ain't you feeling yourself this morning?' she asked, frowning. 'If it's rest tha needs, happen Uncle Ambrose wouldn't mind you beginning your new position the morrow instead—'

'Nay.' Pulling on the cap, Amos shrugged aside her concerns. 'I'm well and good, well and good. A drop too much of porter last night, mebbe.' Puffing out his chest, he nodded. 'It's excited I am to get started, aye.'

'Well, if you're sure . . .'

'Aye. Right, then, I'll see thee later, lass.'

Arms folded, her frown still lingering, Laura watched her father set off for his first day's toil at the coal yard. Ambrose had already left over an hour before; she just prayed he wouldn't work his new employee too hard. A thick head due to ale, she knew, wasn't what ailed her father, despite what he'd said – he never partook in excess to feel the effects the following day. He was exhausted, plain and simple, that was the truth of it, though what could be done if he wouldn't admit to it, stubborn as he was?

Swallowing down her worry, she made her way to the kitchen. Again, the idea of her obtaining employment, thus relieving some of the burden of support from Amos's shoulders, piqued, and she went to seek out Bridget for advice. She found her busy at the fire and was glad she had her back to her, for it afforded Laura a few moments to regain her composure; the sight of the maid had reawakened memories of the noises from her uncle's room last night, bringing with them a deep blush. However, when all was said and done, goings-on beneath this roof were none of her business; she had no desire to involve herself. How folk chose to conduct themselves really was no concern of hers, was it? She cleared her throat and, when the woman turned, fixed in place a smile.

'Morning, colleen.'

'Morning, Brid— Figg,' Laura amended reluctantly when the maid made to protest. 'Sorry, I keep forgetting.'

'Sure, you'll get used to it. 'Ere, you sit yourself down and I'll pour ye some tea.' She abandoned her work and crossed to the table, adding, 'So how are you and your father settling in? Well, I hope?'

'Oh yes. My uncle has shown great kindness in letting us stay.'

'Aye, well. That's Mr Ambrose for thee. Generous as the day is long, is he,' Bridget announced with warm feeling, and Laura felt a tug of pity for the Irishwoman. Was she so oblivious to the way he treated her? Or perhaps infatuation was blinding her to his poor behaviour? Was that it? Was Bridget Figg in love? Somehow, Laura doubted that Ambrose's need for his bedfellow came from the heart.

After pushing a filled cup across, Bridget made to return to her duties, but Laura stopped her: 'Where might I find employment, Figg?' she asked. 'I can't sit around here all day doing nowt and, besides, I don't want Father working hisself into the ground providing for us both.'

The maid sat down and rubbed her chin. 'Well, the cotton factories are your best bet, colleen. Sure, good spinners and reelers and the like are always in demand.'

Though Laura's stomach dropped a little to hear this – the mills seemed such noisy and dangerous places – she nodded nonetheless. If grafting in such a place was what it would take to keep her beloved father's health, she'd do it in a heartbeat.

'I have two nieces who work at Sedgwick Mill just off nearby Jersey Street,' Bridget continued. 'It's one of the better works, so they say. Decent conditions, like, compared to some.'

Laura brightened a little at this. 'Aye? And d'you reckon they'll take *me* on?'

'Ye can but ask.'

'I'll go right now.' Smiling, Laura drained her cup and rose. 'Ta, Bridget.'

'*Figg*. Sheesh, colleen, you'll be the death of me, to be sure!' she lamented theatrically, throwing her hands in the air.

Laura couldn't help but laugh. 'Sorry, I just . . .'

'Aye, keep forgetting, you've said.' Grinning, Bridget flicked her chin towards the door. 'Go on, now. You go whilst I get on with my own work, and good luck to thee. Oh, but Manchester's a mighty big city; you'll not get lost?' she added, biting her lip.

Laura assured her she'd be fine. 'I can allus stop and ask someone the way, should I lose my bearings. Bye for now, B— *Figg!*'

29

The maid's exasperated 'Saints preserve us!' followed a chuckling Laura down the hall and out of the door.

She turned immediately left and retraced the way she and Amos had taken to get here the previous day. She recalled they had passed several mills and factories looming over the district like angry red giants – hopefully, one of them had been Sedgwick. Keeping her eyes peeled for mill gates and the premises' names inscribed thereon, she continued at a brisk pace.

Minutes later, Laura was utterly lost.

Tumbledown lanes snaked like veins in a hand every which way, and she'd followed them blindly, believing they would bring her out at Jersey Street's thoroughfare. She'd been wrong; the warrens of tightly packed houses all looked the same to the untrained eye. She halted at the end of a street and sighed. Though one or two people passed her by, their grim expressions made her hesitant to ask directions. As in her hometown of Bolton, here the slum dwellers could be a vicious lot. Abject poverty and the desperation that came with it drove a body to dark measures – many had no qualms in robbing and beating any stranger fool enough to wander into their territory alone. Glancing about, she chewed her lip.

'I ain't seen thee around here afore. I'd remember a bonny thing like you, aye.'

Whipping around, Laura met a rough-looking man in his middle years. His badly scarred face, proof of pugilistic activity, was hard to read in the poor light that struggled to penetrate through to the cobbled streets. His tone, however, told her all she needed to know. This one was not to be trusted. She took a hesitant step back.

'What's your name, love?'

'I . . . was just leaving . . .' she began, but he side-stepped her and blocked her path.

'Scarpering so soon, when alls I want is to get to know thee? That's not reet friendly, is it?' Face darkening, he seized her elbow.

'Let me go.' But her strength was no match against his brawn. 'I have no brass.'

'Mebbe. Mind, there's more that can get a fella going than money.'

Though her heart threatened to smash from her chest, she forced her voice to remain even, sensing instinctively she mustn't show she was afraid. 'I mean it – leave *go* of me.'

'Bitch.'

Laura opened her mouth to scream but, lightning fast, the man's arm went around her and he crushed her to him. His mouth found hers in a sickening, thick-tongued kiss whilst his hand tugged roughly at the bodice of her dress.

'Get off me!' she managed to scream when his mouth dropped to a now-exposed breast, before his lips clamped over hers once more, smothering her breath. Struggling wildly, she pummelled at his chest, but with little impact, and her panic reached fever pitch. 'Help! Someone, please!'

'Ain't nobody coming to save thee, my lass,' he told her between pants, slamming her back against a brick wall and tugging up her skirts. 'So save your breath and stop struggling.'

'Nay!' With a shriek, she brought up her knee several times in blind desperation. One attempt managed to find its mark and she cried out in sheer relief as her attacker crumpled to the ground with a groan. Clutching his genitals, he glared up at her, teeth bared, but whatever threat he'd been about to make was missed on Laura – not wasting a second, she skidded around on her heel and pelted away.

How much later she couldn't say – lungs ablaze, coughing and gasping for breath, she was finally forced to rest. As her energy returned it brought with it simmering rage that had her shaking. How *dare* he! Who did some men think they were, believing it was fine to treat women exactly as they liked? She was sick to the back teeth of the male species; she was, really. Bar her father, every last one could go and rot, for all she cared!

Looking around through a blur of tears, a flash of black smudged with green lettering caught her attention in the distance. She rubbed her eyes with the heels of her hands and stared harder. It *was*. Oh, thank God . . . Gaze fixed on the familiar sign, she set off at a run once more.

Before entering her uncle's yard she took a few minutes to compose herself. Her clothing was dishevelled, long tendrils of blonde hair had escaped their pins and were hanging around her face, and her eyes felt puffy. When her breathing had steadied and she'd tidied herself up the best she could she fixed in place a smile and passed through the gates. Hopefully, Amos hadn't yet left on his rounds; all she wanted was to see him for just a moment, feel his safe and calming presence, and all would be well again. *Please, Father* . . .

'Lass?'

Laura's heart dropped as the voice called out her name from the direction of the office. Before turning, she scanned the yard quickly for a glimpse of her father and Kenneth, but there was no sign of either. Swallowing down her disappointment, she made her way across to Ambrose.

'What brings thee here? Is summat up back home?'

'Nay. I wanted to see Father.'

'Oh?' When she didn't respond, he held the office door wide. 'Come in, take a sup.'

Despite everything, his offer warmed her somewhat. 'I'd not be disturbing thee, Uncle?'

'Nay, nay.'

She nodded. 'Aye. All right, then.'

Inside, she checked the pot and poured them each a cup of tea. After a few sips of the hot brew she felt a little better. She smiled across the desk at the older man.

'All right?'

'Aye, ta. I'll just finish this and will be on my way, leave you to your work.'

Shaking his head, Ambrose leaned back in his chair. 'No need, lass. I've allus time to spare for kin. So. What's got you in such a state?' He motioned to her tear-streaked face. 'Summat's upset thee. Am I right?'

Laura opened her mouth to offer a denial, then her chin drooped to her chest and she sighed. 'Aye, you are. There was a man. He . . .' She looked up at her uncle's angry murmur and released another long breath. 'I'm all right, really. I . . . hit him where it hurts and he let me go.'

'Where was this? I'll have the whelp hunted down and horse-whipped!'

'I don't know,' she told him truthfully. 'I was out look-ing for work, you see, and became lost. These streets all look the same to me. It was my own fault, really; I shouldn't have wandered so far. Please, I just want to forget it.'

He released air slowly. His eyes travelled the length of her, settling on her chest; glancing down, she saw her bodice was missing a button from her assailant's heavy handling. Blushing scarlet, she drew her shawl closer around herself. 'Really, Uncle,' she insisted in a whisper, 'I'm fine.'

After a long moment during which his gaze remained rooted to her generous bust, Ambrose nodded. 'I think it best we don't mention this to my brother. He'll not stop till he finds the divil and would likely kill him when he does. We'll keep this to ourselfs, aye?'

Laura readily agreed. Amos's love for her often blinded his judgement; Ambrose was right in what he said. Her father's rage would be sure to see him do something he'd later regret, and the beast who had assaulted her wasn't worth a murder charge. 'Ta, Uncle Ambrose,' she said with feeling.

He nodded once more then folded his arms. 'Now, about the matter of thee finding work.'

'Aye. Figg mentioned that her nieces are employed at Sedgwick Mill. That's where I was heading when I got lost.'

'Well, you can put that from your mind, lass. Starting the morrow, you'll work here for me.'

She blinked in surprise. 'Here?'

'You object to it?'

'Well, nay, but . . .' Glancing through the window to the busy yard and the thick-muscled men hard at toil, she bit her lip. 'You really think I'll measure up, Uncle Ambrose? I'm stronger than I look, it's true, but those sacks look awful heavy . . . What?' she asked when Ambrose threw back his head and laughed heartily. 'What did I say?'

'Not out on t' yard floor, you daft bugger, yer,' he spluttered on a guffaw. 'Nay. You'll work alongside me in t' office, here.'

'*Oh*.' She grinned sheepishly. 'That makes more sense.'

34

'It's a ruddy mess, and that's the truth.'

Taking stock of the space, she nodded agreement. 'I'll be tidying and such, like?'

'That's right. And keeping my papers in order – just by date will do if you're not too sharp with the reading – and making brews, that sort of thing. Well, what d'you reckon?'

'I reckon it sounds gradely, aye.' And she meant it. So long as he didn't think to treat her as he did his other staff, that was. She'd give him no cause to complain, of course, and in return hoped he'd show her the same level of courtesy. 'Eeh, ta, Uncle. I'm that grateful.'

'That's settled, then. Now, you get going home.'

'Aye, all right.'

'And lass?'

Laura paused by the door. 'Aye?'

Rising from his seat and closing the space between them, Ambrose fixed his eyes once more on her chest. Then he reached out and prodded between the cleft of her breasts – she squirmed beneath his touch, though he didn't seem to notice. His voice was low and thick. 'Get Figg to repair yon button afore your father notices. Remember, not a word to him about today's antics.'

'Aye, yes, I . . . I will.' Gripping the shawl tightly against herself, she backed off through the door. 'I'll be going now. Goodbye.'

Throughout the short journey home her mind was a jumble of thoughts. That she'd gained a position she was, for her father's sake, happy about. And yet . . .

Her hand travelled to the spot her uncle had fingered; his touch still lingered, as though branded there. Confusion and an odd sense of sickliness washed through her. She frowned. Then her rational side was

35

telling her not to be silly, that she was misreading the situation. He was her *uncle*, for goodness' sake . . . And wanting to believe it, she listened.

Still, she was at a loss as to why the unease coiling her guts remained with her for the rest of the day.

Amos was delighted with the news.

'She'll come to no harm under my watch, brother.'

'Aye, that I know.' He patted Ambrose on the back. 'The lass couldn't be in safer hands.'

Laura offered them a small smile and continued with her breakfast. Her encounter yesterday with the scarfaced varmint in the dark and deserted lane lay heavily on her conscience; keeping secrets from Amos, no matter if it was to protect him, didn't sit well with her. However, Ambrose had been right: her father would be furious should he learn what had occurred, and that would do his health no good at all. Better that they kept it to themselves.

Her thoughts switched to her conspirator and their meeting in the office and her body gave an involuntary shudder. But again, she told herself she had blown this all out of proportion, that if anything *she* was the queer one to be harbouring such inappropriate notions. He was her *uncle* . . . Today marked the start of a fresh beginning for her. Not only would she be earning, but she'd get to see Amos throughout the day when he dropped in at the yard between rounds. It was the perfect position, really. She must do her utmost to see that it worked out.

'Right, then. I'll see youse shortly.' Ambrose rose from the table with a nod to them both. 'Don't you be late, lady,' he added to Laura, winking to his brother, who chuckled.

'I'll not,' she assured him, waving him on his way. Her smile soon slipped, however, when, immediately her uncle left the house, Amos's face contorted in a discomfort he'd clearly been hiding from the other man. 'Father?' She rushed to his side. 'What is it?'

Rubbing his chest with a bunched fist, Amos breathed deeply. 'Nowt, no need to fret. I'll be reet in a handful of minutes, allus am.'

'This has happened afore? When? How long has tha been getting this pain?' He'd appeared fine yesterday upon his return from his first day at his new job. Had that been a mask he'd been wearing, too? 'Father, why didn't you tell me?'

'Lass, I'm all right.'

'But Father—'

'We'll speak on this no more, Laura.' His voice brooked no argument. Taking a last deep breath, he sat up straight and picked up his spoon to resume his meal. 'You see. I'm fine now, just like I said.'

Fear had her gripped in its jaws and, more than ever, she was thankful for her new job. She'd maintain a better watch, see that he took rests between his rounds. Lord but she loved him, *needed* to keep him well.

A short time later, as they walked together to the coal yard, she flicked sidelong glances in his direction to check how he fared, but he looked his usual self. Again, when he climbed atop his laden cart and was about to set off, Laura scrutinised Amos's face – all seemed fine. Breathing a sigh of relief, she watched until he and Kenneth had disappeared through the gates then made her way to the office, her attention now on her own duties.

The morning passed quickly and she found the work pleasant enough. After tidying and sorting into neat piles mounds of ledgers and loose papers she set to organising everything in order of date and filing them away into their relevant drawers. Ambrose, busy directing his workforce in the yard, flitted in to check her progress once or twice only throughout the hours and was happy with the results.

Laura matched his feelings. She knew a sense of accomplishment she wasn't accustomed to, and she liked it. She'd never had to work as Adam's wife – he'd have had a blue fit had she suggested the idea, and incurring his wrath was something she'd striven to avoid at all costs. Earning an honest crust all by herself left a warm glow deep within her that she hadn't expected. She was *good* at something. She knew now that, if she could help it, she'd never be out of work again.

Having dusted and swept, she made a fresh pot of tea and allowed herself her first sit-down of the day. She was sipping her sweetened brew when the door opened once again and her uncle entered. He took stock of the room and slowly nodded his approval.

'You've done well.'

'Ta, thanks, Uncle Ambrose.'

'Any tea going begging?'

Laura went to fetch him a cup. He drained the drink in one then reached for a bundle of papers on his desk.

'I'm away to a business meeting. You'll manage right enough whilst I'm gone?'

'Aye, Uncle Ambrose.'

He nodded, smiled. Then he crossed to her chair and stooped until their faces were level. His eyes, a darker grey than usual, bore into hers. He chucked her under the chin – though if Ambrose meant the action to be friendly or jocular, he was sadly mistaken; Laura squirmed at his touch.

'I've a feeling we're going to work well together, lass, aye,' he murmured.

She tried but failed to offer a response, and the smile she attempted to drag to her lips wouldn't cooperate. Uneasiness had quickened her heartbeat, and the struggle to remain calm, to stop herself from springing from her seat and him, and running from this room, was growing by the second. She couldn't even pinpoint what exactly was going on in this moment. She just knew instinctively that whatever it was, it wasn't . . . *natural* was the only term she could put to it. And she didn't like it.

'Right, then.' Ambrose straightened and strode to the door. 'I'd best be away. I shall be gone some hours. See thee later.'

When he'd left she released air she hadn't realised she was holding. When, moments later, footsteps sounded beyond the door, and believing it to be her uncle returning, having perhaps forgotten something, breath caught in her throat again. However, it wasn't Ambrose's towering form that entered the office but the wiry one of the young man Nathan, his employee.

'Apologies for disturbing thee, miss. Your father . . .'

'What is it?' She was on her feet and hurrying towards him in a heartbeat. 'He's unwell?'

'I reckon so, aye.'

Pushing past him, she sprinted outside and scanned the yard. She spotted Kenneth and the cart by the gates, but Amos was nowhere to be seen. 'Where is he?' she asked of Nathan, who had followed her.

He pointed to a makeshift bench a short distance away. 'I left him there to rest whilst I came to collect thee. He's insisting nowt ails him, mind.'

Laura rushed to the older man, who sat with bowed head, his hands on his knees, as though struggling to catch his breath. She laid a gentle hand on his shoulder. 'Father?'

'Hello, lass,' he wheezed out, and his attempt at a smile was more of a grimace. 'How's your first . . . day going . . . then?'

'Oh, Father.' Tears sprang to her eyes. 'Please stop this pretence. Summat's not right with thee and—'

'I'm fine.'

'But you ain't! I'm sending for t' doctor—'

'Nay.' Amos's head sprang up. His eyes were steely. 'That's an order, my lass. As for thee,' he added to Nathan coldly, 'you see what you've gone and caused? I told yer I was all right, *told* yer not to go running to the girl here, upsetting her.'

'I'm glad he did,' Laura cut in. 'For God's sake, Father, you're not *well.* You need to rest—'

'It's back to work I need to be.'

She could only watch in horror-filled astonishment as her father rose and headed to his cart, on to which men were piling fresh sacks of coal in preparation for his next round. 'I don't believe . . . Why won't he *listen?*'

'He's proud, miss. But he ain't doing hisself no favours.'

Her tears spilling, she turned desperate eyes to the young man. 'What d'you think it is, Nathan? What's ailing him?'

He hesitated at her distress, then: 'It's his heart, I reckon. It's what drew my attention when he arrived back here; he were clutching his chest, looked in mortal pain.'

Gulping back a sob, she returned her gaze to Amos. Still, a deathly pallor touched his features, and anger rose up in her. She straightened her shoulders. 'Right. There's nowt else for it.'

'What will tha do, miss?' asked Nathan, hurrying after her as she strode off towards her father.

40

'Summat that'll make him see sense, God willing. And please, call me Laura.'

'Now, lass, I've told thee—' began Amos when she reached him, but her nod and sweet smile stopped him in his tracks. He blinked in surprised relief that another pestering, as he clearly saw it, was to be avoided. 'Right, then. Good. I'll see thee later.'

'Wait a minute, please, Father.'

Pausing in his task of climbing aboard the cart, Amos turned back with a frown. He was still wearing it when, after hurrying to the office, Laura returned waving an old flat cap she'd spotted in a cupboard earlier during her cleaning. She put it on, tucked her hair beneath it and nodded again. Then she pulled herself up into the space beside her father's seat.

Amos was aghast. 'What are you doing?'

'There's work to be done, Father. You said so yourself.'

'Aye, but—!'

'And you're right: the coal won't deliver itself, will it?'

'Well, nay, but—!'

'Are we all loaded?' Laura asked Nathan, standing in stunned silence, watching the scene unfold. At his confirmation, she lifted her chin. 'Right. Come along, then, Father.'

'Laura, what in the world . . . Have you taken leave of your senses entirely, girl?'

'Nay, Father, you have. That's why I'm being forced to take this action.' Her tone brought Amos's mouth open in shock. Not once in her life had she spoken as harshly to him, had never so much as raised her voice. Her desperation – and steadfastness – was clear. 'You're driving your health into the ground, and I can't sit back and be witness to it any longer. If you're determined to continue toiling like this, then I'm going to help.'

41

'Help? Thee?'

'That's right.'

'Now, Laura, you've gone too far here. I'll not—'

'Father.' She laid a hand on his shoulder and, leaning in close, spoke softly now, soothingly, sensing his mounting humiliation. 'I love thee; oh, more than I can put into words. Please. Let me do this for thee. Let me ease your burden in whatever way I can. Just till you're stronger, eh? No one need know. We'll be discreet, and Uncle Ambrose will be none the wiser. *Please.*'

'Lass . . .'

'I'll not take nay for an answer,' she said, her firmness returning before he could pooh-pooh the suggestion further. Glancing down to Nathan, she added, 'My uncle ain't due back forra while yet; me and Father should be back afore he is. Mind, if Uncle Ambrose should return and find I'm not here . . . tell him . . . tell him I weren't feeling too good and took myself off home. Will tha do that for me, Nathan? Please?'

''Course, aye. Fret none; Mr Todd is allus gone from t' yard forra few hours each day.' He looked over the sacks on the cart then nodded. 'You're all set.'

She passed the reins to Amos, who accepted them with a defeated sigh. His pride was taking a painful battering, she knew, but it was for his own good. Hopefully, he'd see that in the long run. She *must* do this.

As the shire made his steady way from the yard and into the street, Laura pulled her oversized cap lower, obscuring her face. Folk could be funny about the fairer sex involving themselves in heavy trades, were inclined to be untrusting of their capabilities, not take them seriously. Unless it was out of public sight, of course; that was another matter. It was perfectly acceptable for females to work themselves into early graves

42

behind the closed doors of dangerous mills and factories, or labour hard in the fields alongside husbands on isolated farmsteads.

Women, too, had even contributed greatly towards coal haulage, but in an altogether more unpalatable capacity – in the actual mining of the stuff. In one of the toughest, dirtiest, most perilous jobs there was, they had toiled up to fifteen-hour days, six days a week, until the 1842 passing of the Mines and Collieries Act prohibited this, only a few short decades ago.

It was a typical, and rather ignorant, case of out of sight out of mind, that was for sure. Nevertheless, she and Amos could well do without word getting back to Ambrose. Besides, unwanted attention was the last thing she needed with the Cannock brothers still – she was sure – on the search for her. Manchester this might be, but Bolton town wasn't so great a distance away. Perhaps they had discovered where she'd gone, were already on her tail, just waiting for the right time to strike . . .

Quickly, she forced the thoughts away before terror consumed her and concentrated on the task in hand.

Chapter 5

AMOS'S BELLIGERENCE ONLY grew throughout the course of the afternoon. Despite Laura's best efforts, he refused to readily accept her help at every house they came to and mumbled his displeasure non-stop. Taking it in her stride, realising how difficult this was for him, she retaliated with but easy silence and smiles.

Their round took them through the heart of the city, past wharfs and warehouses, mills, brick and timber yards, as well as tanneries, boneyards and gasworks, and culminated in a plethora of fetid smells, depending on which way the wind was blowing. To her surprise, Laura found that she loved the work. Though her arms and back had begun to ache within minutes, and muscles she didn't know she had burned from the unaccustomed toil, she'd pushed through without complaint. By the time only half the sacks of coal remained on the cart, even her father was showing a grudging admiration of her tenacity – it showed in his eyes, though he did his best to mask it.

'We'll be finished afore we know it, Father.'

Amos didn't respond. Drawing Kenneth to a halt out-side the next customer's house, he climbed from the cart, and Laura followed. He dragged a heavy sack towards him then, bending his knees, hauled it up and

44

on to one broad shoulder. Once more, she was waiting. Gripping the bottom of the sack in her two hands, she lifted it high, thus distributing the weight and sharing the burden, and in a shuffled walk they made their way to the circular coalhole cover imbedded in the pavement by the property. This, she knew, like the others they had stopped at on the round, would have been unlocked from the inside in preparation of their visit, to be swiftly secured again on their departure – you never could be too careful in this swarming city, where both desperate and opportunist burglars abounded.

Ingenious, really, Laura thought again, eyeing the silver plate, beneath which lay the resident's coal bunker in the cellar. Thanks to this method, sooty sacks and equally grubby delivery men had no cause to venture inside the house proper, just as these more affluent occupiers desired – though their poorer counterparts were not afforded such luxury.

The last thing these customers wanted was coal dirt, thick and black and smelly, besmirching the beautiful carpets, or large and clumsy men bumping into their delicate, spindly-legged furniture with their dusty sacks. In turn, the depositing holes' location on the street made the coalman's job easier, minimising the distance over which they had to carry their heavy load. It suited all concerned.

Yet to her, more impressive still were the varied designs on the covers themselves. Roughly twelve to fourteen inches in diameter, they were mainly of cast iron, though one or two she'd seen today even included small glass panes and concrete panels. Besides advertising the name of the foundry which had smelted them, each boasted moulded patterns, some more intricate than others, which were raised to prevent them being slippery underfoot in wet and sleety weather. Some bore simple designs; others were more decorative and rather beautiful, depicting bold, interlocking stripes and even images: flowers and stars, suns and diamonds. A mostly overlooked form of art in their own right.

Now, after placing the sack on to the ground and removing the cover, Amos stalked back to the cart and resumed his seat to catch his breath without her having to argue with him. Arms folded, mouth set in a grim line, he stared straight ahead. This acceptance – albeit definitely grudgingly – that she would undertake the next part of the job lightened her heart. Relieved he was finally taking note, she smiled sadly to herself. *It pains me to have to force you to face that you're not as fit as you once were, but it's only because I love you, Father,* she told him with her eyes as she shimmied the sack closer to the hole.

Her first few attempts at overturning them into the small openings had proved difficult – coal had spilled across the flagstones to settle in the gutter, much to Amos's chagrin. Precision was vital. But as with every-thing, practice had become her friend; now, she managed to position the sack's opening directly in place without much bother and was gratified to hear the black nuggets tumble effortlessly down the chute into the house below. Beaming, she looked to her father to see him watching her, a whisper of a smile on his lips, which pleased her enormously. Slowly but surely, his acceptance of her being here was growing, his pride, precious to him, tucked aside, and she adored him all the more for it.

After securing the plate back into position, marvel-ling anew at it – another unique example – she rose, folded the empty sack and deposited it on the cart. Ken-neth, attuned to the daily routine, pawed at the cobbles with a giant, feathered hoof. On instruction from her father, she collected his nosebag, secured the straps around his head and climbed back into her seat. Whilst the horse enjoyed his oats, Laura took the quiet time to reflect on the day thus far – and the following ones to come.

Would Amos consent to her coming out with him again? She wished to make today a regular thing – he appeared much better than he had earlier, due, she was certain, to her help – but how would he take it? And what of her uncle? Could she continue to hide her absence from the yard? Would he discover what was going on? What if he did? They could both be out on their ear. Was this scheme of hers worth the risk? Yet what was the alternative? Allow the man beside her to work himself into an early grave? Never. Not that. She released a weary sigh.

'Tha's done well.'

Laura blinked in surprise at the gruff words. Warmness filled her. 'You really think so?'

Staring straight ahead, he gave a reluctant nod. 'Stood up to muster, aye. You've your mother's stubborn streak in thee, all right,' he added, frowning, but his tone held what sounded suspiciously like pride.

Shiny-eyed, she chuckled. 'I miss her.'

His head bobbed again in agreement.

'Father?'

'Aye?'

'Thank you.'

Now, Amos turned to look at her. 'For what?'

'The sacrifices you made for us, for me. Toiling alongside thee the day . . . I never truly realised how taxing the life of a coalman is. It's hard ruddy graft!'

Out in all weathers. Come lashing rain and winds, snow and sleet and beating heat. Hauling and tipping and humping mammoth weights, the continuous grind, the dirt and the grime. The monotony of it all. It took a hardy will to cope; this she appreciated now completely.

With his usual modesty, he shrugged. 'I'm the fella, ain't I? It's what we do.'

'Nay, not all. Husbands and fathers aplenty fritter their brass on ale or strong porter, on gambling – or worse.' She swallowed hard, picturing Adam Cannock's face. He'd been a husband for the 'or worse' category, all right. 'You chose – choose still – to earn, provide.' Reaching for his massive hand, rough as old leather, she squeezed, repeating in a heartfelt whisper, 'Thank you.'

They were silent for a while, listening to Kenneth's soft snorts as he strove to reach the last morsels at the bottom of the canvas feeder. Then: 'I'm for coming out with thee again the morrow.' Laura let her eyes slope sideward to gauge his reaction, but his face was impassive. 'All right?'

'Aye.' The word left Amos's lips on a dull breath.

She pressed his hand tighter. 'You understand why, Father?'

'Aye,' he repeated, and his eyes were misty, the expression in them one of utter defeat.

Tucking her arm through his, Laura laid her head on his shoulder. Just the two of them, always. Nothing – no one – else mattered.

As they weaved their way through the streets heading back for the poorer part of the district and the coal yard, Kenneth's step lighter owing to the empty cart, Laura had prayed that her uncle hadn't returned and discovered her gone. It wouldn't have looked good, being her first day and all, not to mention the questions it would have raised and possible repercussions upon

48

his finding out about Amos's flagging health. However, she needn't have worried. Nathan had greeted them with a meaningful nod: the boss man was yet to return; their secret was safe.

Nonetheless, her father had stopped her as she made to turn for the office. 'Lass . . . No more.'

'But we agreed—'

'Should our Ambrose discover . . . I'm not ready for the knacker's yard just yet, yer know,' he added on a defiant growl, chest expanding with pumped-up pride. 'No more, and I mean it.'

Laura's mouth, opening to protest, clamped shut abruptly when she spied her uncle entering the yard through the gates. 'We'll speak on this later,' she told Amos through the side of her mouth, disappearing into the office before he had a chance to offer more bluster.

'All right?' Ambrose took off his hat and threw it on to his desk. His smile at Laura's nod slipped slowly away as he took in her face properly, and she frowned.

'Uncle?'

'What the divil has tha been up to, then?'

Blinking rapidly in confusion, not to mention shock – how on earth had he guessed? – she kept her tone nonchalant. 'Up to? I don't . . .'

'Your ruddy phizog. It favours you've done a full shift down the pit.'

Her bemused frown melted and a cherry hue crept up her neck to blaze across her face. Oh God! Peering towards the window and catching her reflection, she baulked to see coal dust streaking her forehead and nose and black lines ingrained in her face. She turned back to him slowly. 'I . . . Well . . .'

'Eeh, I am sorry.' Pulling a sheepish face, Ambrose shook his head. 'A reet mucky hole, weren't it?'

49

Laura could only shake her head.

'The office here,' he elucidated with a sweep of his arm. ''Tain't seen a broom nor duster for more years than I care to admit. By, but you've worked hard, lass, I can see.'

'*Oh.*' To her horror, understanding brought bubbling laughter to her throat. She swallowed frantically to quash its escape. 'Aye, yes. Well . . . ta.'

When he'd gone off again to inspect his workers in the yard, she heaved a sigh. Thank the Lord she'd remembered to return the cap she'd worn to its cupboard. And, owing to her shawl's protection, little dirt had marred her clothing; though her skirts hadn't been so lucky, were rather grubby, she noticed, glancing down. However, she'd forgotten all about her face – and hands, she realised, scrutinising these, too, and pulling a face.

What she needed was a change of clothing to wear whilst out on the cart. An old jacket and her own flat cap. Her father had customised his uniform, and years past had had her mother stitch together scrap lengths of leather which she'd fashioned into a waistcoat of sorts that he wore beneath *his* jacket, which cushioned the bite on shoulders and back from the lumpy coal sacks. Of course, she wouldn't need this, her task being to merely hold up the bottom of the sacks. She could, however, do with some trousers – much more practical than long skirts. Though what Amos would say to this last item of wear she could well imagine. But well, he'd just have to accept it.

For despite his words upon their return, she had no intention of letting him continue his work alone. And she would tell him so, she thought decisively, squaring her shoulders, concern for his welfare lending an angry edge to the vow. If her father thought she'd been hard on him earlier . . . He hadn't seen anything yet.

That evening, as the three of them rose from the table after their evening meal, Bridget hovering close by in readiness to clear away the dishes, Laura motioned to her father to follow her. Leaving Ambrose to head to the room at the front of the house and his comfortable chair by the roaring fire, she led the way upstairs to her room, closing the door behind them.

Arms folded in readiness against the discussion to come, Amos stared at his daughter guardedly. 'I'll not be swayed.'

'Nor will I,' she shot back, voice low but firm.

'Lass . . .'

'We can make this work, Father. I know we can.' She nodded her conviction. 'Uncle Ambrose need never find out. He's away from the office forra few hours each day; didn't Nathan, the employee who tried to aid thee earlier, tell us so hisself? And he'll help cover for us again should we need him to, I know he will—'

'Tha can't expect the lad to do that! He'd get the shove right away should my brother discover he'd been scheming along with us.'

'But he *won't* discover owt. He won't, Father, for we'll be careful. Please, trust me.'

For the next ten minutes, as Amos put obstacle after obstacle in her path as to why the idea was doomed to fail, Laura was armed with ready solutions:

'You can't manage two jobs,' he put to her. 'I'll not see you wear yourself thin.'

'The office work is but filing papers and light cleaning. Hardly taxing, Father.'

'But lass, you're a *lass*. I don't agree with the fairer specie toiling in t' muck!'

'Pah. A bit of dirt never hurt no one. Besides, where there's muck there's brass, as the saying goes, eh?'

'But . . . Ambrose discovering—'

'We've spoke on that, Father.'

'And what of me?' he'd finished on a gruff rush, twin spots of colour appearing on his cheeks. 'I'm done for, aye? Finished with?'

''Course not. I don't think that—'

'Nay? Well, I bloody does! I bloody feel that, Laura! Like a hammer blow to the guts, this is, as well as my pride. I should provide. *Me*, goddammit! I'm the *man*. Aye yes,' he finished bitterly, and there was a catch in his voice, 'the *owd* man, eh? The man now past it. The man what might as well fling hisself in t' bloody canal and have done with it afore I become even more of a burden to youse all!'

'Father, Father . . .' Laura wrapped her arms around him tightly and he hugged her back, his large frame shaking in silent grief. Her own tears flowing, she thought her heart would break for him. 'I'll not hear thee talk so. *Never* think them things. I love thee, need thee, always. All you've done for me – are still doing. Let me give sum- mat back. Let me help thee. Please.'

After a long moment, Amos straightened. He studied her, his eyes soft with anguish but also gratitude. Then his gaze flicked down to her clothing and one corner of his mouth twitched. 'You'll need another rig-out, mind. Them skirts'll not last two minutes with the coal dirt.'

'You mean . . . ?' He was accepting that this was how it must be? She held her breath, not daring to believe it.

'Aye. Aye, lass.'

She threw her arms around him once more. 'I'll call in at Smithfield Market the morrow afore work. I'm sure to find what I need there. They've clothing stalls aplenty – cheap, an' all, a lot of it. Bridget were telling me so the other day.'

'Ahem. Don't you mean Figg?' her father corrected her in his haughtiest voice and pushed up the tip of his nose with his finger, poking fun at his brother's false grandeur ways.

Smothering their laughter, they headed back downstairs arm in arm.

The following morning Laura rose early and, after dressing, made her way from the bedroom quietly so not to disturb the slumbering household. Upon entering the kitchen, she found Bridget up already and busy at work; she smiled at the maid's surprised expression.

'Morning, Figg.'

'Morning, colleen. 'Tis unexpected to see ye at this fine hour.'

Rubbing the last traces of sleep from her eyes, Laura smothered a yawn. '*Fine* hour?' she asked.

'Oh aye.' The Irishwoman glanced through the window to the sky of the newborn morn, its streaking of pearly pink clouds rapidly chasing away the dark. 'This time, just before dawn break, is my favourite. God's hour, I call it; for sure, you'll not find another the whole day long so peaceful, nor beautiful.'

Contemplating her words, Laura nodded, and not for the first time wondered to herself what this gentle-spirited soul saw in her uncle. 'I suppose you're right, Figg.'

Eyes sweeping the heavens one last time, Bridget sighed happily then turned her attention back to Laura. 'So, then,' she said, pouring her tea. 'Couldn't ye sleep?'

Mindful of the need to keep her intentions secret – Bridget might well make mention of it to Ambrose – she

53

sipped the hot brew before answering carefully, 'I thought I might take a walk to the market.'

'Well, you've picked the right time for it. It's always best to get there ahead of the crush, before all the best buys are gone. Are you after purchasing anything in particular?'

'Er, nay, not really. I'd best be away, then,' she told her, handing back her cup and making for her shawl, which was hanging on a peg by the door. 'Bye for now.'

'Aye. And oh, don't let those dealers charge ye top price. The cheek of some, to be sure! Barter, colleen. You'll remember?'

'I will,' Laura assured her, smiling.

'Good. I'll have breakfast ready for ye when you get back.'

Despite the hour, the vast emporium in nearby Shudehill was heaving with traders and customers alike; Laura gazed around with interest. Every manner of produce you could need or imagine was right here under the iron-and-glass roof; the atmosphere buzzed with enthusiasm. Stalls and barrows groaned under foodstuffs and household items of all descriptions, and the air was filled with a cocktail of smells: spices and fruits and beautifying potions amongst a hundred others, all mingling together in a heady scent that plucked teasingly at the senses.

She spotted a second-hand clothes stall up ahead and made her way towards it through the throng of shoppers and market porters, glancing as she passed at other products on sale. She hadn't money to fritter, it was true, but browsing was enjoyable nonetheless. Naphtha lamps swinging from stalls threw their lurid glow on the stock, some of which she hadn't a clue what it was. Who knew so many different things existed? There were foods she'd never seen before, aromas she couldn't identify, items crafted from wood and pot and metal whose uses she couldn't guess at. The city market was an enchanting place; she could have stayed here all day.

Skirting a barrow piled with dead-eyed herring and shellfish, Laura edged her way to the front of the clothes stall, behind which stood a buxom girl busy serving a woman. Handing a bundle of neatly folded material to her customer, she eyed Laura and smiled. 'Be with thee in a moment, love.'

Turning her attention to a pile of jackets whilst she waited, Laura found one right away that looked a good fit. The collar was stained and frayed and the sleeves torn, but that didn't worry her – it was only to cover her own clothes from the muck of the coal sacks anyway. 'How much?' she asked when the stallholder was free to serve her.

'It's in a sorry state . . . Mind, nowt a good scrub and a needle and thread wouldn't cure . . .'

'It's for my brother, and he warned me not to over-spend,' Laura lied, heeding Bridget's advice. 'He needs a rig-out for work. It's coal he toils with, so the condition of the clothes matters none.'

The girl nodded. 'To be honest, I'd likely have a job getting shot of it to many others in that state . . . All right, love, you can have it forra few pennies.'

'Ta, thanks. I also need trousers. Oh, and a cap.'

After sifting through a mound at the end of the stall, the girl returned with two pairs of trousers. She held up some in good-quality tweed, but Laura shook her head, opting instead for the others: a shabbier – and there-fore cheaper – pair in rough fustian. A large cap sporting numerous holes followed the other items into the brown-paper-wrapped bundle.

'Owt else?' the girl asked hopefully, indicating with a sweep of her arm the array of bonnets and hats and shawls. 'How about a few lengths of fine-quality silk?' She fingered a pile of small square off-cuts. 'Make lovely trimming, this would, for a tired-looking blouse. Or this—'

'Mebbe another time when I've the brass to spare,' Laura said with a smile, picking up the parcel of clothing she'd come for and handing across a fraction of what she'd anticipated spending on it. She thanked the seller and turned for home, delighted with her purchases.

She'd almost reached the market's exit when a snippet of conversation nearby made her ears prick. Slowing, she glanced to the two women chatting by a rickety barrow filled with curious-looking ointments and liquids in glass bottles. They were discussing someone's health, she realised, and immediately her father sprang to mind. She stepped closer. 'Excuse me?'

'Aye, lass? What can I help thee with?' enquired the elder woman, her craggy face stretching in smile.

'I . . . Well, it's more my father needs helping really.' Laura pointed to the merchandise. 'Are these medicines?'

'That they are. Herbal potions made by my own fair hands, I have here, to cure every ailment under God's sun.'

Laura's eyes widened with hope. 'Even for the heart?'

'Your father's is bad, aye?' the woman asked sympathetically.

Tears welled. She waited until the other customer had ambled away then nodded. 'Has tha owt on yon barrow for him? Owt at all what might help?'

'That I do.'

'Oh! What?'

'Well, that depends on exactly his condition.'

'He gets pains. And breathlessness, aye.'

'Well, now. If it's attacks wrought by nervousness, a tonic diet and change of air will calm his excitement. Palpitations of the heart can also arise from indigestion?' she added when Laura shook her head – but this second suggestion she, too, dismissed. 'Another cause of rapid pulse easily remedied is that of a luxurious lifestyle or indolence?'

'Nay, nay.' Laura was emphatic. 'We ain't the brass for high living. As for indolence . . . Father's the least lazy person I know. Works his fingers to the bone, he does, allus has. It can't be through that, neither, why he's suffering.'

'Right. Well. I'm guessing his symptoms ain't on account of corsets being laced too tightly . . . Therefore, it might be a plethoric cause.'

Laura's blood turned cold at the frightful-sounding disorder. 'What's that?' she forced herself to ask, dreading the answer.

'Too much bodily fluid. He'll need a purgative.' With this, the herb woman selected a small jar from her collection and unscrewed the lid. Then she reached beneath her shawl and drew out a long chain hanging around her neck, attached to which was a tiny silver spoon. A scrap of cloth from her skirt pocket followed, and she spooned into it from the jar a small amount of the green, powdery concoction. After gathering the material into a pouch and securing the top with a length of string, she held it out to Laura and smiled. 'Guaranteed, God willing, to do your father the world of good. Go on, take it.'

Though tempted, Laura hesitated. Could she really trust her? She'd heard talk of this type of people, quacks

57

and their ilk, who made a living off the backs of folks' desperation. They would promise you the moon – for an extortionate price, of course – when most of the time their miracle cures were nothing more than a useless mixture of random ingredients, void of any health benefits whatsoever. And those with sick loved ones or suffering from their own ailments fell over themselves to procure these 'medicines', clung to the shred of hope that they would work, only to discover too late that all they had got was duped. Unsurprisingly, the law came down on these charlatans heavily.

Profiting from people's misery; was it possible to sink any lower? Frowning, Laura let her arm drop back to her side.

Sensing her uncertainty and the reason why, the woman took Laura's hand and pressed the pouch into it. 'No charge this time, lass.'

'But . . .' Now, guilt replaced her mistrust. 'I can't let you do that. After all, you have a living to make and—'

'No charge,' she repeated quietly, kindly, and hope returned to Laura, threatening to overwhelm her.

'It'll really work?' she whispered. 'What's in it?'

'Oh, a pinch of this and a sprinkle of that. The main ingredient, mind . . .'

Laura was entranced. There was something about this old woman, something behind her sharp hazel gaze that spoke of something higher, some deeper wisdom that most couldn't reach. She dropped her voice further. 'Aye?'

'The purple foxglove.'

'Oh.' The large-belled, spire-shaped bloom, indigenous to the region, grew some four and five feet tall along hedges and copses. Though beautiful, hearing that what she'd anticipated to be some magical, mysterious component was but a humble plant deflated her a little, and the woman laughed.

'Ay now. You and many afore you underappreciate it. But us traditional folk, us herb wenches, we know, aye. The medicinal properties of wild foxglove in dropsy – and on the heart – are well proven, lass. Many a soul have we cured, where doctors have failed, from the dried leaves of yon flower. Gather it myself, I do, from yonder on the city's outskirts, just afore blossoming time.'

'It ain't dangerous, then?'

'Oh aye, that it can be in the wrong hands, which is why it don't get the merit from our modern medical men it deserves. Mind, if it ain't misused and the dosage is right, it'll do what it's meant to without mishap.'

'And this here you've made and measured up . . .' She held the cloth aloft. 'It'll definitely not harm Father?'

'It'll not.'

What did they have to lose? Laura nodded acceptance. 'What do I do with it? How is it administered?'

'You're to prepare it as a single dose of foxglove tea. Add to boiled water, lass, with a little sugar to sweeten if your father so prefers. He's to sup a dram of it, which will bring on violent vomiting. Pass water more frequent, he will, an' all. It's the purge he needs. The badness must be flushed out, you see?'

It sounded dreadful. Laura nonetheless nodded again.

'A very active medicine it is,' the woman continued, 'but one that shall fetch relief, you have my word on that. Afterwards, he's to abstain so far as he's able from owt that could have the condition return: fermented liquor, aye, and animal food should be avoided especially. Too much sleep will do him no good, neither. You'll remember all that, lass?'

59

'Aye yes, I think so.'

'You'll find me here each week – Widow Jessop's the name. Just you come and see me, should tha have the need to.'

'Thank you. Truly.' Tears blurred Laura's vision. She blinked them back and flashed a watery smile. 'My father . . . He's my all.'

'It's lucky he is to have thee. Now, run along home to him,' she instructed. 'Take care, lass.'

Glory be to God, her father had never been a big drinker, so there were no worries on that score regarding abstinence. As for his grub, she'd ask Bridget to plan him a special diet, Laura determined as she hurried back through the increasingly busy streets for home. She'd have to confide in the maid his trouble, must if she was to have the other woman's cooperation, but would swear her to secrecy. The less her uncle knew, the better. Mind you, should Ambrose query why his brother was eating differently to them at mealtimes . . . Well, she'd think of something, would cross that bridge when they came to it.

All in all, the morning had been a successful one. Her own heart lighter than it had been for a good long while, she hurried her step towards the coal yard. She'd stash her new working clothes there ready for later, save her uncle spotting the bundle upon her return to the house, she reasoned. His overseer would have opened up by now in readiness for the day's toil; fingers crossed, she'd be able to slip in and out without detection.

Passing through the gates, Laura made for the huddle of lean-tos that served as stables. Only a handful of workers were present at this hour and, though one or two who now recognised her touched their caps in greeting, no one enquired of her business.

When she reached Kenneth's stall she let herself in and breathed a sigh of relief. Making for the far wall, she buried the package beneath a pile of straw then went to stroke the horse, who stood, watching her curiously.

'Morning, lad.' She patted his thick neck affectionately. 'You'll not tell on me, will thee?' she said with a wink and a smile.

'What would he have to tell, then?'

Laura whipped her head around at the booming question – and seeing Nathan's grinning face, her own relaxed. She wagged a finger at him in mock-sternness. 'Ain't anyone ever told thee it's rude to eavesdrop? Not to mention creeping up on folk; near caused me an injury there, tha did.'

'Sorry, miss.'

'Laura, remember?'

His grin returned. He nodded. 'Sorry, Laura.'

She smiled back, and it grew when she remembered the pouch she still held. She grasped Nathan's sleeve, saying excitedly, 'I purchased medicine from the market, lad. For Father. For his heart. The herb woman assured me it's known to work wonders.'

His eyes softened with sympathy at her fervour. 'Aye? What's in it?'

'Foxglove, would tha believe. Reet good for the heart, so says she.'

'Well, you can but try, eh?'

'Aye.'

'Good luck with it, Laura. I'd best get back to my work afore the boss man catches me loitering.'

Her face fell. 'Uncle Ambrose is here already?' At his nod, she motioned to the door. 'I'd better be getting along with thee – I'd rather he didn't see me, neither.'

61

Quickly, she told Nathan of the clothing she'd hidden. 'Father, he'd rather that Uncle Ambrose didn't know I'm accompanying him on his rounds.'

Nathan nodded understanding. Then his slow grin returned, spreading across a boyish face fresh and clear of muck at this early hour and crinkling eyes now holding a wicked glint. 'I can't wait to see thee in your new rig-out.'

'Get away with you,' she chuckled, ushering him from the stall and following him into the yard. 'It's a sight I'll look, all right. Mind, I care naught for that really, so long as it eases Father's burden, even just a little.'

'Amos is lucky to have thee,' Nathan told her with feeling. He'd paused to look at her, eyes suddenly serious. They deepened with intensity as they stared at one another, and Laura felt something she hadn't known for a long time stir within her. She dropped her gaze and cleared her throat, both surprised and embarrassed.

'The herb wench reckons he's lucky, an' all,' she said, for want of something to break the charged silence. 'It's the other way around, if you ask me. He's a father in ten million. Gone above and beyond for me, he has, since all the trouble—' She clamped her mouth shut, horrified that she'd let her tongue run away with itself.

A frown appeared to tug at Nathan's brow but, if he intended to question her comment, he didn't get the chance – Ambrose, striding towards them, looking none too pleased, shattered the moment. Laura didn't know whether to be relieved at this or not.

'Interrupting summat, am I?'

Concealing the medicine in the folds of her shawl, she masked her disconcertedness with a smile. 'Nay, 'course not, Uncle Ambrose.'

The older man turned to Nathan, saying darkly, 'You,

back to your work. Now.' And when he'd gone: 'You're early,' he remarked to Laura, gaze narrowing slightly in suspicion.

'I thought I'd show willing. I had to visit the market this morning and, well . . . I reasoned I might as well come straight here afterwards, make an early start in t' office, like.' She could feel colour creeping up her neck at the deception but did her best to keep her tone light. 'You don't mind, do yer, Uncle Ambrose?'

He folded his arms across his huge chest, his eyes turning to slits. 'So? Where are they?'

Laura blinked in confusion. 'Where are what?'

'Your purchases? From the market?'

'I . . . They didn't have what I needed after all. No matter,' she added, smiling, and turned for the office, lest he spot the flustered blush now staining her cheeks, too. 'I'll get on to my work, then. Can I brew thee some tea afore I begin?'

He didn't answer. Instead, to her dismay, he followed in silence, his heavy tread seeming to match his mood. When they were inside he closed the door and stood with his back to it, watching her as she flitted to the low cupboard for cups. Then: 'What was it tha needed that the market couldn't cough up? They sell everything a body could ever want or need down Smithfield's.'

She kept her back to him. 'It's . . . private.'

'How so?'

'It just is.'

'Why?'

Reaching the end of her endurance, she spun on her heel to face him. 'Uncle Ambrose, *please*. You're embarrassing me.'

'Embarr—?'

'It was . . . female things I needed, is all,' she cut in,

hoping the lie would work and he'd leave the matter be. *Lord, he was like a dog with a bone . . .*

'Oh. I see.' Shifting from foot to foot, he looked decidedly uncomfortable.

Laura returned her attention to the task at hand. 'Would tha like a sup, then, Uncle Ambrose?'

'Aye. 'Ere, lass . . .' He stepped towards her with a crooked smile. 'I shouldn't be shoving my nose into your business. Sorry.'

Swallowing her relief, she smiled back and motioned her head in acceptance of his apology.

'I really am sorry.'

'It's all right— Oh.' The last word was smothered in Ambrose's chest as he wrapped his arms around her and drew her to him in a too-tight embrace.

Her body stiffening with awkwardness and growing unease, her arms remained by her sides as she waited the moment out. Finally, he released her, and she turned back hurriedly to the tea-making. Behind her, his breathing had quickened and she just knew his eyes were on her – she could feel his stare like two hot embers boring into her flesh. Then, as it always did, her mind told her she was being ridiculous, imagining things – she was his niece, for God's sake – and what was wrong with her at all to keep conjuring up these wild and mucky notions? It was sick, that's what. And still . . .

'I'll not bother with the tea after all,' said Ambrose, breaking through her thoughts, and she released her breath.

Seconds later, he was gone; she closed her eyes and shook her head. Then she straightened her shoulders and got started with her work. Father would be arriving any time now. She must be ready to greet him naturally, with a smile. His state of well-being depended on it.

I'm just being silly. As the minutes ticked on, the rational side of her brain repeated the mantra. Nevertheless, it didn't stop her flesh from creeping, as though home to an army of insects, at the memory of her uncle's touch.

Chapter 6

'so, how do I look?'

'That young lad back at the yard's taken a fancy to thee.'

'What?' Laura had been twisting in her seat on the cart, arms outstretched, showing off her new working clothes. Now, she straightened up and, ignoring the flush of red that sprang to her face, repeated, 'What?'

'Yon lad – Nathan, is it?'

Not trusting herself to look at her father, she kept her gaze on the uniform row of houses they were passing.

'I've seen the way he looks at thee. If you ain't, lass, tha must be blind.'

'He seems a nice enough lad . . .' She shrugged. 'It matters not either way.'

'And why's that, then?'

'Because I'll *never* shackle myself to another fella as long as I breathe.'

Amos said nothing for a few minutes. When finally he spoke again, his tone was low but firm. 'I'll not be around for ever, lass.'

'Father?'

'I'll not see thee cast into this world alone. Not all men are cut from the same cloth as Adam Cannock. Promise me you'll remember that.'

Laura felt tears prick. She knew this, of course she did. She'd been unlucky was all. She should have listened to her judgement – her *father's* judgement. He'd seen through him from the off. *The Cannock brothers.* Her stomach did a few unpleasant flips at the thought of the two siblings still living. Had they given up on her? Were they still hell-bent on exacting revenge? She hadn't the answer, just her prayers that she was free of them at last to keep her going. Pushing their snarling faces away, she switched her thoughts back to the young man who toiled at the coal yard.

Nathan was handsome, she had to admit. And he did seem to have taken a liking to her – something her uncle had also noticed, though he clearly wasn't as accepting of this as his brother was. What was Ambrose's problem at all with his employee? He seemed to detest his very presence. *Or was it that he resented Nathan's attention towards her because he himself . . . ?* Stop, she told her warped musings yet again. Just please stop with this madness!

'Hold up there, lad.' At Amos's command, Kenneth obeyed immediately and the cart rumbled to a halt outside their first customer's abode. 'Ready, lass?'

Nodding, Laura hopped to the pavement, mind now firmly on the job at hand. Her task, her father's health, meant more than all her worries combined. She just hoped he'd agree to take the foxglove tea when she put it to him tomorrow. Being Sunday and thus a day of rest, he'd be able to deal with the sickness that the medicine brought on better at home. *Please, please, let it work . . .*

Arriving back at the yard some time later, the cart now carrying but a pile of empty sacks, they saw Nathan apparently waiting for them; he made his way towards

67

them with his ready smile, and Amos nudged Laura with a knowing look.

'Father, please,' she murmured, her earlier blush resurfacing. Nevertheless, she couldn't quell the secret spark of pleasure. Her own lips stretched a greeting when the young man stopped by her side of the cart. 'All's well?' she asked.

'Aye.' Nathan nodded, cleared his throat loudly. 'I erm, wondered . . . well, what I wanted to ask—'

'Spit it out, lad,' cut in Amos. There was definite amusement in his eyes.

Nathan's cheeks bloomed with colour. He turned once more to Laura. 'Could I . . . ? What I mean is, would you . . . Would you like to come out with me some time?' he asked on a rush. 'The People's Concert Hall is an all right night, have some good acts on at the weekend. Mind, it can get a bit lively at times . . . 'Course, we can try somewhere else if you prefer? Or . . . or we could go forra walk? Not that there's many places to go where it's pleasant round here, mind . . . Or we could—'

Again, it was Amos who broke through his speech: 'She'd like that,' he answered for her. 'Wouldn't you, lass?'

'Father, *please*,' Laura beseeched again, face now ablaze. Meeting Nathan's expectant gaze, she was loath to disappoint him, but this needed nipping in the bud here and now. As she'd said before, she wanted no truck with the opposite sex ever again. It just wasn't worth it. The lies, pain, crushing heartache, *the danger* . . . She'd suffered more than her share where men were concerned; she wouldn't put herself through that once more, however nice he seemed. That's how it started, after all. That's how Adam had been at first. God, how wrong she'd been then. She'd rather face a lifetime

68

of loneliness than risk it. Oh, she would. 'Nathan, listen . . .'

'You don't have to give me an answer right away, nay. Think on it awhile—'

'I don't need to.' She lifted her chin and, though her words were not unkind, her tone was firm: 'Sorry, lad, but the answer's no.'

'Oh. Oh, well. That's all right. No bother. I erm, I'd best get back to work.' He flashed a half-smile and walked away, head down.

Inwardly cringing, Laura turned accusing eyes on Amos.

'No need for that, now, was there? Where was the harm?'

'Please don't ever put me in such an awkward position again. Embarrassing ain't in it! Honestly, Father, I didn't know where to look.' She jumped from the cart and made her way to the office before he could say anything further. An argument was the last thing she desired, but he'd been wrong to do that to her. As for poor Nathan . . .

She stole a look at him across the yard and was pained to see him looking back, his face a mask of forlornness. He put her in mind of a kicked puppy, all large sorry eyes and slumped shoulders. She tore her gaze away and hurried for the sanctuary of the office.

For the remainder of the afternoon, she avoided the window lest she caught another glimpse of Nathan outside, and threw herself into her duties with gusto to keep mind busy as well as hands. She recalled sitting down gratefully some time during the day and drinking a cup of tea, but at which point she'd fallen asleep, she couldn't say. She awoke suddenly. Blinking away the dream fog, she looked about the empty room.

At least she'd thought it was empty.

Ambrose was standing in the dim corner, watching her.

Something in his expression froze Laura's limbs to marble ice. It seemed he hadn't noticed her eyes were open – no wonder, as his dark gaze was fixed firmly on her chest. Then her stare travelled down and she saw to her sheer disbelief that his hand was moving furiously inside his trousers.

A wave of smothering repugnance assaulted her soul – she reared back in the chair as though struck by an invisible fist. Its meaning – *the truth* – was absolute. There was nothing that the logical side of her mind could conjure up to explain away this.

'God in heaven . . .'

'Lass! I—'

'Nay. You just stay back.' Her hands, claw-like, swiped the air between them as he moved towards her. 'Stay *back*, I said!' she almost screamed when he failed to halt, the words punctuated with choking sobs. 'Father will kill thee for this, you just wait and see!'

'I've done nowt, you hear?'

'What? How can tha *say* that when you were—?'

'I touched thee not. Only myself. Go on, deny it!'

Laura's brain spun with the warpedness of it all. 'And that makes it any less grotesque?' she asked incredulously. 'You were . . . I *saw* thee, what you were about. For the love of God, I'm your *niece*.'

'Aye, well.' Not a trace of shame or remorse stirred his features. 'It's not like you're a daughter, is it? Not that closely bonded, are we? That *would* be bordering on foul, I grant thee.' He shrugged. 'I like the way you look. You're a bonny 'un, aye. What? I've done nowt!' he burst out again at the contemptuous curl of her lip. Realising his excuses wouldn't wash with her, his tactic changed. He drew himself up to his full height – a formidable-looking figure enough when at ease, tenfold in anger. 'Go on, then, you go right ahead and tell that father of yourn. Reckon he'll believe thee? Huh! Looks up to me, he does, allus has. Worships me, tha might say. Your words would mean nowt stacked against mine.'

'That's lies! Father . . . he would listen, he would, he—'

'Stake your life on that, would you?'

Though instinct had her head snapping up and down in a firm nod, her inner voice whispered doubt. Just how often had she lambasted herself for what she'd believed to be her wild imaginings? How many times had she dismissed her uncle's improper behaviour as innocent? If she had so little faith in her own judgement, could she say with complete conviction that her father would take it as gospel? Mother of God, if he should think her lying . . . the pain of that would be too much to bear. And what then? Would he disown her? Cast her out through the shame and disgust of it? He'd stood by her unshakably where her disastrous marriage and the Cannock brothers were concerned – but this? His brother? She'd sooner die than lose him.

The corner of Ambrose's mouth lifted at her hesitation. 'Got it cushy, here, youse have. A sound job apiece, good dwellings – you're willing to chuck it all away? Ruin the lot, see our Amos on the streets along with thee? And for what? I never laid a finger on thee. I've women aplenty for that, don't you fear.'

Though her heart was banging with terror and the building rage of injustice, she lifted her chin. 'Like Bridget Figg, you mean?'

'That's right. By, but she's willing enough. With you . . . I were looking, is all. Just *looking*. There's no harm.'

71

'But I don't *want* you to! Never in that way. Not ever. It's depraved, that's what!'

Charged silence hung between them. Her uncle's face was stony; she could glean no clue as to what he would say – do – next. Then he spoke, and the air around her seemed to shatter like glass, the words jabbing at her ears like a physical thing:

'I'll do as I like. Ain't no prissy young doe tells Ambrose Todd what to do.'

'Then you leave me with no choice.' She edged forward towards him and the door. 'Get out of my way.'

'Aye, all right. You seek out our Amos, try your luck. Just know this, missy: I don't take kindly to slander.' He delivered his threat calmly. 'You'll live to regret your folly, by you will.'

Who was this monster before her at all?

Skirting past the desk, Laura made her dash for freedom. 'I wish to God we'd never come here.'

'And why was that, I wonder?'

Her hand froze on the knob. She swallowed.

'Queer, it is. A reet rum do, aye. Upping sticks like youse did, no warning or word to me, hotfooting it to Manchester, just like that.'

Thankful she had her back to him, she closed her eyes. 'I don't know what you mean.'

'Aye? Shall I tell thee what I think's occurring here? I reckon you're running. Oh yes. From what, I wonder? Happen I should make a few enquiries, eh, in yon Bolton town? What says thee to that?'

Her tongue refused to form an answer, be it a denial or otherwise. Her chest felt heavy, her legs weightless. She prayed to the Almighty that she wouldn't pass out.

'So. There we have it. I'm right, eh?'

He couldn't discover the truth. He mustn't know. For if he did, if he informed on her to those men ... It would mean a fate worse than death for her. Worse still, Father, too. No. *No.*

'Well, then. Now we know where we stand ... I'll leave thee to get back to your duties.' As if a switch had been pressed, Ambrose was suddenly changed. His voice was jolly, his face beaming. 'I have some calls to make. See thee later, lass.'

The door slammed shut behind him. Numbness kept her scorching tears from spilling and the sobs confined to her throat.

She released a long breath. Then she crossed the room slowly and returned to her work.

The following morning, Bridget had prepared breakfast before leaving for church, and Amos and Ambrose were helping themselves from the dishes on the table when Laura entered the kitchen. To match her mood, the cloud-heavy sky had released a steady stream of rain since dawn, and the sight of her uncle sitting there smiling, his large stomach resting on the table in front of him, dulled her world further.

'Morning, lass!'

She flicked her eyes to her father and, seeing him watching her, forced herself to smile at the other man. 'Morning, Uncle Ambrose.'

'Any plans the day?'

Reaching for the small teapot, wishing he'd shut up and leave her be, she shook her head.

One thing Laura was sure of: if her father chose to practise what this day was intended for – to rest – and coupled with Bridget away at worship, she would make an excuse – must – for she wouldn't spend the day alone with *him*. No way. The notion caused her stomach to churn and bile to rise. Yesterday . . .

She never dreamed herself such a coward, yet here she was, sat breaking bread with him after all he'd done, his disgusting display . . . And to think that before venturing to this city she'd believed that things surely couldn't get any worse. *Stupid.*

Sleep would be an impossibility later, same as last night, and no wonder. Lying in her moonlit bed, she'd gathered up the coverlet in her bunched fists, raging inside, tears of helplessness coursing unchecked down her face. Ambrose Todd had her over a barrel, and he knew it.

Telling Father what his brother was about would result in nothing but loss for them both. Their dwelling, their jobs, would be no more. Even if Ambrose didn't boot them from his home and business if confronted, Amos would never stay on here and at the yard if he knew. And yet *she* knew that was the best outcome she could hope for. Because the alternative scenarios that could play out were far, far worse.

Her father could kill him. Had he solid proof of the real goings-on, he'd tear his brother's head from his neck, of that she was in no doubt. Then he would hang. Just contemplating this killed *her.* Next, of course, there was the possibility that Amos wouldn't take her revelation as truth. He could side with his brother. Then she'd be homeless, jobless *and* alone. Penniless, destitute, disowned, *destroyed* by the person she loved more than any other. She couldn't – wouldn't – risk that.

And if Ambrose should – nay, he definitely would, oh yes – carry through with his threat of asking their business in Bolton and what had driven them here, reveal her whereabouts to the Cannock brothers . . . Her very life would be in jeopardy – more so than it was now, with no one, without her father's support and protection. She'd be done for, well and truly.

No. There was no way out of this mess he'd created. She *had* to keep her silence, at least for now. At least until she had a way, a plan. *If ever.* It was the safest, most sensible option open to her at the moment. And yet . . . what did that mean for her?

Would he attempt again . . . ? Of course he would. Hadn't he said himself no one told him what to do? He had no intention of stopping what he'd started. He had her in his palm, to play and manipulate as and however he pleased. The horror, fear, made her want to weep.

Damn it, she couldn't let him violate her like that. She couldn't!

'I'm for returning to my room forra lie-down, I think,' Amos announced, slicing through his daughter's thoughts, oblivious of her agonising. He rose and stretched. 'It's what lazy Sundays are for, eh, after all?'

'Aye. Me, an' all,' Laura said, doing her utmost to keep the panic from her voice at the prospect of what she'd dreaded becoming reality: being alone with her uncle. Then she glanced to the very man and her heart dropped as though from a heady height to see him staring at her with a deep and knowing glint in his eye.

Mother of God, surely not. Not at home, with her father in the next room? He *wouldn't* try it here . . . Was nowhere safe?

Crossing the flagged floor quickly, she snatched up her shawl, saying to Amos over her shoulder, 'Actually, I'll take a walk, Father, whilst you're resting.'

'A walk?' Her uncle's interjection was clipped; he

wasn't best pleased she'd thwarted his sick plans, she saw. 'But it's raining. You'll catch your death of cold.'

'Nay. It looks to be clearing,' she said, keeping her eyes averted as she busied herself knotting the ends of the garment beneath her breasts.

'But these streets and lanes ain't the place to be alone, even in daylight hours. There's all manner of madmen in the slums, and you being a lass, to boot . . . It's in danger you'd be, aye. 'Specially if some varmint took it into his head to get a grip of thee, bonny 'un like you,' he added slyly, and Laura knew he was using the attack the day she accidentally wandered into the cluster of alleys when searching for employment to frighten her. Hah. It was here, with the madman that was *him*, that terrified her far more.

Amos was frowning. ''Ere, lass, happen your uncle's right—'

'I'll be fine, Father. I'll be fine,' she repeated reassuringly, seeing his anxiousness, sorry to worry him but loath to have him talk her out of it, to remain here. 'I'll not roam far, have no fear.'

Ambrose's eyes followed her from the kitchen, and it wasn't until she reached the end of the street that she was able to breathe easier. She leaned against the wall of a pawnbroker's on the corner and squeezed her eyes shut, biting her bottom lip to stem her emotion until she tasted blood.

She and her father had promised to accompany the maid to church another time – Bridget, a staunch believer, had been thrilled to discover they practised the same faith. Laura's maternal grandparents had been Irish and Amos, with no solid denomination, his own family lax on the religious front, had converted to Catholicism after falling in love to appease his future in-laws. Laura now wished she'd gone along today to the Hidden Gem, as St Mary's in the city centre was known locally, to offer prayer; she needed all the help she could get. Fortunately, she wouldn't have to suffer her uncle for a few hours next Sunday at least; he followed no doctrine. No surprise there. He'd probably combust if he stepped through a holy door, devilish piece that he was.

Just how have things come to this? she asked of the Lord, squinting skywards through the drizzle. This new nightmare she'd become trapped in was worse than she'd thought. What the hell was she to do? Living and working together, she couldn't avoid that beast for ever; what, then?

'That's it.' Her eyes opened slowly. She nodded. 'We'll move. I'll find me and Father fresh dwellings and a new position for me. Father won't miss my help delivering the coal sacks when I'm gone from the yard, not once he's had the medicine and is well again – the medicine!' She clicked her tongue, remembering. What with everything that was going on, she'd forgotten all about it, much to her shame. I'll prepare it for him later, she vowed, pushing herself from the grubby wet bricks and continuing on her way.

Laura had been walking aimlessly for what felt like days when a voice called her name – Bridget! She hurried to catch up with the Irishwoman and, upon reaching her, had to stop herself from throwing her arms around her neck. Never had she been so happy to see another human being. 'Hello, Figg.'

'Saints preserve us! What are ye doing out wandering the lanes? Sure, you're soaked through to the marrow!'

'I fancied a walk.'

'Fancied a . . . ?' She shook her head in bemusement.

'I don't understand the young of today, I'm sure I don't! Come, colleen. Let's get you home by the fire and a hot drink inside ye.'

Laura gratefully allowed herself to be led. Her clothes and the body beneath them were itchy with damp and her feet throbbed in her squelching clogs. She'd be safe there now she had company. *God above, how much more of this?*

Minutes later, she had a fluffy blanket around her shoulders and was warming her toes before the kitchen fire's leaping flames; Ambrose was nowhere to be seen. Where he'd gone, she neither knew nor cared, was just glad of the fact.

'Ta, thanks, Figg,' she said, taking a steaming cup from her and feeling quietly calm for the first time that day. She just hoped her uncle wouldn't return to mar her mood for a good long while. 'Is my father still abed?'

The woman smiled. 'If the snores I heard coming from his room when I went upstairs to fetch your blanket are anything to go by, he is.'

Laura nodded. She'd leave him to rest a while longer before preparing and taking up to him the foxglove tea. Would he accept it? Would it even work? Time would soon tell. In the meantime . . .

'Figg?'

'Aye, colleen?'

She kept her tone as matter-of-fact as she could muster. 'What was the name of that mill again where you said your nieces work?'

'Sedgwick. But you'll not be needing the use of that place now, will ye? Not since sir gave you a position at his works, kind and generous soul that he is.'

Her false nod of agreement made her want to be sick. Bridget couldn't see him for what he was, all he stood

78

for. She was infatuated, had to be. Laura had heard talk that it happened often with servants and their masters, but dear God, *him*, who spoke to and treated Bridget like muck beneath his boot? Was love really so blind?

'How are ye getting along, then, at the yard? You're enjoying it, I trust?'

Again, she forced a bob of her head. 'Aye yes, I—'

'Sweet Jesus, what was that?' the maid gasped, looking upwards in the direction of the heavy thump that had cut off Laura's answer. The women shot each other a worried glance then hurried from the kitchen.

Laura took the stairs two at a time, heart thumping, and burst into her father's room. She slapped a hand to her mouth. Amos was lying face down on the floor by the bed, unmoving. 'Father!'

'Let me through, colleen.' Bridget moved her aside and knelt by Amos. She took his wrist and checked his pulse whilst Laura looked on, frozen in terror. Then gently, she lifted his head. 'Mr Amos, sir? Can ye hear me?'

'Hmm.'

'Oh, thank God!' Laura threw herself to her knees. 'Father, what happened? What ails thee, what—?'

'Give him a minute to gather his bearings,' soothed Bridget, squeezing her arm. 'He's coming round, see.'

With effort, they helped Amos into a sitting position and propped him against the bedstead. His eyes were glassy, and blood trickled from a small cut above his nose where it had made contact with the floor. Laura dabbed at it tenderly. He peered up at her with a frown.

'Lass . . . What happened?'

'You took a tumble, Father. Fell from your bed, it seems. Lord, seeing you lying there . . . You frickened me half to death. I thought . . . You're all right?' she asked through her tears, scrubbing her face with her sleeve.

'My head. Hurts. Tea . . .' He glanced to Bridget, who nodded. 'Parched.'

'Let's get ye up and back into bed first, Mr Amos, then I'll bring you up a sup.'

Again, between them they lifted him up and half dragged him on to the bed – even with two of them, his considerable size, coupled with his weakened state, made it a struggle. The moment his head touched the pillow he closed his eyes and was immediately back asleep.

Puffing from the exertion, Bridget gnawed her lip. 'I'm not happy with him, colleen. I think we should send for the doctor.'

'He'd cause merry hell; he dislikes owt to do with medical men.' *And if Ambrose should discover* . . . 'He seems well enough, now . . . Or is it just wishful thinking on my part?' Laura was torn. 'D'you really think it's that bad, Figg?'

'I can't rightly say. He could have banged his skull, could have done some damage . . .'

'There's no injuries I can see, bar the one on his nose.'

'Aye. And as ye say, he's stable enough.' The maid nodded. 'We'll keep an eye to him till your uncle returns, see what he decides. I'll fetch that tea.'

Before Laura could beg her silence – the last thing she and her father needed was Ambrose finding out – she was gone. Sighing, Laura perched on the edge of the bed and, taking one of Amos's hands in her own, stroked it softly. Had he simply rolled from the bed in his sleep? Or, as she secretly feared, had he already risen and collapsed whilst conscious? Would he remember when he wakened? Would he admit the truth to her if he did?

Was his health deteriorating? Closing her eyes, she breathed through the rising panic. *Lord, watch him, please.* One thing was clear: she couldn't leave the yard after all, not now. She must be close by to keep an eye to him, to help him in his work. He needed her. *And Father, I need you, now more than ever before.*

Could she really endure her uncle, though, if she was to stay on there?

Her gaze swivelled to Amos's tired face and, of its own accord, her back straightened in resolution.

God help her, she'd have to.

Chapter 7

OCTOBER GALES HAD brought to the city the first shivers of winter. In every Manchester street, court and lane, people kept a watchful eye on the impending season with quiet dread. Cold brought illness, and for the poor in particular, increased threat of death. No money meant no coal. No fire meant no hot meal or drink to stave off the chill. Coupled with inadequate and ragged clothing and dwellings colder than the outdoors, the only healthy thing in the slums was the reaper's trade. If the freezing temperature didn't get to them first, disease would finish the job. Countless people would perish before the birth of the new spring. Such was the way of the world.

Life in the house off London Road continued as usual. The foursome rubbed along beneath the same roof as if nothing was changed – only Laura and her tormentor knew different. With dogged determination, she did her utmost to ignore him as much as she was able and steer clear of him when she wasn't. At home, her bedroom was her sanctuary – Ambrose had to pass his brother's room to reach hers and so, as yet, hadn't attempted it. Being holed in the small office at work, however, made it harder to avoid him but, much to her relief, besides leering looks and the odd lascivious remark, he'd left her be. For now.

The one beacon of hope in her otherwise tense and uncertain world was that the medicine seemed to have done the trick – Amos was fresher, brighter, than she'd seen him in many months. As the old herb woman forewarned, the foxglove tea had made him sick something awful. But soon enough, he was up and about, frowning in discomfort less and smiling more, and for this alone, Laura was thankful of their circumstances.

Then came the day when the situation took a sinister shift. It was a time she'd dreaded. When stares and comments were not enough, and Ambrose upped the stakes in his debauched game.

It was the end of the week and nearing finishing time at the yard. Her uncle had been absent for most of the day and, when he entered the office, he did so on slightly unsteady feet. It was fast approaching the best time of year for men of his trade; fuel was king. Clearly, he'd raised more than one glass in the public houses in celebration that business was increasing and profits were up. Laura took one look at his bleary gaze and slack-jawed grin and felt her guts drop to her toes. She quickly filed away the papers she'd been sorting through and went to fetch her shawl. Wrapping it around her shoulders, she moved to the door, eyes averted, head down.

''Ere. Wait.'

'But I've completed what tasks tha set me for the day—'

'And a gradely job you've done, too, no doubt, as always. Nay, it's not that.'

'Then what?' she forced herself to ask.

'Sit with me awhile.'

'Father . . . Father will be waiting for me, he—'

'I sent him on an errand. We've a handful of minutes to ourselfs afore his return.'

Unease traced prickly fingers up her spine. She licked her lips nervously. 'Aye, well. Nonetheless, I think I'll just be on my way—'

'Sit.'

His tone brooked no argument. After a last look of longing at the door Laura did as she was told.

Ambrose leaned against the desk close by, his knee almost brushing hers, and folded his arms. He chuckled when she shifted her legs to avoid them touching. 'I ain't riddled with the bubonic, lass.'

'What d'you want?'

'To talk is all.'

'What about?'

His eyes trawled the length of her. 'Tonight.'

'What?'

'I'm for coming to you later when you're abed. I'll not waken thee. Be sure to keep a healthy fire in your room so as you've no need for blankets. 'Tain't as fun if you're all covered up.'

She had to be dreaming this whole sordid nightmare, surely? Mouth falling open with incredulousness, she shook her head slowly. 'You're mad – *foul.*'

'I told thee—'

'Now I'm telling thee,' she spat, springing from her seat. 'Come anywhere near me and I'll run screaming to Father. He'll kill you, d'you hear, and it's no more than you deserve!'

'You'll not.'

'I will, I tell you!'

'Then you're a fool. I could make your life very unhappy. I'll see thee with nowt as easy as that.' He clicked his fingers.

Though scared, she forced her chin up. 'Listen to yourself. You're really so arrogant you believe you can bully

84

and intimidate me into going along with your disgusting wishes? I'm not a slip of a lass, Uncle Ambrose, what knows no better and will bend to your will. I'm a grown woman who's known life, known a man. A widow—'

'Aye, I've been thinking on that.'

The calmness with which he delivered his statement – and its subject – threw her. She swallowed hard. 'What d'you mean?'

'How was it again that Adam died? I can't recall.'

'That's because I've never told thee. But if you must know, he was sick. An, an illness took him.'

'Well, that's queer.'

'What is?'

'Well, our Amos, you see, *he* reckons it were a tragic accident occurred at work. He said so hisself out yonder, the day youse arrived in this city. Remember?'

Laura went hot all over. He'd been trying to catch her out, and it had worked. Consumed by her emotions, she wasn't thinking straight, had allowed herself to be tricked. *Stupid, stupid.*

'So? Which is it? Or have I to take myself up to Bolton town, dig out the truth for myself?'

'Just leave me alone. Please.'

Seeing the nervous twisting on her hands, the tears building in her eyes and tremor of her bottom lip, he sighed as though satisfied. 'Later, then. You'll be . . . accommodating, won't yer?'

She stared back dully. She had nothing left to fight with.

'No sticking to your father like a limpet, no lingering in the kitchen till all hours with that bloody maid, *no* avoiding me. You just get yourself off to bed at a reasonable hour the night. You hear?'

'Please . . .'

'That's an order. Ah, here's Amos,' he added cordially, as though nothing had taken place between them, glancing to the yard through the window. 'Run along now and catch up with him, get yourselfs off home. I'll see thee later.'

She fled. Desperate eyes fixed on her father chatting to another worker up ahead, she failed to spot Nathan emerging from the stables until it was too late; she hurtled into him, almost knocking the pair of them to the grubby cobbles.

'Lad! Oh! So sorry, I . . . didn't see . . .'

'That's all right. 'Ere, what's the matter?' Taking in her wild stare and trembling hands, his smile faded. 'Laura?'

'I . . . I just . . .'

'Come with me.' He made to lead her to a quieter part of the yard, but she pulled back, couldn't bear his kindness right now, for she'd break down without a doubt and all would be lost.

'Nay. I'm fine, lad, honest. I . . .' A sudden idea came to her and her spirits lifted ever so slightly. 'Does your offer of going out some place together still stand?' she asked tentatively. She'd embarrassed the both of them a few weeks ago by refusing, although, being the easy-mannered fellow that he was, he hadn't let it come between them – would he still be interested? She needed something to avoid that house of her uncle's for a few short hours and all it had come to stand for. She'd also more than welcome Nathan's calming presence. 'If you've changed your mind, of course, I'll understand—'

''Course I ain't. I'd like that, Laura, aye. I'd like that very much.'

Warmness filled her, threatening to tip her emotions overboard. She smiled, nodded. 'Today?'

His pleased grin spread. 'Aye. Aye, yeah. Where d'you fancy going?'

'Anywhere, I don't mind. You'll call for me at home? You know the address?'

'Aye yes.'

'Say . . . in an hour?' The sooner she could escape its confines, the better.

'An hour?' He seemed surprised. 'Well, I suppose I could have a quick scrub and change of clothing in that time . . . Mind, we'd have to snatch summat to eat whilst we're out, for Mam mightn't have my meal prepared so soon—'

'That suits me,' she cut in, already making her way to the gate, lest he questioned her urgency. 'See you later, then.'

And what of tonight upon your return? For you'll have to go back there some time. He'll be waiting. He'll take his chance, slip across the landing, into your room and— 'Nay,' she whispered fiercely, scattering the loathsome fact from her racing mind. 'I'll not dwell on it!'

'Hello, lass.'

How she commanded the smile to her lips and kept it there, she didn't know. Begging her thumping heart to slow and the tears to stay at bay – this man was her safe harbour; she should have been able to tell him of her crippling struggles, would have done anything for it to be possible but, damn it, it wasn't – she fell into step beside him. 'Good day?'

Amos nodded. 'You?'

A few deep swallows, then: 'Aye.'

'Good, good.'

Oh, Father . . . 'You're well? You've had no pains – breathlessness – at all?'

'Nay, lass. I'm mended, I told thee. No fussing.'

'Sorry.' She smiled again, linked her arm through his. 'I love thee is all.'

'And I thee. Now, then. Young fella-me-lad back yonder . . .' He jerked his head towards the yard and wiggled his bushy grey eyebrows. 'Youse seemed to be deep in conversation back there.'

'He's . . . Well, we're for meeting up later. Only as friends, mind,' she hastened to add when Amos nodded knowingly.

'Well, I'm glad to hear it, lass. He seems a sound sort.'

'Aye, he does.' And she meant it. Perhaps in another time, another place . . . But no. She couldn't, no matter the man, knew she never would again. Adam Cannock and his ways had put paid to that.

It had been a wonderful evening.

Laura cast the gathering darkness a bitter glance. She could have stayed out for ever. And much to her shock and not a little confusion, the reason wasn't only to avoid home and her uncle.

She'd enjoyed herself.

Despite her current problems and those still haunting her mind from the past where the opposite sex was concerned, she'd found herself warming to Nathan in a way that she hadn't anticipated. He made it difficult not to, and she'd quickly given up trying to uphold a distant front. He was cheeky, fun, made her laugh. Most importantly, he was kind and respectful. More than anything else, she'd needed that tonight.

He'd opted for the People's Concert Hall, known locally as the Cass, situated on Lower Mosley Street. A plain, drab-looking building, its edifice soot-blackened like everything else in the chimney-choked industrial towns and cities, it seated upwards of three thousand people. Classes were segregated into separate areas and Nathan had announced that he could stretch to the best seats, but she'd persuaded him otherwise and they had instead made a beeline for the cheapest section. She didn't want him to feel obliged to impress, to fritter his hard-earned brass unnecessarily, and especially not on her.

As he'd previously pointed out, it was a rowdy place. Packed with men and women of all ages, desperate for a brief reprieve from toil and want, it was somewhere they could let their hair down and lose themselves, if only for a little while, in the entertainment of the night. The air was muggy with tobacco smoke, over which hung an ale-laden pall, and the atmosphere had throbbed with joviality. Strains from the orchestra mingled with shouts and guffaws, and the audience had shown their appreciation with foot-stamping and loud applause – or boos and hisses for anyone who didn't pass muster.

Fortunately, most acts had been decent; she'd laughed along with Nathan at the comic performer until her sides ached. Then it was on to a supper room for chops and potatoes swimming in onion gravy, where, to her surprise, she'd found she had a hearty appetite. Later, hands wrapped around mugs of strong tea, watching Nathan laughing as they discussed the night's show, his scrubbed face free of coal dirt shining with animation in the gaslight, she'd known a sudden urge to lean across the table and press her lips to his.

Though fleeting, the moment had alarmed her and she'd blushed to the roots of her hair. Mistaking her flush for the heat of the room, he'd suggested they take a slow walk back to her home, much to her disappointment; yet hadn't she known that the evening must end at some point, Lord help her?

Now, as they stood outside her door beneath a milky moon, pricks of shimmering silver studding the navy sky, her earlier happiness seemed a distant memory and she wanted to weep. She stared up at him, wanting to say so much but knowing she couldn't utter any of it.

'I've had a gradely time, lass.' His voice was husky with feeling. 'Thanks for agreeing in t' end, for giving me a chance.'

'Thank *you*, Nathan. I've enjoyed every minute.'

'Aye?'

She nodded. 'Aye, really.'

'You'll come out with me again, then?'

Her answer needed no deliberation: 'I will.'

Silence hung between them.

'Well.'

'Well.'

'Goodnight, then.'

'Night, lad.'

He dipped his head and planted a swift kiss on her cheek then turned and walked away.

Only when he'd disappeared from view did she force her feet forward and enter the house.

Inside, all was quiet as the grave. For a full minute she stood stock still, listening for the slightest movement, any indication that her uncle was about. None came. Nevertheless, as she moved towards the kitchen, where she knew Bridget would be waiting up for her return in order to lock up, her breaths came in short gasps and her palms grew slick.

Please don't let him be here. Let him have already fallen into a drunken stupor, she pleaded silently, over and over. To her sheer relief, her prayers appeared to bear fruit – the maid, seated alone before the near-dead fire, smothered a yawn and smiled as she entered.

'Sorry to have kept you from your bed, Figg.'

'Tsk, no. Sure, it's not altogether late. Did you enjoy your evening?'

'I did.' Her eyes strayed to the ceiling. 'Father's abed?'

'He is so.'

She wetted her lips in anxious dread. 'And Uncle Ambrose?'

'Aye, sir as well.' She smiled again. 'Snoring away like a pair of wild boars, they are.'

Laura was aware that the maid was still speaking, but the words didn't register, so intense was her relief. Closing her eyes, she exhaled deeply.

'Colleen?'

'Aye. Sorry. What did you say?'

'I asked whether you're for wanting a sup or bite to eat, or are ye away to your bed also?'

She suddenly felt bone-numbingly tired. 'Nay. Thanks, but I think I'll go on up.' Bidding her goodnight, she left and headed for the stairs.

In her room, Laura undressed and slipped beneath the sheets. Despite Bridget's reassurance that Ambrose was asleep, her gaze remained fixed on the door for an age. But sure enough, nothing occurred; no approaching footsteps out on the landing, no turning of the knob, only silence. Eventually, her lids grew heavy. She snuggled deeper in the bed and the memory of Nathan's smiling face carried her to her dreams.

It was the metallic scrape of a belt buckle being unfastened that woke her in the dead of night. Complete darkness, thick and clogging, enveloped the room – disorientated, Laura squinted desperately but could see nothing. Then her uncle spoke:

'No blankets, I said, damn it.'

In a heartbeat, she was out of the bed and springing

for the door. He grasped her shoulder, hissing at her to stop, but she shook him off savagely. Then she raised her arm and, going by guesswork, aimed in the direction of his face. The flat of her hand made contact with his nose, the sound like the crack of a whip rebounding from wall to wall.

Her voice was a guttural growl. 'Get *out* of here.'

'How dare you! Young gutter bitch—'

'Go on, get out!'

'You'll pay for this.'

She felt him rush past her. The blackness of the landing swallowed him up and all was still once more. She closed the door. After some moments, she crossed the cold floor and got back into bed.

As her brain absorbed what had just happened she felt momentarily empowered. Then reality trickled home and she squeezed her eyes shut, sick with dread of the repercussions her actions were certain to produce.

Ambrose would see his threats through. Soon, the Cannock brothers would form part of his vengeful trio.

She was done for.

Chapter 8

'I THOUGHT I'D look around this afternoon for cheap dwellings up for rent.'

Eating his breakfast, Amos paused. He returned the spoonful of porridge to his bowl. 'What's brought about this?'

'Nowt, Father. It's just . . . Well, we can't stop on here for ever, can we?'

'I don't see why not. We've had no complaints from Ambrose so far.'

That very name brought the acrid bite of bile creeping to her throat. She kept her gaze fixed firmly on her own food. 'Even so. I reckon it's for the best. I . . . Well, I miss it being just me and thee. You know?'

His pale eyes softened. He nodded wistfully. 'I still get a hankering for owd Bolton town and our little rooms above Mrs Hanover's shop.'

Tears stung. She, too, experienced a painful pang whenever she thought of all they had been forced to give up.

'We've many a happy memory from them there years. Eh, lass?'

Until I brought the Cannocks into our lives and ruined everything. Her father had become caught up in her mess, even their poor kindly landlady, her livelihood burned to the ground. Who else? How many more lives would she have a hand in ruining before all this was through?

'You sure you're all right, lass?'

Meeting his eye, Laura nodded with a sigh. 'Aye. Tired is all.' That wasn't altogether untrue. She'd remained locked in fear's jaws for the remainder of the night following her uncle's retreat, hadn't slept another wink and doubted she would again. How could she ever feel safe in that room now? And still, she'd uttered nothing to a soul. *Nothing.*

'Lass? Does summat ail thee?'

This, as though he'd read her tumultuous mind, threw her for a moment. Her eyebrows drew together in dread. 'Father?'

'You seem agitated somehow. Like the weight of the world's on yon shoulders. You sure all went well yesterday with that yard lad?'

Laura had already given her father a run-down of her and Nathan's outing. She repeated what she had earlier: 'It were a gradely time we had.'

'Then what? Don't tha know by now tha can come to me with owt?' His gruff tone softened. 'Ain't my listening ear allus open to thee?'

'I . . .' *Tell him,* her inner voice begged. *Make all this stop! He'll surely believe you – has to.* She opened and closed her mouth again. Though the shame wasn't hers to carry, thoughts of putting into words what his brother had done made her cheeks flame. 'It's . . . I . . .'

'Morning, Mr Amos, Mrs Cannock,' Bridget trilled, entering the room, face all smiles, unaware how significant her timing was – Laura was both grateful and regretful for the interruption. 'Are ye for attending church today?'

Before father and daughter had a chance to respond, heavy footfalls from above, heralding that Ambrose had risen, reached them. Laura got in quickly: 'I'll accompany thee, aye. Father?'

'Aye, all right.'

'Grand so! I'll just fetch my shawl and we'll be away.'

'I'm gradely, Father, honest,' Laura told him when the maid had gone. 'I just, well, I worry still at times about that Cannock pair back home is all.' This, after all, wasn't an outright lie – more of an understatement, if anything. The other issue, much nearer to home, that was causing her such misery, she once again buried down deep inside herself. She'd come close to revealing all a moment ago. She was glad she hadn't. No good could come of it, not for her father.

'Tha must try to forget all what's passed,' Amos told her. 'It's finished with, lass.'

Laura nodded, then busied herself with drinking the rest of her tea as a diversion when her uncle entered the room. The last thing she desired, now more than ever after last night, was to look at his hateful face.

'Morning.'

'Morning, brother. We're just away to church with Bridget.'

Ambrose scowled. 'I hope *Figg* has prepared my breakfast afore she goes anywhere.'

'You all right?' asked Amos, and Laura held her breath when her uncle shot a dark stare in her direction. Then, as though remembering himself, he smiled and sighed.

'Gnawing headache is all, lad. Puts a dampener on the mood.'

Amos nodded understandingly – that the older man

had drunk more than was good for him the previous day was no secret.

'I'll see thee later, lad,' Ambrose said as they made to leave. 'I'm for returning to my bed awhile, I think. See thee, lass,' he added before she had time to slip out behind her father, and she was forced to turn so not to appear impolite to the others. The look of pure murder waiting for her in his eyes lodged the farewell in her throat. Black fear gripped her stomach. Lowering her gaze, she inclined her head and escaped as fast as she could get away with.

Laura was still fretting about that glare, about when and how her uncle would exact his revenge, when they reached their destination: an attractive red-brick and sandstone building with rounded windows in Mulberry Street. Entering through the carved arched doorway with its slim pillars and angelic-hosts-sculptured tympanum, however, her racing thoughts stilled as she scanned the congregation.

She spotted Nathan straight away. To her surprise, a small smile pulled at the corners of her mouth. She tried to catch his eye as she headed to a pew, but he was deep in conversation with an elderly woman seated beside him.

Throughout the service, she tried to keep her gaze on the high altar and ornate marble statues of Our Lady and the saints, but she couldn't help casting the young man furtive looks across the room. She hadn't expected to see him here, hadn't realised he was Catholic. And who was the woman in his company? She was surely too old to be his mother.

Again, afterwards, when the worshippers were spilling out of the church, she trawled the sea of faces for a glimpse of him, hoping to grab his attention, but he and the woman had been swallowed up in the crowd; hiding her disappointment, she followed her father and Bridget into the weak sunshine.

'My foxglove potion came good, then, I see?'

Laura turned to see the herb woman from the market winking up at her. Her own face broke into a warm smile. 'Oh, hello! It did, and I've been meaning to come and see thee, to thank thee, like.' She touched Amos's arm. 'Father, this is Widow Jessop, who makes the medicine I got for thee.'

'How's tha fettling, lad?' the woman asked, pumping his hand in a firm shake.

'Gradely, aye.' Though gratitude sounded in his voice, pride lifted his chin slightly. 'Mind, there weren't nowt altogether wrong, nay. The lass, she frets. Strong as an ox, me.'

''Course you are.'

Giving her a crooked smile, Laura drew her aside. 'Bridget, the maid there, cooks him all the right things, as you instructed.' She'd been forced to tell the Irishwoman he was unwell following his fall from bed, had to, to keep her from informing Ambrose, and had sworn from her the promise of confidentiality. Thankfully, Bridget had cooperated and had even done her best to alter the daily menu as inconspicuously as she could to save her employer enquiring over Amos's changed diet. 'He ain't had a turn since, norra one. Eeh, I don't know how to thank thee, that I don't,' she told her with feeling.

'Just keep an eye to him, lass. He's a proud bugger if ever I met one.'

'Stubborn, to boot,' Laura agreed with a chuckle.

'Well, as I've said afore, you know where I am, should you need me. I'll be on my way now, lass, let that young buck making cow eyes at thee have your attention.'

97

'Young buck?' Laura glanced around with a frown, a rush of pleasure going through her to see Nathan waving from the wide church steps. She bade the woman goodbye and made her way across to him.

'Hello, Laura.'

'Hello. I thought I'd missed thee. I spotted you inside, but you were in conversation,' she explained, looking with a smile to the woman still in his company. Bent almost double with age, with flowing white hair, her tiny frame was enveloped in a tattered green shawl.

'This is my neighbour, Mrs Price,' Nathan introduced them. 'She's blind,' he mouthed when she didn't clutch the hand that Laura held out to her.

Her face softened in compassion. 'I'm very pleased to meet thee, Mrs Price.'

'And me thee, lass.' Looking beyond Laura, she flashed a toothless smile. 'Eeh, the lad here's a good 'un accompanying me the day, and him not even Catholic.'

'Tenants across the way from us who normally visit church with Mrs Price moved away last week,' he explained to Laura. 'So I offered to do the honours.'

'Aye.' The woman hooked her arm more securely through his. 'Kindness itself, you are.'

Laura agreed. Her impression of him strengthened further still. Then his words sank in and she gasped. Without thinking, she grasped his hand in excitement: 'You said your neighbours have moved?'

'Aye.'

'The house is still empty?'

'That's right. Why?'

'Me and Father are looking for a place of our own. Where is it youse dwell?'

He shifted uncomfortably. 'Lass, I don't think . . .'

'What is it? What's wrong?'

'Well, it's a bit . . . I don't reckon it'd be much to your liking—'

'It's a stinking hole is what he's trying to say, lass,' the old woman intervened with a wry laugh.

Nathan coloured then shrugged. 'That's the top and bottom of it.'

Did he think her so judgemental, so shallow? He believed she'd pour scorn on his position? She and her father hardly sprang from grand beginnings – until very recently, they had called a few cramped rooms home all her life. Her fingers tightened around his hand, which she realised she still held; embarrassed, she released it, saying, 'We're not gentry, lad.' Then without thinking: 'Anyroad, owt's better than where we are now.'

His brows rose in surprise. 'If that big place of the boss man's ain't up to your standards, then by gum, lass . . . Ebenezer Court would turn your hair white, let me tell thee!'

'Nay, it's not that, it's just . . . Well, me and Father can't put on Uncle Ambrose for ever. Besides, we miss it being just the two of us. You know?'

He was smiling again, the uncomfortableness gone, much to her relief. 'If you're sure . . . ?'

'I am.'

'I'll have a word with the rent collector when next he calls, ask him to speak with the landlord on your behalf. There shouldn't be no problem. He ain't bothered none who dwells in his warrens so long as his pockets don't suffer. The last thing he wants is a house that can be earning standing empty.'

'Oh ta, Nathan. Thanks.' She couldn't keep the joy from her voice. God above, to be free of his den. The *relief*. 'Me and Father will have a walk round when we can, see the place for ourselfs. What were it called again?'

'Ebenezer Court. You might have need to ask folk for directions; it's tucked away between two other courts, and all three sit squashed between Mill Street and Back Factory Street. It ain't easy to find if you don't know the area like the back of your hand.'

'We'll manage, I'm sure.'

'Fancy, though, eh?' He grinned and winked. 'Us, neighbours.'

The truth in his observation – and the underlying meaning – brought for the first time a flutter of panic to her chest. In spite of her growing interest in him, would settling down so close by seal her fate for her? There would be no distance between them, no line; their lives would be even more intertwined. Would he simply assume it inevitable that they would come together? Did she want her future deciding for her? She didn't want to tie herself to another, not again, had told herself often enough. Did she?

'Laura?'

'What?' She shook herself back to the present, forced a smile. 'Aye. Sorry. I have to go, Father's waiting.' She bade him and Mrs Price goodbye and returned to Amos and Bridget, who were standing chatting nearby.

'The lad's well?' her father asked as they passed through Albert Square for home, and there was clear acceptance in his tone.

Ahead stood the impressive Albert Memorial, the large monument recently erected to commemorate the late Prince Consort, and the half-constructed new Town Hall – fixing her gaze on these to avoid looking at him, Laura nodded. Amos wouldn't fail to notice the excitement – and uncertainty – she knew shone from her eyes and, naturally, he'd want to know the reason for it. 'Aye, he is.'

It was wisest that she held off mentioning the empty property in Bridget's presence, lest it got back to her uncle. He mustn't learn they were considering vacating his house just yet, not until they had somewhere definite. Given his unpredictability, who knew what his reaction would be? He'd likely attempt to scupper their plans; through sheer spite for her, if nothing else.

'A Catholic, to boot, eh?' Amos added. 'Your mam would've approved, lass.'

'Father, please. Me and Nathan—'

'Aye, I know, you're just friends,' he cut in, and there was a twinkle in his eye.

'That's right. We are.' That stir of misgiving grew. Even her father had begun to assume . . . *Would* Nathan, too? Should she simply forget all about the vacant house in Ebenezer Court, search elsewhere, for all their sakes? 'And he ain't Catholic, was just accompanying an elderly neighbour,' she hastened to point out, half hoping this would quell Amos's design of them coming together.

'Aye? Well. Now there's a selfless deed, if ever I heard one.'

It was evident the statement had had the opposite effect and that the lad had gone up a notch further in Amos's estimation – Laura had to fight the urge to throw her hands in the air in frustration.

Though aware she was being unfair – Nathan was an all-round decent fellow – she couldn't help feeling peeved by the whole situation. She didn't want her future mapping out for her by others. Even she didn't know what she wanted, was finding it impossible to straighten out in her mind the conflicting thoughts. There was too much going on at present to focus rationally on any one thing. She was exhausted with it all.

That night, after a tense few hours of doggedly

avoiding Ambrose around the house, she slipped across the landing to her father's room to further discuss them moving out. She'd decided she would inform him of Ebenezer Court after all and see what he thought about it. The ever-worsening atmosphere here had made her mind up for her – she *had* to get out.

Amos patted the edge of the bed and she sat down. He listened to her news without interruption. When she'd finished, he rubbed his chin.

'A court?'

'Aye.' She nodded understandingly. Consisting of several enclosed, poor-quality dwellings huddled around a small yard, courts were notoriously cramped and dank places to live. 'But a home is what you make it, Father. We'll have it looking presentable in no time. Let's at least look at it, shall we, afore making up our minds?'

He shrugged in agreement. 'What our Ambrose will make of it, mind, I don't know. We've perfectly decent lodgings here.'

Laura kept her quiet. As far as she was concerned, her uncle could think what the hell he liked.

A little later, when their conversation had turned to reminiscences of the past, she noticed Amos's eyelids growing heavy. He dozed off with a small nostalgic smile on his lips and, reluctantly, she made to head back to her own room. Then visions of the previous early-hours antics stopped her in her tracks and she backed away from the door. Ambrose Todd wouldn't get to play out his depravity a second night.

She returned to the bed and, as softly as she was able, so not to disturb him, curled into a ball beside her father. His safe presence and steady breath on her cheek lulled her into a heavy sleep within seconds.

*

102

Nathan hadn't been wrong – Ebenezer Court took them an age to locate.

On the spur of the moment, they had taken a detour here after finishing the afternoon delivery round; fingers crossed, Ambrose wouldn't arrive back at the coal yard before them and notice their absence.

Even with directions from passers-by en route, the deeper into the city they went, the denser the maze of alleyways, lanes and courts became, sloping off the thoroughfares every few seconds; one wrong turning and they were lost again in another tangled pocket.

'It'll fair be a miracle if we ever make it back to Kenneth,' Amos grumbled as they made down yet another dark entry. The passages hereabouts were so narrow that they had been forced to leave him and the cart by the roadside on the main street. Hopefully, the nosebag her father had attached to him would keep him occupied long enough that he didn't grow restless and decide to wander off.

'It must be around here somewhere— Ah!' Laura exclaimed suddenly when a faded sign above an arched entranceway caught her eye; she could just make out the name. 'This is it.'

She knew a mild sense of awkwardness being on Nathan's home turf, but this wasn't to last – as they stepped through the opening, whatever else she'd felt quickly melted into despair.

A thin strip of open drain, overflowing and clogged with refuse, ran down the centre of the yard; puddles, stagnant and evil-smelling, dotted the cobblestones. Doing their best to avoid them, they halted and looked about through the gloom.

To their left and right, resembling rows of decaying teeth, slouched six or so miserable, grime-blackened houses crumbling with neglect. The few steps leading to the broken doors were worn and cracked, several long-since-smashed windows were boarded up with mouldering card, and rags and old newspaper were stuffed into the rotten frames to keep out the draughts.

Ahead, a high brick wall blocked off the adjacent street, limiting further what little light managed to squeeze through the cluster of rooftops above. Hemmed in one dim corner was a shared privy, in the other a pump for gathering water, and this, as far as Laura could see, completed the features. She glanced behind her to the slim stretch of alley through which they had entered and wondered if they had stumbled by mistake into hell.

Like every other court in the slum districts of Manchester, Bolton and beyond, it was a crowded and confined, sunless, airless square patch of grinding poverty and squalor. And they were actively volunteering to live here? They must be stark staring mad!

Her voice lacked all trace of her former enthusiasm. 'So, Father . . . What d'you think?'

Lifting his flat cap, Amos scratched his head. 'I think it's a midden, that's what.'

'Aye,' she was forced to agree. Then a familiar craggy figure appeared at one of the doors and, despite herself, Laura's slumped spirits lifted slightly. She stepped forward.

'Who goes there? Hello?'

'Afternoon, Mrs Price. It's me, Laura. We met yesterday at church.'

'Ay aye. Young Nathan's friend in search of fresh dwellings, I remember.' Her milky eyes creased in pleasure. 'Having a gander around the place, then, are thee?'

'That's right, with my father, Amos.'

'Well, now, let's see.' She pointed a gnarled finger in

the general direction of the houses as she spoke: 'There dwells Bee O'Brien and her brood; eleven or so, I think she has,' Mrs Price revealed, much to Laura's shock – how on earth did twelve people fit into such a small property? 'Then there's a newly-wed couple, the Andersons, and their babby at number three. John Goode has the one next door with his boarder, another John – well, he says it's just his boarder, but we all know there's more to it than that, if you get my meaning,' she added conspicuously through the side of her mouth. 'But we mind none about that, nay, for they're golden-hearted fellas, aye.'

Next, she jabbed her thumb behind her. 'This, as you've likely gathered, is my home, and I take in lodgers when I can, in fact we all do; needs must for the brass to keep body and soul together, you see. There's Nathan's one, where he dwells with his mam and brother,' she continued, indicating the house opposite. 'And that 'un there is what you'd occupy.'

Following her nod, Laura hid a sigh and dared not look at her father and what his expression at this news would surely be. The house nearest the privy – of course, it would have to be that one, wouldn't it? The poisonous stench from the excreta of over twenty people, literally on their doorstep . . . God above.

'You're welcome to come in and get an idea of the empty place – mine's identical in layout,' she suggested, opening her door wider. 'It's sorry I am that I can't offer you a sup, mind. I'm all out of tea and milk.'

Feeling obliged to accept out of politeness – they just couldn't live in this court, they couldn't, would have to keep searching – Laura thanked her, and she and Amos followed her inside.

'Now, then.' Settling into her chair by the crackling

fire, Mrs Price gave a sweep of her arm. 'Go on, feel free, and look where you like.'

As they took in their surroundings, Laura and her father shot each other a pleasantly surprised glance, eyebrows raised. The little house was bright and homely and everywhere spotlessly clean – a sharp contrast to the wretchedness outside.

Amos was suitably impressed. 'You keep a very nice home, Mrs Price.'

'Ta, lad. This is Daniel's doing, aye. Maintains its condition regular, the best he can: mends owt that needs it, fresh whitewash on t' walls, that sort of thing. And all out of the goodness of his heart.'

'Daniel?' asked Laura.

'Aye, Nathan's brother. An admirable job their mother, Joyce, has done with them. Salt of the earth, they are, the pair.'

The appreciative spark in her father's eye didn't go unnoticed by Laura. Only this time, it brought no trickle of irritation; she shared his positive view. However much she tried to dismiss it, Nathan was a good catch – and now she had proof he also came from decent stock if this about his brother and mother were anything to go by. Every mention of him, from no matter whose lips, showed him only in a more favourable light. She could, so she had learned only too well to her cost, do much worse.

'One of Bee O'Brien's lasses, young Mary, nips in once a day to dust and sweep the place,' Mrs Price was saying now, 'and another, Lizzie, fetches my purchases from the shops and helps me when preparing meals. They're a gradely lot here, aye. It's the workhouse I'd of finished up many a year ago, if not for my friends. Us Ebenezer Court folk look after our own. Stick together, we do.'

'Everyone sounds nice. I don't reckon it'd be too bad dwelling here.' And Laura meant it. 'Well, thanks, Mrs Price, for your time,' she went on. 'Me and Father had better be going. We've left the horse and cart on t' street.'

'It were my pleasure. Mind, I'd be hotfooting it back to yon beast quick sharp if I were youse. There's many a desperate soul – and plenty more just plain wicked – what would have them away soon as your back's turned.'

Father and daughter shared a worried look. Eager to get back to Kenneth, they bade her a hasty farewell.

'Goodbye for now. I'll tell young Nathan tha called.'

Leading the way, Laura turned through the entrance and hurriedly left the court. Amos had asked the landlord of the public house they had parked the cart outside to keep an eye to it from his window, and though he'd agreed, it would only take a passing opportunist half a heartbeat to have them away.

'It were foolish of me to leave them out there,' Amos said as they navigated their way back through the countless turnings and ginnels. 'I'll murder any swine what's dared take my lad.'

'He'll be fine, I'm sure— Oh no!' she added on a cry when their horse's unmistakable whinny, high in distress, rent the air from nearby. 'Quick, Father!'

'Kenneth!' Amos whispered, wide-eyed, setting off at a run.

Emerging into the street, they almost collided with a tall, blond-haired young man heading in the same direction. He reached the cart before them and it was then they saw the small grey dog – his dog – darting in and out between a terrified Kenneth's legs, barking wildly.

'Heel, Smiler!'

The dog paid him no heed. With a growl of his own, he thrust a hand beneath the horse and plucked out his animal by the scruff of its neck. It squirmed and whined to be set free, but he hooked it securely under his arm, ordering, 'Enough, you divil!' He turned to Amos and sighed. 'Sorry about him. It were a rat scuttling in the gutter, you see. He gave chase afore I had chance to stop him—'

'That thing should be on a rope if tha can't control it.' Amos was incensed. 'Vicious little swine, it's nowt else. And look here, see what it's done!'

The man stooped beside him to assess the trickles of blood running down one of Kenneth's hind legs. 'He's caught but a nip from Smiler's teeth.'

'A bite's harm enough!'

'It shan't lame him.'

'You'd better pray you're right. This here horse is my livelihood and more besides. Should that be deeper than it looks when I get him back to the yard, or later turn infected, I'm coming looking for thee, d'you hear?'

'Well, you'll not have far to search – I dwell but minutes from here at Ebenezer Court.'

Laura had been occupied in stroking the fair, silky hair of the shire's neck and murmuring in his ear words of comfort. Now, her head snapped around. 'Ebenezer Court, you say?'

He glanced her way. 'That's right, lad.'

Lad? She frowned. Then, glancing down at her working apparel, her brow cleared. Coupled with her coal-dust dirty face, it was easy to understand why he mistook her as male. Too busy musing over who he might be from Mrs Price's earlier listing of the court's occupants, she nodded without bothering to correct him.

'I am sorry.' He'd turned back to Amos. 'As I said, you know where to find me, but I reckon a bathe of the wound will see him right as rain.' He touched his cap and swung away towards home. 'The name's Daniel, by the way,' he called over his shoulder before disappearing through the entry.

'Blockhead,' muttered Amos as he climbed aboard the cart. 'Irresponsible, that's what it is.'

Satisfied that Kenneth had calmed, Laura took her seat beside her father. 'That's who Mrs Price spoke so highly of. Nathan's brother.'

'So it seems. Mind, *I'd* not use "salt of the earth" to describe that one. "Cocksure young whelp" is closer to the mark, aye.'

Seeing that his mood was still up and eager to pour oil on troubled waters, Laura changed the subject. At this moment, Amos wouldn't react too well were she to admit her first impression of the light-haired, dark-eyed, confident younger man was favourable. He'd held his hands up to the incident, after all, made no attempt to dodge responsibility. And he'd apologised – twice. Though of course she understood her father's anger – Kenneth was more than mere economic value, he was one of the family.

Urging the horse on, they kept a slow pace back to the coal yard. They found Ambrose waiting for them; thinking on her feet, Laura sent Amos straight off to see to Kenneth's leg, saying she'd explain their absence to her uncle. Naturally, she excluded any mention of Ebenezer Court. Her account of Smiler's antics proved sufficient; he accepted it without question.

'A lad who'd witnessed the whole thing called at the yard saying Father needed assistance, you see, and I took the message. I hurried to where he was and helped calm Kenneth,' she continued as a way of explaining why she'd been with him on his return. Fortunately, she'd rinsed her mucky hands and face in a public horse trough on the journey back. And she always wore her work clothes over her dress, had managed to strip herself of them on the cart.

'Aye, well. You just get back to your duties here. I don't pay thee good money for nowt, you know,' he barked before slamming out.

She was thankful he hadn't pressed the matter. Even more so that he'd left her once again in peace. She'd seen him for only a few minutes this morning before he'd left the yard on one of his usual calls. A foul temper he'd been in, too – had he tried his luck last night but found her missing from her room? She hoped so, prayed with all that she was that he'd eventually get the message.

A full-grown woman who could only find comfort in sleeping beside her father – it was ridiculous. She'd feigned innocence to Amos upon awakening, insisted she couldn't recall falling asleep, and he'd chuckled, saying the same, and suggested they both needed to get some earlier nights. If only he knew. *Oh, if only*. What had Ambrose reduced her to? Her strength of mind had improved steadily since regaining her freedom following her husband's death; now, she was back to square one, it seemed. Her uncle was chipping away at her budding independence, was ruining her. She loathed him for that most.

And still there was tonight to get through; and the next night, and the next after that . . . God help her.

Now, memories of Ebenezer Court filled her with quiet excitement. The poverty of the place had switched to paradise, the squalidness to sanctuary.

She'd persuade Father somehow. She'd make damn sure they got that house if it killed her.

Chapter 9

AS NATHAN'S BROTHER had predicted, Kenneth's injury proved superficial and caused him no further problems. Work continued as usual and Laura was glad of the distraction from continually worrying about the outcome of the new abode. Finally, when she entered the coal yard one morning, Nathan was waiting for her by the gates. She raised her eyebrows expectantly.

'The house . . .'

'Aye?'

'It's yours if youse still want it.'

'Oh, lad!'

'Rent collector will call in t' court with the key in t' morning. Mam will take it in for safekeeping if you can't be there.'

Overcome, she threw her arms round his neck and, laughing, he lifted her off her feet and spun her around. 'I'm that pleased, I am.'

'Steady on. It ain't a palace you've been offered, lass.'

No, it's a haven, she told him with her eyes. *You've helped me more than you think, saved me, almost.* Then out loud: 'Thank you, Nathan. Truly.'

'What would tha do without me, eh?'

She thought about his statement frequently for the remainder of the day. Though said in jest, it had struck

111

a chord within her, and the ever-recurring answer that came when she searched her mind was unchanging: she really didn't know. He was a true friend. She'd never really had many, and especially not male ones. He made her feel secure. She was content in his presence. She really couldn't – and didn't want to – imagine not having him around now.

That evening over dinner she and her father broke the news to Ambrose.

He listened without expression or interruption. For a long moment, he looked from one to the other, his normally florid face taking on a purple hue. Then he leapt to his feet, sending the crockery on the table clanging in protest: 'A stinking bloody court? Have you taken leave of your senses entirely?' he exploded.

Amos was stunned. 'Brother, brother. We couldn't very well stay on here for ever more, could we? It's not fair on thee. Being a confirmed bachelor, an' all, you surely miss your space. It's true I weren't altogether taken with the new place at first,' he continued when Ambrose resumed his seat, 'but Laura managed to convince me.'

I bet she did! his eyes screamed.

'I think the lass hankers for somewhere we can call ours again, misses keeping house, being her own mistress, you know? Women can be funny about that sort of thing. It means a lot to them, aye. And well, court or no, a home's what you make it, and Laura will make it homely. Besides, who's to say it's for ever? We can allus search for summat more decent eventually.'

Though his voice was calmer, quieter, Ambrose spoke through gritted teeth. 'I'll not see no kin of mine living in such a place when you've a perfectly good home here with me.'

'We're indebted to thee, brother, for everything. But

it's time. If it's what the lass has set her heart on . . .' Amos shrugged. 'I'll be content anywhere if she is.'

Such unwavering loyalty, support. Laura couldn't have loved her father more in this moment if she'd tried. She reached for his hand and squeezed. Then she lifted her eyes to meet those of the demon's and for the first time since this nightmare began didn't shudder with nerves or bow her head. Instead, she held his gaze steadily, saying with poise and new-found control, 'We've made up our minds, Uncle Ambrose.'

He scraped back his chair and left the kitchen.

Sighing, Amos nodded to Bridget, hovering by the scullery, that they were ready to be served. The leg of mutton, dishes of vegetables and crusty loaf made Laura's mouth water. Victory had brought on a fierce appetite; she'd never felt so ravenous.

'He'll come round, Father,' she told Amos afterwards, seeing that the corners of his mouth still held a down-at-heart droop. *He'll just have to. Please don't bend to his manipulation now.*

'Aye.'

She kissed him on the brow then, crying a headache, escaped upstairs to pack.

Laura knew Ambrose would come to her room that night.

When the door creaked open in the pre-dawn, she was sat up in bed, ready for him. This time, there was no loitering in the shadows, no fumbling of his trousers – he made straight towards her.

'You're going nowhere. Does tha hear me?'

'Get out.'

'Come on, now, lass. Now you know youse are better off here—'

'Get *out*.'

113

'But we're family, lass. Does that mean nowt to thee? Hm?'

That he had the gall – *him* – to speak of such things. 'It's over. Does *tha* hear *me*? The morrow, I'll be free of here – and the yard,' she added as a sudden after-thought, and was gratified to see him blanche. 'Being a stinking bloody court, as you call it, the rent shall be manageable enough on just Father's wages.' This was true enough. Why hadn't she thought of it sooner? 'It's over,' she repeated.

'What wages would they be, then? If you go, he does!'

'As you like. There's coal yards aplenty would be only too glad of his labour.'

His breathing was ragged with pent-up rage. 'I'll find out what it is you're running from in Bolton.'

This was it, the moment she'd been planning through-out the small hours. Though her heart threatened to leap from her chest, she lifted her chin. The risk was worth taking. 'You do that. You go on up there and probe till you're blue in t' face. I've nowt to hide.'

'Aye, you do. I'll *ruin* you.'

'Just you pray I don't ruin you first!'

His eyes bulged in utter fury. Cajoles and threats hadn't worked. His desperate attempt to keep her under his rule, keep her in easy access for his foul fancy, was scattered. Belying his size, he sprang forward, throwing himself on top of her, pinning her at an awkward angle against the wall. 'Bitch!'

'Nay,' she gasped. 'Nay, please!' as he grabbed pain-fully between her legs.

'Shut it.'

His massive bulk was crippling. Dragging into her compressed lungs as much air as she was able, she screamed at the top of her voice.

Time seemed to freeze. Her uncle's mouth fell slack in astonishment at her show of defiance. Swinging his head to the door then back to her, fear had replaced lust; he scrambled off her and bolted from the room. Moments later, a tousle-headed Amos appeared in the doorway.

'Lass? What is it, what's occurring?'

'A nightmare, Father.'

'You're all right?'

'Aye.' The darkness hid her determined tears. 'Fret not. It's over now.'

'It's for the best. Someone needs to be home during the day to clean and have a meal ready for when you return from your toil. The arrangement worked for us well enough in Bolton, eh? Let's give it a trial run and, if brass proves too tight, I'll find employment somewhere again. I'll still help with the afternoon coal round, same as always, will meet thee each day outside the yard.'

'But lass, quitting without giving notice? What will your uncle say? You'll be leaving him reet in t' lurch – and let's be fair, he deems us having abandoned him as it is, us vacating his house as we are.'

'Nay, nay. I spoke on it with him. He's reet about it.'

'Aye?'

Smiling through the guilt which the lies that seemed to trip from her tongue ever more frequently of late brought, she nodded, eager to reassure him. Ambrose's reaction to their moving out had hurt her father and she'd do all in her power to salve his conscience. He'd sacrificed so much for her already. If for Amos's peace of mind she must sing that devil's praises – false as they may be – she would. 'Honest, Father. He was understanding, said as how I had his support. Kindness itself, he was.'

'Ay, that's our Ambrose for you.' Mollified, Amos crossed the room to collect his cap. 'Right, well, I'd best be away to the yard, else he'll wonder where I am.'

'I'll have everything ready for when you get back,' she said, glancing down the hall at the pile of their bits and pieces ready for the off. Amos would call here with the horse and cart after his first coal round of the day and take their possessions to Ebenezer Court. 'There's just a few more items upstairs need packing and then we're done.'

She began work the second he left and, as promised, had everything sorted upon his return and was waiting in her shawl by the front door. They had the cart loaded within minutes. Before climbing aboard, they went to say their goodbyes to Bridget, who was waving from the step, dabbing at her eyes with the corner of her apron.

'It's an eejit I am, making a spectacle of myself, so. But sure, have I not taken ye both to my heart in the short time you've been here? We'll miss youse, the sir and I.'

For a horrifying moment Laura thought Amos would change his mind about the whole thing – the mention of his brother had brought a flash of uncertainty to his eyes – and she laughed quickly to lighten the mood. 'We're but a short walk away, Figg,' she told her, giving her a hug. 'You're welcome to visit us if ever you're free.'

'And as I said to our Ambrose, the same goes for him,' added Amos, much to Laura's dismay, 'so, you see, you're not getting rid of us that easy.'

Happy with this, the maid saw them off with a smile. Laura felt a pang at leaving her. Then Kenneth picked up the pace and the house and all it had stood for were out of sight and an overwhelming surge of relief warmed her like a mother's embrace. She closed her eyes, savouring every inch of distance that was put between them.

As with before, they had to leave the horse and cart on the street – this time, Amos was taking no chances and offered a passing lad a penny to guard them, along with instructions to keep a tight hold of the bridle. Then arming themselves with as many items from the cart as they could manage, they navigated their way to the court.

It seemed Mrs Price was awaiting their arrival; she turned her head towards the entrance as they emerged into the yard: 'That you, Laura, lass? Amos?'

'Aye,' they puffed, dumping their loads on the least mucky patches of ground.

The old woman nodded. She reached behind her into the house and brought out a broom, which she used to knock on next door's window.

A large woman appeared in a flowery apron, a child clamped to each hip. Spotting Laura and Amos, her round face spread in smile. 'Hello there! I'm Bee. It's nice to meet ye.' She motioned to their possessions. 'Is that the lot?'

'Nay, there's more on t' cart up yonder,' Amos told her.

'Right you are. You, lass, call at Joyce's for the key and get the house opened up,' she instructed Laura. 'Meantimes, I've a swarm of kiddies inside that will give a hand to your father. The men of the court are away at their work, else they'd have mucked in, but no bother. My lot ain't afraid of hard graft. Sure, you'll have the cart emptied in the shake of a lamb's tail.'

Laura was touched. Thanking her, she made her way to the house Mrs Price had previously indicated was Nathan's. Introducing herself to the willowy woman with soft brown hair and eyes who answered her knock,

Laura was suddenly self-conscious. She smiled politely, keen, given who she was, to make a good impression. 'I'm Laura, very pleased to meet thee. Nathan said you'd kindly offered to take in our key?'

'That's right. By, the lad weren't far wrong; you're a bonny 'un, all right.'

Both glad of and embarrassed by the compliment – and the knowledge that Nathan had spoken of her to his mother and so favourably – she laughed quietly. 'Well, thank you. I'd better get the house unlocked and make a start. Father must return to work once the cart's unloaded and I'd like the place looking as decent as I can afore he returns this evening.'

Joyce nodded approvingly. 'You're a sound, clean sort, I see. Not like the last lot we had there, nay. Housing a pig indoors, I ask you! Fair shocked the life out of me when I glanced inside one day whilst passing and spied the thing snoring away in bed with the kiddies! A right rag-bag lot, they were, aye.'

Laura looked aghast at her new home. 'Oh my dear God . . . What state must they have left it in?'

'I shudder to think, lass. But worry not, for I'm willing to help thee, if you'd like? We'll have everything straightened out in no time. I'll have a word in our Daniel's ear, an' all, ask him to give the walls a whitewashing for youse. That'll brighten up the rooms no end. He'll not mind none, nay, is good like that.'

Given Amos's understandable but ill-natured display, she'd refrained from mentioning to Nathan the encounter with his brother. It was a real pity that their fresh start here had already begun on the wrong foot. Would Daniel be willing to help his new neighbours when he discovered who they were? She doubted it, but thanked Joyce anyway. The woman's offer to help her clean the house, however, she accepted with much more enthusiasm – what generous souls these strangers were proving to be. She hadn't anticipated this at all.

'I'll give young Mrs Anderson a yell, too. Bee won't mind watching her babby for a few hours whilst she helps out. What d'you say? Many hands make light work, and all that.'

'Oh aye, yes. Ta, Joyce.'

'Right, then. Let's make a start. I'll fetch a pail to fill at the pump and shall set it to heat on my fire. Meantime, get yon door opened, lass, and we'll see what we're up against!'

'What a welcome committee, eh, Father?' Laura whispered happily soon afterwards, pulling him aside when he'd carried through the last of their things. As she'd feared, the house was in a sorry state, but with the women's help, she was confident that the clean-up wouldn't take too long. 'They're all so kind and accepting. I'm so glad we moved here.'

He smiled agreement, but it didn't quite reach his eyes.

'Father? What is it?'

'Nay, there's nowt wrong. Bit breathless with humping that lot is all. I'll be reet in a minute. Now, I'd best return to Kenneth and get back to work.'

Frowning worriedly, she reached for his hand as he made to leave. 'Wait. Are you sure you're well?'

'Aye, aye.'

'Your heart's not—?'

'Enough with the fussing, lass. I'll see thee later.'

'I'll meet thee outside the coal yard this afternoon, like we planned!' she called after him as he walked away.

Amos raised a hand and waved, and Laura returned it. When he'd disappeared out of the court she stood for a moment, biting her lip.

Fret not. The medicine did its job, didn't it? He's been healthy for weeks, she reminded herself.

Rolling up her sleeves, she went to continue with her own work inside the house.

'I don't know how to thank thee.' Too choked with emotion to convey her gratitude adequately, Laura let her tear-filled gaze linger over the room.

Though they had all worked like Trojans throughout the morning, it had been far from finished when she'd left to help Amos with his round; they had done wonders in her absence. Every nook and cranny was scrubbed and swept. The rag rugs were strategically laid to cover the odd cracked flagstone, their sparse furnishings arranged and highly polished, and the odd picture and aged ornaments they owed adorned the walls and mantel. The women had even hung the curtains and got a nice fire burning to take the chill from the air.

'We worked like a pair of demented wasps to get it finished for when tha returned,' Joyce laughed.

'Aye, buzzing hither and thither till we were fit to drop!' Mrs Anderson put in. 'Aye, but it were worth it to see your face, lass.'

''Ere,' added Joyce, 'just you mind yer don't sully the place again, afore you've had time to wash!'

Still wearing her working clothes, Laura had made to sit in the chair by the gleaming, black-leaded fireplace – she straightened quickly with a guilty grin. 'You're right. I'll go and swill my face and hands at the pump and, when I've got changed, I'll make a well-earned pot of tea.'

Stepping outside, her mouth stretched in a smile as she imagined her father's reaction when he set eyes on their dirt-free, cosy dwelling. She could hardly believe things were running so smoothly, had been expecting something to go horribly wrong, as it always seemed wont to of late. But no. Glory be to God – dare she trust it to be true? – their run of good fortune showed no sign of abating. *Please may it continue.*

To her relief, Amos had appeared refreshed, his energy restored, when he'd emerged from the yard with his cartful of sacks to find her waiting, as promised. Throughout the delivery he'd given no indication that he felt unwell, and by the time they had finished and she'd set off back to Ebenezer Court, she was convinced she'd been fretting unnecessarily. Hopefully, the new house would lift his spirits further. She planned to make his favourite meal this evening, wanted their first night here to be just right.

'Oh, Lord, not you. Now see 'ere, lad, it were nobbut a scratch yon horse received from Smiler here, so if it's compensation your father's after, you can just tell him to go and whistle. He ain't getting a single farthing out of me.'

Releasing the pump's long black handle, her ablutions now forgotten, Laura turned to find Daniel glaring down at her, his dog sitting obediently by his side. For a moment, she didn't know how best to answer. He still thought her a male, and no wonder: she was once again in his presence in her ragged, too-big cart clothes and, after all, she hadn't corrected his false assumption last time, had she?

She suddenly felt the strongest urge to laugh, but one more look at his face and her mirth died. He thought her here on instructions from her father to demand money for damages from him – and he wasn't best pleased about the fact. He might very well thump her one, if she wasn't careful. She stepped forward. 'You're mistaken. Father never sent me. The horse is just fine, just as tha said he'd be.'

'Oh.' The antagonism left his face. 'Then what's your business? Well, speak up, lad.'

'That's summat else you're mistaken about.' Moving back to the pump, she cranked the handle with one hand and with the other splashed the gushing stream on to her face, scrubbing the coal dirt away. She turned back towards him, reached up and removed her flat cap. Set free from its confines, her long hair fell with a swish, uncoiling about her shoulders like liquid butter. 'I'm no lad. *Lad.*'

Daniel's lips parted in shock. He blew air through them slowly. 'So you ain't. But last time—'

'I should have told thee, aye. But well, now you know. Didn't you suspect owt when I opened my mouth?' she asked, a bemused smile hovering.

'Some lads take a time longer than others to mature, don't they, and . . .' He shrugged. 'Nay, it never crossed my mind. Well, it wouldn't, would it?'

'I suppose not.' She motioned to her trousers and jacket and held up her cap. 'I help Father on his coal round. These save my own clothes getting dirtied and it's easier to hop on and off the cart with no skirts getting in t' way.' She held out a hand and, reverting to the maiden name she much preferred, said, 'I'm Laura Todd. Your new neighbour,' she finished, nodding towards her house.

'*You're* Laura?' A look she couldn't identify flashed in his eyes and a frown appeared. 'Our Nathan speaks of nowt but thee.'

'He's a sound lad,' she said quietly, cursing her blush. 'Aye.'

The silence stretched as they stared at one another.

Then something at the end of the court squeaked, and a barking Smiler – their resident rat-catcher, so Joyce had informed her earlier – raced off in pursuit, breaking the stillness.

'Well. It's nice meeting you. The *real* you, I mean.'

'And you,' Laura told Daniel's retreating back – he'd already turned and was making for his house, opposite. He disappeared inside without a backward glance and, when the door closed, she headed inside her own home, feeling somewhat deflated.

From what she'd read in his demeanour he wasn't overly keen on his brother's new friend. Which was a pity, for her initial opinion of *him* hadn't changed at all.

Chapter 10

THE THREE WOMEN were on their second cup of tea when the rattle of the front door opening heralded Amos's return. They smiled at each other in readiness, picturing his amazed expression when he entered the room – Laura, in particular, was giddy with anticipation – but they were swiftly disappointed.

His hollow-eyed gaze didn't seem to register the improvements, nor did he appear even to notice their neighbours' presence. Without a glance at either of them, let alone a greeting, he crossed to the fire, cap scrunched tightly in his fist. Resting an elbow on the mantel, he stared mutely into the yellow-blue flames.

'Well,' said Joyce awkwardly, placing her cup on the side table and rising to her feet, 'I'd best get myself off home and prepare the lads' evening meal. Bye for now.'

'Aye, and me.' Mrs Anderson was right behind her. 'My husband'll not be best pleased if his grub's not on t' table when he comes in.'

Murmuring her thanks, and expressing a silent apology with her eyes, Laura saw them out. When she re-entered the room, her father hadn't moved a muscle; he seemed lost in a world all his own. Trepidation worked cold fingers up her spine – something was clearly wrong.

What? She'd never known him like this, was almost too afraid to ask.

'Father?'

Nothing. She placed a tentative hand on his shoulder. 'Father, what is it? What's happened?'

The choked answer that fell from his lips turned her veins to ice: 'Ambrose.'

He knew. Dear God, how? That low-down beast hadn't the courage, the decency, the *stupidity* to confess his depravity. Did he? Then again, had he twisted the way of things, concocted some wild and devilish tale of untruths, placed the blame that was his alone squarely at her feet? Or had he followed through with his vow to visit Bolton? Did the Cannock brothers know of her whereabouts? What was it? *What?*

'Ambrose. He said . . .'

'He said what, Father? *Tell* me.'

'He's given me the shove.'

'He's . . . ? Oh, nay!' Hadn't he warned he'd do just this if she left? But she'd believed it an idle threat, never thought he'd do it. This would shatter the man before her completely. How could he? 'Oh, Father . . .'

'He reckons I'm not up to it.' Amos swiped a sleeve across his nose. 'Past it, I am. That's what he thinks. I'm fit for nowt.'

'Nay – he *knows* nowt!' she told him fiercely. 'You possess more drive in your big toe than any other worker in this city, I'll be bound. Well, to hell with him. There's merchants aplenty what will take you on and feel the lucky for it, you just watch and see. We managed just fine afore without him, and we'll do the same now. We don't need nowt – nowt at all – from Ambrose Todd.'

Amos allowed Laura to guide him to a chair. She placed a filled cup before him, but though he lifted it absently, he made no attempt to sip the sweetened brew. Staring into space, his features were wreathed in raw misery. She could have wept for him. She *could* have quite happily killed her uncle with her bare hands.

'We're the both of us out of work – with rent on top of everything else, now, to find. Then there's Kenneth. We can't expect Ambrose to keep him on at the yard, not any more. There's fresh stabling needs securing, the cost of his grub to consider. How will we cope?'

She'd never seen her father so flat, so defeated, and it both scared and enraged her in equal measures. *Damn* that blackguard to Lucifer's flames! Another level of hatred towards him was born this day; she'd get even with her uncle if it was the last thing she did. 'Don't despair so, *please*,' she beseeched Amos, taking his hand in both of hers, desperate to infuse a little of her passion into him. 'God is good; he'll deliver, you'll see. *Summat* will come up, it allus does.'

But it was as though her words were falling on deaf ears: 'How could he cast me aside like that?' he continued to lament, almost to himself.

He's punishing you to get back at me. He's not the person you think he is.

'My one and only brother. I'd never of believed it possible.'

I'm sorry. So sorry . . .

'I told him I were well, told him it wouldn't happen again, but he'd not listen.' Amos squeezed shut eyes swimming with tears, his hold on Laura's hand tightening to near-painful proportions. 'I'll not *leave* thee on this Earth like this with nowt!'

The last part of his speech had been barely audible, but she'd grasped enough for it to make sense. Her gaze narrowed in deep confusion, this slowly giving way to dreaded suspicion. 'What d'you mean? What ain't tha telling me?'

'I'm going forra lie-down.'

'Father, please tell me—' The slamming of the door swallowed her pleas and she crushed a hand to her mouth with the unknown fear of it all. Dear God, what was he hiding from her?

She had bolted from her chair and was hurrying for the bedroom to press him further when a familiar whistle echoed through to her from the court. She paused. *Nathan.* Then she was rushing outside to meet him.

'Laura! I planned to call in on thee later, see how youse were settling in . . . You're crying.' His wide smile melted. 'Eeh, what's wrong, lass?'

'Father. Father, he . . . Summat's occurred and he'll not say what. It's his health, I'm certain. Was it at the yard? Did you witness owt the day? Please, Nathan, I must know!'

'Ay now, sshhh. Don't take on so, else you'll be the one ill.'

'So he is unwell? I knew it! What happened?'

Putting his arm around her shoulders, Nathan led her to the court's narrow entrance, where they could talk in private. 'There were an incident, aye. Your father arrived back from his afternoon round breathless and in pain with his chest. I went to his aid, but he wouldn't admit he needed assistance. He were trying to hide the truth of it, same as afore, but I saw through it – as did your uncle. He'd spotted Amos from his office window. He ordered me to help his brother inside. That's all I know. When the shift was over and I went to find your father for us to walk home together, I were told he'd already left.'

'But he was fine when I left him.' Laura dropped her

127

head in her hands. 'The foxglove tea worked, it did, I saw the change in him with my own two eyes. It's a medical marvel, works wonders on the heart, the owd herb woman said so herself. She'd no reason to tell untruths, even refused to take my brass . . . Why relapse now, when he was doing so well? I don't understand!'

'Talk to him. I've a feeling he's been keeping more from thee than tha realises.' There was sadness in Nathan's eyes when Laura jerked her head up to look at him questioningly. He lifted one shoulder in a shrug. 'Amos wants to protect thee. If that means bending the truth when he needs to . . . he will. I'm sorry, would do owt to take away your pain. Talk to him,' he repeated in a whisper, taking her body, shaking with silent sobs, into his arms.

'Uncle Ambrose dismissed him,' she told Nathan through her sniffs minutes later as they walked back to their homes.

'He never did! Oh, lass.'

'I've given up my position, and if Father ain't strong enough to work . . . What will we do, with no brass coming in? Who'll keep an eye to him if I'm forced to seek other employment?'

'We'll worry about that when we need to. For now, go and be with him.'

She paused to look up at him. The gathering darkness threw the cobbled yard in shadow, but the curve of white moon, sitting in the small patch of sky visible above them, cast its glow on to his handsome face, showing him to her clearly. 'We?' she murmured.

'You're not on your own, Laura. Not now you have me.'

A sense of security, warm and wonderful, thumpthumped in her breast. 'Eeh, lad . . .'

Their lips found each other. His hand on the back of

her head drew her closer still and, blissfully, she felt herself slipping from reality, from the pain and fear and uncertainty. For just this one brief moment, troubles didn't have to exist and all was beautiful with the world. His tongue sought hers and she matched his fervour without restraint. He was here, and she needed him. They were meant to be, had been all along. She'd been blind to it at times, but not any more. Nathan loved her. And she . . .

Forced coughing sounded behind them and the here and now crashed back with a thud; she sprang away from Nathan with a gasp.

'Sorry to interrupt . . .'

'Nay, lad. We were just . . . talking, is all.'

Daniel gave his brother a wry look. 'Aye, 'course youse were.'

If the ground could have opened up, Laura would have dived headlong into it, would have welcomed it swallowing her up – her embarrassment was absolute. What on earth had she been thinking, carrying on like that? Right here, too, in public view . . . God alone knew what the neighbours must think. The shame!

'Mam sent me to warn thee your meal's on t' table,' Daniel continued, 'though how long for remains to be seen. She's threatening it'll be inside Smiler if you're not indoors in the next minute.'

'Mam saw . . . ?' Nathan nodded to Laura.

Daniel fixed Laura with his steady green gaze. 'Aye, from the window.'

'Oh 'ell.' Nathan's guffaw brought a smile from his brother, but Laura was far from amused.

This was all some big lark to him, was it? She'd let her guard down, given herself up to his attentions, his love – *trusted* him – and it had meant nothing? A grubby

129

game was all it had been, was that it? She felt loose, cheapened, used – so bloody foolish.

'I'll see thee later, Laura?' Nathan called after her as she turned on her heel and hurried for home.

She didn't answer. The way she felt at this moment in time, if she never set eyes on him again it would be too soon.

Amos was still in bed when she entered, but she knew he wasn't sleeping. She went across and sat beside him. He lay with his back to her and for a long moment she didn't speak, simply stared at him, her heart breaking. Then: 'Why didn't tha tell me, Father?' Her question held no recrimination, only heavy sadness.

'I couldn't. You were that convinced . . . I had to let thee think yon medicine had worked, couldn't wipe the happiness from your face.'

'Oh, Father, Father . . .'

'Don't cry, lass.'

Enveloped in his thick-armed embrace, she emptied out her sorrow into his broad chest. 'The day me and Bridget came to your aid . . . you didn't fall from bed in your sleep, did you? You became breathless again and passed out. That's the truth of it, ain't it?' she asked through her tears.

'Aye.'

'There's been other times, others I know nowt about?'

'Aye,' he murmured again, rocking her comfortingly as one would an infant.

'I believed the foxglove had worked.'

Laura felt him shake his head.

'I just learned to hide it better. I'm that sorry, my lass.'

She felt bitterly let down, deceived. Above all, she was utterly devastated. Her heart felt like it had shattered to dust. *She was going to lose him.*

130

Desperation had her grasping at any possible shred of hope: 'Happen your bad turn today . . . . Happen it were just the strain of the house move, of you lugging our possessions.'

'Nay, lass.' Amos was shame-faced. 'And me haranguing Ambrose for letting me go? Well, I were looking for someone to blame, weren't I? He were right in what he did. I can't keep lying to myself no more as well as to thee – I'm finished.'

No. 'I could visit Widow Jessop at the market again. Another dose might—'

'It'd not do no good, lass.'

She didn't want him to say this. Why wasn't he reassuring her that all would be well, as he always had? She felt she was drowning in terror, couldn't comprehend the truth of it. He was her haven, her safe place. She had no one but him. She'd die, too, without him, surely?

He was speaking again: 'It weren't meant to be like this. I agreed to Ebenezer Court for your and young Nathan's sakes, figured it would bring the two of you closer – mebbe we should have stayed where we were. You're going to have to lean on your uncle when I'm . . . It's all gone *wrong*.' His voice rose, his breathing quickening in panic. 'Look at us. No positions, very little brass . . . I'll not see thee alone and destitute. Never that! Summat . . . summat needs to be done, and soon, aye, else—'

'Father. Father, please,' Laura soothed. 'You'll make yourself ill. Don't fret over me.'

'But of course I do! I do, day and night! Lass . . .'

'I'll wed Nathan.' The words were out before she had time to understand what she was saying. Now, there was no biting them back. Nor did she want to – not if it

131

helped ease her father's mind. She nodded determinedly. 'If he asks me . . . I'll accept.'

The stress seemed to leave him in a drawn-out sigh. Closing his eyes, he sagged with undeniable relief. 'It must be for thee, mind. Tha have to want to, Laura.'

'I do.'

'You'd never shackle yourself to another fella, you said—'

'Aye, well,' she cut in quickly. 'Happen I were being hasty, there. Nay, I know I was,' she insisted, in what she hoped was a tone of certainty.

'Then my heart is gladdened again. That it is, lass.'

And hers was because Amos's was. And later that night when he was sleeping and a knock came at the door she put aside her earlier annoyance and disappointment with Nathan and welcomed him with a smile.

They sat close together on stools outside her front door. Neighbours were by their hearths, enjoying the precious hours of rest before a new working day began at dawn, and the court was quiet. Above, the moon had shifted from view. Barely touching the night, flickering candles from the windows and the single gas lamp bracketed to the wall by the entranceway threw the only dull strokes of light on to the cobblestones.

'Mrs Price reckons she remembers when great chunks of this city were grazing pastureland and open meadow. In the last century, like, when she were just a slip of a lass. Imagine that.' Nathan spoke in a hushed tone. 'Our generation and our parents afore us ain't known nowt but greyness, have we? Grime and chimney stacks, that's our lot. And the smoke. There's no forgetting the smoke. No getting away from that, is there?'

Though his words held no bitterness, there was an underlying edge to them, as though the usual acceptance

132

of things for the poor wasn't something that sat well with him. Laura stared at him keenly. 'Nay.'

'And these squalid little courts, shoehorned in between squalid lanes and streets, with their squalid little burrows that the nobs have the gall to call dwellings . . . That's our lot, an' all, eh?'

'Looks that way, aye,' she responded, frowning slightly. She hadn't heard him speak as deeply before. He was usually carefree, his ready smile never far away. 'Nathan? Is tha all right?'

Turning suddenly, he took her hands in his and held them to his heart. Though she couldn't see his face properly in the darkness, the passion in his voice was clear: 'I want to take care of thee. This – our lot – there's no changing it, nay. But we could still find happiness amongst it all. We'd make our own, the two of us. Once we'd shut away the outside at the day's end, it'd be just us together, and the misery beyond the front door couldn't touch us. You see?'

'I . . . don't know, I . . .'

'I don't pretend to be a man of greatness, Laura. I'm more brawn than brains, for sure. I ain't like our Daniel; he's the thinker of the family. He's employed as an overlooker in a cotton mill, did you know? That's some responsibility, aye,' he continued when she shook her head in answer. 'An achievement, to boot, landing such a position, and him only in his middle twenties. Me? I'll likely allus shovel coal, and that's all right. It's honest work and regular brass; folks'll allus need fuel. Anyroad, it could be worse. I'd prefer the yard above ground any day over working the coal face in the Earth's bowels extracting the stuff – awful toil, mining is.

'D'you know, with the wages we're fetching in betwixt

133

us, we could afford to get Mam out of here and into summat a bit better, but she'll not hear of it. The court's been her home for ever – she'll not budge and there's folk aplenty what share her view. Our lot . . . It is home, aye.'

He paused for a moment as though he'd trailed off course and was searching for the right words to bring his point back on track. 'What I'm saying is this: I reckon I love thee. Nay, I know it. We could make this life we're saddled with a better one, for the both of us, if we put in the effort. What d'you say, lass?'

Say to what? she wondered. That hadn't exactly been a proposal of marriage, had it? Though it probably amounted to the same thing. A husband-and-wife team was what he was driving at and, in all honesty, it sounded a solid idea. Sensible, aye. Secure. And he loved her. Well, he reckoned so, at any rate, and that was enough. For if she was to answer the same question regarding him, with all honesty . . . Aye, Nathan loved her. And she . . . She loved her father, and a promise was a promise.

'Lass? Say summat.'

'I . . . We'd make a good team, I think, Nathan, aye.'

His teeth flashed white in a delighted smile. 'Eeh, lass.'

'So if you're asking . . . Aye. I'll marry thee.'

He held out his arms. She leaned towards him and he held her in a soft embrace.

'By,' he murmured into her hair. 'You'll not regret it, Laura.'

That night, she found herself locked in a terrible dream.

It was snowing heavily. In the spiralling flakes, Ambrose stood laughing at the entrance to Ebenezer Court.

His bulk barred all chance of escape. Alone in the

centre of the cobbled yard, she knew it was pointless banging on the doors of the darkened houses. No one would come to her aid. Not her father, not Nathan, for both were lost to her for ever. She was trapped.

Though she screamed on in terror, it made no difference – her uncle simply laughed harder. Then two figures loomed into view over his shoulders and her heart ceased its beating. Unable to breathe, to speak, she watched the Cannock brothers' faces come into focus.

Their features held no amusement. They were snarling, eyes pinpricks of red, their murderous intentions palpable. Ambrose had brought them here. They were drawing closer, closer, and she couldn't move an inch, was rooted to the spot. She was going to die, was going to die . . .

In the moment that the four rough hands made a grab for her, the scene changed.

She was lying in her old marital bed in Bolton. Though she tried to stop her eyes straying to the space beside her, they wouldn't obey, and she gazed, petrified, at the unmoving shape beneath the bedclothes. She saw her hand reach out and pull back the covers. Adam's dead grey features and glassy stare greeted her and again she was screaming. But his voice reached her anyway.

The same words. Over and over in a gravelly scratch: 'A.C. and L.T. Remember. A.C. and L.T. Remember . . .' And on and on. Until the world spun, faster, faster, and she slipped into blackness.

She awoke drenched in perspiration, tears streaming into her soaked pillow. But the knowledge that it hadn't been reality brought no comfort.

Though she couldn't answer why, she knew without

135

question that it had been more premonition than nightmare.

Bad things were coming. There was nothing she could do to stop it.

The burning question of when would terrorise her waking hours more than any dream could.

Chapter 11

IN THE FOLLOWING days, Laura couldn't settle her mind to anything. The meaning behind the opening of that nightmare had been clear: Ambrose still posed a very real danger. She'd prayed he was all bluster, but she wasn't so confident about that now. After all, had he not seen good his threat in sacking her father? What next? The possibilities made her nauseous with worry.

However, it was the second part of her imaginings, involving Adam, that she found herself replaying more; the ambiguity made her head ache. Why must she remember their initials? Had he really the power to reach her from beyond the grave? Did his ghost know she planned to marry Nathan? Had it been a warning, his way of telling her she'd never be free of him, that she was his still? But that was ridiculous, surely. And yet the thoughts continued, relentless.

Adding to her troubles was Amos. The news that she and Nathan were betrothed had injected him with a renewed sense of purpose – weddings cost money and he was determined to contribute to make it a decent one. Deaf to her protestations, he'd gone off in search of fresh employment and, to her consternation, had secured a position within the hour at another coal merchant's.

Eyes sparking with determination and that old stubbornness she recognised so well, he'd told her in no uncertain terms that his one wish left on this Earth was to see her settled and, if needs be, he'd toil until he dropped to see it happen. Nothing she said would dissuade him and so she'd had no choice but to accept his decision – albeit with a condition of her own. She'd accompany him on the cart same as before, only this time she'd be present on every delivery. If it meant breaking her back by doing the lion's share of the work, so be it. She refused to lose him sooner than she must for the sake of male pride.

Then, on the morning he was due to start, the snows came. It brought with it an eerie realness almost, as though the dream had nudged a step closer to coming true, and her dread intensified.

After gulping down a breakfast of bread and dripping and a cup of piping tea, Amos was impatient to be off, but Laura stopped him. Inclement weather coupled with his precarious health was a recipe for disaster – she was taking no chances. 'Wait a minute, Father.'

'Come on, lass, afore I'm late. It's a good impression I'm for making. Besides owt else, folk need their fuel the day, 'specially so, thanks to the white stuff. I'll not have families freezing to death on my conscience.'

'And I'll not have *you* ending up the same way on mine,' she told him, securing his rough jacket closer around him and pulling his cap lower to shield his face from the biting breeze.

As with the arrangement at her uncle's yard, Amos's new employer had agreed to stable Kenneth on his premises – now, as they picked their way along the slippery streets to Ambrose's to collect the horse and cart, Laura's stomach churned painfully with nerves. The last thing in the world she wanted was to see him, but needs must. She couldn't have let her father face his brother for the first time since their fall-out alone. He needed the stress like a hole in the head; she'd make damn sure that devil created none.

Thankfully, Ambrose wasn't present when they arrived, and as Amos harnessed Kenneth to the cart with Nathan's assistance, Laura wandered back to the gates to wait. Just being on *his* ground made her flesh creep – the sooner they were away from here and for good, the better.

'Nasty business, that fire.'

The icy shiver that travelled the length of her spine had nothing to do with the cold. She forced herself to turn towards the man towering behind her. 'What did you say?'

'Oh aye.' Ambrose nodded slowly. 'Very nasty business indeed.'

The inferno the Cannock brothers had ignited as she and her father left for Manchester . . . The thought exploded inside her head. *But that was impossible – he couldn't know. He couldn't—*

'Nice owd bird is that Mrs Hanover,' he added, shattering to pieces in an instant Laura's hopes that she was wrong. 'Such a shame that the wench were caught up in your trouble.'

She had to push her response through trembling lips: 'What have you done?'

'I reckon it's *you* should be answering that, hmm?'

'Listen to me.' Her heart was beating so fast she could barely feel it. 'If you've run your mouth off in Bolton as to my whereabouts . . . Dear God, I'll be *done* for – and my father along with me!'

'Eh?' The intensity of her desperation had clearly thrown him. 'Just what the divil is tha hiding?'

'Please.' Her breaths came in jagged gasps. '*Tell* me what you've gone and done.'

'I visited Bolton town, aye. And yes, I asked around about thee.' He lifted his chin defensively. 'Didn't I warn thee I would if tha crossed me? Well, didn't I?'

'You made mention that I was in this city?'

'Might've done, and what of it?'

She couldn't breathe, was drowning . . . 'Ebenezer Court? You . . . You were specific about Ebenezer Court?'

'What . . . ?'

'Answer me, goddamnit!'

His mouth fell open at her tone and, once more, his expression was one of slight concern. 'I had a few pots of porter in the local inns and taverns, got talking to one or two people – that's how I learned of the shop you dwelled above being burned down – but I can't rightly remember . . . what exactly I might've . . .'

'Try,' she ground out through gritted teeth.

His brows drew together as he tried to recall just what he might have divulged to any listening ear in his drunken stupor. Finally, he shrugged. 'I don't . . . I don't know.'

'Nay . . . Nay, you can't have . . .' Silent tears fell from her frantic eyes and splashed to her cheeks. 'Have you any idea what you've done?' she rasped.

'Laura, I—'

'Save your breath.' An apology from him at any time would have carried little impact – now, with this, it meant even less than nothing. 'May God forgive thee, Ambrose Todd.'

Just then, Amos appeared, killing any further dis-course. He drew Kenneth to a halt beside them. 'Brother.' He nodded an awkward greeting to Ambrose. 'I'm glad I caught thee. It's a sorry you're owed.'

'Lad . . .'

'Nay, hear me out. You were right, I'm norra well man. It were sensible for business that tha let me go. I bear thee no ill will.' Eyes soft, Amos held out a hand. 'We're . . . all right?'

'Aye. Aye, lad,' said Ambrose quietly, his gaze flicking to Laura. He took the proffered hand in both of his.

How she kept her tone even, she didn't know. 'We'd best be off, Father.'

'Aye.'

Taking her seat beside him, she stared straight ahead as her father waved goodbye to his brother. Only when they had turned the corner did she let her shoulders sag – she wouldn't have that poisonous fiend witness another second of her anguish.

As they bumped along the snow-cushioned cobbles to the new coal yard, she closed her eyes. And she prayed like she'd never done before.

'All right, lad?'

If the devastating meeting that morning with Ambrose hadn't been enough to put her in a black place, the day's work had certainly contributed. Desperate for a hot drink and dog tired – and there was still the evening meal to prepare yet – she hadn't the spirit to drag a smile to her lips at Daniel's quip. She mumbled a greeting and continued for home, head down.

She was frozen to her very marrow. Deliveries had taken longer than usual, owing to the careful pace they had to set Kenneth – one slip of a hoof could have disastrous consequences. Moreover, the snow, which had fallen steadily for most of the day, had quickly swallowed the pavements and she'd been forced at every house they stopped at to sweep clean with her bare hands the flagstones for the buried metal coal plates. As it was a new round, it had been guesswork as to their locations – right now, she doubted whether her fingers, blue with cold, would ever regain feeling in them.

'I heard about your betrothal,' Daniel added as she reached her front door.

Joyce had been to offer congratulations and her pleasure that she'd soon be joining her family, but of her elder son, Laura had seen nothing. She turned to face him. He wasn't smiling now, but his voice hadn't been unkind. 'Aye.'

'I just wanted . . . Well, congratulations. Nathan's a sound fella.'

'Aye,' she said again. 'Well, I'd better . . .' She indicated her working clothes and her need to get changed and washed. 'Bye for now.'

'Laura?'

'Aye?'

Searching her face, a frown appeared. 'You're all right?'

She nodded. 'Tired is all. It's been a long day.'

'Whitewashing.'

Laura had entered the house and was closing her front door when Daniel called out yet again. She poked her head back outside. 'What?'

'Mam said the walls of yon place could do with it. I don't mind. Call it my way of saying sorry to your father for our Smiler's antics with his horse.'

'That's kind of thee. Although you already apologised that day, if I recall. Twice.'

'Your father weren't having none of it, mind.'

The corner of her mouth lifted. 'He has a temper on him when he chooses, 'specially where Kenneth's concerned. He loves him almost like a child.'

142

'Where is the owd man, by the way?'

'Settling the horse in at the yard. Father insisted I weren't to wait outside for him in this weather but was to go on home in front. I'll tell him of your offer when he returns. I'm sure he'll be most grateful, as am I.'

Daniel nodded, raised his arm in farewell and walked away. A smile still playing about her lips, Laura turned and went inside.

She'd scrubbed the day's toil from her skin, changed into her usual wear and had just finished peeling vegetables for the broth they would have for their meal when she noticed the time. She frowned. Father should have arrived home by now.

Donning her shawl, she went to the front doorstep and scanned the end of the court, but there was no sign of him. Her frown grew, along with her worry, with the passing minutes. She'd just decided to go in search of him when three figures emerged into the tiny yard through the entranceway.

The first things to crash through her brain were memories of her nightmare. First the snow, now the three demons out to destroy her, just as she'd dreamed . . . But the scream that had risen to her throat died when she noticed that the person in the middle was being supported by the other two. Bent double, he was leaning on them heavily, as though unable to walk unaided. Who . . . ?

They drew closer and now, the cry she'd been holding back was given life. Those clothes, the white hair . . . It was Amos. *Dear God.*

'Father!'

'There's been an incident, lass,' one of the men told her, breathless from the exertion, as she rushed towards them. 'We need to get your father inside and by the fire. He were lying in the snow Lord knows how long.'

'Lying in . . . ? But why? How? What happened to him?'

'Hurry and get yon door open, lass. And fetch blankets. As many as you can lay your hands to.'

Knowing they were right and that her questions could wait – right now, Amos needed tending to – Laura dashed off in front. As she threw open her door Nathan emerged from his facing and called her name, and she ran to him. 'Oh, lad. Father . . .'

Taking in the situation, he ushered her back to her house. 'I'll go and give the fellas a hand. You wait for us inside.'

She was scrambling about collecting blankets, as instructed, when they entered. They carried Amos to his chair by the fire and she quickly covered him up then rubbed his arms and legs vigorously, desperate to instil some warmth into his frozen frame. His face was the colour of bleached bones, his lips tinged a terrible shade of purple. His rapid breathing was harsh and laboured.

'Father? Oh God, Father, please speak to me!'

'Lass . . .'

'I'm here. I'm here, Father. What the hell's occurred?' she asked tearfully of the two strangers now hovering nearby. 'You found him collapsed?'

'That's right.' The elder stepped forward. 'I'm Mr Howarth of Howarth's Yard, his new employer. Amos had fed and shut in the horse and, after wishing me goodnight, he headed for home. Some time later, Jim here,' he continued, indicating the man beside him, 'left the yard and was himself homeward bound when he spotted Amos lying prone in an alleyway. He came and fetched me and we helped him here. That's all I know, lass.'

144

'Happen he slipped on t' ice, banged his head, like,' offered Jim.

Though Laura didn't voice it, she suspected otherwise. This was his heart again, had to be. Why hadn't she waited for him instead of going on ahead? *Why* had she agreed to him working again in the first place? She'd known he wasn't up to it, had let him talk her into him providing for the wedding; now look what had resulted. She should have put her foot down, insisted he wasn't to toil any more. This was all her fault. She'd never forgive herself for this. Never.

'I'll be away now, if you don't mind, only the wife will be wondering where I've got to,' said Jim.

Mr Howarth moved to the door with his employee. Taking a last look at Amos, he shook his head. 'You'd do well to send for t' doctor, I reckon, lass.'

When they had gone Nathan pressed Laura's shoulder. 'I think he's right. Your father . . . he really don't look too good, lass. I'll fetch him, shall I, the doctor?'

'Aye,' she choked. They couldn't continue trying to handle this by themselves any longer. Medical intervention was needed and not before time, whether her father approved or not.

'I'll not be long. I'll ask Mam to sit with thee whilst I'm gone.'

'Ta, Nathan.'

Alone with him, Laura stroked his weathered cheek. 'I love thee,' she whispered. 'Please don't leave me, Father. Please.'

'Lass . . .'

'Sshhh. Everything's going to be all right.'

'I must . . . Lass . . .'

Tears streaming, her breast throbbed in anguish as she watched him struggle to speak. 'Please, Father. Rest.'

But Amos was insistent: 'They . . . *They* . . .'

'They who? What are you trying to tell me?'

'They're . . . here. In . . . In . . .'

'Father?'

'In . . . danger.'

Her blood froze in her veins. She blinked rapidly. 'What?'

'You're . . . in *danger.*'

'The Cannock brothers?'

He managed a pained nod.

'They're in Manchester? They did this to thee!'

'Lying . . . in wait. Wanted to . . . know where tha was. Wouldn't . . . tell them. *Never.*'

Laura was shaking all over with a mixture of terror and fearsome fury. 'They hurt thee?' she forced herself to ask, though she couldn't see any obvious injuries on him.

'They . . . didn't have to.' He tapped his breast.

The stress had brought on a severe and devastating attack. *Those bastards!* My God, she was dying inside . . .

'I'm sorry. Can't . . . protect thee . . . no more.'

'Oh, Father. *Father.*'

'Lass . . .'

Wracked with dry sobs, she buried her face in his chest. Moments later, she felt beneath her cheek the tired heart, as big as an ocean, cease its beating.

Unearthly wails tore from her. She clung to him and drowned in blind despair.

'Laura? Come away, now. Come on, lass.' Joyce drew her from Amos's limp body and wrapped her own arms around her, murmuring soothingly. 'Eeh, you poor love.'

'Father's dead.'

'A crying shame, it is.'

'I can't . . . I can't . . . live without him!'

The older woman didn't say any more, just let her cry and release the anguish threatening to suffocate her. At some point, Nathan returned and he ushered her across the cobbles to his own dwelling whilst the doctor carried out his preliminary examinations.

Neighbours drifted in and out, alerted by the buzz of activity in their private court. Here was like another world all their own – they rarely got outsiders wandering in or otherwise. Sensing her pain, Smiler stuck close to her, his warm body pressed up against her leg. Someone put a cup of sweet tea into her hands and she sipped it absently. Then the doctor was back, speaking quietly of the likelihood of a defective valve and mitral disease, which he informed them meant heart failure, and offered his condolences along with, last but by no means least, his fee.

Talk of necessary arrangements, of laying out the body, of candles and coffins and undertakers, hummed above Laura's head, but she took in little of it. Matters moved swiftly in such circumstances. Death was a common occurrence; folk grew accustomed to loss in the slums. Grief would come later; now was the time to be practical.

'Me and Bee O'Brien shall see to the laying out,' announced Joyce. 'Haven't we both buried a husband apiece, and a handful of children betwixt that besides? We've the experience, aye.'

'I'll see to the undertaker, will call round there the morrow.' Nathan was talking now. 'And I'll visit Mr Howarth's yard whilst I'm at it, inform him of the sad tidings.'

'Good lad. 'Ere, what about kin?'

Nodding, Nathan rose. 'I'm for going round to see Ambrose Todd now—'

'Nay!' Laura cut in.

'Lass?'

All eyes were on her. She shook her head wildly, sending fresh tears spilling. 'Not now, not yet. I'll tell him myself the morrow.'

'But lass, the boss man's his own blood brother. He deserves to—'

'I said nay, Nathan.'

She'd be the one to inform her uncle. And by God, he'd pay for this. They all would.

As this vow was made, the queerest sensation overtook her. She at once felt calmer, clearer of mind and heart. Revenge would be her crutch now in the black days ahead, and she welcomed the fresh purpose with open arms. Anything so long as she needn't focus on life without him. *Anything*.

'There's also the matter of where you'll sleep the night and the next few days to follow, lass.' Joyce's voice was gentle. 'Tha can't be alone with the . . . with your father. Wouldn't do your mind no good, that wouldn't. I'd have thee here in a heartbeat, only given the circumstances with you and the lad, it wouldn't be right and proper, like, youse sharing a dwelling afore you're wed . . .'

'The lass will stop with me,' announced Mrs Price. 'I've no lodgers at present so can spare the room. And I'll not take nay for an answer.'

On instinct alone, Laura reached across and pressed her thin, aged hand. 'Thank you.'

Some time later, she roused from her numbing thoughts and, glancing around Joyce's homely kitchen, saw that she and Nathan were alone. He put his arm around her and rubbed her back in silent comfort.

'Father died in my arms.'

'I'm sorry.'

'I don't know what I'll do without him.'

'I do know how you're feeling, Laura. When I lost my father—'

'It's not the same.' Hugging herself, she shook her head. 'You still have a parent left. A sibling, too. I have no one.' Never had she felt so wretched and alone.

'Aye, you do. You have me. I'm going nowhere, I promise thee.'

'Oh, lad.'

'And there's your uncle, of course. He's fond of thee, aye.'

She closed her eyes. She'd have to tell Nathan about Adam and his brothers, reveal the truth about Ambrose. She must if she was going to be his wife. They couldn't start their marriage with secrets between them. And yet, as much as she loathed the prospect of dragging him into all this, of their involvement possibly placing him in danger, she prayed he wouldn't give up on her. Not now, for she really would be on her own. Selfish, she knew it to be, but desperation had a habit of bringing out the unpleasant in people.

'You know I'm a widow?'

'Aye. Adam died in an accident at work.'

'Nay, he didn't.' She waited for a response, but Nathan simply stared back in silence. 'I first caught Adam's eye one day at the market back home. He was there every week after that, pursued me for months. It weren't long afore I discovered he was from a lawless family with the reputation to go with it, but he convinced me he wasn't like them, that he was different, decent. He was handsome and charming and I wanted to believe him, despite Father's warnings. Father saw through his deceit from the beginning, pleaded with me to see sense, only I was too blinded by love to listen. Turned out Adam was as

149

bad as the rest of them. I'd been duped. I felt so foolish that I kept my silence for a long time, hated admitting I'd been wrong.'

Nathan was frowning deeply. 'He hurt thee?'

'Aye. Once that ring was on my finger, he turned into a whole other man. Or rather he discarded his mask and revealed the real one beneath. I'd beg him to go straight, give up the criminal activities, the stealing and scheming and drunken brawling, but he wouldn't. He didn't want to, nay.

'One day, he struck me. It became a regular thing after that, but I never gave up trying to change him. I was sure that if he'd only steer clear of his brothers, he'd be better. They're another level of rottenness. Poisonous to the core. They . . . They boasted to have murdered folk, Nathan, and I believe them. They have a touch of insanity about them, aye. And now, they're after my blood. That's why me and Father came to Manchester. We were fleeing *them*. And today . . . today . . . His death is their doing!'

Eyes wide with horror, Nathan shook his head. 'How? *Why?*'

'The night Adam died, we argued. He'd been gone from home two days – up to God alone knew what with them brothers of his – and when he returned I beseeched him once again to change his ways. He grew mad with rage when I wouldn't shut up. He ran at me with his fist raised and I bolted for the bedroom to escape the blows. Only he caught my skirts and dragged me back. I . . . I just . . . I kicked out. Panicked. Didn't want him to hurt me. The thump as he tumbled backwards and hit the stairs was like a gunshot – I've never heard owt so loud in my life. He wasn't moving. I tried to waken him but he wouldn't get up.'

Nathan's voice was a whisper: 'What did you do?'

'Ran for the doctor. He confirmed what I knew: Adam was dead. Police and his family rushed round; it was chaos. I never mentioned we'd rowed, were petrified they would blame me. All assumed he'd just fell in a drunken stupor. Well, all except his brothers. Them two were still out drinking somewhere and couldn't be tracked down. They made their appearance the next morning. Banging at my door fit to burst it from its hinges and screaming all sorts of threats unless I answered their questions, they were.'

'They thought you'd killed him?'

'But I didn't, lad, didn't intend . . . I knew I faced the same fate if I stayed. I scarpered through the back way and made for Father's in the centre of town. All too soon, the Cannock brothers discovered where Father dwelled. They burned the place to the ground. I've been running ever since.'

Releasing air slowly, Nathan dragged a hand through his dark hair. 'Jesus, Laura. You must have been that frickened . . . How have you *coped*, lass?'

'Father,' she answered simply, and hot tears flooded her eyes. 'Though he'd have had every reason to and I'd not have blamed him for it, he refused to give up on me. He gave up his dear home and the precious memories it contained and brought me here, to safety; no one knew of my uncle's existence. At least we hoped it would be safe. Now, Father's dead and it's my fault. Adam's brothers discovered our whereabouts. They must have been scouring the area and spotted him making his way home. The devils that they are, they ambushed him, an old man on his own and twice their age. He must have been so scared.' She was sobbing hard. 'His heart just couldn't take it. He died protecting me to the last.'

'My love . . .' Nathan's arms went around her tightly. 'They'll get what's coming to them, have no fear—'

'Nay, lad!' Jerking back to look at him, she grasped the front of his jacket in her fists and shook him hard in terror. 'You mustn't, for they'll kill you as surely as they did Father. These ain't men, Nathan, they're demons straight from hell! Please. Promise me you'll not go seeking them out. *Promise* me.'

'But—'

'Promise. Else I'll leave this minute and you'll never see me again. I mean it. I'll have to, to keep you and yours safe.'

'So they gets away with it? And what if they find thee, what then?'

'I . . . don't know. I just . . . I want vengeance, of course I bloody do, but . . . Oh, I just don't know! What I am certain of is this: I'll not see thee hurt. I can't have that on my conscience as well, lad. Manchester's vast – we can but pray they'll grow bored of searching and leave me in peace. But Nathan, if tha chooses to end what we have right here and now, I'll understand, honest I will.'

'Laura . . .'

She'd had to give him the choice. She held her breath, dreading his response. Once more, her selfish side rose to the fore and her mind screamed out to him: *Please don't give up on me. I need you, can't do this alone.* Then he spoke, and she flopped in blessed relief:

'I've said it once and I'll say it again: I ain't going anywhere.'

'Thank you,' she choked, throwing herself against him and hugging him tightly. 'Thank you.'

'There's summat I can't fathom,' he said, brows furrowing in suspicion when they drew apart. 'How have

them swines discovered where you are? You said yourself they hadn't knowledge of Ambrose Todd.'

Her mouth opened and closed but refused to bear
life to the truth. She lowered her head. She couldn't
utter it. The horror, the shame of it . . . How could she
speak of her uncle's actions, that he'd blabbed in Bolton through sheer hatred of her, and the reasons for it?
The war it would create, the disgust it would bring forth
in all who discovered it . . . She just hadn't the strength
for the repercussions of that as well, not this day.

Besides, that felt like one battle she must fight – and
win – alone. He'd brought the brothers here. He'd
killed her father as surely as if he'd snuffed him out
with his own two hands.

Ambrose would answer to her. *She'd* be the one to
make him pay – some day, somehow.

On this, she was hell-bent and nothing would dissuade her now.

Chapter 12

'COLLEEN! IT'S GRAND to see ye, so it is—'

'Is my uncle home?'

The maid's delighted smile slipped. 'Sure, it's mighty early – he's still in his bed.' She held the door wide. 'Will ye come in?'

'Ta, Bridget.'

Clearly sensing that something wasn't right, she didn't correct Laura's usage of her given name. 'Everything well? You seem—'

'Not really, nay.' Feeling tears well at the Irishwoman's concern, she swallowed them back desperately. She couldn't – wouldn't – crumble. Not today. Not here. 'I must speak with my uncle urgently. Will you waken him, please?'

'Right so.'

As she waited in the hall Laura took the time to steady her breathing. Maintaining composure and self-control were vital; she wouldn't give him the satisfaction of her anguish, not ever again. Her weakness would be her undoing, and she was damned if she'd let that happen.

'To what do I owe this pleasure, then?'

'Father's dead.'

Midway down the stairs, Ambrose juddered to a halt

154

with a gasp. Mouth falling slack, he shook his head. 'You're a liar. A barefaced, stinking little—!'

'Orphan, Uncle Ambrose, is the word you're looking for.'

'Nay . . .'

'And you're to blame. Ain't yer?'

He stumbled down a stair or two. Then his face contorted into a look of such murderous rage Laura took an involuntary step back. With a roar, he thundered down the remaining stairs and, seizing her round the waist, bundled her into the kitchen. She broke free, panting with her own anger and not a little fear, and scurried to put the table between them and thus gain her some seconds of breathing space until she figured out what to do.

But Ambrose made the choice for her. He sent the door crashing shut. Then he slid his back down it and crumpled in a heap on the flagged floor. He buried his face in his hands. 'I don't . . . What's . . . ? *How?*' he gabbled in broken snatches.

She hadn't expected this. His vulnerability momentarily threw her; she'd never seen a chink of weakness in his hardened armour before.

'The lad's really dead?'

'Yesterday. It was his heart. And your little jaunt to Bolton is the cause of it. Adam's brothers have been on t' warpath since Adam's death – they wrongly believe I killed him,' she revealed, figuring she might as well spill the history now. What was there left to lose, after all? 'Your careless talk must have got back to them and they came to this city in search of me. Only they got to Father first. Their threats were enough to bring about an attack of the heart.

'*Why* did you *do* it?' she continued on a tortured rasp.

155

'Malice? Revenge? And for what? Because I refused your filthy advances? I deserve this – Father deserved to die – because a disgusting beast wants to mess around, in the worst possible way, with his own niece? D'you hear that? D'you hear how it sounds? Well, do you?'

'The lad, I never meant . . . Mine's but healthy urges, that's all. A fella has needs—!'

'Rancid, that's what you are,' she cut in, throwing the words at him like blades. 'I thanked Christ that Father hadn't had to know about his brother, knew it would have finished him off for sure. Well. You've put paid to that, ain't yer? You killed him anyroad. You killed him!'

'Let me make it up to thee.' Ambrose had risen, was making his way towards her. 'Let me—'

'Get back! Don't you dare come anywhere near me!'

'Lass . . .'

'I want nowt from thee. Nowt at all!'

'Our Amos would want me to see right by thee. I'm all the kin tha has left. Now then. You'll leave that dirty court this very day and move back in here. I insist.'

Laura's laugh was hollow with loss, but her eyes burned with a hatred she could never have contained. 'You're serious . . . I'd sooner die myself.'

'You need me, and you know it.'

'I need a depraved madman like thee? Huh. I'd rather starve in the gutter than depend on you for support, financial or otherwise.' She lifted her chin. 'As it happens, you're wrong about summat else, an' all: I do have other kin of my own. Least I will have shortly.' She nodded at his frown. 'Your employee, Nathan, has asked me to marry him and I said yes. So you see, *Uncle*, I neither desire nor require a single thing from you – not now, not ever again.'

'You'll not wed that bombastic young buck! I'll . . .
I'll . . .'

'You'll do what? You don't get to tell me what I can
and can't do – I'm of age, remember, don't require a
guardian or the permission of one, neither. Besides, it's
what Father wanted.'

'And what of thee? I notice there were no talk of love
in that there speech?'

His sly smile and the flush it brought to her cheeks
had her shaking with frustration. Damn him! How she
loathed this man. Why, in the name of God, had she
and her father ever come here? If only she could turn
back the clock. Somehow, she'd see him pay for all he'd
done, if it was the last thing she did.

'I'm right, then, aye? You're marrying that pup for
security, nowt more. But you see, you've not the need to
do it, for you have it here, with me, in abundance—'

'Get out of my way.'

Laura pushed past him and stalked to the door.
Before she could wrench it open and make hasty her
exit, however, Ambrose threw a final gambit that
stopped her in her tracks. She turned slowly.

'Aye, that's right.' Puffing out his chest, her uncle
repeated, 'You marry that lad and he's finished at the
yard. I'll see to it that he never finds work with another
coal merchant this side of the Irwell whilst I'm at it.
You'll be penniless, done for.'

He meant it. She had no doubts on that. If he could
as easily dismiss his own brother as he had, he'd have
no qualms with a man he'd always shown disregard for.
Nathan enjoyed his job; hadn't he spoken so himself
only last week? What on earth would he do without it?
How could this man do this? *Why* was he intent on ruining her and all she held dear?

'Just try me,' Ambrose added, taking her silence as a sign she was wavering.

But no, never. As sorry as she was for Nathan, she could never return to this house, to him. She shook her head. 'You're good at that, eh? Cutting off your nose to spite your face. Chucking out members of your workforce on a whim. That's all you've got, the only power you can wield. You really are pathetic. So, do as you like. Your evil can't buy me back. I'd happily live on them mean streets out there with him than dwell here with you.'

'I'm warning thee—'

'Nay, Uncle. You don't get to do that no more. I'm going now, and I don't ever want to see your face again. And another thing: don't show up to Father's funeral, for you ain't welcome.'

'We'll see about that! He was my brother!'

'Aye, when it suited thee. Just you steer clear.'

'Upstart bitch! I hope them brothers-in-law of yourn find thee! D'you hear? I hope they tear your head from your neck!'

'Goodbye, Uncle Ambrose.'

'You'll be back, mark my words. You'll be back!'

Without another word, Laura stalked from the kitchen and left the house. She'd gone a few yards when a voice called her name. She glanced back to see Bridget motioning for her to wait. The maid closed the door to behind her and hurried into the street to meet her. She was pale, her eyes red-rimmed, and her lips were all aquiver. It didn't take a genius to work out that she'd picked up from outside in the hall what had just passed between her master and his niece.

'Colleen . . .'

'Aye.' It was all Laura could lay her tongue to. What else was there to say?

158

''Tis mortal sorry I am. About your father. About . . . everything.'

'Why do you stay, Bridget?' She flicked her gaze to the house. 'That man in there is wicked beyond words. He cares naught for no one but hisself. No one,' she reiterated, and nodded when the Irishwoman blushed to the roots of her hair. 'You ain't the only one who's overheard . . . things,' she admitted quietly.

'May Mary, Mother of God, forgive me.' Bridget dipped her head. 'I just, I live in hope that one day . . .' She lifted her shoulders in a miserable shrug.

Love really was blind. Deaf, dumb and daft at times, too, aye. Didn't she know all about that? Hadn't she herself fallen victim to its curse with Adam Cannock? She pressed the older woman's hand. 'You know where to find me. Take care, Bridget.'

'And yourself, colleen.'

Arriving home, Laura passed Nathan in the court leaving for work. She swallowed hard. Would he even have a position to go to? Figuring it was pointless either of them worrying unnecessarily until the worst had happened, she assured him all had gone well with her uncle and saw him on his way with a smile. Then, sighing, she made her way to Mrs Price's humble abode.

The old woman had been kindness itself. She'd sat up with Laura until the early hours last night, simply offering a listening ear and a comforting hand, as Laura cried and railed at the unfairness of life, talked of her childhood and reminisced of years and people gone by. In fact, everyone at Ebenezer Court had been genuinely lovely and understanding of her loss.

Outsiders could say what they liked about who they deemed the lowly, the savage, the undesirables – slum folk, in other words – but they themselves knew different.

Bad apples grew amongst them, of course they did, but you found that in any walk of life. Truth was, you'd be hard pressed to find a more loyal and supportive class of souls in the whole of the world.

Times like these highlighted this more than ever and made Laura proud to be one of their number. They banded together in the face of difficulties like never before, ensuring no one felt alone. That she and her father were relative strangers made no difference. She was humbled and more grateful than she could put into words.

'How's tha fettling this morning, lass?' asked Joyce, who was sat enjoying a cup of tea with the old woman by the fire.

Removing her shawl and draping it over the back of a chair, Laura shrugged. 'I don't really know. Numb, I suppose.'

'Aye, well, it's to be expected. It's a fair fearsome shock you've suffered and it'll take time to sink in. You have us lot, whether tha likes it or not, in t' meantime.' Joyce winked softly. 'You remember that.'

'Ta, thanks,' she murmured past the lump in her throat. 'I don't know where I'd be without youse all right now.'

'Eeh, poor love.' Mrs Price felt around the table until her hand brushed the teapot. From years of practice, she expertly filled a cup without spilling a drop and passed it across. 'Come on, sup up. It's a reet tough morning you've had, you having to break such tidings to your uncle.'

'How did he take it, love?' added Joyce.

Laura lifted then dropped her shoulders again. 'As well as you can expect,' she said eventually, her attention on her tea. 'Mrs Price, I was wondering . . . would you mind very much if I stayed on here with thee? Just till the wedding, I mean? My uncle did offer me my owd room back at his but I . . . Well. I like it better here. Please?'

'That tha even had to wonder on it! 'Course tha can.'

They sipped their brews in companionable silence for a few minutes until Joyce asked, 'Have you given thought as to what you'll do with your house in t' meantime, lass? Heaven only knows that landlord of ours won't stand for it if the rent ain't in his grubby paw on time. What with you not in work and your father, God rest his soul, gone . . . You'll be hard pressed to keep the place on.'

'I shall just have to find employment. I'd hate to lose the house and, besides, me and Nathan will need somewhere of our own to live once we're wed.'

They nodded at one another in agreement, then each glanced to the door as a knock sounded. Joyce went to answer it and a comely young woman with dark hair and deep brown eyes followed her back inside.

'I don't think youse have made acquaintance proper as yet, have yer? Laura, love, this is Lizzie, Bee O'Brien's eldest – or Busy Lizzie as she's known, for she never sits still, nay. Allus on t' go, she is.' She chuckled. 'Lizzie, meet Laura, our Nathan's intended.'

'Laura: eeh, that's a bonny name.' Lizzie's smile lit the room. 'Pleased to know thee, I'm sure.'

Laura liked her instantly. 'Aye, you too.'

'I am sorry about your father.'

'Ta, thanks.'

''Ere, but many congratulations on your betrothal. Nathan's a good 'un. They both are.' Lizzie's gaze swivelled to Joyce then, and of her, she enquired, 'Daniel's well?'

161

Seeing the girl's eyes sparkle at Joyce's nod, Laura knew a queer sense of unease. That Lizzie carried a liking for the elder brother was evident. Did he reciprocate her feelings? And what on earth did it matter to her?

'Any idea as yet when the wedding will be?' Lizzie chirped, bringing Laura back to the present. Plonking herself down at the table, she reached for the teapot. 'Sure, I'd be happy to bake your bride's cake for the occasion.'

'The lass here's what you might call a master confectioner in t' making,' said Joyce. 'Never have I tasted owt as light and delicious as what Lizzie here creates. Am I right, Mrs Price?'

'Oh, that you are, wench.'

The girl blushed a pleasant shade of pink. 'Go on with youse! Sure, they're not that good,' she insisted modestly, but it was clear she was delighted with the praise and passionate about her craft.

'Thanks, aye. That's kind of thee.'

'My pleasure, Laura. Now then,' she added, turning to the old woman, 'do you want owt doing, Mrs Price?' And she was up again, shifting from foot to foot, as though being idle was for her an impossibility. 'Owt fetching from the shops, like? A bit of dusting or sweeping in here, mebbe?'

Mrs Price was about to answer but Joyce interrupted her – something outside had caught her attention. She rose slowly with a frown. 'What the . . . ?'

'What is it?' Laura followed her gaze to the window. Spying Nathan crossing the cobbles sent her guts lurching in cold dread. *God above, Ambrose had done it.*

'What's that lad of mine doing home, then? He's barely been gone a few minutes!'

'I'll go,' Laura murmured as Joyce moved to the door.

Hands thrust deep in his pockets, Nathan was pacing back and forth across the tiny yard, his face a picture of disbelief and confusion. He didn't seem to hear her saying his name and only paused when she touched his arm. He stared down at her blankly.

'Lad?' Though she knew exactly what troubled him, she asked anyway. 'What's wrong? Why you not in work?'

'Your uncle. He . . . He's let me go.'

She closed her eyes in despair.

'Why, lass? *Why* would he do it?'

I loath you so much I can taste it, she inwardly raged. *Why are you doing this to us?*

'He gave no reason, none at all. Just told me to collect my things and leave, for he didn't need me no more. I just don't understand it. Why now? You'd think with me soon to be family and all . . . It's ruined everything.'

His devastation – and that she was the cause – crushed her. 'Nay. Nay, it hasn't, it—'

'We can't marry now. Least not yet. How will we afford a wedding, a home of our own, with no brass coming in?'

'Nathan, lad.' She struggled to hold back her tears. 'I'm sorry . . .'

'Hey, nay. Don't you be blaming yourself just 'cause he's your kin.' Regaining his composure in the face of her anguish, wanting to reassure her because that was the positive sort of person he was, he took her hands in his and brought them to his chest. 'The man's a swine; this is his doing and his alone.'

'We . . . crossed swords. Earlier, when I went to inform him of Father's passing.' She tried to pick her words carefully so as not to give away the whole truth. She couldn't bear Nathan – couldn't bear anyone – knowing . . . *that.* God no. 'He don't like the idea of us wedding. So you see, I can't go round there and try to appeal to his better nature on this, can't reason with him to take thee back on, for he'd not budge.'

'Reckons I'm too beneath thee, eh? Pompous owd goat, he's nowt else. And anyroad, I'd not go back to his crummy yard now for a gold watch. He's never taken to me, that's the top and bottom of it. It's a miracle he's kept me on this long.'

'I hate him, Nathan. I *hate* him!'

'Well, he don't do hisself no favours, does he? He makes it nigh on impossible *to* like him; he'd try the patience of a saint, aye. But 'ere,' he added, smiling now, 'you're not to worry none. We'll find a way. As for your father's funeral . . . this won't affect nowt. I intended to pay for it myself out of what I've been saving. We'll give that good fella a decent send-off, you'll see.'

'You'd do that for me?'

''Course, aye.'

'I don't . . . don't know what to say.' Now, her emotion spilled over; she covered her face with her hands. 'You're so kind, so kind . . . I don't deserve thee.'

'Now that's daft talk. I'm the lucky 'un, bagging thee. You deserve all I can humanly offer and more besides. I'd do owt for you, Laura. I love you.'

'Eeh, lad.' Though she didn't, couldn't for the life of her, say it back – she wanted to so much, but the words just wouldn't form – she portrayed her gratefulness to have him in a hug. 'I were contemplating selling Kenneth and the cart to cover costs. After all, with Father gone, there ain't the use for them . . . now . . .' She licked her lips in excitement as a thought occurred. 'That's *it*.'

'What is?'

'Have you been to see Father's employer yet?'

'Nay. I planned to call in t' undertakers then on to

Mr Howarth's yard during my dinner break today. Why? What you thinking?'

'I'm thinking you could take over the round.'

'Me, deliver coal?'

'Aye, why not? You said yourself that toiling in black gold is your life – well, you'd still do that, only you'll be humping sacks of the stuff rather than shovelling it. There's the horse and the cart sitting there ready. And I'd accompany thee if you'd like, till you learned the ropes. What d'you say?'

'I say it's a bloomin' marvellous idea.' Nathan's grin stretched from ear to ear.

'Come on, then.' Taking his hand again with a smile, she hurried him out of the court. 'There's no time like the present.'

She'd show Ambrose. If he believed he could best her that easily, he had another thing coming.

Thirty minutes later, it was settled.

The job was Nathan's if he wanted it. Laura could have cried with relief.

Mr Howarth had offered his condolences regarding Amos and shrugged when the idea of the younger man taking over his position was put to him. So long as someone was available to keep his customers supplied with fuel, he was satisfied with the new arrangement.

'You'll not let no one turn your thinking, sir, will you?' Laura had beseeched tentatively as they were leaving. 'My uncle, you see, he . . . don't much care for the lad here – not that there's a reason for it, you understand? – and well . . . he might try and twist thee into letting him go. But there'll be no truth to owt his mind might concoct as reason for it. He's nobbut a rotten liar, that's all.'

'I judge a man on what I see with my own two eyes, lass, not what's fed to my ears by others,' he'd assured her. 'If the lad passes muster, then we shan't have a problem.'

And that had been that. After thanking him, she and Nathan had continued on their way for the undertakers with easier hearts.

At one point during the journey guilt had crept in to dim her quiet happiness a little. Father wasn't even resting in the ground yet and already they were filling his shoes. But she knew her feelings to be unwarranted. Amos would have accepted wholeheartedly, would have urged them to strike before the grass grew under their feet. Moreover, he'd have been delighted that Kenneth was to stay in the trade, and particularly in the family. They had made the right decision.

Choking tears came immediately they entered their next port of call; Laura gulped them back desperately, but it did little good. The oppressive room, three walls of which were lined with coffins of varying size and quality, pressed down on her like a physical thing, making it difficult to breathe, and she almost turned tail and ran at the magnitude of her reason for being here. *Father was dead.* Then an arm went about her and stayed there, its warm firmness holding her safe, and she nodded. So long as Nathan was by her side, she could see this through.

The sombre-faced undertaker listened to their request with small nods and expertly timed sympathetic sounds. That he'd been in the industry of death for many years and knew exactly how to handle strangers' raw grief was clear to see. He knew precisely what his customers wanted even before they did.

'Plain deal wood, I think.' He spoke to himself,

166

scribbling notes into a large, leather-bound book. 'Unlined. No coffin furniture.'

'Coffin furniture?' Laura asked.

'That's right, my dear. Raised metal embellishments to the sides and lid. Such ornamentation lends a classical kind of charm. Images of angels, urns of flowers, even death's heads and crossbones, that sort of thing.'

And a bonny penny that would cost, no doubt. Amos would have been horrified at the extravagance. She shook her head. 'Nay, thank you. Summat simple, as you say.'

'Yes, yes. That can certainly be arranged. Now, may I have the deceased's particulars, to be engraved on the breastplate? Name, age and date of passing, if you please.'

'Amos,' she murmured. 'Amos Todd.'

The undertaker lifted his eyes from his desk. A small frown pulled at his dark brows. 'Amos Todd?'

'That's right.'

He sifted through some papers to the side of him, extracted one and ran his gaze over it. 'Amos Todd,' he said again. 'Of number five Ebenezer Court, Manchester?'

'Aye, but . . .' Laura looked to Nathan in bewilderment. 'How . . . ?'

'A Mr *Ambrose* Todd arrived here requiring my services for the self-same departed man not half an hour ago.'

Well, of all the . . .

'Let me see,' the undertaker went on, running his finger down the page. 'Ah yes. Carved oaken coffin, black crêpe lining, decorative brass screws and handles . . . It's all here.'

She breathed deeply. How *dare* he! She'd let it be known in no uncertain terms only that morning that she wanted nothing from him. This ostentatious gesture was nothing more than a means to salve his conscience. She'd sooner sell every possession she owned, the very clothes off her back, to pay for her father's send-off than be beholden to her uncle. He just had to meddle, couldn't help himself. Well, she'd soon rectify that.

She turned back to Nathan, intent on insisting they wouldn't accept this, her uncle's blood money, when she suddenly remembered. It *wasn't* her funds that were paying for this, though, was it? It was the lad's here. How could she ask him to hand over his hard-toiled-for savings still now? Then Nathan was speaking and she could have wept all over again:

'Sir. This 'ere's Amos Todd's daughter and my wife-to-be. *We'll* be covering the fee the day. You can return his brother's money in full, for it's not needed.'

'But lad, is tha sure?' she whispered, grasping his arm.

Nodding, he dropped a feathery kiss on to her brow. 'I am.'

'Indeed. Well.' Clearly puzzled, unused to such scenarios – and no doubt somewhat piqued that profit from this funeral had plummeted considerably, though he did his professional best to mask it – the undertaker cleared his throat. 'Of course, if you're sure.'

'We are, aye.'

'As you wish. Now then, where were we . . .'

'I'll pay you back,' Laura told Nathan earnestly, drawing him to a halt when business was conducted and they emerged outside. 'Every copper coin, I swear it.'

'Now don't talk daft. What's mine is yours, now, lass.' He laughed. 'That ain't much and never shall be, I'll be bound, but you're welcome to it all t' same.'

She really had struck gold with him. So why couldn't she answer even to herself whether she loved him? And did it matter?

Folk from across all walks of life seldom married for that one, unadulterated emotion alone. More a question of convenience, in all its forms. Be it for security, companionship or a means of escape, unions were often gone into on the whisperings of the head rather than the heart. And in time, if you were lucky and treated well, what you started out with usually grew into something deeper – love, hopefully.

Would she learn to love him? Laura pondered as they made the short journey home.

Again, she hadn't the answer. But she was willing to give it a damn good try.

Chapter 13

AS NATHAN HAD vowed, Amos Todd was laid to rest on a crisp November morning in a manner befitting the person he'd been: decent and dignified. They had done him proud, as he deserved.

Nathan and Daniel, along with their neighbours the two Johns, had carried the light-wood coffin with its posy of pale flowers atop through the court to the cart, where Kenneth, his polished harness adorned with bows in black ribbon, was waiting to pull his master on his final journey. A fitting tribute, they all agreed.

Laura had sat up front with Nathan, who took the reins, whilst the small trickle of mourners – Mrs Price, supported by Joyce and Lizzie; Daniel; the Johns and Mr Anderson – followed on foot. Mrs Anderson and Bee O'Brien had stayed behind to prepare the food they had managed to scrape together for the funeral tea. As the poor did in such times, Ebenezer Court's residents had contributed what precious pennies they could spare to the burial collection; Laura was humbled by their generosity.

Throughout the service, she'd kept one eye on the church door, convinced that at any moment her uncle would make his grand entrance, but he didn't, and the emotionally wrought event was eased somewhat by its smooth running, for which she was thankful. Her snubbing of him with the undertakers looked to have worked. It seemed at last he'd got the message, and this lent her strength. He could put as many obstacles in her path as he chose – she refused to be cowed, to be beaten. That she had an ally now – her future husband – and wasn't alone in this was a comforting thought.

Now, after making their solemn way home, all but Nathan filed into Joyce's house – he'd gone to return Kenneth and the cart to Mr Howarth's yard. Laura murmured her gratitude for the spread to Bee and Mrs Anderson then went to sit by herself near the fire. She was mentally and physically wrung out, hadn't thought it possible to shed so many tears as she had. Even now, she couldn't rid the image of the box holding her precious father being lowered into the winter-hardened ground. He truly was gone from her for ever. The pain of it was indescribable. Dear God, what would she *do*?

'Laura?'

She looked up to find Lizzie standing over her, smiling gently. In her hands was a tin jar.

'I made a little summat for the occasion, thought you could do with a sweet treat,' the girl told her, revealing a small round honey cake that smelled delicious and was beautifully baked. She'd even gone to the trouble of spelling out in currants on the surface a sweeping 'A' for Amos. The sight brought a lump to Laura's throat.

'Thank you, lass. Truly.'

'They favour tiny cobs of coal, don't they?' Lizzie said, nodding to the dark fruit lettering. 'I reckon it would have made your father smile, that.'

'They do. And aye, it's a fair nice touch. I only wish

171

Father was here to see . . .' She bit her lip as it began to tremble. 'Ta ever so.'

'He is here in a sense, have no fear of that. Our loved ones never leave us completely, you know.' Lizzie gave her shoulder a squeeze then left her to compose herself. 'I'll go and cut thee a slice, love.'

'The O'Brien girl's a likeable lass,' Laura told Nathan when he came to sit beside her upon his return.

He nodded then chuckled. 'Not that our Daniel seems to notice.'

'Oh?'

'Lizzie's been battling for his attention for years. Smitten, she is.'

'And your brother ain't interested?' Glancing across the room, she watched Daniel talking with Mr Anderson whilst, nearby, Lizzie shot him frequent adoring looks from beneath her lashes.

'He's fond of her well enough – as you say, she's a likeable sort – but not in that way, I don't reckon. Mind, he's a funny 'un, our Daniel. Quiet and brooding, he is, much prefers his own company to that of others. I can't ever see *him* finding anyone he's drawn to enough to wed, somehow. Not like me, eh?' He took her hand and caressed it. 'I'm one lucky fella, aye.'

Laura smiled but couldn't stop her gaze from flitting back to the other man. There was no denying his aloofness but, still, he was nice enough, had been kind from the start to her. Poor Lizzie, though. She really ought to focus her attention elsewhere, find someone who would reciprocate her feelings. She deserved that, was a real bonny lass and lovely-natured to match. And a great cake-maker into the bargain, Laura discovered later – Joyce and Mrs Price hadn't been exaggerating. Though in her current state of mind she only managed a few nibbles of the rich slice, she had to agree it was the best she'd ever tasted. Daniel really was missing a sound catch with her. So why couldn't he himself see it?

'You'll be all right the night, lass?' Nathan asked Laura that evening as she rose to leave with Mrs Price, and she was glad of his concern.

She nodded. 'It's sleep I need, I think. I'm worn through.'

'It'll do thee the power of good, aye. I'll see thee the morrow, then, bright and early?'

'The morrow?'

'Aye. Mr Howarth's yard. I start work there in t' morning, remember?'

What with all that had happened, she'd forgotten about that entirely. 'Oh aye, 'course.'

'I'll manage fine if you're not up for accompanying me on t' round as tha suggested . . .'

'Nay, I'd like to. Really, I would.' And she meant it. Though it would be painful being atop the cart beside Nathan and not her father, it was preferable to sitting idle at home with her doomy thoughts. 'See thee then. And lad?'

'Aye?'

'Thanks for today. For everything. I couldn't have seen it through without thee.'

She dreamed of Amos that night. They were sitting facing one another by the hearth in their room above Mrs Hanover's shop; him snoozing, her darning by the light of the fire. Comfortable, safe; a scene they had played out thousands of times in years gone by. Then he opened his eyes and beckoned her across.

She knelt by his feet and held his hand, and his lips moved but she couldn't hear the words he was speaking. She leaned in closer.

173

Clear as day, in his quiet gruff tone, she heard it: 'A.C. and L.T. A.C. and L.T. . . .'

She awoke with a frown etched in her brow. Those initials. Hers and her late husband's. Just like before, with her dream of Adam in bed . . . But *why*? It made no sense. Why did her father, of all people, want her to remember them? He'd hated Adam Cannock with a passion. It was he who had *wanted* her to wed Nathan, wasn't it? So what on earth did it all mean? *What*?

The sky beyond the thin curtains was the darkest of blue, but faint sounds of industry could be heard from somewhere in the distance – the city was slowly stretching its legs in readiness for a new working day. Pushing back the covers, she climbed from bed and padded downstairs.

After raking out the dead ashes as quietly as she could so as not to disturb the sleeping Mrs Price, she built a fresh fire and went to fill the kettle at the pump outside.

Lost in recent thoughts of Amos, she was halfway across the moonlit yard when she spotted the man ahead of her. Stripped to the waist, he was bent forward with his head under the wide tap, one arm moving up and down glinting white as he cranked the handle.

Unable from his position and the darkness to make out his identity, believing it to be an outsider who had wandered into their court, she swallowed a gasp and had begun to back away when she spotted Smiler by his feet. Daniel.

Realisation should have calmed her racing heart. She should have turned and headed back indoors until he'd finished his ablutions. However, for reasons unknown to her, neither of these things happened. She simply stood and watched, transfixed, as he gave himself a final rinse and flicked back his head, sending a silver spray of water through the air to land with gentle *pip pip* sounds on to the cobbles. He wiped his face on his forearm and ran his fingers through wet hair now darkened to the colour of caramel. Then he whistled to the dog and turned for home – stopping dead to see Laura standing behind him.

Neither spoke. After some seconds, he crossed the space towards her.

'Morning, Laura.'

'Morning.'

Despite the dawn air's winter bite, he didn't seem to notice the cold on his bare skin. Droplets of water made their slow track down his shoulders and smooth torso and, for the briefest moment, she had the overwhelming urge to put her tongue to them. The shocking impulse acted like a slap to the face and now, her gasp was given life. She tore her gaze from him with a shudder of mortification and not a little shame.

'Sorry if I kept thee waiting.' He motioned to the kettle swinging limply in her hand. 'Go ahead. I'm all done, now.'

'Ta, thanks.'

Yet still she made no attempt to leave – what the hell was wrong with her? Until, that is, movement to their right caught their ears and she turned to see Nathan standing watching them.

His eyes flicked from his brother to her as he walked towards them; it was only then she realised her state of undress. Her long nightgown was open at the neck, revealing the clear swell of her breasts; and her hair, normally drawn back from her face and secured at her nape in a neat knot, flowed freely over one shoulder.

She attempted a smile but failed. What must he *think*

of her, out here, at this hour in the secluded dark, with his half-naked brother? If his expression was anything to go by, she could well guess. She made to utter an explanation, but Nathan was already addressing Daniel:

'You'll catch your death of cold parading around the court like that.' There was an edge to his tone.

'I'm not parading, lad. I were having my wash.'

'Aye, well.' Nathan then trained his gaze on Laura. 'You an' all, for that matter.'

'You're right, we just, me and your brother, we crossed paths when I came to fill the kettle.' She held it up to reinforce her words. 'I'd best get on, else Mrs Price will be up and about and wanting a sup of tea,' she told him, edging to the pump and cursing the flush that sprang to her cheeks as her arm brushed Daniel's on her way past. 'I'll see thee later.'

Daniel nodded to her a farewell, but Nathan didn't respond. She hurried to the pump and busied herself with her task, and by the time she turned back for home the court was deserted. She stole a glance at Joyce's door. Then, releasing a slow and shaky breath, she made back inside.

The old woman hadn't stirred; the kitchen was still empty. Laura put the kettle on the heat and lowered herself into a chair at the table. Her tumbling thoughts ran on and, again, her cheeks flamed with the memory of her actions – or lack thereof. She covered her face with her hands.

What she'd wanted to do just now . . . more to the point, with whom . . . She was wicked, that's what! How would she be able to look either man in the eye now? Where on earth had those sudden and mistaken desires come from? Nathan deserved so much better for a wife!

Her mind was still in disarray and her guilt still

lingered when he knocked for her some time later. She opened the door with an apologetic smile, but she needn't have worried – to her relief, it was like nothing had occurred. Nathan wore his usual grin and greeted her warmly.

'Ready, lass?'

She nodded. 'I'll just fetch my shawl.'

'I'm excited about this, you know. It's going to work well, I can feel it,' he said as they approached Mr Howarth's yard.

'A fresh start,' she agreed.

He met her stare and his eyes held none of the recrimination from earlier. Now, they shone with only happiness, hope and affection. 'For the both of us.'

How she'd missed this.

Taking in a lungful of sharp air, Laura leaned in closer to Nathan with a contented sigh.

The feel of the wind in her hair, the sulphurous smell of the black nuggets wafting from the sacks, the clop of Kenneth's hooves on the cobblestones . . . It made her feel alive. Of course, it had been difficult at first, owing to the fact her father wasn't here now to share it with. But she knew he saw, and she was certain he was proud, and she soon rediscovered her love of the job. Delivering coal was in her family's blood, and they were damned good at it – that she was keeping up the tradition in Amos's memory was an honour and brought tears to her eyes.

They had experienced no hiccups. Nathan had taken to his new role like he'd been born to it, even seemed to be enjoying himself in the process. Naturally, the horse was a little agitated to begin with at the strange hands working the reins, but he soon settled down. And though by the end of the first round he still swung his long lean head around occasionally with soft, puzzled whinnies in search of Amos, which tore at Laura's heart, he was well on his way to accepting Nathan as his new master.

They had restocked the cart at the yard with fresh supplies and had set off on their afternoon delivery when Laura spied a familiar stooped figure heading towards them down Carruthers Street. Her mouth set in a hostile line. Though part of her told her she was being unreasonable, that true culpability lay not at this person's door, the stir of resentment refused to abate and she pointed her out to Nathan.

'That there's the herb woman, Widow Jessop. I don't know how she has the gall to hold her head up in public.'

'Now, I know you're upset, but—'

'Upset? That don't even come close to it. Her medicine was meant to help him. Stop the cart.'

'Laura—'

'Stop the cart, Nathan. I must have an explanation.'

With a sigh, he drew Kenneth to a halt at the roadside. Swallowing back the lump that had sprung to her throat, she climbed down and waited for her to reach them. However, as she drew nearer, Laura saw that her features were wreathed in misery and her own anguish, the anger along with it, faded. Frowning in concern, she raised her hand: 'Widow Jessop.'

The aged eyes squinted into focus. Then recognition dawned and the herb woman's face spread into a gladsome smile. 'Hello there, lass!'

'Is everything all right? Only I couldn't help but notice . . .' Laura faltered as, to her consternation, the woman instantly crumpled with emotion, as if she'd been holding it back all day and one kind word had been enough to shatter the dam. 'Widow Jessop, whatever's the matter?'

'Oh, lass. Oh, what'll I do?'

Putting her arm around her thin shoulders, Laura hushed her soothingly. 'Tell me what's afoot. Happen I can help.'

Gulping down her sobs, she shook her grey head. 'Tha can't, lass. I'm done for, you see. It's the poorhouse for me come the morrow. Oh! How will I bear such a place!' she cried, and again she dissolved into a flurry of tears.

'The workhouse?' Laura was horrified. 'But why?'

'They're closing up my cellar, lass. Summat to do with the New Streets Act what were passed or some such, the sanitary inspector said. Slum clearance, aye. Not fit for human habitation, they reckon. They're clearing up the whole city of cellars used as dwellings; what in the world will all us residents do? Nigh on thirty years I've lived there and now they've taken it. Aye, it's but a hole in the ground, but it's mine, you see? Love that place, I do.'

A solution to the woman's dilemma formed in Laura's mind immediately, but she hesitated. Still, a niggle of bitterness lingered deep within her and she was unsure if she could put the idea – that Widow Jessop lodge with Mrs Price – forward. Could she reside with ease, in the intimate confines of the court, with someone towards whom she harboured such bad feeling?

Misplaced blame, that's what this is, her inner voice whispered, and she knew it spoke sense. This woman had gone out of her way to aid Father. She'd offered advice, acted as a friend, didn't even charge for her services. She'd offered no hard guarantees, simply did her best with what she had. No one else was to blame but those Cannock devils and Ambrose. Let the animosity go. Help her, as she endeavoured to help you.

Holding her closer, Laura gave life to the suggestion: 'The lovely wench I dwell with takes in lodgers. She'd put you up, I'm sure, till you find summat else, like?'

Widow Jessop's eyes lit up. She wiped her face on the corner of her shawl. 'Eeh, lass. Where?'

'A court up Ancoats way.' Despite her own misgivings when she'd first set eyes on the place, she'd since developed a queer kind of protectiveness for it and, now, she felt the need to defend it. Every abode within it was scrupulously clean and presentable – good housekeeping made all the difference to a person's surroundings. Of course, not much could be done outside in way of improvements – you couldn't make a silk purse out of a sow's ear, after all – but the decent lot at Ebenezer Court did their best. 'It's norra bad sort as courts go, ain't bursting at the seams with folk like most. I reckon you'd like it.'

'It sounds gradely,' the old woman breathed with genuine excitement. Given what she was used to, Laura realised – cellar dwellings were notoriously terrible places, which only the poorest and most desperate members of society inhabited – it was little wonder. 'And you sure she's got the room?'

'Aye. And she'd be glad of the brass. You'd be doing each other a favour. Another thing: it's no great distance from the market so it'd be no hardship getting there to sell your wares.'

'I don't know what to . . . how to thank . . . Eeh, I've been that worried. You're an angel, what are thee?'

Laura smiled. 'Well, I don't know about that. I'm just happy to help. I tell you what . . .' She looked to Nathan, who, guessing what she was about to propose, nodded.

'How's about you go on home, Widow Jessop, and pack your things? Me and Nathan will clear things with Mrs Price when we've finished our round then come and collect you and your belongings on t' cart. Will that do thee?'

'It will, aye. I haven't much, really, bar my jars and potions. 'Ere,' she added, clicking her tongue. 'Listen to me prattling on with my own woes and forgetting the manners my dear mam taught me: how's that father of yourn?'

'He . . . He died, Widow Jessop. Last week. Summat to do with a bad valve in his heart, so said the doctor.'

'Oh, lass. Eeh, I am sorry. Sadly, them herbs of mine can't work the unworkable, not with complaints that are out of the control of human hands.'

'I understand,' Laura assured her, meaning it. 'You did your best.'

'You handled that good, lass,' said Nathan when the old woman had given them her address and left for home and Laura rejoined him on the cart.

'Aye, well. Fault lies not with her, really, does it? Besides, I couldn't see her – anyone, for that matter – destitute when there was summat I could do to help. Kindness costs nowt, after all.'

'That's you, all right. Generous with everyone.'

Something in his tone made her turn to look at him. His eyes were straight ahead, concealing his expression, but a pulsating muscle in his jaw hinted at . . . was that annoyance? At what? By 'everyone', did he mean his brother? The thought struck her suddenly. Or was her guilt having her read things into the situation that were not there? Her cheeks reddened in memory of their encounter, of what she'd longed to do, and she lowered her head. Then the moment was gone and Nathan was speaking again in his usual cheery way, convincing her she was paranoid:

'Right then, let's get this lot delivered and go and see Mrs Price. Ged up there, Kenneth lad!'

Tired and cold but with warm satisfaction in their breasts, they headed for home at the day's end arm in arm. The remainder of the shift had gone as well as the beginning – they could really make a go of this new position, of that they were both confident. The future didn't seem so bleak any more, in spite of Ambrose's best efforts to the contrary. Finally, they were on the up.

They had taken Kenneth to the yard for a rest and a nosebag of oats whilst they called on Mrs Price, and would collect him again soon for the short trek to Widow Jessop's home. Passing through the narrow alleyway that led to Ebenezer Court, Laura was crossing her fingers that Mrs Price would agree to the other woman staying when Nathan drew her to a stop. He looked down at her for a long moment and there was an intensity there that she'd never seen before.

'Lad?'

'Sshhh.' He leaned in and brushed the tip of her nose with his. Then his lips were on hers, his kiss ardent.

Taken by surprise, it was all she could do not to shrink from him. However, feeling his fingers move inside her jacket to tweak her nipple, common sense returned to her and she pulled back. 'Lad, we shouldn't ... Someone might come this way and see.'

'They'll not,' he whispered against her mouth, his breathing heavy. He put his free hand on her buttock and pulled her closer to him. His hardness pressed against her stomach and he groaned. 'Laura, Laura ...'

'Nathan, please. Stop.'

He jerked back as though she'd struck him. The dim

light held his face in shadow but his words, low and clipped, portrayed his mood perfectly: 'I bet you wouldn't say stop if—' He cut himself off and his deep swallow was audible.

If I were Daniel. Is that what he'd been about to say? Was this merely her imaginings again?

'If what, Nathan?' she made herself ask.

'If . . . If we were married.'

'Oh. Well, aye, 'course that would be different—'

'Then let's do it. As soon as possible.' There was a sense of almost manic desperation in his tone, as though he feared if he didn't claim her soon, he'd lose her. Which was silly – she'd already promised herself to him, had she not? 'It's what we both want, ain't it?'

'It is. But—'

'But what?'

She blinked several times as an odd sense of alarm took hold of her. 'Well, we haven't the brass, for one. And there's the timing: won't it look a bit distasteful, us entering into celebration so soon after Father?'

'Nay. It's what he'd have wanted. He'd want thee to be happy. Ain't that so?'

'Aye,' she had to agree.

'Then it's settled? Shall we say Christmas?'

'Christmas? But that's only a few weeks—'

'Christmas Day! Eeh, now that would be nice. Extra special, like, that is. I could stretch to the upkeep of the rent on that house of yourn lying empty till then – we'd have a home all ready to move into. What says thee? You happy with that?'

'I . . .'

'Please say yes, lass.' His tone had softened to one she recognised. He brought her hands up and squeezed gently. 'You'll not regret it.'

'I'll wed Nathan.'

'Then my heart is gladdened again. That it is, lass.'

Her and Amos's last conversation on the matter, his final wish, whispered to her like a breath on the breeze. She nodded.

'Aye?' Nathan's voice was full of wonder.

'Aye. There's nowt I want more than to marry thee, lad.'

'Oh, Laura . . .'

'You're right,' she murmured, returning his embrace. 'It is what Father would want.'

That her alarm had swelled to panic, she chose to ignore.

Chapter 14

OF COURSE, MRS Price had been all for Widow Jessop staying and, immediately upon meeting, the two elderly women had struck up a genuine friendship. Evenings in the small house at number one were now filled with laughter and chatter as, wrapped in their ancient shawls, they reminisced about the 'good owd days' over tea and toast by the fire.

Warm, contented, safe – Laura would watch them with a small smile, the winter frosts shut out, the soft candlelight lending the room a cosy glow. She'd be sad to leave them. They had taken on the role of mother figures and, once she set up home with Nathan, she'd sorely miss them.

Days had rolled into weeks and Laura allowed herself to be pulled along with the upcoming nuptials. Joyce, overjoyed with the news, had taken over the planning, and Laura was content to let her. Her take on the matter had switched to that of apathy – marry they must and so she awaited the festive morning with quiet acceptance.

Today marked ten days until the event, and Laura was whiling away the slow Sunday at number five with Lizzie. It felt strange being in what she still deemed her and her father's house – Bee O'Brien's was bursting at the seams with children, and Laura had given Lizzie the use of her kitchen to bake a birthday treat in peace for a friend of hers.

Wiping the back of a floury hand across her brow, Lizzie smiled. 'Ta for this, Laura. It'd take me twice as long to make this at home, what with the little 'uns careering in and out every two minutes and getting under my feet.'

'That's all right.'

'Eeh, smell that,' said Lizzie appreciatively, closing her eyes with a long sniff as the heady tang of hot lemon cake permeated the air. 'It'll be browned in a minute and ready to take round to Eliza's. Has a bad leg, she does, and it's been playing her up – bring a much-needed smile to her, will this. I've been saving for the ingredients 'specially.'

'You're a kind soul, lass.'

'Nay.' Modest to a fault, Lizzie would take no claim of the compliment. 'Anyone would do the same.'

'Well, I say you are, and you are! And another thing: Daniel's blind if he can't see thee for the sound catch you are—' She paused and bit her lip as colour rushed to Lizzie's cheeks. 'Sorry. I didn't mean to put my nose in your business . . .'

'It's all right. It's no secret, I suppose. I like the lad, aye. I like him a lot.'

She nodded awkwardly. What was there to say? That Daniel didn't share her keenness was also common knowledge and the sting of this was clear on Lizzie's face – she shouldn't have brought the subject up. It had nothing to do with her, after all. She busied herself with clearing away the dirty bowls and spoons whilst Lizzie turned her attention back to the finished bake.

'Sorry, lass,' Laura said again later, breaking through the silence that her statement had created. 'I really ought not to have said owt.'

186

The girl's smile returned. She shrugged. 'It's all right. 'Ere, come on. Help me spread on the sugar icing.'

Job done, and when the topping was dried and hardened, Laura motioned to the broad knife she'd used. 'Why don't I scratch an 'E' on t' top, as you did with that one in Father's memory? Be a nice touch, that will.'

'Aye, go on.'

Whilst Laura fulfilled her suggestion, Lizzie brought up the subject of her and Nathan's wedding and, as they chatted, the knife continued to move over the surface as though it had a life of its own. Laura wasn't aware of what she'd done until Lizzie's gasp broke through her daydreaming – she looked from the girl to the cake and her puzzlement swiftly turned to horror.

'Oh! I've ruined it. Sorry, Lizzie, I didn't realise—'

'Nay, leave it,' she insisted, rescuing the knife as Laura made to try and smooth over fresh icing to conceal her handiwork. 'Just look at that. How in the world . . . ? I love it!'

In the centre was the promised letter 'E'. But it was the carved shapes around the edge that set the whole thing off: a pattern of diamonds with a pearl border, neat and perfectly symmetrical.

'A work of art, that's what it is.' Lizzie was full of admiration. 'That's a rare talent you've got.'

Laura recognised the design instantly as that on a coal-hole cover she'd seen on her rounds and often admired. She'd pointed it out to Nathan several times, along with others she admired, but it was plain he hadn't the same enthusiasm in the artworks as she, though he did indulge her interest with smiles. 'How queer – I didn't even plan to do that; my hands took over without me! You sure your friend will like it?'

'She'll love it.' Studying it further, Lizzie laughed. ''Ere, we should team up, me and thee. We'd make a fair handsome living flogging baking as good as this. If only we had the means, eh?'

'What would we need?' Laura asked, and though Lizzie laughed again, she pressed, 'Tell me, lass. Means for what?'

'You're not serious?'

'And why not?' She nodded thoughtfully. 'You just said yourself they'd sell.'

'Aye, mebbe, but . . .'

'But what?'

'Well, it's just . . . folk like us don't try at things like this. It's the shop owners, the fancy confectioners and the like, what do this forra living. What would two lasses from the slum have any business doing, trying to compete with that? It'd never work.'

A spark of proud defiance brought Laura's chin up. 'We're as good as anyone else beyond them court walls, lass, and don't forget it. We seem to be good at this – at least we could be, with practice. Us, working together. We'd start out small at first, like, you know . . . ? Our own business. Just *think* of it!'

'But how? Who would we sell to and where?'

'I don't know,' Laura admitted, 'not right now. Not till I've had time to plan. You'd be for it, though, lass? You'd want to give it a go should I figure out a way?'

'Aye. Oh, Laura, it'd be a dream come true. D'you really think we could?'

Before a grinning Laura could assure her further, the door sounded and they turned to see Daniel entering the room. Forgetting herself in her excitement, she hurried towards him and took his arm. 'Come and see this, Daniel. What d'you think?'

He lifted an eyebrow at their creation. 'That's gradely.'

'You really think?'

'Aye. The detail really is very good. Did you do that?'

She nodded then blushed, suddenly feeling self-conscious. Then she caught sight of Lizzie's gaze, full of desperation to be noticed by him, and her eyes creased in pity. Hoping to shift the praise, she shook her head. 'How it looks ain't nowt on how it'll taste, mind. Lizzie here has the real talent.'

'I don't much care for cake, to be honest. Too sickly for my liking. That design, though . . . Well done. I'm impressed.'

She'd succeeded only in making matters worse – the girl was crestfallen. Didn't he realise how hurtful he was being? Laura shot Lizzie an apologetic look and was about to sing Lizzie's skills further when, once again, the door opened, and in walked Nathan. His smile for Laura fell away slowly to see his brother present.

'What are you doing here?' he asked the older man.

If Daniel sensed any animosity, he didn't show it. 'All right, lad? I came looking for thee, thought tha might like to come forra jar at the inn.'

'I've been at the yard, feeding the horse. And nay, sorry, I can't. I came to ask Laura if she fancied a walk somewhere.'

'Aye, I'd like that,' she said quickly when Nathan turned to look at her, keen to kill the tension. 'Where was tha thinking?'

'I thought Alexandra Park. It's a fair trek, but worth it; a bonny spot, it is. Oh, er . . . youse are welcome to join us,' he added to the others, and it was evident he'd merely offered out of politeness, for his face fell at Daniel's nod. Clearly, he hadn't expected either of them to accept. 'Oh. Well. Right, then.'

189

'A better choice than what I had in mind, lad. After all, ain't it said that the park were built to keep Manchester men from the alehouses on their day off?' Daniel flashed a lopsided smile. 'You can bet we'll be able to count the working fellas there the day on one hand, mind.'

'You'll come, an' all, won't you?' Laura asked Lizzie, but the girl shook her head.

'I've to get this to Eliza, remember?'

'You can take it round to her later, can't you?'

She glanced to Daniel, as though in the hope he'd give some indication he wanted her to accompany them. Receiving none, she shook her head again. 'Thanks, but nay. Some other time, mebbe.'

Hiding a sigh, Laura bade her a quiet farewell and went to fetch her shawl. Then she and the men set off on the somewhat awkward jaunt.

Their afternoon was as uncomfortable as she'd feared.

She'd had no option but to spend most of the time talking to Daniel, couldn't very well have ignored him, as Nathan chose to trail behind in sullen silence. She could, to a point, understand his churlishness – it had been rather tactless of Daniel to accompany them on what had clearly been intended to be an intimate walk. But Nathan *had* asked him along, after all. The least he could have done was put a civilised front on it.

He'd been right about one thing – the triangular-shaped public space, recently opened by the mayor, was a definite beauty spot. Covering some sixty level acres of lawn with curved and oval walkways, lodge, sunken bowling green and raised terrace complete with clocktower, all interspersed with flower gardens and ornamental features, she would in different circumstances have enjoyed promenading in such pleasing surroundings. Instead, she found herself willing the time away and couldn't contain a relieved breath when it was decided they should be making their way back to Ancoats.

Nathan lagged again on the return journey and, after several fruitless attempts to let him catch up, Laura gave up and walked ahead with his brother.

When St Mary's bell-tower appeared in the distance, it was releasing its deep chimes to the bleak sky, and she pointed: 'Mrs Price and Widow Jessop shall just be leaving – have we to walk across, see them home?'

Nathan shrugged, Daniel nodded and Laura led the way to the church. They spotted the two women by the door and, after exchanging greetings, they were all about to set off for Ebenezer Court when someone else caught Laura's eye. 'I'll not be a minute,' she told them, before hurrying after the beshawled figure.

Bridget jumped and sprang round when Laura tapped her on the shoulder. Her face creased slightly in pleasure at seeing her, but her downcast mouth refused to budge. 'Hello there, colleen.'

'Your eye.' Laura was horrified. She reached out to touch the dark swelling but the Irishwoman shrank from her. 'What happened to thee?'

'Oh this?' As though a switch had been flicked, Bridget pooh-poohed her concern with an easy chuckle. ''Tis nothing. Sure, weren't I an eejit yesterday and took a tumble in the kitchen? Tripped over my own feet, so I did, and received this from the corner of the table for my clumsiness.' She let out another laugh then pressed Laura's arm. 'And how are ye? Keeping well, I hope?'

Laura wasn't fooled in the slightest. She shook her head. 'What really occurred, Bridget? Please, you can tell me.'

'Colleen . . . It's as I said,' she insisted, but her gaze had gone suspiciously bright. 'The table, and . . . and not watching my step—'

'I'm sorry, but I don't believe thee. This is Ambrose, in't it? He did this to thee.'

The woman released a long, slow breath then dissolved into silent tears. 'Aye,' she whispered. 'Aye, he did.'

Despicable, bullyish, rotten old swine . . . 'Come on,' she said, taking her elbow. 'You're coming home with me for a brew and a talk, and I'll not take nay for an answer.'

When the six of them were squashed into Mrs Price's kitchen with Joyce, who had seen them all entering the court and, figuring something was amiss, had joined them inside, Laura took some steadying breaths. She'd decided the time for honesty had come. Bridget knew her secret and, should her injury somehow be the result of being privy to it – which Laura half suspected it was – she'd rather the sordid revelation came from her lips than those of the Irishwoman. These people – her neighbours, friends, soon-to-be family – needed to know the truth. But by God, how would she utter it? She was overcome with queasiness just contemplating it.

'Here, wench. Get that down thee.'

Taking the cup from Widow Jessop, Bridget thanked her and took small sips of the sweetened tea. After a few minutes, it became clear that she was using this as a distraction to put off what must be said, and Laura prompted her gently:

'This . . . is it due to what you overheard the day I came to tell Uncle Ambrose of Father's passing?'

The Irishwoman nodded and her words were barely a whisper. 'I finally confronted him about it. He flew into a fearsome fury. He struck me, warned me never to mention it again.'

192

'What's this?' Nathan was looking at them both in turn. 'Ambrose Todd inflicted that shiner? Overheard what?'

'Lad . . .' The shame was unbearable; Laura couldn't bring herself to meet his eye. 'My uncle, he . . . tried things with me that he shouldn't. Unnatural things – *warped*.'

'The bastard what?' He was livid. Even Daniel looked as though he'd like to dole out to Ambrose the kicking of his life.

'The first time it happened . . . I'd been to the market, had been up early, and what with doing double the work – helping out Father on the round alongside my duties at the yard – tiredness caught up with me. I dropped off to sleep in t' office and when I awoke . . . I tried to stop it but he'd not listen, and I were so frickened, so confused and ashamed and disgusted, and I couldn't tell a soul, not even Father, for I didn't . . . didn't know what to do and . . . and . . .'

Nathan's arms went around her, killing her distressed and garbled speech. Clinging to him, she opened up her heart, right there in front of everyone, and it felt so good. The relief in sharing her crippling burden was immense.

'I'm going to kill him.'

'Nay, lad.' She'd feared this, knew he'd want to exact revenge, to defend her honour. Yet there was a tiny part of her that was relieved he believed her. She'd fretted that no one would, had put off telling Amos for mainly that reason. But also because he, too, would have murdered that lecherous devil, had he seen the way of things. She wouldn't drag another soul into her troubles. Look what happened last time, the terrible fate that had befallen her father. She wouldn't have another death on her conscience. 'It – *he* – ain't worth dangling

193

at the end of a rope for. I'll not see thee swing. Please, leave it to me. I'll have my day with him yet.'

'But—'

'Promise me. You must, Nathan, for I'll not know another minute's peace till you do.'

There was silence. Joyce was the one who broke it. Taking Laura's hand, she shook her head. 'That's not how we do things here, lass. Folks cross the line and folks have gorra pay. You're one of us, now, and we stick by the ones we love, in good times, but 'specially during the storms, whatever the cost. That filthy piece you call kin needs teaching a lesson. No law, mind – our lot, our class, don't work like that. We settle scores our way. We'll be the ones to dole out his punishment. Aye, and one he'll not forget.'

She glanced to her younger son then continued, 'The lad confided in me about them brothers what are on yon tail and the reason why. Now, don't be vexed with him,' she added soothingly when Laura threw Nathan a disappointed look. 'He were worried is all, needed his mam's guidance. That pair, we'll think on as and when the need arises; seems they've left for now. This Mr Todd, on t' other hand, ain't for curbing his antics any time soon. As far as I can see, he's caused grief enough and must be stopped afore he creates any more. Question now is how.'

Mrs Price and Widow Jessop were nodding agreement, as was Nathan, whilst Bridget sat staring at the floor, biting her lip. Only Daniel appeared unconvinced, and Laura wanted to run to him, to shake him and tell him to reason with the group, who seemed intent on taking dangerous matters into their own hands. She pleaded to him with her eyes to speak up for her but he merely sighed quietly and looked away. She turned back to Joyce.

'We can't act as judge, jury and executioner, *can't* go wading in there to cause him injury or worse, much as he deserves it. We'd be the ones to suffer a more fearsome fate, don't you see? He's powerful. He's got standing, money; we touch a hair on his head and one word from him and we'd be hauled off to the gallows. No court in the land would listen to our side, not us, not over a successful man of business. Nay. I'll not risk it. There has to be another way.'

Why couldn't she just live a life of peace? Why did God hate her so? What had she done to deserve this hellish existence but fall in love with the wrong man? She seemed to draw enemies to her like a moth to a flame. It was all so unfair, and she was bone weary of looking over her shoulder, of running, being afraid, all of it. Would it ever end?

'I'd best be on my way, else sir will wonder where I've got to, so he will.'

Though Laura wanted to reason with Bridget, tell her not to return to that hell house, she knew it wasn't her decision to make. It was Bridget's life, Bridget's call. She loved the man, that was the crux of the matter. Whatever anyone said, the Irishwoman had to follow her own way. Laura walked her out and, when they were in the privacy of the yard, said, 'You know we'd help thee, Bridget, put thee up, if ever you choose to leave his employ.'

''Tis kind of ye to say, colleen.'

'I mean it.'

'I know. Only I can't,' she said simply, a look of such longing in her eyes that it tore at Laura to witness.

'He'll never wed thee, Bridget.' She had to say it. It seared to have to hurt her with the words but she had to give them life. 'He's incapable of love, I think.'

Blinking back tears, the Irishwoman smiled. 'I live in hope. It's all I can do.'

'Remember,' Laura told her, giving her a quick hug, 'I'm allus here. And Bridget?' she added, when they drew apart. 'You'll not inform him of what you've heard us speak about the day, will thee?'

After a long hesitation she shook her head. 'No, colleen.'

When she'd gone Laura leaned against the house's cold bricks and heaved a long sigh. Would she keep her word? Only time would tell. She'd discovered in the most painful way possible what happened when you crossed Ambrose Todd. Heaven help her should he get to hear she was planning his downfall. But how, *how* would she achieve it if not by brute force, as those inside believed to be the answer? What other route was there to make him pay? For pay he must, there was no debate on that front at least.

'They want only to get you justice.'

Laura glanced around and nodded to Daniel, who had appeared beside her. 'I know.'

'When one of our own are wronged, it becomes a matter for us all. You see?'

'Aye. It's just . . . There's other ways than turning to savagery, surely?'

'Aye, if you've the means. Do you?'

'Nay,' she was forced to admit. 'But I'll not give up until I do. I vowed I'd ruin him, and I will, one day. Ruin, not maim or kill, you understand?' she murmured, turning to face him again, and was gratified when he nodded. 'Violence . . . I shrink from it, avoid it at all costs. I suffered enough as Adam Cannock's wife. I can't condone it inflicted on another for my sake.'

'It's the only language some people understand,

though. It's my way of thinking that your uncle's one of them. But if you say nay to it . . .'

'I do.'

'Then we'll find another way.'

'We?' He'd come to stand in front of her and she gazed up at him in hopeful disbelief.

'Me and thee. Together.'

'But Nathan, he . . .' Laura knew her intended wouldn't be too pleased with her teaming up with someone who he'd begun to see as competition, brother or no. His jealousy of late if she and Daniel were so much as in the same room together was palpable. 'He . . .'

'Don't need to know.'

'Keep it a secret from him, you mean?'

'In a manner of speaking, aye. The lad's too hotheaded to fight with his brains – his fists are the only weapons he knows how to win with. He'd be for the noose, as you said, and I'll not see that happen. So we say nowt.'

She nodded. He'd moved in, close enough that she felt the breath from his words fan her cheek.

'You act like the matter's on t' backburner for now, convince him nowt's to be done till you say.'

His face was so near she could see the new growth of fine-coloured hairs at his strong jaw and chin. Her heart was hammering. 'I will.'

'Meanwhile, I'll start doing some digging about Ambrose Todd.'

'Yes.'

'And Laura?'

'Aye?'

'You know, don't you, that for two pins I'd slay every last swine what's ever caused thee hurt if you asked me to?'

She didn't answer, simply stared back, lost in the captive depth of his green gaze.

'We'd best get inside afore we're missed.'

This wasn't deceitful, not really, she told herself as she followed Daniel back to Mrs Price's. It was for Nathan's own good, that's all. They were doing him a kindness, saving him from himself. So why were her palms clammy and her stomach in knots with the knowledge that she and his brother shared something that was just theirs? A secret that was his and hers alone . . .

And what he'd sworn he'd do for you should you but ask? her mind whispered. *The burning urge to kiss him that gripped you just now? You're going to convince yourself that was innocent, too?*

Closing her eyes and ears to the accusation – *the truth* – Laura forced the troubling thoughts away.

Chapter 15

SMITHFIELD MARKET BUZZED with Christmas spirit and left a glow in all who passed through its doors. It mattered not if money was in short supply, whether turkey, roast beef, goose or the cheaper options of boiled sheep's head or offal broth would grace the family table on Wednesday afternoon – the festive anticipation was felt by all.

Stalls were decorated with sprigs of shiny-leaved holly and the traders were more enthusiastic than ever in urging the shoppers to buy, their cries as they advertised their wares mingling above the heads of the crowd in an unintelligible garble. Of course, the poorer folk of the city were careful not to be drawn into parting with the little they had, not today. Instead, they would swarm here in their droves on Christmas Eve, when the best bargains were to be had. Sellers keen to offload their remaining stock would drop their prices considerably at the last minute, and eager buyers knew it. For many, needs must, and the late trek home in biting temperatures was worth it to save a farthing or two.

Laura wasn't much feeling the cheer. This would be her first Christmas without Amos and she was missing him more than ever. A chance for kith and kin to gather together, that's what the time of year was meant for. You couldn't make that happen when everyone you'd known and loved were not on this earth any more, could you?

She had Nathan and her friends at the court, but it just wasn't the same, though of course she didn't tell them so. Everyone was being so kind and understanding that it would appear ungrateful of her to put words to her emotions. But by God, how she longed to confide in someone, to spill her heart and release some of the pent-up pain of her loss.

Then there were her disturbing feelings concerning Daniel.

Sighing, Laura gave a pile of material on a nearby stall a cursory glance, but her attention remained on the deeply concealed thoughts hounding her brain. He was on her mind constantly – yet oddly, it added only to strengthen her resolve to marry his brother.

Guilt had her seeking out Nathan's company more than usual and, in doing so, she'd got to know him better and to see even more what a thoughtful, loving, all-round decent fellow he was. He could make her laugh until her ribs ached and he loved her. Oh, he did, and it felt good to be needed. More than ever, she realised how fortunate she'd been to find him. Nevertheless, that didn't stop the other man from creeping relentlessly into her consciousness and she'd given up trying to banish him. It was all such a worrying mess, and one she was at a loss how to resolve.

'Remember to tell the ribbon seller you're a friend of mine. You'll get what you're after at a better price.'

Laura assured Widow Jessop that she would. She'd accompanied the old woman to work in order to purchase the last few items for the wedding. Of course, she couldn't stretch to a new dress, but one or two carefully chosen adornments would make all the difference.

The market would stay open late tonight and, being the last Saturday before Christmas, it was busier than usual – it seemed that half of Manchester was here. In addition to their regular shop, many were on the search for small, inexpensive trinkets to give to their relatives on the twenty-fifth, and the stallholders were doing a roaring trade. That included Widow Jessop. Business was always good this time of year, owing to the numerous winter ailments that plagued people young and old and, already, her barrow was almost empty.

After fighting through the crush to the appropriate stall and selecting a length of silky material in pale yellow to wear in her hair on the big day, Laura moved on to the next. Here, she opted for a handful of cheap artificial flowers in a similar shade to fashion into a bouquet. Several minutes later, she'd begun making her way back to her friend when a stall selling cakes caught her eye and she paused, her interest piqued. Changing direction, she headed across.

The sweet treats were carelessly arranged and looked less than appealing. Some hadn't risen sufficiently, whilst others were burnt around the edges, suggesting the heat of the oven in which they were made was too fierce. Worst of all, most looked to be bordering on the side of stale – discreetly, Laura pulled a face.

The none-too-clean-looking woman serving offered no smile and sighed at Laura's request, as though customers and work in general were some big inconvenience to her. With a fingerless gloved hand and long, grubby nails, she plucked a slab of plain sponge, wrapped it carelessly in brown paper and handed it over.

Unsatisfied with the cost – it was much too overpriced for its condition – Laura was nonetheless willing to give the woman the benefit of the doubt until she'd at least sampled the product. As she'd expected, it was bland-tasting, due to low-quality ingredients. All in all, a heavy, stodgy, inferior bake.

She and Lizzie could do so much better than that. And what was stopping them? Excitement stirred. She must talk to the girl about this, see what she thought. Surely Widow Jessop could help them in acquiring a stall ... Could they really do it? They would need capital to set things up – money for equipment, ingredients, that sort of thing. Would it be possible? Could they make a success of it?

Questions were still whirring around her head later when Nathan came to meet them to walk them home, and Laura was disappointed when, upon reaching the court, she saw that the O'Briens were already abed and the house in darkness. Her proposition to Lizzie would have to wait until morning.

'Just four more days and you'll be my wife,' murmured Nathan, pulling her into a hug when Widow Jessop had disappeared inside and they were alone in the yard.

She smiled. 'I can hardly wait.'

'Will I see thee the morrow?'

'Aye, all right. We could go forra walk somewhere if you'd like?'

'Aye. Only keep it to yourself, eh? We don't want a certain someone tagging along next time, do we?'

Laura remained silent. Truth be told, she would have welcomed both men's company, though of course she couldn't say so.

'What time shall I call round for thee?'

'Whenever tha likes. Oh,' she added as she remembered, 'I plan to call at church tomorrow, though, and catch Bridget afore she leaves. I'd like to invite her to the wedding – it slipped my mind entirely last week when she was here.'

Nathan's eyebrows met in a frown. 'Is that wise? Happen she tells your uncle? I've not rushed round there and smashed his skull in yet for your sake alone, for you've begged me not to. But I warn thee . . . If he shows up at that church, Laura, I'll not be responsible for my actions—'

'He'll not. She won't let on to him.' At least she prayed so, for all their sakes. 'Right, well, I'd best get in afore Mrs Price pulls the bolts across and locks me out,' she teased, dropping a quick kiss on to his cheek.

'Let her. There's plenty of room for you in my bed.'

'Cheeky!'

Winking, he flashed a wicked smile. 'Eeh, lass. Four days . . .'

'Goodnight, God bless, lad,' she said with a chuckle, and grinning, he headed for home.

As she lay in bed that night his words flitted back to her – allowing herself to imagine the wedding night, she blushed in the darkness. However, her embarrassment wasn't born from the idea of the lovemaking itself; no, no. She was a widow, after all, had known a man before. Rather it was because if she allowed her mind to wander too far, the face in her thoughts changed to that of another.

'Daniel . . .' she whispered to the emptiness.

Just what was she going to do?

Bridget didn't show up at church.

Laura waited outside long after the last worshippers had disappeared for home, but there was no sign of her. Dread coiled her guts into knots. Something was wrong – she hadn't known her to miss a service once since she'd known her.

Glancing in the direction of Ambrose's street, she chewed at her lip, agonising whether to call round and check the Irishwoman was well. But would she just make matters worse? What if Bridget was merely a little under the weather and that's why she hadn't attended? Was she reading something into it that wasn't there? Then the image of Bridget's bruised eye, coupled with the recollection of her uncle's wrath when a black mood took him – hadn't she borne witness to it herself more than once? – trickled into Laura's mind to torment her, and she nodded. She must make sure that everything was all right.

Once more, when reaching Ambrose's residence, she found herself hanging back for an age. Seeing the place again had brought to her memories – both good and bad – she'd rather not dwell upon, and her legs refused to take her further. Her uncle creeping to her room with depravity in mind in the dead of night, his threats whenever he managed to get her alone, the pleasant evenings wiled away in the warm kitchen with Bridget, the cherished midnight chats with her father in his bedroom and, later, snuggling close to him as he slept and drifting into an easy slumber . . .

A sob caught in her throat and she crushed a fist to her mouth. So much had happened. So much had changed. What was yet to come? Just as she had sworn vengeance, her uncle seemed intent on doing all in his power to destroy her, too. Like her, was he still scheming to find a way to achieve this? And which of them would succeed? Lord, how she wished he'd been the one to die instead of her father. The wrong brother was no more; this time, God had got His plan devastatingly wrong.

She had forced herself to the door and was lifting her hand towards the knocker when a voice hissing her name from behind stopped her in her tracks. Turning, she frowned in surprise to see Daniel beckoning to her from the roadside.

'How did you know I'd be—?'

'What the *hell* are you doing?' Taking her arm, he drew her aside, none too gently.

'Daniel, you're hurting me!'

His face changed instantly. He dropped his hold and ran his hand across his mouth. 'I'm sorry. I'd never . . . You've had me worried out of my mind. What the divil were you thinking, coming here alone?'

'Bridget, she weren't at church. I were fretting about her, wanted to make sure nowt had happened. How did you know where to find me?'

'When Nathan returned from your walk earlier without thee . . . Well, let's call it a hunch.'

'I told him when we reached the church on our way back to carry on to the court, that I'd follow once I'd spoke with Bridget. He had no idea I were coming here. I had no *intention* of doing. I still need to know she's all right, Daniel. You saw for yourself her face last week, what he's capable of. I'll not rest, else.'

He flicked his eyes to the house. Then he nodded. 'Aye. But first, let me go alone. You might make things worse for her, should your uncle see thee,' he hastened to add when Laura made to protest. 'He don't know me; our paths ain't ever crossed. Trust me. I have an idea.'

Hiding out of sight, she watched him walk away. He knocked at the door and she held her breath – what on earth did he have planned? Then there stood Ambrose. Arms folded, he listened as Daniel spoke. Though she was too far away to hear what was said, whatever it was had the power to steal all vestige of colour from her uncle's face. His mouth dropped open in disbelief. Then, with a roar, and much to Laura's astonishment, he pushed past Daniel and thundered down the street as though hell's hounds were at his back, leaving the door flapping wide. When he'd vanished, she made her way to the house and a smiling Daniel.

'How in heaven . . . ? What did tha say to him?'

'Oh, just that he'd best get down to his yard sharpish, as the place was up in flames.'

Nervous giggles bubbled in her throat. She clamped a hand to her mouth. 'You never did!'

'That's got him out of the road forra few minutes, eh? Now then, let's get inside and check on your friend.'

'And be quick about it. He'll not be in the sunniest of moods, I'll be bound, when he realises it were a pack of lies. I for one wouldn't like to be here when he returns. Oh, Daniel, thank you,' she added and, on impulse, hastily pressed her lips to his cheek. 'Come on!'

They made straight for the maid's domain – the kitchen – and burst inside. The space was empty. Laura motioned for Daniel to follow and headed for the stairs.

A minute later, they were back in the hall, breathless and disappointed. Their search of the whole house had proved futile – Bridget was nowhere to be found.

'I don't understand. She *must* be here.'

'We checked every room, Laura.'

Her head swung in confusion. 'But where could she be?'

Suddenly, heavy footsteps reached them from outside. *Someone was approaching the house.* They looked at each other in dread.

'Colleen?' Wearing a look of amazement, there stood the maid, in her ill-fitting clogs and thick shawl, a wicker basket in the crook of her arm.

'Bridget? It *is* thee!' Laura ran to her. 'Eeh, I were that worried!'

'Worried? About me? Sure, I'm grand, so.'

She *did* appear well. Even the bruising was almost faded to nothing. 'But . . . tha weren't here, and . . .'

'I've been down the way, visiting one of my nieces, for she's mighty sick, poor love.' She held up the basket. 'I took her some foodstuff – a bit of beef tea, that sort of thing – to build up her strength.'

'Oh. Aye.' Glancing to Daniel, Laura bit her lip.

'Where's your uncle? Does he know you're here?'

'He . . . had to rush out.' Despite herself, Laura felt the giddy laughter rising again, and it grew at Daniel's soft snort. 'We'd best be away.'

Still frowning in bemusement, the Irishwoman walked them to the door. 'Have I to give your uncle a message . . . ?'

'Nay. Nay, don't do that. He mustn't know I were here. Oh, and Bridget,' she added, remembering why she'd wanted to seek her out in the first place, 'I'm getting wed. Christmas Day. You'll come, won't yer?'

'Ay, I'd be delighted, colleen! 'Course, it shall have to be a flying visit, for I'll have to get back to prepare the festive lunch for your uncle—'

'Speaking of Uncle Ambrose: he ain't invited. So please don't say owt to him.'

A cloud of sadness for how things had turned out passed over her face. Nonetheless, she nodded. 'As ye wish.'

Looking left and right up the street before stepping out, and relieved to see there was no sign of her uncle,

Laura took Daniel's sleeve. 'Come on.' Grinning, they hurried for Ebenezer Court.

''Ere, give me a minute to catch my breath.'

Panting and laughing, Laura sagged against a ginnel wall beside him. The excitement – the risk – was exhilarating. She'd never felt so alive. She turned her head on the rough bricks to face him. He was gazing back, cheeks rugged from the exertion, his eyes twinkling. For a long moment, they simply stared at each other. When their mouths met, it felt like the most natural thing in the world.

It wasn't a hungry kiss; there was no passion involved. More a mere joining of two friends brought together in the moment. Just one soft press of lips against lips, then they were grinning once more and running again for home.

Lizzie, crossing the yard as they careered through the arched entry, stopped to stare. Laura's laughter slowly fizzled as real life – contrition along with it – slammed home. Just what was she thinking anyway, cavorting around the lanes like a slip of a lass? More to the point, with Daniel, whose company she had no business being in alone. Lizzie was bad enough, but what on earth would Nathan have thought, had it been he they had happened across instead?

She smiled guiltily. 'Hello, lass. We were just . . . I went to ask Bridget – you remember Bridget? – to the wedding. It slipped my mind when she was here last week, what with her injury, an' all. I met Daniel on the walk back.'

Glancing to the man himself then back to her, Lizzie's face relaxed, the mild hurt at seeing them together leaving her eyes. She flashed a smile of her own. 'Will she come, your friend?'

'Aye.'

'That's good. Eeh, not long, now! You must be a bundle of nerves – I know I would be!' Once more, her gaze flicked to Daniel then away again quickly. 'I'll be making a start on your bride's cake soon, Laura. I hope you like it.'

'I'm sure I will— Oh! I've been meaning to talk with thee,' she added on a rush, suddenly remembering the idea that had struck her at the market. 'Eeh, lass, we could make a success of it, I just know it!'

'What's this?' asked Nathan, emerging from home and catching the tail end of the conversation. Reaching them, he kissed Laura's cheek in greeting. 'A success of what?'

'A market stall.' Laura nodded eagerly. 'I reckon me and Lizzie could run our own, selling cakes. I sampled one yesterday whilst I was there and, oh, it were just terrible. We could do better than that with our eyes closed. We'd make a killing! 'Course, we'd need to plan, figure out how much brass we'd need to set up, that sort of thing, but . . .' Grinning, her eyes sparkled. 'I really reckon we could do this.' She raised her brows expectantly. 'What d'you say, lass?'

'Us? Our own business?' The stunned girl looked terrified.

'But . . . You were all for it, not long since.'

'I thought it just talk when you mentioned the idea afore. Oh, Laura. Oh, I don't know . . .'

'Why not? People aplenty do it; why *not* me and thee?'

Before Lizzie could stutter a response, Nathan spoke: 'And what of the round?'

'Well, I . . . Now you've learned the ropes and Kenneth's taken to thee . . .'

'I thought tha enjoyed us working together?'

'Well, I do, 'course I do—'

'There you are, then. You'd not have time to deliver coal *and* flog cakes, would yer?'

Her enthusiasm melted. Blinking back her dismay, she looked away. 'I suppose not.'

'Nathan's right, Laura. We couldn't compete with others in the trade. Then, as tha said, there's the money involved. It were a nice idea, but well . . . It's best to know our place, eh? Dreams ain't meant for folk like us.'

'Folk like . . . ?' Her shoulders slumped in crushing disappointment. Lizzie had no belief in herself. *Nathan* had no belief in his future wife. The pair hadn't an ounce of ambition or adventure between them. Her voice was flat. 'Aye. Youse are right. It's nobbut daft talk. Forget I mentioned it.'

Daniel had remained silent throughout the discourse. Now, when Laura escaped to Mrs Price's, he followed. He stopped her with a hand on her shoulder as she made to enter the kitchen. 'Wait.'

Alone with him in the minuscule hall, she avoided his eye as she struggled to hold back her tears. 'Can this wait till later? I'm tired and—'

'Don't you dare let them – let *anyone* – trample on your aspirations. They know nowt. Me, I have faith in thee.'

The lump in her throat was the size of a tomato. 'You do?'

'*Carpe diem.*'

She frowned at his usage of the Latin phrase.

'It means seize the day.'

'I know what it means. But lad, it's hopeless.'

'Let me help. I've a bit of brass put by, will loan you what you need.'

Laura was aghast. 'I couldn't let thee do that! Anyroad, there's no point, you heard the lass—'

'I'll talk Lizzie round.'

'Charm her into agreeing, you mean?' The words were out before Laura could stop them. She wouldn't see the girl manipulated. 'Lizzie's in love with thee, you know.'

He looked away. 'Aye, well. I'm sorry for her for that. I ain't never encouraged it.'

'And your brother? You'll sweet talk him into agreeing, an' all, will you?' Shaking her head dully, she sighed. 'Thanks, but let's just forget it, eh? They're right. It were a fantasy.'

'Laura—'

'Daniel, just please go.'

He hesitated then turned and left the house. She closed the door quietly and made straight for her room, desperate to be alone.

In the distance, the future tapered like a cloying, stifling, yawning void over which she'd very shortly have no control. A feeling of drowning was upon her and she was powerless to shake it.

Chapter 16

WHILST THE MAJORITY of Manchester gathered around their tables for Christmas dinner, Laura was putting her mark to paper. It was legally binding, done. She was officially Mrs Clough. She'd fulfilled her father's wish and, for that, she was happy.

Her neighbours had brought a tear to her eye upon her entering the church. Aware she hadn't a soul in the world besides her uncle – and the least said about him, the better – they had planned between them on the journey there to split themselves between the couple. And so, expecting the bride's pews to be holding only the figures of Widow Jessop and Bridget Figg, Laura had been surprised and touched to see seated there also the two Johns, Mr and Mrs Anderson, and Mrs Price and Lizzie. Bee O'Brien and the rest of her brood, along with Joyce and Daniel, had taken their places on the groom's side.

The ceremony had gone without a hitch and Ambrose had kept his distance. Even the weather had held out. The day couldn't have run any smoother if it had tried. So why did Laura feel so oddly numb and detached from it all? Even she hadn't the answer.

Now, as she and her husband made their way home-wards on the horse and cart, the guests following on foot – bar Bridget, who had had to return home to work – she glanced behind and her gaze locked with Daniel's. His eyes creased ever so slightly in a smile and she acknowledged it with the briefest of nods. Then she straightened back around to continue for Ebenezer Court and to begin married life with Nathan.

The wedding tea was roast chicken and all the trimmings at Joyce's house. On a variety of chairs and stools, the group squeezed around the two tables – Bee had loaned hers, along with her best cloth, to make room for them all – and there was barely space to swing a mouse in the stuffy kitchen.

A small barrel of ale had been acquired, and this the men made a beeline for whilst the women dished out potatoes and vegetables. The children, meanwhile, looked longingly at the far corner, where stood Lizzie's promised creation: a traditional bride's cake with dark fruit filling, decorated on top with white heather, which fittingly symbolised luck and protection. Though Laura appreciated this thoughtfulness behind the blooms' gesture, she couldn't stem the pang of regret over their market stall that would never be, and that such confectionary talent was going to waste.

'To the bride and groom,' announced Joyce, lifting her mug, voice cracking. 'I wish youse nowt but health and happiness.'

'Hear hear!' chorused the rest.

'Eeh, my own youngest lad wed. I'm fair overcome.' Joyce shot him an affectionate look, bestowed the same on Laura, then turned her smile to Daniel. 'And there's praise owed to thee, lad,' she told him, nodding. 'Stepping up as tha did in place of poor departed Amos and offering to give the lass away.'

He flashed a small smile, whilst Laura turned her

213

attention to her meal. The stab of something she couldn't identify had returned and she breathed slowly.

She'd first felt it earlier when Daniel had indeed made the proposal. It had struck deeper into her guts, like the twisting of a hot blade, as she walked beside him down the aisle. And when he'd taken her hand and given it to Nathan, voluntarily passing her over to another man, she'd wanted to double forward from the pain.

Of course, she wasn't stupid. She knew precisely what affected her. His face, which seemed to have become a fixture in her mind; her shameful yearnings for him these long weeks past; the kiss they had shared in the ginnel . . . She knew, all right. Admitting it, even to herself, was another matter. And completely and utterly pointless. The issue, she now realised, wasn't that she'd become Mrs Clough. It was whom she'd agreed to make her thus that was the problem.

And yet . . . she was really very fond of Nathan, felt a sense of betrayal merely considering their union a mistake. So just what did she want? Did she know? And after today, did that even matter? Father had thought him a sound catch, and he'd always known best. He'd be bursting with quiet pride to see her now. *God, how she missed him.* That, she told herself determinedly, was good enough for her. She had a husband, a duty. Yes, she did. She'd do her utmost to uphold her vows to the letter and fulfil her wifely role. Nathan deserved no less than that.

'Come on, then, youse two.' Grinning, the two Johns held out their hands to Laura and Joyce for a dance. The meal finished, the tables had been cleared and dragged outside into the courtyard to make a space. 'Give us a song, Bee!'

In an accent thick as soup, the rotund Irishwoman

belted out an old number from her younger years in her much-missed Isle. Soon, most of the room had paired up – the children, in fits of laughter, waltzing together in dizzyingly fast circles; Mrs Price and Widow Jessop holding hands and swaying to the music; the young Anderson couple locked in each other's arms, their eyes full of love for one another as they moved around the room. Then Nathan held out his hand to Bee's teenage daughter Mary and swept her off to join the rest, and only Daniel and Lizzie remained.

Laura watched discreetly over her dance partner's shoulder. Lizzie was shooting Daniel desperate furtive glances and, finally, he turned to her and said something. She nodded and her smile lit up her face. She put her hand in his outstretched palm and he placed his other arm around her waist, drawing her buxom body against his. Suddenly, he looked across the room to settle his gaze on Laura. She stared back. His expression was one of open loss, and she knew she wore it, too.

Her step faltered as if to go to him, but of course she didn't. Then Bee started up a livelier song, John and Nathan swapped partners, and she found herself wrapped in her husband's arms. Now, the crush of people obscured her view of Daniel and she turned her attention to the man who was holding her. He smiled down at her tenderly and something stirred in her breast, a warmness for him that both pleased and puzzled her in equal measures.

Just *what* did she *want* at all? Was it possible to love two people at once? She was beginning to believe so. The answer as to whether it was morally right, however, she was in no doubt: it certainly was not. Even more so given that the men were siblings. And Daniel felt the same for her; she knew this without question.

Two brothers loved her, and two brothers hated her.

What a dangerous mess. She shuddered to imagine how this tangled web could turn out.

Later, by some unspoken agreement, she and Nathan slipped out of the kitchen and walked the few yards across the court to their own home. The marital bed was already prepared. Without a word, they removed each other's clothing and slipped between the fresh sheets and, by the glow of soft candlelight, they made love.

There was no awkwardness; the binding of their commitment came together with ease. Laura found it pleasurable, satisfying even, and as she lay in his arms afterwards she knew a sense of contentment.

'I love thee,' Nathan murmured on the cusp of sleep.

'And I love thee,' she responded, this time without attempting to question it.

Before sleep claimed her, too, Daniel's face floated on the outskirts of her mind, as it always did, and her inner voice repeated the same declaration to him. *And I love thee.* Because she did. *She did.* And so long as neither man found out, was there really any harm in it?

'That smells good.'

Placing Nathan's breakfast of fried red herring in front of him, Laura stifled a yawn with the back of her hand then shot him a crooked smile when he grinned. 'It's not funny, lad. We've the round to see to the day.'

'Aye, well. I were all for an early night last night so as to wake up bright and ready for the first day back at work. Only someone would insist on ravishing my body till the early hours.' He winked when she swatted his arm with a click of her tongue. 'By, but it were worth it.'

Her pretence at being offended melted and she chuckled. 'What am I going to do with thee?'

'I don't know, but I'm looking forward to finding out,' he growled, then ducked, laughing, when she raised her hand again. 'Save it for later, though, eh? We'd best get going, else we'll be late.'

They had barely surfaced from home in the two days they had been married – one another's company had been enough. The sunlight hours were taken up with sorting through and rearranging their few possessions to make the house their own, eating meals together, talking about their pasts and making plans for their future. And at night, they would lie in each other's arms in bed and take their time exploring each other, familiarising themselves with every inch of the other's body, as was every husband and wife's right. But real life had returned for them today – money must be earned if the necessities of life were to be had.

The sharp air felt good in Laura's lungs, and as they passed through the frost-whitened streets, she drew in several deep breaths. However much she'd enjoyed time spent in their private cocoon, it was nice to get back into some order of routine and out of the court for a few hours to stretch her legs – clearly, Nathan was of the same mind.

He had an air of fulfilment about him and a lightness to his step that she'd never seen before. He was happy. That's what it was. Despite any misgivings she might have had in the weeks leading up to the wedding, so was she. She actually was, and she was relieved.

'*Once we'd shut away the outside at the day's end, it'd be just us together, and the misery beyond the front door couldn't touch us,*' he'd said to her the night he proposed. It seemed it was proving correct.

No, this wasn't a mistake, as she'd feared it might be. It felt right, and she was glad she'd listened to her father.

Kenneth swung his head up and down and pawed the ground in greeting. Mr Howarth had seen to his needs whilst they were off work, but it was clear he was happy to see them. Laura stroked his nose and Nathan patted his muscular back, his own face relaying his affection for his new partner. Then they were away on their round, the familiar smell of coal and horse in their nostrils, and it was like they had never been away. Snuggling in on the cart's seat, both for warmth and the desire to feel closer, they shared a contented smile and set off through the busy streets.

There were only one or two sacks left to deliver, and Laura was looking forward to returning to the yard to gulp down a cup of hot tea whilst the cart was reloaded ready for the next round, when she saw them. For a long moment, her eyes refused to believe it and she could only gaze, suspended in a state of horror-filled awe, towards the public house in the distance. *God Almighty. Please, no* . . .

Feeling her grow rigid beside him, Nathan turned to look at her. 'All right, lass?' he asked lightly.

'It's them. It's them.'

'Who?'

She slithered down from the cart on legs that felt like melted wax, and Nathan followed. Lifting a hand, she pointed out the hellish duo who had hounded her, in every possible sense of the word, for months. 'There. The Cannock brothers.'

Nathan's narrowed stare scrutinised the surrounding people. Then his eyes settled on the two similar-looking men and his face hardened like a flint. 'Oh, *is* it, now!'

'Nay!' She made a grab for his sleeve as he made to stride across. 'You can't—'

'Watch me.'

'Lad!'

'After what they've put thee through? They murdered your father, for God's sake!'

'And they'll kill thee, too, should you front them out. They're the divil's servants, capable of owt. I'll not lose thee, an' all. Lord, I should never have told thee!' She leapt frantically back on to the cart. 'Please, come away, come on, afore I'm spotted. I beg of thee.'

But Nathan didn't follow her, didn't take his place in the seat. Instead, he mouthed to her that he loved her. Then he brought his palm down on Kenneth's rump with a resounding slap.

The horse reared with a sharp screech of confusion and fear, sending the few sacks hurtling over the back of the cart and coal raining across the flagstones, and set off at speed down the road.

With a cry of her own, Laura grappled for the reins and pulled with all her might: 'Stop!' But the horse was too lost in blinding panic and refused to obey and, like a helpless captive, she was hauled against her will from the scene and from Nathan.

She contemplated jumping from the cart, but one glance over the side at the whizzing cobbles and she quickly abandoned the idea. She'd break her skull for sure, then what use would she be to her husband? Why had he *done* it?

As she twisted in her seat for a look of him, she got her answer when he lifted an arm to her. He was waving goodbye. He'd spooked Kenneth with the intention of getting her out of harm's way whilst he confronted the Cannock brothers. He had, it was true – he'd turned and was running towards the pub.

'Nathan! Nay!'

Again, she tried desperately to bring the horse under

219

control, but her yanking of the reins only frightened him more and he sped up further. Before they careered around the corner and out of sight, she looked back.

The brothers were gone. Nathan, on the other hand, was still there. He was in a heap on the ground in a pool of red. A crowd was gathering around him. And she could do nothing but scream and scream, until the blackness descended and she crumpled in a dead faint.

Mr Howarth's face swam into focus. Kenneth had made his way back to the yard, he told her. In a right state, he'd been. But the lads managed to calm him. They had given him a rub down and he was safe in his stable, munching on his oats. So she wasn't to worry, no harm done. But what had occurred to make the normally mild-mannered beast act so? She'd been lucky, could have tumbled from the cart in her unconscious state. She was all right, wasn't she? Not injured at all? Aye, a miracle, that. Could she sit, take some tea?

Laura couldn't make sense of the questions. She saw that she was lying on a blanket on the office floor. She ached and a spot above her temple throbbed. She allowed the coal merchant to help her up, felt a cup at her lips and drank. Snatches of sight and sound tapped at her brain then flitted from reach. She lurched sideways and brought up a stream of bile.

'Aye, see if he's at home,' she heard Mr Howarth say to a person unseen. 'The lad should have been with Kenneth on t' round – God knows what's afoot. That's right, Ebenezer Court. Tell him to come quick sharp, that she's mighty unwell.'

'Yes, boss. I'll not be long.'

'Lass?' The coal merchant was speaking again, this time to Laura. 'Your husband's on his way, so you're not to fret. More tea? There now, that's it, take another sup . . .'

Then she was being carried through the streets. The steady step echoed in the evening mist, and coldness bit. She shivered. The arms tightened around her. Her husband. He *had* come to get her. Her husband was all right.

'Nathan?'

'Don't try to speak. You've had a nasty knock to the head.'

'Lad . . .' Dizziness swooped. Her head lolled and she closed her eyes, sending tears of all-consuming relief spilling down her face. 'I thought you were dead. I thought the Cannock pair had done for thee.'

'Sshhh,' was his only response.

Familiar sounds of the court filtered through some time later and her lips twitched in a ghost of a smile. They were home. All would be well again, now. All would be well . . .

Wailing, full of raw agony, was coming from somewhere nearby. It was Joyce, Laura realised. And Laura laughed. For it didn't matter, because Nathan was here. He was all right, and all was well with the world.

Chapter 17

STABBED IN THE *throat. A flick knife, over in seconds. Hadn't stood a chance.*

'I don't believe you,' Laura whispered to the empty room as the words Daniel had uttered earlier pierced their relentless pitchforks into her brain. 'It's all a lie, for Nathan's well. He'll be home soon.'

She waited. She watched the dawn reborn, followed its track as ribbons of opal light crept through the sky. Then voices downstairs, hushed and weary. She strained for Nathan's, but it didn't come. Not yet, but it would. Nodding, she waited patiently.

'Sorry, but I must nip home. There's the babby to see to, my husband's breakfast to prepare . . .'

'It's all right, Mrs Anderson. I'll sit in with Laura.'

'Your mam?'

'She's sleeping, finally,' Daniel replied. 'Bee's with her.'

A muffled farewell and the front door clicked shut. Then footsteps sounded on the stairs and Daniel entered the room. He came towards her. 'Laura?'

'You shouldn't be here. Nathan will have a blue fit to find us alone together.'

Daniel perched on the bed beside her. 'Laura . . .'

'He's jealous, you know. He suspects I have feelings

for thee. I do. I love youse both. But he mustn't know, it's too cruel. You won't tell him?'

Daniel's mouth had slackened in disbelief. He shook his head.

'It won't stop me being a good wife to him. I vowed to do my duty, and I will. When's he coming home, lad?'

'He's here already.' The words were scratchy-sounding, full of despair. 'He's across the way at mine and Mam's.'

'Oh. Oh! D'you see? What did I tell thee!' Laughing brokenly, she swung her legs from the bed and hurried from the room. Daniel followed at a slower pace. She flew across the cobbled yard and into Joyce's house – and stopped dead in her tracks.

Stretched out on a door atop the table was her husband. He was covered with a blanket up to his neck. The face above was chalk white and his eyes were closed. She turned her mildly puzzled gaze on to Daniel.

'The landlord of the public house the lad were found outside . . . he gave us the lend of the door from his premises. It's what we used to carry him on to get him home.'

'I don't understand.'

'I knew. I just knew.' Daniel's voice faltered with emotion. He cleared his throat. 'When Mr Howarth's employee came to tell us you'd arrived back at the yard alone, the horse in a right state . . . I knew summat terrible had happened to him. I traced your delivery round on foot, found him within minutes. He were already gone. The stab wound . . . it were too deep. Nowt could have been done.'

Tears glistened on her lashes. Frowning, she turned back to Nathan, put her head close to his. 'Lad? It's me. I need thee to come home. Come home, now, eh? I'll prepare your favourite meal and, after, we'll go to bed. We'll talk and we'll make love, and we'll fall asleep in each other's arms like afore. Please, lad.'

'Laura. Lass, please, don't . . .'

Feeling Daniel's hands on her shoulders, she spun around and pleaded with him: 'Wake him for me. Go on, for he'll not listen!'

'Lass, lass . . .'

'Try, Daniel, please!'

'He's *gone*, lass.'

Dragging an arm across her eyes, she shook her head. Faint weeping reached her from the direction of the fire. Looking across, she saw Bee, tears streaming down her plump cheeks as she watched the scene unfolding. Laura went to her instead.

'Daniel'll not listen, Mrs O'Brien. You'll waken the lad for me, won't thee? Please?'

'Oh, poor, sweet Laura . . .' The woman buried her face in her apron and sobbed harder. 'Poor, sweet girl . . .'

'Nay. Nay, you must help, you must . . . Joyce! Joyce, please, I . . .' Spotting her mother-in-law hunched in the chair by the hearth, she fell to her knees and clutched at Joyce's skirt. 'My husband won't waken. Tell him, please,' she pressed, her voice rising in desperation when Joyce stirred from her sleep. 'He'll listen to his mam. He'll listen to thee, he—'

'Stop it, Laura! Stop it!' Daniel cried out across the room.

'But he must waken! He *must*.'

'Come here.' Hauling her to her feet, Daniel shook her hard, sending her teeth rattling. His wet face was creased in anguish. 'He's dead, lass. Dead. D'you hear? Look at him. Do it!' He forced her to turn. 'See him, *properly* this time. Nathan's *gone*.'

As though someone had swiped away the floor from under her, Laura's legs buckled and she fell, howling, into Daniel's arms.

'He died because of me.' Clutching a cup, the tea within long since grown stone cold, Laura stared into the fire's flames. 'I told him nay. I warned him, *begged* him, not to go to them, and now he's dead. He died alone, must have been so frickened, in so much pain. He sent me away, thought he was saving me. He wasn't. He wasn't, for how will I live now?'

Daniel let her talk, understanding she needed the release. Sometimes, her speech was disjointed as she struggled in vain to make sense of the tragedy, and all of it was peppered with bursts of uncontrollable sobbing. But he made no attempt to interrupt.

'Two days we were wed for, and he's gone. They've taken another person I loved. I murdered one of theirs, or so they think, and they've murdered double that of mine in retaliation. We were just getting to know each other properly, me and Nathan. I miss him already. Just what am I going to do?'

The grief made her hurt all over, caused her very bones to ache. Her hoarse weeping was the only sound for several minutes. Then: 'Daniel?' she whispered with a sense of urgency.

'Aye?'

'I want to kill them.'

He glanced towards the chair at the opposite end of the room, where his emotionally exhausted mother was sleeping again, with the help of a dose of laudanum. Bee had gone home to her own family and he'd told the rest of their neighbours not to call on them for the rest of the day, that he'd look after Joyce and Laura. When he turned back to her, his mouth was a hard, thin line. 'So do I.'

'This can't go on. Them two will never stop unless made to. Your mam, the rest of the court . . . they were right. It's time I did things their way. Getting vengence by biding your time, using your wits, don't work. Sometimes, you must fight fire with fire, for as you said yourself, it's the only language hell dwellers understand.

'The police would be of no use,' she continued. 'This whole city is crawling with all manner of villain and crook – violent altercations, even them resulting in death, are as common here as night follows day. They'll not have batted an eyelid over this, just another slum skirmish to them. And the Cannock brothers will be long gone by now. Anyroad, they'll have an alibi, some false story all neatly sewn up. It's down to me to see they pay.'

'Us,' Daniel ground out.

'They might kill thee, an' all. I have to say this, can't have the blood of yet another on my hands, must warn thee what you're getting yourself into.' Her tone was measured, purposeful. 'If you know the facts and are still in agreement . . . Then on your head be it.'

'I make my own decisions. *I'm* accountable for my actions. Whatever occurs, you'll not be to blame.'

She nodded. 'They'll have quick-footed it back to Bolton town to lie low. I know where to find them.'

He took a deep breath. Then he squared his shoulders and lifted his chin. 'Right, then, that's settled. We leave the morrow. Them bastards won't know what's hit them.'

She'd slept longer than she thought she would. The small clock on the bedroom mantel showed the time was just shy of seven – rubbing her eyes, she climbed from the bed.

Daniel had insisted last night that she sleep at his, that she shouldn't return so soon to her own home alone, and she'd been glad of the offer. She doubted she'd ever be able to face the marital bed ever again, not now. Not without her husband to share it with.

Her gaze swivelled to the far side of the room that, until recently, the brothers had shared. The single bed that was Nathan's before he'd moved out to live with her was still there. Her feet took her towards it and she sat on the edge. Gathering up fistfuls of the counterpane, she brought it to her face and breathed deeply. It still held his scent; a hard ball formed in her throat. She rose quickly and smoothed out the dark material until the bed was as neatly made as before. Then she dressed and made her way to the kitchen.

Deep and simmering rage was her motivation now, what was keeping her going, feeding her soul with strength. She couldn't give in to the agony of grief. She had to remain focused until she'd made those accountable for tearing her life to shreds pay. She *mustn't* fall apart, not yet.

Last night, on Daniel's instruction, the men of the court had carried Nathan home, his presence here being torture for his poor mother. Now, as Laura's eyes went to the table, she was glad of the decision. If she looked upon his face today, she'd crumble, the plans for the Cannock brothers along with her. No, no. That couldn't happen.

Flitting about the space with light steps so not to disturb Joyce and Daniel sleeping in the fireside chairs, she collected the teapot and cups then went to fill the kettle. Once she'd made a brew, she'd wake Daniel.

A quick sup and they would be on their way. There was, of course, Joyce to consider – she couldn't be left alone the state she was in – but the neighbours would rally round in their absence, Laura was sure. Nodding decisively, she slipped outside.

She was reaching for the pump's handle when she heard the privy door bang shut. She turned her head and there stood Lizzie, an empty chamber pot in her hand. It was the first time they had seen each other since the terrible loss and neither knew what to say. Then the girl's bottom lip wobbled, Laura's followed suit, and each rushed to throw an arm around the other.

'I'm so sorry, Laura. I'd have come to see thee, only Mam said to leave it a while and . . .'

'It's all right, lass. I weren't much up to visitors. It's took me some time to accept . . . to accept he's gone.'

'Eeh, love.'

Gulping down her emotion, Laura drew back. 'I'd best get in.'

'Aye. I'll call and see thee later, shall I?'

She and Daniel had decided to keep their plans concerning Bolton to themselves, figuring the fewer folk who knew what they intended, the least chance of further worrying the distraught Joyce. 'Aye, mebbe.'

'Right, well, bye for now, love. You make sure that fiancé of mine looks after thee.'

Laura's hand stilled on the doorknob. She swivelled around slowly. 'Your . . . fiancé?'

The girl's face had pinkened. She nodded. 'The night of your wedding, Daniel asked for my hand. I said yes.'

Mumbling something that sounded vaguely like congratulations, Laura made her excuses and escaped indoors. She leaned against the hallway wall, struggling to catch her breath. And yet, she had no *right* to these feelings! None! Her husband was lying cold just yards away and she . . . She was foul, wicked. She deserved what she'd had dealt to her, and more. A second widowhood was her punishment for developing feelings for Daniel. It was. She hated herself!

She moved towards the kitchen but didn't enter. Head pressed against the doorframe, the forgotten kettle swinging loosely in her hand, she watched mother and son for an age.

She'd wreaked so much pain and destruction upon this family since arriving here. She'd already lost Joyce a son – she wouldn't allow her remaining one to put his safety at risk, too. Daniel had the chance to forge a happy life with Lizzie. She had no business being here any more. Father was gone, as was Nathan. There was no one – nothing – left for her in Manchester.

After forcing herself into the room, Laura paused again. The dark bottle of laudanum atop the windowsill caught her eye – following the plan, which she now must see through alone, she lifted it down.

'I'm so very sorry, for everything,' she mouthed to the woman.

A last, lingering look at the slumbering man and Laura slipped from the house.

Once more, she halted. Looking to the dwelling opposite, the home in which she and her husband should have been together, now and for always, she allowed a tear or two to fall. Letting herself in, she headed straight upstairs and, again with the plan in mind, changed into her coal-stained working clothes. Along with what little money she possessed, she slipped the tincture of opium she'd taken from Joyce's into her jacket pocket.

Emerging into the murky sunlight, she pulled her cap low. Then she was running, from Ebenezer Court, from the memories, regrets and recriminations, from what was no more, whilst her heart withered to ashes.

'Please, don't ask me to explain, there ain't time.' She'd taken a risk and it had paid off – gripping Bridget's hand, she sent up to God a silent thank-you that the Irishwoman had answered her knock and not Ambrose. 'I need thee to do summat for me.'

'Sure, of course I will, colleen, but . . .' Bridget's face was wreathed in concern. 'I must know. Are ye in some mode of trouble? For if so, perhaps your uncle should be told—'

'Nay.' Bridget wasn't yet aware of Nathan's death, that much was plain, and this suited Laura. She hadn't the strength to go into that; not here, not now. 'I'm fine, honest. Inform him of nowt. Please just trust me.'

After some deliberation she relented with a sigh. 'All right. Although I have to say, I don't like this; something feels wrong . . . What is it ye want me to do?'

'Deliver a message to Mr Howarth at his coal yard. Tell him . . .' She swallowed hard. This definitely hadn't been part of the plan. However, circumstances were now drastically altered. This was, she was certain, for the best. 'Tell him that Kenneth and the cart are his. I haven't the use for them no more.'

'But why, colleen?'

'I'm going away.'

'Going? Going where?'

'I . . . can't say.' Nor did she reveal that she had no intention of returning. There was nothing for her here any more. 'Please,' she continued before Bridget could fire more questions her way, 'will tha do that for me?'

'Aye, but—'

'Thank you, Bridget, truly. Oh. And should Daniel

230

come here looking for me . . . Tell him I no longer need his help. Tell him to go home.'

'Colleen, wait. Just what on earth—?'

But Laura didn't hear, had already turned tail and was running down the street.

Chapter 18

NOTHING HAD CHANGED, and yet everything had. Gazing around Bolton's town centre square, Laura breathed deeply.

Every minute of the train journey here had been mental torture – continually, she'd agonised whether she was doing the right thing. However, Amos and Nathan's smiling faces would appear each time she wavered, reminding her that she was, that this whole despicable mess must be resolved once and for all, and another layer of hatred towards the Cannock pair would pile in her grief-scarred mind.

She knew where they would be: Breightmet, a small rural township some two miles north-east. Made up of sloping hills, farms and woodland dotted with relatively few homesteads, it was a pleasant spot. Other than the odd coal pit and sandstone quarry, and the handful of small-scale weaving and cotton-spinning, calico-printing and bleaching establishments, it was as yet largely untouched by industry. She'd enjoyed dwelling there during her marriage.

Neither brother was wed – nor for that matter had they shown signs of even thinking about settling down – the last time she'd been in contact with them. Chances were they would be exactly where they had always been: in the decrepit cottage they shared with their mother.

With the memory of Dotty Cannock, Laura's upper lip curled in distaste. A drunken, foul-mouthed, vicious slattern, completely lacking in morals and common decency – it was little wonder her children had turned out the way they had. Laura had tolerated her for Adam's sake, had done her utmost to be civil. Dotty, on the other hand, had never attempted to disguise her detestation for 'the uppity bitch who had snared her last born', as she'd referred to Laura from day one.

Now, fingering the bottle in her pocket, dread and not a little terror rolled through her guts at the events to come.

Praying for strength and purposely avoiding Ashburner Street, loath to see the burnt-out shell of Mrs Hanover's shop that was once her beloved home, she set off for the demons' lair.

As she'd suspected, she arrived at Red Lane to find the cottage empty. No matter the time of day, there was only one place you'd be certain to find Dotty: propping up the counter of some low inn or other. As for her sons, God alone knew where they would be – up to their criminal activities somewhere, no doubt. However, it had been best to make absolutely sure and, after a last squint through the grimy window, and satisfied no one was home, Laura headed out towards Bury Road, where it was busiest.

After checking one or two beer houses without success, she pushed open the dark-wood door of the next and, peering through the gloom, scanned the occupants. Several bags of bones clad in rags huddled around the small open fire, but Dotty wasn't amongst them. Then Laura trained her gaze in the opposite direction and there, alone at a stained table, a glass clutched to her breast like a suckling babe, was the beshawled figure she sought. Laura smiled grimly. Pulling her cap lower still over her eyes, obscuring her face, she crossed to the counter.

'What's your poison, lad?'

She put on her deepest voice. 'Er . . . porter,' she told the innkeeper, thinking on her feet – it was what Adam used to drink. She took the filled tankard from him with a nod, paid and went to sit in a secluded alcove. Pretending to sip the foul-smelling drink, she kept her eyes on her former mother-in-law across the room. The woman looked to have been supping since dawn, was slurring a ribald song to herself and swaying precariously in her seat. *She'd be ready for home soon. Not long, now.*

As the minutes ticked on, Dotty's voice grew in pitch until, eventually, another down-and-out customer yelled across to her to 'shut tha bloody trap'. She in return screeched back a stream of profanities, which caught the innkeeper's attention, and Laura prepared herself for the imminent departure.

'Right, Dotty, let's be having thee,' the aproned man told her sternly as he came to stand over her, hands on hips. 'I'll have no ruckus on my premises. Go on home and sleep it off, there's a good girl.'

'Good girl? Who the bleedin' hell d'you think you're talking to?' She lashed out with a clogged foot, catching him on his shin. 'Ha! Serves thee right, an' all,' she cackled gleefully as he yelped in pain. 'Good bleedin' girl, I ask thee. It'll be poor bloody Bob for *you* when my lads hear of this and get a grip of thee. Ah aye, that's knocked the bolshiness from yer sails, ain't it?' she added with a smirk when he blanched at the threat.

'Now then, Dotty. No need to bother your sons with

this, is there? Another gin afore you leave?' he simpered, and Laura ground her teeth to see the level of power that loathsome duo exerted, over everyone, it seemed. *Aye, well, not for much longer . . .*

Some thirty minutes and *two* drinks later, Dotty finally lumbered to her feet. She staggered to the door and disappeared outside. Several seconds later, Laura rose and casually followed.

She kept a reasonable distance between them, which required walking at a snail's pace – the drunken woman could barely stay upright, was zigzagging her way homewards at an agonisingly slow rate. At one point, midway along a rutted footpath leading to Red Lane, Dotty's feet seemed to become tangled and she stumbled sideward in a floppy trot, landing headlong in a hedgerow. She lay for a time hooting with laughter, and it took her a good few minutes to crawl out and right herself again. Reaching the end of her patience, it was all Laura could do to stay out of sight and not drag Dotty the remainder of the way by the scruff of her neck.

After what felt like hours they arrived at the cottage. Whilst Dotty was busy fumbling with the lock, Laura took the opportunity to scan the area to make sure they were not being watched. Then she crept up behind the older woman in readiness.

Dotty got the door open and ambled inside – Laura was right behind. Before Dotty slammed it shut, Laura slipped into the cottage behind her and flitted to the corner of the kitchen, where stood an ancient dresser, which concealed perfectly her crouching form. It wouldn't have done to break in. Damage to door or window would have been spotted right away; no one must suspect a thing. Fortunately, the idea had worked perfectly.

Heart hammering, she watched Dotty go to the fire-place and lift from the mantel a quart bottle of spirit. She removed the stopper with her teeth, spat it across the room and fell with a grunt into a sagging chair by the hearth.

After a few sips of the fiery liquid Dotty's eyelids began to droop in her flabby face. This was what Laura had been waiting for. Quiet snores told her the time was right – she emerged from her hiding place and crawled noiselessly across the flagged floor.

Upon reaching the chair, she glanced back around towards the door and prayed the Cannock brothers wouldn't arrive home just yet. Then she took the laudanum from her pocket.

She removed the cork carefully and peered inside the bottle at the reddish-brown contents. She chewed her lip. How much to administer? Ten drops? Thirty? Despite being sold legally by even respectable druggists and its wide usage amongst all classes – it cost around only a penny an ounce, the same as a pint of beer – ingested in high amounts, the poison could be lethal; it was a common killer. She didn't want to murder Dotty, just induce sleep, suspend her in a heavy state of narcotism for a while so she wouldn't get in the way of Laura's main objective. She didn't really deserve death – unlike her sons.

Daniel would have known the dosage. The thought tapped at her mind, but she shut it out quickly. He wasn't here and she wouldn't think of him. No. She refused to. She was on her own, now, and that was that. Cursing the lump that had crept to her throat, she returned her attention to the task in hand.

It was extremely bitter to the taste, but the brandy would mask that – Dotty wouldn't notice anything untoward . . . would she?

Laura hesitated a few moments longer. Then she held straight the bottle lying loosely in the woman's hand and tipped into it the entire contents of the laudanum.

After hurrying back to her hiding place, Laura took a series of deep breaths. Then she raised her hand and slapped the flagstones hard. The action had the desired effect – Dotty wakened with a start and, puzzled, squinted around the space. Spying nothing, she shrugged. Then she glanced down and, remembering the brandy, brought the bottle to her lips.

As she glugged on the laced drink Laura crossed her fingers that it would work. She didn't have long to wait.

Dotty grew drowsy and, shortly afterwards, appeared in a half-dazed state. She began babbling incoherently – had she fallen victim to the drug's hallucinogenic properties? Laura suspected so. Then suddenly, Dotty's head lolled and she fell into a death-like sleep.

Laura crept across. She lifted one eyelid then the other. The woman's pupils were greatly constricted. Panic rising, she put her ear to her chest and listened. Her breathing had shallowed alarmingly. Dotty had slipped into unconsciousness.

Had she given her too much? Would she die? Laura fretted. She glanced around the room in the grip of confusion, unsure now what to do.

You've come this far. You can't back out now, her inner voice commanded. *Follow the plan. Do it. For Nathan, for Father.*

Her face hardened and she nodded.

She turned and bolted up the stairs to hide.

Waking to a flurry of activity downstairs, Laura blinked in the darkness. It took a moment for her befuddled senses to return and, as remembrance slammed back,

237

she swallowed hard. She was in the Cannocks' house. And it sounded like the brothers had just arrived.

True, she hadn't known enough rest last night, but still . . . how on earth had she fallen asleep with all that was going on? Shaking her head at her own stupidity – the men could have discovered her and she'd have been done for – she scrambled to the bedroom door and craned her neck to listen.

Someone was stabbing viciously at the kitchen fire in a vain attempt to tease some life into the dead embers. A loud curse rang out then the clang of metal reverberated off the walls as the poker was slung across the room.

'Look at her! Fast akip, no fire in t' grate and bugger all to eat on t' table.'

'Aye,' the younger of the two agreed. 'She's a bone-idle sow if ever I saw one. 'Ere, mind out; I'll waken her.' His footsteps thumped as he crossed angrily to his mother – Laura held her breath.

Dear God, the laudanum. Was she . . . ? *Had* she killed the woman?

'Mam?'

Nothing.

'Mam, wake up! D'you hear me?'

To Laura's sheer relief, a gargled groan from Dotty sounded. *Thank God . . .*

'Ah, leave her be, lad. There'll be no getting sense from her till the morrow, when she's slept the drink off.'

'Bloody slattern, she's nowt else.'

'Check that there pot on t' fire,' said the elder brother. 'Happen she made some grub earlier. It'll be stone cold by now, but owt's better than nowt.'

There came the scrape of a pan lid, then: 'Ay! Good owd Mam.'

'What is it?'

238

'Beef steak and onions, by the looks of it.'

'Fetch it across, then. I'll get the bread.'

For the next few minutes the scratch of spoons on bowls, intermingled with the occasional burp, filled the silence. Then one of the men began to speak and the hairs stood up on the back of Laura's neck:

'What I'd not give to get my hands on that Todd whore. That haul we made away with . . . we'd be set for bloody *life*, now, if not for her!'

'Aye. Instead look at us. Barely a ha'penny to our names, sat here eating what favours stewed dog spew.' He breathed deeply in fury. 'Don't fret, lad. We'll track down the thieving little slut if it's the last thing we do. She can't hide for ever. I'll snap her bleedin' neck once we've reclaimed what's rightfully ours.'

Thieving . . . ? What haul? What were they talking about?

'That mystery fella Mam overheard in that tavern in Bolton town were right enough: Laura *was* in Manchester.'

God damn you, Ambrose . . .

'And spotting her father as we did proved it. Mind, we didn't get much information from that quarter, did we? Silly owd bastard. Fancy him keeling over like that afore we could get her whereabouts out of him.'

Laura had to bite down hard on her bottom lip to stop herself from crying out. *Father, Father. I'm so sorry.*

'But who's to say she ain't moved on since? The bitch could be anywhere by now.'

'Aye. We'd be taking a gamble stepping foot back in that city again after the trouble last time.'

'Nowt's come back on us, has it? Nor shall it. We were away afore possible witnesses could get a proper look at us. And it's not like the swine what came at us will squeal, eh? After all, dead men don't talk.'

239

Oh, Nathan.

'Anyroad, he asked for that blade in his windpipe. Charging at us as he did, fists swinging; what the bleedin' hell did he think would happen?'

'Aye. What d'you reckon it were about, then, that?'

'God only knows. Probably some sod what couldn't hold his ale thinking hisself tough and looking for bother.'

They didn't know he'd confronted them for her sake. Her husband hadn't even had a chance to explain. Oh, lad . . .

'Weren't so much the big man when we'd finished with him, mind, were he?'

Their laughter rent the air and Laura squeezed her eyes tight. Shut up, she silently begged. *Shut up.*

'Bleating for his mam as he clutched at his throat,' the younger brother spluttered on a guffaw. 'Fancy it. The daft bloody babby.'

Dear Lord, no! Shaking her head, she clamped her hands over her ears. How could they mock, and with such contempt, something so terribly tragic? For the first time, she was thankful that Daniel wasn't here, for this would have killed him inside to hear. This pair were the devils through and through. By God, they were. They deserved all they had coming to them, and more.

'Who's that, then?' one of the men asked suddenly. 'D'you hear it?'

'Aye.'

Laura's eyes widened. Where they referring to her? Had she created a noise without realising it, given herself away? They were speaking now in hushed tones – she slunk further from the bedroom to hear them properly.

'There it is again,' a brother hissed to the other. 'Listen.'

Laura knew then they didn't mean her – she hadn't made a sound. Now, she listened, too. When she heard it, her mouth fell open in astonishment – and sheer, gut-wrenching horror. *No.*

'A dog.'

'Some bastard's loitering outside the cottage.'

Oh God, oh God. What should she do? She'd know that bark anywhere. *Smiler.* That could only mean one thing . . .

What the hell was he doing here? Should she cause a distraction? Do something – anything – before the brothers discovered him? But what? *What?*

In the next moment, all hope was lost when a knock came at the door.

'Evening, lads.'

The sound of Daniel's voice brought conflicting emotions and tears to her eyes. You *foolish* man; why put yourself in danger like this? But by God, it's so good to hear you . . .

'And what can we do for thee?' The younger brother's tone was low with aggression.

'Well?' demanded the other.

'I trekked to Breightmet this afternoon on t' promise of work, but it's fell through – farmer whose land I were for labouring on don't need me after all. Now I'm stuck here, you see, and in need of lodgings for t' night. I've been asking hereabouts if anyone has the room but ain't had no luck so far.'

'Oh aye?' The suspicion was clear. 'What farm were that, then?'

'The one behind the little school down Roscow Fold way,' Daniel answered easily without hesitation – it was evident he'd done his research before approaching here.

241

'And from whence d'you spring?' shot back at him the other brother.

'Blackburn town, and I've missed the last train. I'll be away again home the morrow. So, have you lads the room to spare? I've brass to pay, of course.'

This last statement looked to do the trick – the men, in the penniless state they had mentioned earlier, whispered amongst themselves in consideration. Then: 'We've a place you can lay yer head, aye.'

'You can take Mam's bed,' explained the elder brother. 'She'll not surface from her chair, there, the night.'

'Ta, thanks.'

There came the sound of money being exchanged, then the brother spoke again: 'Well, come in, then. I'll show thee upstairs.'

Laura looked about wildly then darted for the bedroom she assumed was Dotty's. Daniel's voice, saying that Smiler would do well enough stopping outside, floated up to her and she breathed in relief. One whiff of her scent and the dog would have given her away instantly.

A battered old wardrobe slouched against one wall and she scrambled inside it. Secreted amongst the musty-smelling garments, she kept watch through the thin gap between the rickety doors. As she waited, her gaze flicked about her surroundings, coming to settle on the wall opposite in cold dread. Hanging there was an aged biblical print, depicting an image of Daniel in the Den of Lions – what were the chances? Was this a hint of things to come? *Dear God* . . .

In the next moment one of the brothers entered the room. Then there he was, following closely behind: *her* Daniel. She almost cried out at the sight of him. Despite her fear for him, and her anger that he'd followed her here, she'd never been more thankful to see anyone in her life.

The brother pointed to the bed, Daniel thanked him, then the former left the bedroom, banging the door shut behind him. Alone, Daniel's cool demeanour vanished – dragging his hands through his hair, he began pacing the floor, his agitation palpable as he agonised what to do next.

Laura was quick to put him out of his misery. She pushed open the wardrobe door and whispered his name. The expression on his face as he whipped around to look at her was one of disbelief swiftly followed by utter relief.

'You shouldn't be here, lad.'

'Thank *God*.' He was at her side in a heartbeat. His arms went around her. He held her close against him for a moment then drew back to stare into her face. 'Thank God,' he said again. Then his brows drew together. 'You say I shouldn't be here? What the hell were you thinking, coming here alone, Laura? Anything could have happened to thee—'

'Well, it ain't, has it?'

'Why did you go off like that without a word? When I wakened and you weren't there ... I just thank God them bastards downstairs swallowed the tale I concocted to get me into the house. We were meant to do this together, had *planned*—'

'Aye, well, I changed my mind.'

'But why?' he demanded.

Jerking her head to the door, she held a finger to her lips. 'Keep your voice down.'

'Why did you change your mind?' he pressed, albeit in a more hushed tone.

She shrugged. 'It matters not. Besides, this is summat

243

I need to do on my own. It were daft of me to drag thee in on it to start with. The first opportunity you get, I'd like you to go. You must leave this to me. Return to Manchester, to your mam . . . to Lizzie.'

He opened his mouth then closed it again. His gaze flicked from her to the floor. 'Ah. You know, then.'

'About you and Lizzie?' She felt tears bite. 'Aye, she informed me this morning. Why didn't you tell me?'

It was his turn to shrug. 'Happen I didn't think it the right time. I don't know. Does it matter?'

'Of course it matters, Daniel! It changes everything, don't you see?' Her tears spilled over to run down her face. 'You . . . have a responsibility now . . . to Lizzie . . . and . . . and you need to leave. I'll not see you risk getting yourself hurt or worse—'

'I don't love her.'

'What?' She shook her head.

'Lizzie. I don't love her.'

The wave of gladness his admission brought made her hate herself even more than she'd begun to of late. She was rotten to the core. Here she was, widowhood but a day old, secretly joyous that, just possibly, everything wasn't lost after all, as she'd feared, with another man. A man she loved still, despite knowing – *feeling* – to the depths of her soul that it was wrong. Who was she at all? Even she didn't recognise this stranger she'd become.

'It's the truth, Laura.'

'Then why ask the lass?'

'I have my reasons.'

'It's *cruel*, that's what!'

His mouth hardened. He swung away from her with a frown. 'Don't fret, I'll not shirk my duty. Although I regret it, I did ask for her hand, and I will see the marriage through. I'm a man of my word, if nowt else.'

She itched to go to him. What had his reasons been? Did he honestly regret it? Would he really wed Lizzie regardless? More to the point, why was she still asking herself these questions? It was no concern of hers. None at all. She must *stop* this. 'Well, tha must do what tha must. It's none of my business, after all.' Then, though it pained her to say it: 'I wish youse both luck and happiness.'

'Thank you,' he murmured flatly.

'But the fact remains . . . You have to go home. It's just not safe here.'

'I'm not going anywhere. We see this through together then we leave together, as we planned. Right?'

That she had no intention of returning to Manchester she kept to herself. He'd learn the truth of that soon enough. 'Lad, please listen to me, you must—'

'Sshhh. What was that?'

They glanced towards the door then back to each other with terrible dread. Someone was coming up the stairs.

'The wardrobe, quick,' Daniel hissed, bundling her towards it.

Laura barely had time to climb inside when the bedroom door burst open and one of the Cannock brothers stormed into the room. Her heart was banging like a drum – she was certain he would hear it – and she had to hold a hand to her mouth to stem her heavy breathing. However, if Daniel shared her terror, he didn't show it:

'Summat wrong?' he asked, his voice conveying only mild puzzlement.

'Get your arse down here, you,' the brother snarled. 'Move it!'

The game was up. They knew what was afoot, must

245

have overheard her and Daniel talking. Lord, they would kill them for sure. *Think*, her mind screamed. *Do something!*

Daniel folded his arms. Though he spoke as calmly as before, she saw through the gap in the wardrobe doors the nervous lick of his lips. 'Eh? Why?' he asked.

'Why, tha asks?' The man crossed the floor towards him. ''Cause that bleedin' dog of yourn's creating merry hell outside, that's what. Yowling and scratching at the door for thee, it is. We'll none of us get a wink of kip with that racket going on. Get and see to it afore I boot it into next week – and you along with it!'

Daniel stiffened at the threat. A muscle throbbed at his temple, hinting at his fury, and for a horrifying moment Laura thought he would lunge at the brother. When instead he forced an apology and followed him out, she sagged in relief. Moments later, he was back, Smiler at his heel. He closed the door, then leaned his forehead against it, fists bunched tight by his sides.

Laura emerged from the wardrobe and, after giving the excited dog a quick stroke, went to Daniel. What it must have taken just now for him to scrape to his brother's murderer, to swallow every instinct in him and not pummel that face to a pulp, she could only imagine. She touched his shoulder. 'Lad?'

'May God forgive me, I'm going to get so much pleasure from ending that set of bastards!' he spat in a whisper.

'They suspect nowt?'

He heaved a long breath then turned to face her. He shook his head. 'Nay, I don't think so.'

'Come, sit down.'

They went to perch on the end of the bed, the dog settling down between them. Not long afterwards, movement sounded again on the stairs – two sets of footsteps this time. Once again, Laura hurried to hide, but the brothers didn't put in an appearance. They made straight for the room they shared next door and soon their loud snores pushed through the adjoining wall.

She and Daniel shared a look. *A little longer,* they told each other with their eyes. *Let the pair reach a deep slumber and then we'll strike.*

When finally they rose and moved to the door, Laura was shaking from head to foot. Daniel didn't look much better. Despite his earlier impatience to exact revenge, his face was now ashen and, before turning the knob, he released several steadying breaths. He nodded to her, she returned it, and they tiptoed on to the tiny landing.

They paused outside the brothers' room. Daniel reached inside his trouser pocket and brought out two flick knives, one of which he passed to her. Then he opened the door slowly and they crept inside.

Both brothers lay on their backs, mouths wide, fast asleep. The high moon's silver sheen pouring through the curtainless window lit the way as she made for one bed, he the second.

The weapons were poised ready at their victims' necks. Laura and Daniel glanced across at each other.

'For Nathan.'

'For Father,' she mouthed back.

In a rapid, simultaneous sweep, they drew the blades across the tender flesh.

Laura could only watch in numbing horror as the younger, more vicious brother, whom she'd attacked, opened his eyes wide with a sharp gasp. Then he was leaping from the bed, roaring like a crazed bull. With

247

a cry, she dropped the knife, sending it clattering to the bare floorboards to become lost in the shadows. He came towards her and she staggered back on legs that felt like melting jelly, hands outstretched to ward him off.

Dear God, she hadn't done it right! The blade hadn't penetrated; she'd barely drawn blood.

'What the ... ? What the ... ! *You*?' Taking in her face, he swung his head incredulously. Then he bared his teeth. 'You whore, I'll kill thee!' he screamed.

'Nay, you stay away from me! Daniel!' she added on a shriek, not daring to take her eyes off the one advancing towards her. 'Daniel, help me!'

Frowning, the man paused – clearly, he'd thought her alone – and scanned the opposite end of the room. Picking out his brother's bed, his expression dropped slowly. 'Bastard ... Nay!'

Laura followed his gaze. His brother, making soft gurgling sounds, wild eyes gazing at the ceiling, was clutching at his neck with both hands. Blood, almost black in the dim light, covered him, the bed, the walls. Standing above, the knife still poised in his fist, was Daniel, frozen with shock, as though not quite believing he'd inflicted the injury in front of him.

'You've done for him! You've slashed his throat!' The younger brother was dragging in each breath painfully and pulling at the hair at his temples, almost delirious with panic. 'Why? Who the hell even *are* you?'

'He's my brother-in-law.' Choking with sobs, Laura ran to Daniel's side. She turned murderous eyes back on the younger Cannock. 'The fella youse stabbed to death in Manchester the other day was my husband. This, this,' she added, swinging round to jab a finger at the dying man, 'it's your comeuppance! You killed

248

Daniel's brother and now he's killed yours! I only wish I'd done a better job and seen *thee* off as well!'

All vestige of colour had left his face. He stared back dumbly in stunned silence.

'Burning down Mrs Hanover's premises. Father, Nathan, now him,' she went on, tears pouring freely down her cheeks. 'All gone. So much destruction and death, and for what? I had *no part* in Adam's demise!'

'You reckon you'd still be breathing if I thought that?' he bellowed back. 'What the bugger are you talking about?'

'The ... the accident. His trip on t' stairs. You believed me responsible. You came for me afterwards, forced me to flee for my life. You *said* you were going to kill me!'

'Aye, because of the brass, yer brainless bitch!'

'But ... But I ...' A terrible, terrible feeling washed through her, making her stagger. This was all some sick ruse. He was lying. This couldn't be happening, it couldn't! 'What brass?' she stuttered.

'Don't act gormless, you sneaky, lying whore. You know exactly what I'm talking about, and I want it back. Every last penny, d'you hear?'

'I don't know. I don't!'

The conversation she'd overheard. They had mentioned a haul that would have set them up for life, had called her a thief.

Dear God, he spoke the truth. All of this. All of it, for all this time ...

Their vendetta against her had nothing to do with them thinking her to blame for Adam's death. They believed she'd stolen from them. That was it. Everything that had happened, the terrific level of loss ...

'This whole thing ... It's been about nowt but *money*?' she rasped.

249

'*My* money, aye. And I want it back!'

Her legs threatened to give way; she grasped on to Daniel to stop herself from falling. She'd lost her home and her father, her husband, her freedom, *everything* she'd ever known and loved . . . for money? This was some horrific nightmare, surely? This *couldn't* be real.

'We need . . . need to get out of here,' she murmured in a daze to Daniel, tugging at his jacket.

'Youse are going nowhere.' Fumbling at a tall chest, the brother pulled something from the top drawer. When he held it aloft, Laura felt the blood drain from her face and knew the threat to her life in light of this new development had far from diminished. She was still in as much danger now as she'd ever been. 'Nowhere, you hear?' he added in a low growl, pointing the gun directly at her. 'Unless you fancy the contents of all five chambers of this revolver emptied into your head, that is.'

Charged silence crackled between them. Then a groan rent the air and they turned as one in surprise to the bed.

'He's alive?' the younger brother asked in disbelief. 'He's *alive*, he is! Quick, there might still be time. Now, you bitch!' he shouted, prodding the gun's barrel into the small of her back. 'Tend to him. *Do* it!'

The seemingly miraculous resurrection appeared to snap Daniel from his stupor – galvanised, he sprang into action. He lifted his victim's head whilst, by the guttering light of the candle the younger brother had produced, Laura assessed his injury.

'I need water,' she said, and Daniel hurried for the pitcher on the washstand by the window. 'You, fetch me the sheet from your bed,' she told the weapon-wielding Cannock. This he did, and she tore it into strips. 'Now, mind back, give me room to work,' she instructed as she wetted a rag and turned her attention to the brother's wound.

'Well, Laura?' Daniel's voice eventually broke through the silence. 'Is he . . . ?'

'Aye, he'll live.'

The younger brother wasn't the only one to emit a breath of relief – Daniel visibly sagged. Seeing it, Laura knew for the first time a touch of thankfulness that the man had survived. She'd agonised over what the hell she was doing as she battled to save her enemy; surely he'd be better off dead, his sibling along with him, for both their sakes? But what would it have done to Daniel? The guilt of knowing he'd taken someone's life would have ruined him, of that she was certain.

Unlike some, he wasn't capable of such evil. He was a good man, and good men didn't go around murdering others, no matter the provocation or how much they might deserve it. She should never have suggested they come here. What an utter mess she'd made of everything – things were now ten times worse.

'You're sure he'll pull through?' demanded the younger brother.

She nodded. 'The blood made it look worse than it were; he lost a fair bit. He has two cuts and they're quite deep, but I've patched him up well enough.' She checked again the improvised bandage she'd fashioned from a left-over piece of the sheet. Satisfied it was secure, she focused next on the injured man's pallor and pulse rate. The former wasn't too good, resembling the colour of old dough. But his skin wasn't clammy; his temperature seemed fair. Furthermore, his breathing was steady. Nor did he look to be in much discomfort.

She rose from the bed and lifted her gaze slowly to the younger brother. He in turn stared from her to

251

Daniel. The gun followed his eyeline, pointing at them alternately. He cast the man resting in the bed another glance. Then he jerked his head towards the door.

'Youse two, downstairs. Move it!'

Laura led the way. In the kitchen, she awaited the next instruction with crippling dread. They were not for getting out of this alive, she and Daniel, she just knew it. How had she been so naive as to think their plan could work? Blinded by rage, terror of further reprisals and the need for revenge, she'd taken the pair of them straight to the slaughter. She'd been such a damn fool. Now, she and Daniel would pay the ultimate price.

'Sit,' the brother ordered Daniel, pointing to a chair. When Daniel had obeyed, he went to stand in front of him. In one swift movement, he swung the weapon, smashing the butt with brute force across Daniel's head.

Laura cried out and as Daniel slithered to the ground, made to rush forward, but the young Cannock sprang in her path. Then he was lifting his arm again and she hadn't the speed to dodge.

She knew a moment of fierce pain, then darkness claimed her, too.

Chapter 19

LAURA AWOKE TO dull throbbing in her skull and an intense dragging in her shoulders. The candle had burned out and the dark room was ice cold. She attempted to stand but found that she couldn't, and when she tried to lift a hand to the tender spot on her head it refused to obey.

Drowsiness threatened to sweep her off again and she was about to let it when a small voice murmured from far away, urging her to waken. She forced her eyelids back open.

Twisting this way and that, she slowly began to understand her situation. The tightness in her shoulders and her inability to rise seemed to point to her being constrained. The bite of rough rope at her wrists and ankles confirmed it. She was tied to a chair. And she wasn't alone. Breathing was coming from somewhere behind her.

Daniel? It had to be. Overwhelming relief flooded through her. *By some miracle, like her, he was alive.* Gulping back tears, she whispered his name.

'Aye, it's me.' He sounded groggy, his voice scratchy like gravel. 'Is tha . . . all right?'

'I think so. What happened?'

'I'm guessing we've been out of it forra good while.

Christ, my head.' He sucked in air sharply. 'Are you hurt, an' all?'

'Aye. The revolver . . . he hit us with it, must have restrained us whilst we were unconscious. Where is he? Have you seen him?'

'Nay. His mam's not here, neither. We're the only ones.'

A small whimper escaped Laura. She bit her lips. 'What's to become of us, lad?'

'I don't know,' he admitted after a pause. 'We're just going to have to tough this out. Can tha move at all?'

'Nay.'

'Try, Laura. There's no way tha can break loose?'

'Oh, I can't!' she finally cried when a few minutes of pulling against her bonds yielded no result. 'What are we going to *do*?'

'Tell the truth, that's what,' a voice said from the stairs.

Laura and Daniel craned their necks, but the darkness obscured the speaker – though it didn't take a genius to work out who it was. Then a flare of light punctured the gloom as a candle was lit and they found themselves staring into the hate-filled eyes of their captors.

The brothers perched side by side on the end of the table then reached forward and pulled the wooden chairs Laura and Daniel were imprisoned in around to face them. Folding their arms, they looked from one to the other in silence.

'What are youse going to do to us?' Laura forced herself to ask. They didn't respond. 'Please, let us go. I know nowt about any brass—'

A sharp slap across her face shattered her speech, the sound rebounding off the walls like a thunderclap and bringing stinging tears to her eyes.

'You bastard!' Enraged, Daniel bucked and yanked

254

against the rope and tried to throw himself forward at the men, but it was no use – he was powerless and they knew it. They laughed in his face, bringing from him a roar of frustration. 'Lay one more finger on her and I swear to God, I *will* gut you like the hog that you are – and I'll do it right next time,' he promised the elder Cannock, who had delivered the blow. 'We should have left you to rot, you evil swine, yer!'

'Aye, but you never, and more fool you,' he shot back on a guffaw. For all his bravado, however, he looked terrible. Beads of sweat pricked his temples and brow and his complexion was a sickly grey. Though he tried to mask it, it was evident he was in some pain.

'You've not the bottle for it, you see,' the younger brother added to Daniel, shaking his head with a grin. 'Not like us. We did a right number on your brother, aye. Finished *him* off good and proper, we did—'

'Stop it, stop it, please!' Laura cried over their manic laughter and Daniel's heart-rending howl. 'Just let us go! Please, let us *go*!'

'We want our money.' All trace of mirth had gone – the snarling brothers loomed towards her. 'You're going to spill to us where you've hidden it, or God help thee.'

Not *this* again? She closed her eyes in hopeless dread. For how long would they keep up the impossible interrogation? How could she give them the answers they sought when she hadn't a clue what they were talking about? And yet their lives very possibly depended on her telling them what they wanted to know. But how? *What* money?

'Adam was the last person to see that haul. You were the last person to see him alive. You *know* where it is – now tell us!'

'The night he died. You'd done a . . . job?' she asked,

255

using the term Adam had to refer to their burglarising activities, desperate to piece this together and, God willing, figure out a way to bring it to an end.

'One of our biggest yet. We'd been planning it for months, chose a wealthy property miles from here so as to better avoid any comebacks, and all went without a hitch. When we arrived back in Bolton Adam insisted we shouldn't keep it at home, that it were best to play it safe in case the police did somehow think to fit us to the crime. He reckoned he had the perfect hiding place for it.'

'Aye, and never imagining he were soon to meet his maker,' said the other brother, picking up the thread of explanation, 'we anticipated no problem and didn't think to question where this were.' His nostrils flared in bubbling anger. 'We've searched and scoured every possible spot we can think of since, and nowt! But Adam ain't took the answer to his grave, has he, for you know, don't yer? He's *got* to have mentioned it afore the fall, so bloody well *tell* us!'

He hadn't, but they were not about to believe that. Nor, now, did she want them to. An idea was forming in her mind and she nodded to herself as a glimmer of hope returned.

She took a deep breath. 'If I do tell thee . . .'

'I *knew* it! You scheming little—!'

'Strike me again and *I'll* be the one taking the money's whereabouts to the grave,' she cried, squeezing her eyes shut and turning her head away as the younger brother threw back his fist. When she thought it safe, she hazarded a peep and was relieved to see he'd lowered his hand.

'Well?' he ground out.

'How do I know you'll let us leave once you have it?'

She could feel Daniel's surprised frown boring into her but ignored it. 'What's to say you'll not just kill us anyway?'

The elder Cannock brother rose to his feet. He bobbed his head in a solemn nod. 'If we get that brass back, you're free to go. You have my word on it.'

She glanced from one to the other. 'Aye?'

'Aye.'

'These bastards tried to kill thee and you're just going to let them off scot free?' his brother burst out, face twisted in fury. 'Not to mention dosing Mam up to her eyeballs – she could have snuffed it, an' all. Oh aye,' he continued to Laura, groping in his jacket and producing the empty laudanum bottle – he must have rifled through her pockets whilst she was unconscious – which he threw at her. 'We know about that, aye. Thought you had it all worked out, didn't youse? But you can't best us, whore. No one crosses us and gets away with it—'

'Enough,' the other man interrupted his rant.

'But she—!'

'I said, *enough*. This ends the day.' Then to Laura: 'You have my word,' he repeated. 'Now, tell me where it's hidden.'

'I can't; it's buried underground and it's hard to explain exactly where. You'd never find it alone. You'll have to let me show thee.'

'Right, then.' Pulling out a small knife from the top of his boot – was that the self-same weapon used to murder Nathan? Laura wondered, bile and anger rising – he moved behind her then stooped at her feet, severing the rope. 'Up. The lad'll accompany thee.'

'I want Daniel there, too,' she hastened to say.

'What? Frickened I'll blow your head off once the

brass is in my hand? Or is there another reason why you're worried about being alone with me?' asked the younger brother with a leering wink.

'I just . . . I'd feel safer if he came with us.'

'Nay.' The other man shook his head. 'He stops here with me. He goes nowhere till you're back with the loot.'

No . . . What now? She hadn't betted on this, had thought that the brothers, in their desperation to get their hands on the money, would have adhered to whatever condition she put forward. She couldn't leave without him, wouldn't! But how . . . ?

'Just do as they say, Laura.' Daniel spoke quietly, but there was a spark of something, meant just for her, in his stare. 'Trust me. Everything's going to be all right.'

Movement caught her eye. She flicked her gaze down then up again quickly. He was ever so discreetly teasing at the rope binding his wrists. She nodded. Then the younger brother was shoving her towards the door and she allowed herself to be ushered from the cottage.

The pre-dawn air was biting. Wind buffeted them as they trudged down the moonlit lane and whipped her hair around her head like a thrashing wave – she'd misplaced her hat somewhere at the house. Watching her struggle to bring the golden tendrils under control, the Cannock brother finally rolled his eyes and removed his own cap. He threw it at her without a word and she put it on, pushing her hair beneath it.

'Which way?' he demanded when they reached a drystone wall.

Swallowing her panic, she pointed randomly and they turned left and set off across a field.

Think! her mind screamed – what the hell was she going to do? She couldn't just keep him wandering around aimlessly for long; he was bound to realise this

258

was nothing but a wild-goose chase eventually. Then what? Would he turn the gun on her? Most probably. She was certain they had only kept her alive this long to squeeze information out of her – they would have no further need of her once they discovered she'd been lying about the money's whereabouts. *Think, think* . . .

She'd counted on Daniel's aid to get them out of this, had banked on them somehow giving the brothers the slip once on open ground, but that wasn't to be, now. She was completely and terrifyingly alone, and so was he. There really was no way out of this. She must come clean. Perhaps if she begged on her knees, the Cannocks would find it in their hearts to spare them their lives . . . *Fat chance*, her inner voice immediately scoffed. That was an utter impossibility: their chests were void of such organs, after all.

'How much further?'

Hauled back to the present, her every nerve jarred at his harsh tone. Buying herself some precious time, she pretended not to have heard.

'Oi, you listening?' he yelled. He dragged her to halt. 'I said, how much— Uh, you bitch!'

She'd kicked him, square between the legs. What had possessed her, she didn't know – she shook her head, dumb with shock. She gazed down at him, groaning on his knees, for a split second longer then she was off. His roars of threats and curses snapping at her heels, she flew full pelt towards a line of trees up ahead and disappeared through the thick branches.

Her lungs burned and her legs grew weak, but she didn't slow her pace. Nor did she look back. Some minutes later and fit to collapse, she spotted a hedgerow in the distance and dragged herself on. She dived behind it and lay on her back on the marshy grass, eyes closed, panting like a whelping dog.

'Daniel . . .' The name floated through her lips. She must find help, free him from that cottage. 'I'm coming, my love,' she croaked, hauling herself up and peering around the green-grey expanse of field and sky.

Which way to go? There wasn't a building, dwelling or otherwise, in sight.

She was stumbling on the spot, agonising what to do, when what sounded like the beat of footsteps reached her ears. She stopped dead and listened harder. It came again and she swung her head round for a glimpse of what – or who – it might be.

'Laura!'

'Lad? Lad! Oh, thank God!'

Daniel, Smiler in tow, threw himself into her arms, the force knocking them both to the ground. They lay in a breathless heap for a few moments until Laura gabbled in disbelief, 'How did you do it? How did you manage to get away, I don't . . . *how*? I—'

'Quiet. They might be close by.'

'You've been running from them both?'

He nodded. 'Their mam roused after you'd left. Her son went up to check on her and the next minute, Smiler came bounding downstairs – they must have locked him in t' bedroom when we were out cold. I'd been working on the rope, had managed to loosen it a bit, and the dog did the rest.' A quick smile touched his mouth. 'He tugged at the thing with his teeth and I were able to break free. I were barely out of the cottage when that bastard came thundering down the stairs after me. I just ran blindly in search of thee, hadn't a clue where you'd gone, were worried out of my mind . . .' He paused and closed his eyes. 'Thank God you're all right.'

260

'And thee, lad. Eeh, I were that frickened.'

'We ran into the other brother being sick in a field. What occurred? How did tha manage to give him the slip?'

'I had to lead him about for a bit, for I've no idea where that brass really is. In t' end, I finished up kicking him . . . down there . . . and ran for my life.'

Daniel winced. 'And a sound job tha did, an' all, by the looks of him. But now they've joined forces, could be anywhere. We're going to have a task on our hands getting out of here and back to Manchester in one piece.'

Scorching tears pooled in her eyes. She shook her head slowly. 'What were I thinking, lad? Why did I ever suggest seeking them out? The danger I've placed thee in—'

'Nay, it were my decision to come.'

'But I planted the idea in your head. It's my doing, all of it, and now look at us. I'm sorry, so sorry . . .'

'Ay, that's enough of that.' His voice was soft, his touch as he cupped her cheek and brushed away the tears with his thumb gentle. 'We're going to be all right, you hear? I'd never let owt happen to thee, Laura. Never.'

'Oh, Daniel.' She received his kiss with a sorrowful sigh. 'Please don't. Not now. Everything's changed.'

He made to respond but, just then, angry voices filtered through a clump of trees to their left and they froze. Holding a finger to his lips, he took her hand.

'Let's go.'

Steps light, heads lowered, they hurried off through the mid-winter mist towards the adjoining field and, God willing, escape.

After a time, the brothers' yells faded to nothing, and Laura and Daniel allowed themselves to breathe a little easier. They reached a gurgling spring and he hopped over it in front, holding out a hand to help her across. Before continuing, they turned to encourage Smiler to jump the narrow stretch of clear water, but it was as if he didn't hear.

He'd turned back towards the way they had come and was staring intently towards a high thicket. Then he lowered his head and released a rumbling growl from deep in his throat, and Laura and Daniel flicked wide eyes at each other. The Cannocks? Had to be. They had dared to hope they had lost them but, all along, the men had been trailing them; the dog had picked up their scent. They turned as one and sprinted off.

Laura noticed Daniel fall before the noise of the gunshot registered. He hit the ground with a groan whilst, overhead, a flock of screeching birds darted through the sky for cover. She whipped round to see their whooping tormentors running in their direction, the younger brother brandishing the still-smoking revolver above his head triumphantly.

'Get up! Quick, lad!' she cried, flinging Daniel's arm about her shoulders and heaving him up. However, when he attempted to put weight on his injured leg, he let out a cry and crumpled back to the grass. 'Nay, please, we must hurry!'

'Go.' He clenched his teeth through the pain. 'Go, get out of here!'

'I'll not leave thee!'

'Now, Laura. *Now*, else they'll kill thee!' He sent her stumbling with a push. 'Run and don't you dare stop. Go. Go!'

Doing so might just save his life, she realised with sudden clarity. It was she the Cannock brothers wanted to exact revenge upon; he'd merely been caught up in

262

the fray, wasn't the real enemy. If she diverted their attention away from Daniel, perhaps they would spare him. She must have them come after her alone. Hopefully, she'd manage to hide somewhere and, in the meantime, Daniel would have time to crawl to safety.

She cast him a last, lingering look. Then she bolted away, zigzagging for a rutted track to lead the brothers out of Daniel's path.

It worked – they immediately headed after her and she sent up a thank-you to God. Picking up speed, she hurtled towards a wooded patch in the far distance.

By now, dawn light pierced the scudding snow clouds. At some point, looking behind her, she discovered she was alone – the brothers were nowhere to be seen. Frowning, she slowed her pace a little and scanned the area again, but no: they were gone. Unsure what to do, she crouched in the grasses to catch her breath. Then movement sounded nearby and she sprang up, once more taking off at a blind run.

A quarry's boundary wall seemed to loom from nowhere and she skirted it, arriving in a rocky clearing that at first sight appeared deserted. Then she saw him, and her heart tripped over itself in several galloping beats.

The bandage she'd applied to his neck earlier was stained crimson and he was wheezing heavily, his colour deathly. Laura flicked her eyes behind him towards the sloping delph edge, but of his brother there was no sign. Then an arm went about her neck from behind, squeezing the air from her, thick muscle crushing her windpipe so she thought she'd pass out. She clawed at her captor's sleeve, but it was a feeble attempt and her eyelids began to droop.

'Scheming, snidy little *bitch*.' The younger Cannock

released her, sending her with a shove to the hard ground. 'We bested thee, eh?'

Retching and coughing on all fours, she stared up at him with wild eyes. Like a hunted rabbit, they had skilfully ambushed their prey. There was nowhere left to run. They had her cornered and, now, she was done for.

Desperation had her skidding to her feet to make a dash for it, but the man was prepared – he grabbed her once more, this time around the waist, pinioning her back against his chest, and she sagged in defeat. She was no match for his strength.

The elder brother in front of them raised his arm and pointed the revolver directly at her head, and she closed her eyes. This was it. At least it would be a quick death, she consoled herself. Quailing, she held her breath.

'Go on, lad, give it to her,' the younger Cannock encouraged eagerly. 'Be sure to save a bullet, mind, for t' other one. We'll pick him off on t' way back.'

Laura's eyes opened in sickening realisation. He meant Daniel. Once they had disposed of her, they would track him down and he'd face the same fate. *No.* But what could she do?

The gun winked in the gathering light as her assassin moved in. It was now or never – she took her chance. She thrust up a foot and, on a cry, kicked out with all her might.

The element of surprise, coupled with his weakened state, had him staggering backwards at an alarming speed. Face holding a look of puzzlement, arms flailing, he hurtled towards the yawning mouth of the quarry.

'Nay!' The younger man released Laura and launched himself forward, landing on his belly and grasping his brother's arm just in time before the cavern could swallow him completely. With beast-like grunts, the veins in his neck bulging with the strain, he struggled to haul the other man to safety.

Laura could only watch on in numbing horror. She could hear the older brother's boots scrabbling at the rockface as he tried desperately to gain a foothold. He seemed to succeed – his upper body rose over the lip of the drop. But it was to be a momentary advantage. There came a rumbling scrape as the stone gave way beneath his weight. Feeling himself slipping, and in blind terror, he grabbed at his brother, dragging the both of them into the hole.

Mirrored screams journeyed with them into the bowels of the quarry, followed by two dull thuds, then all was still. Laura bent double and heaved up the contents of her stomach on to the gravelly ground.

It was an age before she could bring herself to look. Forcing herself forward and dropping to her knees, she peered through the dark depths to the delph base. In a shallow bore, the Cannock brothers' broken bodies lay side by side in a pool of blood. Laura rose. Unseeing, she turned and headed back towards the fields.

She located Daniel close to where she'd left him, unconscious beneath a tree. A forlorn Smiler sat by his master; Laura lay down close on the other side and shut her eyes. And as the first flurry of snow spiralled calmly down, she awaited their deaths with quiet acceptance.

Shortly, the elements would carry them off and they, too, would meet their maker. Just maybe, if she held on to Daniel's hand very tightly, he'd have the power to lead her with him and she'd not have to meet Lucifer for her sins. Her father and mother would be waiting; Nathan, too. There would be no more pain or loss or abuse, no more anguish, fear; only peace. And they would dwell together in the Lord's kingdom for ever.

Daniel moaned and she shushed him softly.

'It's all right, my love,' she told him, laying her cheek against his. 'Rest easy, now. We'll be home soon.'

Chapter 20

'LAD?'

'It's all right, Laura. We'll be home soon.'

Daniel had echoed her words. He believed in her hope for them both, that all would surely be well. She smiled. They would all be together as one in no time at all.

He was carrying her, and his limping gait bobbed her lightly in his arms, lulling her to the eternal sleep. She trailed a hand around his back to caress the hair at his nape. She'd never known such a sense of completeness like this before; it warmed her from the inside out and her eyes again grew heavy. Her mouth curved once more.

She was vaguely aware of several stops and starts, then he was murmuring her name and asking if she could stand. They were approaching the bustle of Bolton town, he told her, and folk would surely wonder at her health. The less attention they drew to themselves, the better, so could she try? he urged, for they must hurry if they were to catch the train.

Train? Nevertheless, Laura obeyed with a nod, and he lowered her gently to her feet. She followed him without dissent to Trinity Street.

Daniel was pale and quiet on the journey he'd insisted they must make, and she didn't question it, simply let him drowse, for it was what she knew he needed. Rest easy, she'd told him as they had lain beneath the tree's snow-stroked branches. She did the same, closing her eyes, and the chug motion carried them closer to their final destination, which she'd been awaiting for what felt like for ever.

They alighted at Manchester Victoria Station and still she was silent, allowed Daniel to lead her into Miller Street and on to Swan Street without a word of protest. However, something niggled at the back of her brain, something she couldn't reach to analyse at any depth but which was there all the same, and was growing in increasing insistence the further they walked.

Ebenezer Court.

She paused to peer at the scuffed sign. Daniel made to disappear through the archway, but she grasped at his jacket. This wasn't right. How had they got here?

A terrible mistake had occurred somewhere along the way. A cruel and confusing wrong turn had snared them from the correct path. This wasn't heaven. There was no Amos, no Nathan, beyond that entrance. Happiness lay not here, not for either of them. She must inform him, *warn* him of their folly. She must . . .

'It's all right, Laura.'

'But . . .'

'Everything's going to be all right,' he soothed, taking her hand. 'It's over, lass.'

Why wouldn't he listen? They shouldn't *be* here. 'Daniel, wait. I must tell thee—'

'Not now. All that can wait. Let's just get inside.'

The courtyard was empty and they made it to Laura's house without being seen. Daniel immediately collapsed into a fireside chair and scrunched shut his eyes, his mouth pursed in obvious pain.

'Lad?'

'I'm all right. Just . . . need to catch my breath.'

Frowning, Laura went to him. Stooping, she turned her attention to his left thigh, which he was gripping, his breathing heavy. 'Let me see.'

'I cauterised it the best I could after you'd gone, but . . . Jesus, it's agony. I must have passed out a few times afore finally waking with thee under that tree.'

Watching him take down his dark trousers and push aside the muffler he'd tied tightly around his leg, she stared in sheer confusion at the bloodied, circular hole. Her thoughts were muggy and drifted from reach like smoke when she attempted to focus her brain on one. 'What . . . ? I don't understand.'

Daniel sucked in air. 'It'll be the shock. Your mind's likely shut itself off, to protect thee from the horrors of the day. Give yourself time. The memories will come back.'

His explanation was like the turning of a tap – the mist cleared from her head in an instant. She sat back on the hearth rug and pulled her knees to her chin. 'We were in Bolton.'

'Aye.'

'I killed them, Daniel.'

He stared at her in silence and she nodded, wrapping her arms around herself. 'The Cannocks . . . It all happened so quickly. I kicked out, for one had the gun to my head, and he tumbled backwards into a quarry. He was holding on to the edge, and his brother rushed to haul him out, but . . . but they both went over and they're dead. I just stood there and watched it unfold. I couldn't help them. I didn't *want* to. I hated them, still do. I'm a murderess.'

'That's why tha wanted to die?'

He'd spoken quietly. She glanced up to gauge his reaction but his face was expressionless. 'I thought . . . I'm so tired of it all, you know? I'm just so tired. I miss those we've lost, and I know you do, too. We might have been happy, me and thee, had the frost carried us off—'

'Nay.' He was leaning forward, his eyes flashing steel. 'Don't you ever say that, d'you hear? Your father, our Nathan . . . their deaths ain't your fault. Aye, the loss is a constant, physical pain now, but it'll ease with time, Laura, it will. It's happened, and nowt will fetch either of them back. Nowt,' he pressed, placing his hands on her shoulders, and there was a catch in his voice. 'We can't cut short *our* lives over this. Where would the world be if folk gave up as easy as that? There would be no one left, that's what. We ain't the only souls to have known heartache.'

'But lad, I killed *them*. And Adam, in a sense, aye. He died from my actions, an' all. I lashed out with him and he fell, too. Today, I did it again with the same outcome – only this time, it's resulted in two deaths. Three men. Three brothers – *three*, Daniel! – have perished at my hands. I'm a monster!'

'Nay. Tha meant not for it to happen. They all came at thee – you were protecting yourself. Self-defence, aye, that's what it was. It were them or thee.'

'It don't change a thing in here, though,' she choked, stabbing at her temple with her finger. 'The guilt, recrimination, *disgust*, is here still. And you'd be the same if this were you we were discussing,' she added in a knowing tone. 'I saw how you felt when you believed your*self* a murderer – you hated yourself forra while in t' bedroom of that cottage, didn't you?'

He looked away. 'That's different. I knew exactly what I were doing back there. I purposely put that knife to his throat. I wanted him dead.'

'Then you changed your mind. Well, didn't you!'

'Aye.' He dragged a hand across his mouth. 'Aye, all right, I did.'

'So you see? How am *I* meant to live with the truth of it, of what *I've* done? You answer me that.'

'I *did* regret it,' he continued in a murmur, as though he hadn't heard her. 'And shall I tell thee for why? Because I don't have it in me to be wicked, Laura. And neither do you. That's why the cut *you* inflicted to the other bloke's neck barely nicked the surface. You couldn't do it, neither. Not really, not well enough to end life, however much your hatred of them or how much you were hurting. That they died later anyroad is neither here nor there. You didn't *mean* it. D'you see the difference?'

Blinking as his words took effect – he was right; she hadn't actively *wanted* to kill anyone, had she? – she nodded. 'I thought I *did* want them dead but . . . Good God, lad, I never actually wanted to *kill* anyone . . .' She groaned in confusion. 'Does that make sense?'

'It does to me. D'you know, lass, if anything, you should be proud.'

'Proud?'

'Aye, for you're a hero. *My* hero.' Eyes bright, he took her face in his hands. 'You saved my life.'

'Oh, lad. Oh, it's been horrible, *horrible*!' The flood gates finally opened and she crumpled. 'Will I ever get past this?' she sobbed, putting her arms around him. He held her back tightly and she clung to him. 'I just want to put it all behind me. I just want to forget.'

'You shall. But you must *let* yourself let it go, Laura. You'll never be free of the past if you don't.'

And that goes for you, my love, her heart whispered to him. *I have to let you go, too, must if I'm ever to hope for a fresh start. You don't belong to me, never have. If either of us are to have a future, I must set myself free.*

The vow brought an odd sense of calm to her mind. Savouring his touch, for it would have to last her a lifetime, she held on to him a few precious moments longer then rose to her feet.

She crossed to the corner and the coffin holding her husband, kissed her fingertips and pressed them to his marble cheek. Then she turned back to his brother with renewed focus. The future started here.

'Right, lad, we'd best get that leg seen to. I'll fetch Widow Jessop. She'll know what to do.'

There wouldn't be any comebacks from today's events. They were all confident of that.

No witnesses meant no investigation, and dead men didn't speak, the court's residents had pointed out later, when Laura and Daniel brought the whole story to light.

Crammed into Mrs Price's kitchen, they had discussed it at length whilst Daniel rested by the fire, the bullet safely removed and the wound cleaned and stitched up neatly by the herb woman's expert hand.

Dolly Cannock had seen nothing and, thanks to the laudanum, would remember less. Any possible sightings of them arriving at or leaving the cottage in Breightmet would yield no results. Daniel was an unknown out-of-towner. As for Laura . . . well, she hadn't been there as herself, had she? Should the authorities get a whiff of a suspect, they would be on the look-out for a young man, thanks to her working clothes, not her. They were in the clear.

Moreover, everyone was in full agreement that the deaths had been unavoidable. Besides, the brothers had got all they deserved, the neighbours insisted

272

vehemently, after the evil they had wreaked on Amos and Nathan. They might have been spared the gibbet for all they had done but they couldn't escape punishment altogether.

Their unshakeable support meant more to Laura than she could ever express. She was one of their own, she belonged, and they would always have her back. Now more than ever, she reciprocated their loyalty tenfold and knew she always would.

'We'll pay a visit to Bolton in a day or two, see how the land lies,' the two Johns had offered. 'If nowt else, it'll put your minds at ease. We'll be discreet, lass, don't fret,' they assured Laura, and she'd thanked them profusely with tears in her eyes.

'I'll rest better in my bed the night, knowing them bastards have paid the ultimate price for what they did to my boy,' Joyce had choked, clutching Laura's hand in gratitude, and they had wept together. 'You're my daughter still, lass, and allus shall be – more so after today, you saving my other lad's life. Just you remember that.'

'He's so brave,' Lizzie murmured later, her adoring gaze fixed on the dozing man across the room. Only she and Laura remained – the others had returned to their respective homes, and Mrs Price and Widow Jessop had retired to their beds. 'Thank the good Lord he's all right. I don't know what I'd have done if . . .' She broke off, her bottom lip wobbling. 'Oh, I shouldn't have said that, not to thee, not when you've lost . . . Eeh, that were reet insensitive of me. I'm sorry, I am.'

Laura reached for her hand. 'It's all right, lass. As for Daniel, he'll be back on his feet in no time. And soon you'll be wed, and you'll be the happiest couple in t' whole of England and beyond, I just know it,' she told her, for in that moment, it felt right. Surely Daniel hadn't really meant what he'd said about not loving Lizzie? He must feel *something* for the lass? He'd been caught up in the moment, that was all. Anger made you spout things you didn't mean. A man didn't ask for a woman's hand in marriage if he didn't want it, after all. Particularly not decent breeds like Daniel. The two of them were going to be just fine, she was certain.

That Laura knew no stab of pain nor trace of envy when speaking these words was like a balm to her soul. She felt reborn almost, clearer of mind than she'd been in a good long while. She was in control of herself, and the relief of it felt so good.

Never again would she allow her fragile heart to rule her head. She'd learned some valuable lessons recently, had matured for sure, and she was all the stronger for it. The time for looking back was mercifully gone.

And what of her future? Where did that lie? She'd sworn to herself she'd finished with Manchester and all that went with it, hadn't she? That aspect, she admitted to herself, was still questionable. She'd remain, for now at least. Who knew what fate would decide to throw her way? However, she was content to wait and see for the time being. She had her friendships here, and that was more than enough for the moment.

'Ay, give over, Laura. You'll have me bawling like a babby in a minute,' Lizzie laughed with a sniff, though the joy in her eyes was clear. 'Ta, that means an awful lot.'

They shared a gentle smile, then Laura rose from the table. 'I'd best be getting across to Joyce's. You'll be all right keeping an eye to him on your own?' she asked – Widow Jessop had insisted Daniel stay the night beneath her roof, where she could be close at hand if need be. 'You've only to say if you'd rather I stopped and kept thee company?'

'Nay, love, you go. I'll be fine.'

Laura bade her goodnight and let herself out. Alone in the star-pricked darkness, she looked around the familiar yard slowly. Her home. Memories. Her loved ones' spirits, captured for a lifetime in the very brickwork.

She filled her lungs with the essence of the place, nodded, and continued on to her mother-in-law's.

Indoors, Joyce was sleeping. After checking on her, Laura closed the bedroom door softly and padded down to the kitchen. The fire burned low and she sat, alone with her thoughts in the dim light, for what seemed an age. By the time she rose for bed her future felt a lot clearer.

Halfway across the room, remembrance sparked. She paused and lifted a hand to her head. Like shedding the last link to all that had endeavoured to harm her, she removed the Cannock brother's cap with quiet assuagement and threw it into the grate. Soon, small flames licked around the edges. By morning, there would be nothing left but ash. And she knew a sense of finality.

They committed Nathan's body to the ground on the first Thursday of the new year 1873. And the next day, the two Johns brought information that helped lay an altogether more unpleasant aspect of Laura's past to rest.

The *Bolton Evening News* had reported that her tormentors had been found.

A quarryman made the grim discovery upon arriving for work the morning after the fall and later deposed to the identity of the deceased. The county divisional coroner had held an inquest at the nearby Hare and Hounds Inn the following afternoon.

Though one of the victims had sustained an unexplained injury to the neck prior to his death, it was concluded that it hadn't contributed to his demise. Neither had the loaded revolver, found with them at the bottom of the quarry, played a part. There was, however, no evidence to show how the fatalities *had* occurred, and the jury therefore recorded open verdicts of 'Found dead'.

Done. Over with, just like that.

The Cannock brothers were gone. Retribution had been served.

Chapter 21

'I HOPE YOU'LL not live to regret this, Daniel.'

He stopped blowing into his cold hands to throw Laura a smile. 'You'll be fine. Like I told thee, follow Lizzie's lead and you'll not go far wrong.'

She pulled a face then nodded. 'I'm being churlish, ain't I? Sorry. I do appreciate you putting in a good word for me, lad. It's just I ain't the first idea about spinning, ain't never worked in cotton afore, and I don't want to let thee down.'

'Now don't be daft, you're not to worry on that score. Every mill hand makes the odd mistake in t' beginning. You'll take to it in no time.' He turned to the other woman walking beside him in the dark January morning. 'Ain't that right, Lizzie?'

'Oh aye.' She gave Laura an encouraging wink. 'Just you yell should yer need me.'

'Ta, thanks. Mind, you might regret saying that, lass!'

The idea of factory work had occurred to her the night she'd sat by Joyce's hearth and assessed her future. What with the coal round no longer an option – her father and Nathan were gone and she'd never manage the heavy sacks alone – she'd decided that a new course of employment was necessary. As cotton was king, the city's mills were in abundance – it made sense to try her luck down that path first. And when Daniel heard of her plans he'd been only too willing to help, had used his position as overlooker to secure her a job at his place of work. Laura just prayed she'd be up to the task.

She'd called in to see Mr Howarth the week before to talk about taking back ownership of Kenneth. He'd seemed genuinely pleased to see her and, when she explained she'd been rash in her decision, that she was to stay in Manchester after all, he'd understood completely, much to her relief. In exchange for using the horse and cart for his business – with a new driver at the helm, of course – Mr Howarth had agreed to keep him on at the yard and see to his upkeep at no expense to her.

Naturally, she'd accepted straight away. Even his oats she could ill afford. After paying the rent on her house and feeding herself, she'd have very little left over for anything else. Though if it had come down to it, she'd have sooner starved than give him up. That shire was her last link with her father, her childhood. The thought of losing him, too, struck like a physical pain. She was therefore delighted to have him back and endeavoured to visit him as often as she could.

She must also try to get to see Bridget Figg soon, she reminded herself, feeling a pang at how she'd left things the last time they met. The Irishwoman had been frantic with worry for her, it had been plain to see. Laura had asked Mrs Price and Widow Jessop to give Bridget a message at church last Sunday to let her know she was back, she was well and that she would meet up with her shortly. Laura just prayed she was all right, that she'd suffered no further viciousness or violence from that uncle of hers.

Now, factory operatives on their way to work steadily

swelled in number, the noise from hundreds of wooden clogs mingling into one collective clump seeming to shake the very streets. Yet it was nothing compared to what awaited her at the mill.

Stepping inside the spinning room, Laura stopped dead in her tracks. It wasn't like anything she could have imagined. After the biting cold outside, the unbearably high temperature smacked her full around the face. She'd been told the hot and humid conditions were necessary to prevent the yarn from snapping, but dear God . . . What it must be like in the height of summer, she shuddered to think. How did these people endure such long hours in this stifling nightmare?

A thick cloud of cotton dust clung to the air and within seconds had clogged her throat, making her cough and her eyes stream. However, it was the sound and sight of the mules themselves that filled her with the most horror – the din of the terrifying-looking monsters was terrific.

Daniel said something she didn't catch then disappeared to begin his own duties. She turned her helpless gaze to Lizzie, who led her to a long row of machines.

Spinners, or 'minders', as they were known, were paid according to the amount of thread they produced. Each worked a pair of mules facing each other, which at six o'clock sharp were brought roaring to life. The crash of the carriages, which carried over a thousand whirring spindles, and shunted backwards and forwards as they spun and wound the thread, was relentless; the overwhelming racket was enough to make your skull rattle.

Soaked with oil from the machines, the boards were treacherous underfoot – following Lizzie's lead, Laura removed her clogs. In no time, her naked feet and ankles were stained dark brown. Rather that and the stab of the odd splinter, however, than an accident. Slips could easily result in crushed bones and mutilation, even death. Catching a hand or arm in the gears was not uncommon. If lucky, you'd escape minus a finger or two but at least with your life.

Lizzie's own mules standing idle, which Laura had expressed worry about, for less productivity meant less wages – though Lizzie had assured her she was a fast spinner and would catch up – she patiently taught Laura what was required.

For the next hour, she slowly began to get the hang of it. Though there was one aspect of the job she doubted she'd ever grow accustomed to: the children. Stunted boys and girls of all ages, their pointed little faces locked in expressions of dull stupor, dashed hither and thither through the gaslit gloom.

Watching the smallest, employed as scavengers for their nimbleness, crawl beneath the machinery to clear away accumulated cotton fluff, had Laura wincing in dread. Then there were the piecers, whose responsibility it was to mend broken threads, darting heart-stoppingly close to the mules to join swiftly with deft fingers the snapped ends. Though horrified at the dangers, Laura had to admit their speed and skill were impressive.

Her own piecer was a girl of around sixteen – and surly-faced, to boot. She'd been shooting Laura regular dark looks, for no apparent reason, since she arrived, and Laura was nearing the end of her tether. When another was thrown her way, she'd had enough. Turning towards her with a frown, Laura mouthed to enquire what her problem was – operatives had to learn the art of lip reading quickly to be able to converse above the incredible noise – but received a stony rebuff for her trouble. Shrugging, Laura turned her attention back to her work.

At eight o'clock, every machine shuddered to a standstill. Ears ringing, the workers trooped off gratefully for their first break of the day – a half-an-hour stop for breakfast. Laura fell into step with Lizzie and they made their way to the mill yard with others to have their food in the fresh air – her piecer had remained behind to eat at her machine.

Preoccupied with savouring the peace and the delicious breeze on her clammy skin, they were midway through their meal before Laura brought up the matter of the girl's attitude.

'Ah.' Lizzie smiled knowingly. 'I think I can guess what's up with her. Mind, I can't blame her, if I'm honest.'

'What is it, lass? Is it summat I've done?'

'In a manner of speaking, aye.' Seeing Laura's face fall, she patted her hand. 'Don't fret, love. It's nowt to do with your performance – you've done gradely picking up the work as fast as you have. Nay, nay. It's more the position itself that's the issue.' Lizzie went on to explain that mule spinners were usually men, but she herself had shown such aptitude for the work that she'd managed to climb from big piecer to spinner a few years ago. 'I reckon that girl of yourn were hoping to do the same.'

Laura nodded understanding. 'Only I came along out of nowhere and snatched her promotion from under her nose and she resents it.'

'It's to be expected; she's toiled as a piecer for years. She came here from another mill only last month in t' hope of snaring a minder's role, weren't getting nowhere at the other place. It's a good position and better paid, after all.'

Laura felt bad, to say the least. Thanks to Daniel, she'd got an unfair shove up the ladder without doing a thing. Something else plagued her, now, too: was he expecting she'd take to it as well as Lizzie had? The pressure not to let him down bore heavily on her shoulders. Problem was, she hadn't the desire for it, like the other woman appeared to. She'd hated every minute of it so far, if truth be told.

When they returned to their work, she made a special effort to be extra nice to her piecer, but the girl was having none of it.

So intent was Laura in wracking her brains for a way to make it up to her and quell her own building guilt, she failed to realise her lapse in concentration. Suddenly, she felt her hair grabbed from behind; she hadn't noticed it had escaped its knot.

It took a moment for her to understand that the thundering mule had seized her and was dragging her into its hungry jaws – she screamed in absolute terror.

A cry went up. Productivity ceased abruptly. Then Lizzie, white with horror, was at her side. Mercifully, owing to her knowledge of the mechanisms and her calm competence, she soon had her freed, and Laura collapsed, sobbing, into her arms.

'Sshhh,' she soothed, stroking her back. 'Come on, let's get thee out of here.' Over her shoulder, she added to the triumphant piecer, 'You, Millicent Figg, see to them mules.'

Though her tears had subsided, Laura was still trembling when Daniel came running outside. He rushed over to where they were sat and dropped to his knees in front of them. His face was grey with concern. He reached for her hand.

'I've just been informed. You're all right, Laura?'

'I think so. And it's all thanks to Lizzie, here. If not for her quick actions . . .' She broke off with a shudder. 'I could have been scalped.'

'But you weren't. That's the main thing. Next time—'

'Nay. Nay, lad, I can't go back in there. I can't do it!'

He nodded. 'If you're sure?'

'I am. I'm sorry.' Her piecer would welcome this news, at any rate, she thought fleetingly. 'I'll have to look for summat else. I'm just not cut out for t' mill.'

'Come on, I'll see thee home.'

'I can't drag thee from your work. I'll manage—'

'I insist,' he cut in, taking her arm. He nodded to Lizzie, who returned it and flashed Laura a sympathetic smile. Then he guided Laura across the cobbled yard and through the mill gates into the street.

Arriving at Ebenezer Court, he ushered her into her house and straight to bed. 'Stay put, and that's an order,' he told her when she protested she'd be well enough in a chair in the kitchen instead. 'You've had a nasty shock and need rest. Now make yourself comfortable. I'll fetch thee some tea.'

She undressed, realising she was still shaken as her hands struggled somewhat with the fastenings, and climbed beneath the covers. Then Daniel was back; smiling, she took the cup he held out to her and he went to sit on the end of the bed.

'You gave me quite the fright back there,' he said after some moments, watching her sipping at the hot drink.

'Aye, and me!'

'When I heard what had occurred, then that it were thee . . .' He lowered his eyes to his clasped hands in his lap. 'I don't know what I'd do if owt were to . . . to happen to you, Laura. I—'

283

'Lad. Please.' She looked away, her colour rising.

'I care for thee. I care for thee a lot.'

'And I thee,' she responded cordially, desperate to lighten the now-charged atmosphere. Yet there was no dismissing the intensity of his stare. Blushing harder, she scrambled around inside her head for something – anything – to say: 'You're ... Well. You're like the brother I've never had.'

'That's really how you see me, is it?'

She was taken aback by the bitter edge to his tone. She nodded, squirming beneath his gaze. 'How else would I see thee?'

'You once told me that you loved me.'

The blood drained from her face at a dizzying speed. *It wasn't true.* 'What? When?' she rasped.

He made to shoot back an answer then seemed to think the better of it. He shrugged. 'Forget I said owt. I'm likely mistaken.'

'I want to know, Daniel. When did I say that?'

'The day Nathan was ... the day he died. You were confused in your mind, were saying all sorts, I ... I'm sorry. I shouldn't have said anything.'

'He's jealous, you know. He suspects I have feelings for thee. I do. I love youse both ...'

Her words came back to her with breath-stealing truth. She closed her eyes. 'Nay. You're not mistaken.'

'You remember?'

She nodded.

Excruciating silence throttled the air between them.

'I'm your brother's widow,' she said finally.

'Aye.'

Even if, by some miracle ... It was impossible, forbidden.

Marriage not only bound a husband and wife but

284

their families, too. In the eyes of the law, her union with Nathan had connected her and Daniel as though they were of the same blood – brother and sister, for life. A relationship between them, therefore, would be deemed as incestuous.

Nothing could change it, not even widowhood: despite Nathan's death, she and Daniel could never wed. No church in the United Kingdom or her colonies would permit it. Of course, there was always the answer of marrying in another country – though obviously not for people of their class, who hadn't the money for such a venture. And living in sin was certainly not an option; they just couldn't. Hopeless, hopeless . . .

But why was she even wasting her time thinking all this? It couldn't be in any case, no matter what: 'You're betrothed to Lizzie. You're going to *marry* Lizzie.'

'Aye,' he whispered again.

'This ain't right. We shouldn't be talking like this.'

'I know.'

'I loved Nathan. I did, aye. And Lizzie's a good woman, don't deserve this—'

'D'you not think I know that?'

'Well, then.' She spread her arms wide.

'Nay, Laura. It's not that simple. For I can't stop thinking about thee, *wanting* thee . . . It's like a disease and you're the cure. I need thee. I can't exist, else.'

Panic was setting in, but she quashed it resolutely, steadfastly refusing to entertain this. His declaration meant nothing, would blow over. He was simply caught in the heat of the moment. The accident, that's what it was. Worry had temporarily turned his thinking, aye.

'Laura—'

'Enough of this. I'd like you to leave, now.'

'Lass, we must—'

285

'Please, Daniel. Please go.'

The door clicked shut behind him and she released a long, shuddering breath. Then she put her face in her hands and gave the pent-up tears free reign.

When a knock came later that evening and it was him once more Laura could have cried all over again. But he seemed different, easy of mood, and he was smiling. Nothing was said of their earlier discussion – it was like it had never taken place – and she was thankful of it. She invited him inside and went to brew fresh tea.

'I've been thinking,' he announced as she scalded the leaves in the pot.

'Oh?'

'About your future.'

She paused in her task to look at him. 'What about it?'

'Come and sit down. Hear me out.'

She did as he asked and he explained his idea in detail. When he'd finished, she simply stared at him, speechless.

'Well, say summat,' he said eventually.

'I don't . . .' She was numb with shock. 'You'd really do that for me?'

'Aye. Well, you and Lizzie.'

'Oh. Aye, of course,' she agreed quickly, cursing her slip of the tongue and that her cheeks had grown hot. 'But lad . . . the cost . . . and Lizzie's job – won't she miss it?'

'We've talked through all that. The bit I've got put by should cover most of the expenses to get youse up and running. And Lizzie's all for it. Giddy, in fact. She just lacked confidence to believe she could be a success.' He smiled. 'I think I've succeeded in making her see sense.'

Their own cake stall.

It was really happening, finally.

'The incident this morning at the mill: you were right. It's not for thee, is it?' he continued. 'Yet still, you gave it a try, and I admire you for it. But you're better than that. Lizzie, an' all. You're hard-working, the pair of you, and you've skills that are going to waste. You just need to catch a break, aye. And I'd be honoured if you'd let me help give youse the step up you need, so to speak.'

Laura clapped her hands like an enraptured child, making him chuckle. 'I'll pay back every farthing once the profits start coming in, I promise thee.'

'So it's a yes, then?'

'Aye. Aye! Thanks ever so much, lad.'

'*Carpe diem*,' he murmured, smiling.

Oh, indeed. She intended to seize the day by the scruff of its bloomin' neck!

Chapter 22

'AYE. YOU'VE A sound spot, here, lasses.' Widow Jessop nodded appreciatively. 'Daniel did well.'

Laura and Lizzie exchanged an excited smile. They had risen early and walked with the old woman to work to see what was soon to be their new stall at Smithfield Market.

'Eeh, I can't wait!' Lizzie trilled, and a grinning Laura clasped her arm in agreement.

Widow Jessop was right: it was in a prime location and decent-sized into the bargain. How Daniel had managed to arrange this, they didn't know; though he had hinted about a friend owing him a favour. To be honest, Laura didn't care, was just grateful beyond anything she could put into words for all he was doing for them. Their own business!

She and Lizzie had spent the previous day hunting for new but cheap baking utensils, cake boxes and boards. Standing outside one high-end shop, they had gazed in wonderment at the new-fangled devices in the window, the sign proclaiming that such labour-saving inventions were a boon that 'kitchen staff in the best establishments' couldn't do without. But of course, *they* must – the eye-popping prices were way off their budget.

'Maybe one day,' Lizzie had breathed dreamily,

pressing her nose to the sparkling panes. And Laura had wholeheartedly concurred. Who could say where this venture would take them and what the future held?

For the briefest moment as they walked away she'd found herself wondering about the stolen money the Cannock brothers had been hunting for, where Adam might have hidden it and what she and Lizzie could do with such a sum. But the musings were quickly scattered from her mind, along with the terrible memories associated with it, and she endeavoured not to dwell on such things again.

One thing Lizzie refused to scrimp on was ingredients. Only the highest class of butter, the freshest eggs and the best grade of flour would do, she insisted, as it made all the difference to the finish and taste. Now, after bidding Widow Jessop goodbye, they headed off to purchase what was required.

'Refined white sugar for the frosting we need, as well,' Lizzie puffed some time later, moving her laden basket to her other arm to give the aching one a rest. 'And fruit – good quality, mind. None of the bruised or, God forbid, worm-riddled rubbish some like to try and palm off on to folk.'

Next, they bought colourings and flavourings to add to the mixes, as well as candied peel and nuts for decoration to tempt the customers' fancy. They also selected an assortment of knives and skewers with differing widths and tips for Laura to use in creating her designs. Finally, tired but happy, they headed back to the court for a well-earned slice of bread and dripping and a cup of tea.

The following day was taken up with sifting and beating and whisking, trying out different recipes and practising unique patterns in Laura's kitchen. And two days later they were once again up with the larks for the start of their brand-new job.

Almond and English plum cakes, meringues, sponge and pound cakes, and thick gingerbread, amongst others, were packed carefully into wooden crates and piled on to the back of the cart. Mr Howarth had agreed to them using Kenneth to transport their stock each morning, so long as they had him back in time for his first coal round, which Laura had promised to do. Hearts hammering in nervous anticipation but with faces stretched in eager grins, they set off at a steady pace for the market.

Recalling the cake seller Laura had encountered here before – and using her failings as a guide of what not to do themselves – they took their time in arranging their wares.

Their conscientiousness made all the difference: the stall looked magnificent. The delicious smells and eye-catching designs immediately caught people's attention. Within seconds, half a dozen women had flocked across. Then came the moment she and Lizzie had been waiting for: they made their first sale. Laura had tears in her eyes as she watched the happy customer walk away.

'We did it, lass,' she whispered to an equally emotional-looking Lizzie.

By late morning, they had completely sold out. The jangle of coins in their pockets was a wonderful sound.

Frank Higson, a man in his late twenties who ran the next stall, was suitably impressed. 'You've done gradely, girls, just gradely,' he told them, his gaze lingering on Lizzie, as it had all day.

They really had done good, Laura thought with warm accomplishment on the journey home. Nathan's handsome face came to her mind and she smiled softly. What would he have made of all this? He hadn't exactly been accepting of the idea, had he? Yet, somehow, she imagined, if he could see her now, he'd have been proud.

After hearing how their day had gone and congratulating them on their success, Daniel drew Laura to one side. He seemed agitated and she felt her stomach flip in dread. Surely nothing could go wrong again, not now, when things were at last looking up?

'I need to speak to thee.'

'What about?' she had to force herself to ask.

He glanced across to Lizzie, resting her aching feet by Laura's hearth, and shook his head. 'Not now. I'll slip across later tonight.'

For the rest of the evening, Laura was on pins. His knock finally came and she let him in him, bombarding him with questions the moment she shut the door: 'Well? What is it, what's afoot? Is it summat to do with the Cannock brothers? Have we been caught out? For you see, I've been fretting about the knife and laudanum bottle and my cap that we left behind. Have they somehow traced them back to us?'

'Nay, there's no way. As far as anyone knows, them items could be the brothers' own property. Put thoughts of that from your mind.'

'It's not your mam, is it? She's not poorly? You, you're not sick, are yer? Or is it summat to do with the stall?'

'Nay, none of that.'

'Then what, lad?'

'It's your uncle.'

Her brows drew together in a frown. 'Oh. What about him?'

'I said, didn't I, that I'd keep an ear to the ground concerning him. Well, I've learned summat the day. He's in debt. Badly.'

She lowered herself into a chair. 'Aye?'

'Underhand dealings, bad investments, overspending – he's neck deep in the lot. Add to the list a raging gambling habit and it don't paint a pretty picture, does it?'

Laura was stunned. 'How d'you know all this?'

'Let's just say he suffers from one hell of a loose tongue when filled with drink.'

She nodded. She was well aware of that, all right. 'Spouting his business in the inns and taverns, was he?'

'That's right. Bloke I know were telling me today.'

'I can't believe it. He allus comes across as comfortably off.'

'A rich man's tastes with a poor man's pockets, by all accounts.'

'Come to think of it,' she said, eyes thoughtful, 'he was hardly ever at the yard. He was forever disappearing to some meeting or other – or so he said.'

'Gambling dens, more like. You never noticed owt untoward when you worked in t' office? No incriminating documents, things like that?'

'Nay. My duties were mainly sorting papers by date – anyroad, I'm not a strong reader,' she admitted.

'He's set to lose the business, you know, in time. Maybe the house, an' all.'

'No! Really? It's that bad?'

Daniel nodded. 'He's borrowing left, right and centre to stay afloat, but it'll not last. So there you have it. You know what this means, don't you? You'll have the last laugh, all right. He's made sure he'll get what's coming to him all on his own without you needing to lift a finger.'

'Aye. I suppose he has.'

Going over what she'd discovered in bed later, Laura was still struggling to process it. Ambrose Todd penniless. Those words just didn't fit right together in the same sentence. However, the most surprising thing of all was she didn't know how she felt about it. He'd wronged her in so many ways, caused her untold misery, and yet now . . . Now, she just couldn't seem to care.

But that didn't make sense, did it? There had been times when her very essence had ached for his downfall. When she'd have done anything to have him suffer for everything he'd done, see he got his comeuppance. And soon, she would. She'd bested him. So why was she so indifferent?

The answer was quick to come.

She'd had enough of being bitter. Revenge was an ugly thing. Soul-destroying, and with the potential to be deadly. Certainly, she'd found that out to her cost. She was simply bone-weary of hating. It caused nothing in the long run but misery to the one who harboured it, left you locked in its black and inescapable hold.

She wanted only to continue moving forward. She was done with all that had gone before.

What a day it had been, she thought as she drifted to sleep. Her success paired with her uncle's defeat. By, but it was a funny old world at times.

As the weeks rolled by the business went from strength to strength. Not only had they begun to build up regular customers, but the buyers had told their friends, who in turn told others, and soon Laura was having to lend Lizzie a hand in the preparation of the cakes in order to fulfil demand. Not that they were complaining, oh no. Things were going better than either of them could ever have envisaged and they thanked God for it in their prayers every night.

One chilly morning at the beginning of February, they were busy as always at the stall, selling to and chatting with customers, when the strongest wave of nausea washed through Laura out of nowhere.

Occupied with rearranging gingerbreads, she paused with a frown and slapped a hand to her mouth. Within seconds, the sensation had gone. Shrugging, she thought no more of it and continued with what she'd been doing.

However, minutes later, the same thing happened again – this time, she was forced to dash to a corner behind the stall to be violently sick.

'You all right, love?' asked a concerned Lizzie when Laura returned to her side, pale and shaking.

'It must be summat I've ate.'

'I can manage here if you want to get off home?'

'And I'm here to lend the lass a helping hand,' Frank called across from his own stall, receiving a shy smile of thanks from Lizzie in return.

But Laura shook her head. 'Ta, but nay. I feel much better now, honest.'

And yet she was mistaken – the queasiness lingered for the remainder of the morning, though she kept quiet so as not to create a fuss.

By the day's end, Laura was utterly exhausted. On the walk home she turned to Lizzie with a grimace. 'I think I am poorly, after all,' she was finally forced to admit.

'Eeh, love. You're to take the day off the morrow. I insist.'

Too weary to argue, she nodded. 'You will manage?'

'Aye, I should be fine. Anyroad, Frank's there if I need him.'

She gave her a sidelong glance. 'He's nice, Frank, in't he?'

'Oh aye,' agreed Lizzie. Again, the little smile from earlier touched her lips. 'Aye, he's all right.'

Laura was sure he'd say the same about her friend,

too. He hung around their stall more than his own these days, and all the while could barely tear his eyes from Lizzie. That he'd taken an instant shine to the sunny-natured girl was as clear as the nose on your face – a fact that surely couldn't have gone unnoticed by Lizzie herself?

'Frank's mam's Irish as well, you know?' she was saying now as they neared Ebenezer Court, though Laura was barely listening; the rolling in her guts was back and it took all her focus not to heave up her lunch at the roadside.

'Oh?'

'And his father passed away when he were but a kiddy, an' all, like mine. Siblings aplenty, he also has, too. 'Ere, and you'll never guess what else—'

'Sounds like you've a lot in common, lass,' Laura interjected, desperate to bring the conversation to a close – she was definitely going to vomit again. 'Sorry, Lizzie, but I must go and lie down.'

'Eeh, you're a shocking colour. Are you sure you're all right?'

Mumbling assurances that she was, that a nap would set her right, Laura hurried across the cobbles for home.

She headed straight upstairs. Crawling into bed – shawl, clogs and all – she immediately fell fast asleep.

She awoke to children's voices filtering through from the yard below and for a good half a minute hadn't a clue what she was doing here or why. Then remembrance drifted back and she smiled. At least she felt better; great, in fact. That little rest had done her the power of good – and a short one it must have been, she thought, for the sky beyond the window still held some daylight.

With a stretch and a yawn, she rose and headed down

to the kitchen. She made herself tea and went to stand on the front step for some air. She was smiling, watching Bee O'Brien's giggling offspring playing a spirited game of tag, when their mother appeared at her own door.

'Hello, Laura. Sorry if this lot woke ye.'

'Nay, not at all.'

'Our Lizzie said you were taken unwell. You're feeling more yourself, now?'

She took a sip of her brew. 'Aye, much better.'

'That's grand to hear. And you're not to worry over the stall – it's in safe hands with Lizzie.'

'Oh, I'll be well enough for work the morrow after all. Will tha let her know, please?'

Bee blinked in mild amusement. 'Tomorrow's already here, lass, and Lizzie's away at the market.'

'What? But it can't . . .' It was then Laura noticed properly the small expanse of sky visible between the rooftops. It wasn't one of late afternoon, as she'd assumed, at all, but that of early morning. She shook her head. 'I dreamed right through to a new day?'

'Ye did. Aye, you must have needed it!'

'I suppose I did.' She must have been sicker than she'd thought. 'I've never afore slept as long as that.'

The older woman had been chuckling, but it suddenly petered out. Her eyes creased with empathy and she bit her lip. 'Laura? You couldn't be . . . ?'

'What, Bee?'

'Well, *you* know.' She motioned to Laura's midriff.

It was like an invisible pail of icy water had been emptied in her face – she sucked in an almighty gasp. 'My God . . .'

The sickness, exhaustion. The lack of monthly bleed, which she hadn't realised until now that she'd missed,

296

what with all that had been going on. It was clear as crystal – how had she not seen it? This couldn't be happening. Just what was she going to do?

'Laura? Are ye all right?' Bee came across and put her arm around her. 'It's a lot to take in, I know.'

'My husband dead, no mother to help me . . . I feel so alone and so very, very afraid. How will I manage – how?'

'Ay, lass. Have I to fetch Joyce?'

Of course. Her sensible, straight-talking mother-in-law would know what to do. 'Aye, please do.'

When Bee returned with Joyce minutes later Laura was standing anxiously by the fireplace wringing her hands. At the woman's concerned expression, tears immediately sprang to her eyes. 'Oh, Joyce . . .'

'What, lass? What is it, what's to do?'

'I've summat to tell thee. Please sit down.' She did, and Laura sat facing her. 'I think I'm . . . I'm with child. I'm having Nathan's babby.'

'Oh my . . .' Joyce shook her head. Then she was on her feet, her astounded laughter following her around the room as she performed an overjoyed jig. 'Oh, tha don't know what this means, how happy you've made me! Oh, my bonny, bonny lass! Come here.' She pulled her to her feet and held her with such warmth and care it made Laura want to weep with the relief of it. Which she did. Then Bee joined them in their embrace and, as they cried and laughed together, Laura knew she could do this.

She wasn't on her own, nor could she ever be, so long as she had her new family, her friends. Her child would never be wanting in attention and love.

Her child. Laura's heart tripped at those two little words. She was going to be a mother! And by God, she'd make sure she made the best job of it that was humanly possible. That Nathan wouldn't get to see his baby and experience the privilege of parenthood tore at her like a physical pain, but she would love this child enough for the both of them. And she'd endeavour to see that he or she never forgot him. *Oh, lad, how I miss thee . . .*

'Our Daniel will be fair overcome when he learns of this,' Joyce said, breaking through Laura's thoughts. 'A little piece of his brother still with us . . . Eeh, I can hardly believe it.'

She struggled to raise a smile. It felt wrong even to hear his name mentioned right now. This was her and Nathan's moment. Mother and father. Husband and wife. Daniel had been the secret third party, with them in the background from the outset, it was true. But not now. Not with this.

Never again, for that time had passed, and the past was where it belonged. This miracle life was her future now.

Chapter 23

DANIEL CRIED WHEN Joyce broke the news. Genuine, breath-snatching tears that made Laura, despite her earlier vow, want to wrap her arms around him. His happiness was absolute. He smiled at her and mouthed a thank-you. She nodded, squeezed his shoulder then moved to the door.

'You're not stopping for tea, lass?'

Laura shook her head. 'I'll get back home, if you don't mind, Joyce, and rest.'

'Aye, all right. Ay, you must take care of yourself, now. Just you shout me, should you need owt.'

Assuring her she would, Laura left the house and headed back to her own. Indoors, she stood for a long while in the doorway, picturing scenes now gone; precious memories created and contained in this room of the two men whom she had loved and had lost. This evening, the emptiness seemed heavier somehow and she wrapped her arms around herself, wondering how on earth she was meant to bear being alone for ever more. Of course, she had those in the court, and would soon have her child. But it wasn't the same, was it?

Her father's death, she was slowly coming to terms with. You expected to lose your parents, after all – it was the natural workings of the world, wasn't it? But a husband, and so young? No. That wasn't and would never be right. That *wasn't* how it was meant to be, and she'd never accept it. The loneliness of that only grew with time; it never went away.

To have someone lie beside you every night and be there with a good-morning smile upon awakening. To have meals with and conversations in the evenings by the fireside. To share fears and hopes, good times and bad. To love and be loved as only man and wife can. To be wanted. Yes, to be wanted. She missed that most of all.

She'd prepared and was picking at a late dinner when tapping sounded at the window. Frowning, she rose and went to open the door.

'Evening, lass.'

'Mr Howarth!' She smiled in surprise. 'Please, come in.'

'I'll not, if you don't mind.' He twisted the hat he'd removed in both hands. 'The reason I'm here . . . It's the horse, lass.'

The hairs on the back of her neck rose in dread. 'Kenneth? He's all right, ain't he?' she whispered.

His rugged face answered for him. He lowered his gaze and Laura released a soft whimper.

'He's . . . dead?'

'I'm sorry, lass.'

'Why? How?'

'It were his age, I reckon. Just general decay, lass. I'm sorry,' he said again, shifting his weight from one foot to the other, his awkwardness at the tears now coursing down her face clear. 'If it makes it easier, he suffered none. Went in his sleep, he did. I made the discovery myself as I were leaving the yard.'

'I want to see him.'

'Aye.'

She plucked down her shawl from the nail in the wall and stepped outside, pulling the door shut behind her. Then she and the coal merchant set off through the dark evening to his premises nearby.

He looked peaceful, at least.

Dropping to her knees, she stroked his mane and placed a soft kiss on the hard-working giant's nose. Then she thanked him for his dutiful service, whispered goodbye and told him to go and be at rest, that Amos was waiting.

When she rose shakily to her feet she could barely breathe for crying and Mr Howarth opened his arms to her. She clung to him for a long moment whilst terrible, terrible thoughts raced through her mind.

Why did *everyone* have to go and leave her? Would the child? Black terror seized her.

She'd be too afraid to love it for fear of it being snatched from her, like everyone else had been, she just knew it. *Please God, no.* Why – *why* – wasn't she allowed to have anyone? What was wrong with her? What had she done that was so very bad?

'Come, lass.'

Laura went with Mr Howarth to a small office, where he eased her into a chair and brewed them both a cup of tea.

'I shall miss him,' she choked when they were sat facing one another. 'He's all I had left of my past, my family. It feels almost . . . almost like I've lost Father all over again. Does that sound daft?'

'Not at all. I know that feeling only too well, aye. All my loved ones are dead and buried. My parents, siblings. My dear wife, my children . . .' Staring into his cup, he sniffed and shook his head.

'I'm sorry.'

'Such is life, lass.'

She nodded. 'I just . . . I'm frickened to get close to anyone, Mr Howarth, for they all leave me in t' end. I can't bear the pain of it any more, I can't.'

Why was she telling him all this? They got along, it was true, had become friends since Amos's passing, would share a cup of tea and a natter whenever she came to visit Kenneth, but still . . . And yet, he was nodding understandingly. He wasn't judging or trying to soothe her with the line that she was mistaken and being maudlin, as those at the court would have done in their well-meaning but unhelpful way. He was easy to talk to, and he listened. She found herself relaxing.

'But what a life we'd have if we didn't take the chance, eh, lass? How lonely if not to let folk in? We must. And we appreciate them whilst we have them, for however long that might be. It's all we can do.'

Nodding again, she wiped her eyes. 'You're right. It's just . . . *This* time, with this one . . .' Her hand snaked to her stomach protectively. 'I'm with child, Mr Howarth. And should anything . . . I don't know if I could go on, and that's the truth.'

'Eeh, lass. Congratulations to thee. All will be well, I'm sure.'

'You really think?'

'I do, as must you. It's the only way, you know?'

'Aye.' Surprisingly, his advice had struck her in a way she hadn't expected. 'Think positive, eh?'

'That's the one. Can't harm none, can it?'

'Nay.' But it might just go some way to keeping her sane, if nothing else. 'Nay, it can't.' Smiling, she put down her cup and stood. 'I'd best be away home now, Mr Howarth.'

302

'Not on your own in this city you're not. I'll walk thee, lass.'

'I don't know how we'll manage, Lizzie. Look at the struggle we had getting the stock to the market this morning on that rickety old handcart of Widow Jessop's – it's just not adequate. What will we do without Kenneth and the cart?'

It was mid-afternoon and the two women were making their way homewards after another successful day on the stall.

'Fret not, love. I've sorted it,' Lizzie announced, and Laura turned to her with a smile of surprise.

'You have? How?'

'Frank said he'd help us.'

Of course. She might have guessed. 'Oh?'

'He'll call at the court for the cakes each morning and take them to the market for us. It'll have to be early, mind you, so he's time to set up his own stall after.'

'You sure he don't mind, Lizzie?'

'Nay. It were his idea. Kindness itself, he is.'

Nodding, Laura studied her friend discreetly. Lizzie had a look about her lately that she'd never seen before. A sort of . . . quiet confidence was all she could describe it as. Though she had her suspicions as to what – or who – was causing it, she didn't feel it her place to ask outright. It really was none of her business, after all. Still, she couldn't help but feel there were troubled times ahead.

'Will tha come in for a sup of tea, love?' Lizzie asked now as they reached her door, but Laura shook her head.

'I'll not, ta. I've Mr Howarth coming round shortly.'

'The coal merchant?'

'That's right. He's been so helpful and understanding

303

with Kenneth, I thought it only right to offer to cook him summat to show my thanks.'

Lizzie wagged a finger – and knowing what was coming, Laura rolled her eyes with a chuckle.

'Don't you be overdoing it, love—'

'I know, I know, I'll not,' Laura reassured her, touched by her concern. Lizzie had squealed with delight upon hearing about the baby and had insisted since that Laura do as little as possible on the stall. Naturally, Frank Higson had backed her up. However, though she was grateful to have folk around her who cared, it sometimes irked somewhat to be treated like fragile china. 'I'll be fine. It's but a bit of grub, after all.'

'Aye, well. Just you make sure you rest well after, all right?'

'All right.'

'I'll see thee the morrow, then, love.'

After waving her friend goodbye, Laura hurried indoors to begin preparing the meal. Mr Howarth – or Edwin, as he'd insisted she call him – had accepted her invite as he'd walked her back last night with a surprised smile. She'd decided on her father's favourite of back bacon, had bought potatoes to go with it on the way home, and now set to peeling the vegetables. Edwin would be glad of the hot meal after toiling all day at the yard in the cold.

She'd laid the table, the food was warming by the fire awaiting his arrival, and she'd just decided to make a pot of tea when she noticed the kettle was empty. Clicking her tongue, she headed outside to fill it.

She was queuing at the pump when she felt a hand on her shoulder. She turned with a welcoming smile, but it wasn't Edwin she saw behind her but Daniel. 'Oh, it's thee.'

He laughed. 'Why? You expecting someone else?'

'As a matter of fact, aye.'

'Oh?'

She talked as she cranked the pump's handle and had just finished explaining when Edwin appeared through the archway. She waved, he returned it, and she turned back to Daniel. 'Here he is. Well, I'll be seeing thee, lad.'

'Evening.' Edwin touched his cap to Laura. Then he nodded to Daniel, who returned it curtly. 'Not kept thee waiting, have I, lass?' he asked her with a smile.

'Nay, nay. Come on in.'

'Ta, thanks. By, summat smells good.'

Before closing the door Laura looked across the yard to see Daniel still standing where she'd left him, staring at her house. Frowning, she asked if he was all right. He answered that he was and, inclining her head in farewell, she closed the door.

The evening was an enjoyable one. Edwin was a good conversationalist and she found she very much liked his company. He told her of his life and long-departed family, and he discussed his work with such passion she found herself warming to him further. Coal was a topic she was comfortable with, one she'd grown up hearing about and had missed since Amos's passing – in fact, Edwin much reminded her of her father. And when, later, he rose to take his leave, she was sorry to see him go.

'I've had a gradely evening, lass,' he told her, pulling on his hat.

'Me, an' all.'

He hesitated then reached for her hand and squeezed. 'Well. Goodnight, God bless.'

'Goodnight, God bless, Edwin.'

'Laura?'

She'd begun closing the door – at his call, she popped her head back outside. 'Aye?'

'Would tha let me return the compliment?'

'Return . . . ?'

'Allow me to thank thee for tonight by coming to mine for dinner.'

'Aye.' She nodded in pleasure. 'I'd like that.'

'Eeh, I'm glad. Say . . . the morrow?'

'I'll meet thee at the coal yard, shall I?'

'Aye. See thee, then.'

'I look forward to it.'

Edwin walked away whistling, and she returned indoors with a smile.

Early next morning, as she and Lizzie waited out in the court for Frank, they met Daniel leaving home for work.

'Morning, Lizzie, Laura.'

'Morning,' they said in unison, though Lizzie's gaze barely flicked in his direction before returning once more to the entranceway.

'I were wondering, today being Saturday and half-day at t' mill, whether you'd fancy a walk to Alexandra Park,' he asked his intended.

Her head snapped round to face him and, now, she gave him her full attention. A sunny smile slowly lit her face. 'Aye, Daniel. I'd like that.'

'Good, good.' Then his stare moved to Laura. 'How about thee, lass?'

The small sigh that Lizzie exhaled didn't go unnoticed on her. Her friend was now looking out for Frank's arrival once more – Laura could have kicked Daniel for his insensitivity. 'I can't,' she told him, trying to convey with her eyes that he'd upset Lizzie by asking her along

on what the girl had clearly hoped to be a private ren-
dezvous between the couple, and to try to make it up
with her.

However, he appeared not to grasp the message,
pressing Laura instead, 'Oh? Why's that, then?'

'Because I'm having dinner with Edwin at his house.'

'Who?'

'Mr Howarth? The coal merchant?'

'Oh, right.'

'So you see, I can't, but thanks anyway—'

'Edwin, now, is it? I didn't realise youse two were *that*
familiar.'

Daniel had delivered his interruption in such a scath-
ing tone that, for a moment, Laura was too surprised to
react. Finally, her lips drew together in a tight line. 'And
what's that meant to mean?' she asked quietly.

'Nowt. It means nowt. Well, then.' He nodded to them
both and strode away.

'He's in a queer mood this morning,' Laura said
mildly when he'd gone, trying to lift the atmosphere
but failing miserably.

'Hmm,' was all the other woman offered in way of a
response.

At that moment, to the relief of both of them it seemed,
Frank appeared. His cheeky grin and attentiveness
brought the light back to Lizzie's eyes immediately –
and Laura couldn't blame her for it.

The obvious attention with which this new man show-
ered Lizzie was what she lacked, and always had, from
Daniel. She'd begun to notice it and, it was evident, was
less willing to put up with it than she'd been in the
past. It was no wonder she was being drawn instead
towards someone who took pains to show her she was
special. Laura knew if Daniel wasn't careful, it was

possible she'd drift too far and he'd lose her lovely friend for good.

Within minutes of them setting up at the market the rush began, as it always did, and the women were kept busy for the next hour or so. Laura's feet soon ached from standing in one spot for so long and at the first sign of a lull, seeing an opportunity to stretch her legs, she offered to quickly fetch them some pigs' trotters from a nearby stall.

Clutching the hot snack wrapped in brown paper, Laura was heading back to Lizzie through the crush of customers when she suddenly came face to face with Bridget, out making purchases. They laughed in delight.

'Hello there, colleen!' The Irishwoman drew her into a hug. 'Sure, it's grand to see ye.'

'And thee. How are you, Bridget?' she asked, guiding her through the bustle in the direction of the cake stall.

'Well, aye.'

'That's good. I'm sorry I ain't been to see thee, only I've been that busy . . .' Smiling, Laura indicated the stall with a flourish.

'Yours?'

'Mine and Lizzie's, aye.'

'Sure, I wish ye every success!' the Irishwoman trilled.

'There's summat else.' She smoothed her hands across her still-flat stomach then laughed when Bridget, gasping, pulled her into her arms again.

'Oh, colleen! Oh, what a time of joy, to be sure!' Then her eyes slowly creased in sympathy and she took Laura's hand. 'I was so very sorry to learn of Nathan's passing.'

'Who told you?'

'Your uncle. He heard the terrible news from Nathan's old friends at the yard. A mighty tragedy, that's what it is. Did they ever catch anyone for the crime . . . ?'

Laura shook her head.

'Sure, the blackguards want stringing up! How are ye coping?'

'Some days are easier than others, you know?'

'Ey, colleen. I'd have called in to see you at the court, only I . . . what with one thing and another . . .'

Ambrose. That's what the maid meant. He'd ordered Bridget to keep away from her; it was written all over her face. He'd no doubt relished the news of her husband's demise. Low-down demon that he was.

'It's glad I am that you're back,' Bridget added, pressing her hand again.

'I realised Manchester is my home after all.'

'Aye.'

An awkward pause grew between them. That both were hiding information from one another was plain. Of course, Bridget wasn't aware Laura had guessed she shouldn't be talking to her. Neither did she know that Laura had heard all about her uncle's crippling financial problems. Just what would happen to *Bridget* when the creditors took everything of his? Laura worried again now, as she had frequently since learning the truth from Daniel. She'd surely be out of a job and home, and Laura couldn't see her destitute. She'd have to keep her ear open to developments, put Bridget up, if need be. Her uncle, of course, was another matter. He could finish his days in the gutter, for all she cared.

The Irishwoman's eyes were flicking about nervously, as though she was afraid Ambrose might somehow emerge from the crowd of customers at any moment and discover her disobedience. 'Well, I'd best be getting home, colleen,' she announced, backing away. 'My niece will wonder where I've got to.'

'Your niece?'

'Aye. She's dwelling with me.'

Sickly dread knotted Laura's insides. She was immediately suspicious. 'At my uncle's house?'

She lowered her eyes from the recrimination screaming in Laura's. She nodded.

'Bridget, why? You *know* what he did . . . How could you risk your own flesh and blood?'

'It was her decision; she nigh on begged me to let her stay on. She had your uncle's backing – what could I do?'

'But how did this even come about? What was she doing there in the first place? Bridget, wait, please,' Laura pleaded as the Irishwoman made to turn and leave. 'Please, we must talk about this—'

'I'm sorry, I must go. It was nice seeing ye, colleen.'

'I don't like the sound of that, love,' said Lizzie, frowning, when she'd scuttled away.

Laura tugged at her lips in apprehension. 'Nay, nor me. Summat's definitely afoot there.'

And she was determined to find out what.

Bridget and her young niece were still on Laura's mind later, as she made her way to Edwin's yard.

Ambrose was most certainly up to his depraved tricks again, had to be, to offer for his maid's kin to dwell in his home – he did nothing through the sheer, innocent goodness of his heart. Thoughts of him violating another vulnerable girl, of someone else suffering the hell he'd put her through, made her jaw clench in fury. That Bridget, knowing full well what he was capable of with his *own* niece – he'd have no qualms whatsoever with hers! – was allowing it to happen right under her nose made her angrier still.

For the poor lass's sake, she had to try to put a stop to

this. No one else was willing to, it seemed. She couldn't live with herself knowing she'd sat back and done nothing whilst he went on to ruin another with his abuse. She couldn't.

'Afternoon, lass!'

One look at the coal merchant's smiling, bewhiskered face, and now Laura's worries tucked themselves away in the back of her mind. He really was a tonic. Even without saying anything in way of comfort or advice, his presence alone was enough to put her troubles to bed. Just like her father, she thought with warmness. He, too, had had that rare quality.

They headed the short distance to his modest but scrupulously clean home on Rochdale Road. He showed her into what he called the parlour: the 'best room' at the front of the house, stuffed with dark furniture, gaudy ornaments and faded paintings, which folk fortunate enough to have one used mainly on high days and holidays – though Laura would have been perfectly happy in the kitchen, as she was accustomed to. Then he disappeared to make a pot of tea.

'Grub'll not be long,' he told her upon his return, settling on the horsehair sofa beside her. 'I prepared it this morning – it needs but a warm through.'

'You cooked it yourself?' At his nod, she gazed at him amazed. 'I assumed tha had a woman who came in daily to do that for thee.'

'To see to the cleaning I do, aye. The cooking I see to myself.' He shrugged. 'I enjoys it.'

She'd never heard the like before in her life. Most men would sooner starve than be seen to so much as look in the direction of a pan. Laura was suitably impressed.

The pea soup and crusty loaf they ate in the kitchen.

Afterwards, Edwin made a fresh pot and they retired once more to the parlour.

'That were delicious, Edwin.' And Laura meant it. The food had been cooked to perfection. 'Thanks for inviting me the day.'

'It's me what's thankful that tha accepted. I . . . I enjoy your company, lass.'

She smiled. 'I enjoy yours, an' all.'

'Aye?'

'Aye.'

He cleared his throat. 'I know this will come across as sudden, but here goes it. You're lonely, lass, as am I. On top of that, you've a babby on t' way and will need support. I could help with both them things if you'd let me. A home, enough brass to live comfortably . . . I could even offer love. Aye, that's right. For I think I'm falling for thee, Laura. And aye, I'm fifty-eight, and you're . . . well, a lot younger; but must age decide happiness? I'd be a fair husband to thee, you've my word on it. And I'd raise the child with as much care as any father could. What d'you say?'

Her mouth hung loose in complete astonishment. His speech had seemingly come from nowhere and she was at a loss how to respond. She simply gazed back in silence.

'You need time to mull it over. I understand, lass.'

'Aye. Aye, I . . . I have to go.' She rose unsteadily to her feet, her mind awhirl.

Edwin followed her to the door then stood gazing at her from the step, wringing his hands. 'I'll see thee soon?'

She nodded. Then she turned and hurried down the street for home.

'Laura?'

At the voice, she stopped and glanced around and was surprised to see she was in Ebenezer Court. She couldn't even recall getting here.

'You all right?' Daniel pressed, pushing himself away from where he stood in his doorway and crossing the space between them. 'Lass, speak to me. What—'

'Not here. Come inside.'

Frowning, he followed her indoors.

'Edwin – Mr Howarth – has asked me to marry him,' she blurted the moment he closed the door.

'He *what*?'

Nodding, she began pacing the room.

'How did he take it when you refused him?'

'I didn't, didn't know what to say—'

'No – that's bloody what!'

'Daniel—'

'Are you actually considering this?' He took her shoulders, forcing her to a halt. 'Laura?'

'Nay, I . . . don't know, I . . .'

'Christ's sake!'

Yanking free, she glared at him, eyes blazing. 'What's it to thee, anyroad? You don't own me, you know. You don't get to tell me what I must and mustn't do. Just because I'm carrying your brother's child—'

'That's not the reason and you know it.'

'Oh, I see. Now we're getting to the truth of it. You're jealous, is that it? Answer me, goddamn it,' she cried, grasping his jacket when he turned away.

'You know I am. You *know* I love thee. And you feel the same; go on, deny it.'

'Keep your voice down,' she hissed, jerking her chin to the wall adjoining the O'Briens' abode. 'Lizzie might hear.'

Daniel stormed across the room and dropped into a

chair at the table, resting his head in his hands. 'Don't do it,' he rasped. 'Don't wed him. Please.'

'You knew, didn't you? You knew he were set to propose; that's why you were distant when he came here for dinner last night and short with me this morning when I told thee he'd invited me to his.'

''Course I bloody knew. He'd have been a fool not to have tried his luck. What man wouldn't with thee?'

'I didn't anticipate it at all. I didn't. I enjoy his company, like him as a friend, nowt more than that. But then again, in time ... why not?' she added after a pause. 'We have companionship to offer one another. He'd take care of me. I do like him—'

'Not in the way it matters. You don't *love* him. It'd be cruel, Laura, cruel—'

'That's rich coming from thee. You're a fine one to talk about wedding for love, ain't yer, Daniel? Why did you do it, eh? *Why* ask for Lizzie's hand if you don't love her?'

'Because I couldn't have thee!' he shot back. There was a world of pain in his voice. 'Because I couldn't have thee. Do you know what strength it took to walk thee down the aisle?'

'But you offered—'

'Aye, I did. For your father was dead and it pained me to know you had no one. I did it to ease your heartache. I suffered handing over the woman I loved to another man *for thee.* I love the lad, God knows I do, but I prayed all through that service, prayed you'd change your mind, refuse to go through with it, flee – *any*thing. But you didn't. And later, when you disappeared from the party, disappeared here to your marital bed, to make love to him ... Imagining ... You killed summat in me.' He tapped his chest. 'And I knew you were gone from me.

'Lizzie ...' he went on, raising his eyes to the ceiling

314

in despair. 'It were a madcap, spur-of-the-moment decision that I regretted the second the question were out of my mouth. I couldn't bite the words back. I can't still. So you see, I've made a fair mess of everything. I must wed her. And you . . .' A ragged breath tore from him. 'You, too, must do what yer must. If that means marrying Edwin Howarth, I'll not stand in your way.'

Through a blur of emotion, Laura walked towards him. He lifted his head when she stopped in front of him and they locked eyes. Tears glistened on both their lashes. When he threw his arms around her waist and buried his face in her chest, she held him tightly. Their bodies rocked in unison with sobs of regret, of yesterdays and of now and what must be for the rest of their tomorrows.

They shared a deep and lingering kiss, which told without words what could never be, one that finally signalled the end. As they drew apart, the heavens opened and rain battered the window, and it was as though the very angels wept in sympathy at their parting.

Chapter 24

HAVING HELPED LIZZIE all morning with the cakes for tomorrow's stock, Laura was free later to honour her own duty. Mouth set in determination, she donned her shawl and headed off for church to catch Bridget and her niece.

Throughout the long, sleepless hours last night, three men had been with her in mind continually – now, they were no nearer to leaving her in peace. One she loved but couldn't have, the other she liked but didn't want. As for the third . . . *Him* she loathed with everything that she was, would rather that he didn't exist at all.

Men were nothing but trouble, she ruminated as she made on for Mulberry Street. All of her life's strife and heartaches had been wrought by them – by men both bad and good – one way or another. Uncle Ambrose, the Cannock brothers – Adam included. Her father and Nathan, Edwin Howarth. Daniel. *None more so than Daniel.* Whether they hated or loved you, they were guaranteed to cause you nothing but pain in the end. She was just mightily fed up of them all.

Pausing by the church wall, she kept a watchful eye on the doors. She moved closer as people began to stream out, then there was Bridget. Sighing in relief that she'd attended today, Laura picked her way towards her.

'Hello, Brid— Oh.' Laura frowned in surprise at the sight of the girl she recognised in the Irishwoman's company. What on earth . . . ? 'Youse two know each other?'

'Sure, this is my niece.'

'Your . . . ?' Slowly, Laura's brow smoothed as she remembered. Lizzie's instruction that fearful day when escorting her from the mill: '*You, Millicent Figg, see to them mules . . .*' Of course. She'd been so distracted with the accident that she'd failed to take notice of the surname, to fit two and two together. Well! She hadn't expected this, that was for sure. 'Nice to see thee again, Millicent,' she told her former piecer with a nod.

'And thee,' the girl murmured. She appeared just as amazed to see Laura. Amazed and . . . was that guilt lurking within her blue eyes?

'*You* know each other?' It was now Bridget's turn to ask.

'We met recently at the mill where Millicent's employed.'

Bridget's chest puffed with pride. 'Just been promoted to minder, the lass has. In charge of her own pair of spinning mules, now, so she is.'

'I thought she might,' said Laura, hiding a smile, and Millicent's awkward blush deepened further. *It's all right, really, no hard feelings*, Laura was quick to reassure her with her eyes.

''Tis glad I am to see ye, colleen,' Bridget said now. 'Rushing off as I did yesterday at the market . . . I'm sorry, Laura, I just . . .'

She nodded understanding. 'Please, don't dwell on that. Mind, I would still like to talk with you, if you can spare the time?'

Catching her meaning, Bridget glanced to her niece then emitted a sigh. 'Aye. Aye, all right.'

317

Laura motioned that they should follow, and the three of them set off for Ebenezer Court.

That Millicent trotted along with them without question spoke volumes about her relationship with Ambrose. Wouldn't Laura herself once have done anything to avoid being alone with him at home?

When they were seated in her kitchen with steaming cups of tea, she hesitantly brought up the subject of Millicent staying at her uncle's. 'How did it even come about?' she asked.

The girl went immediately on the defensive. 'What business is that of yourn?' she shot back before Bridget had a chance to answer. 'What is all this? My aunt's friend you might be, but that don't mean you've the right to poke your nose—'

'Ambrose Todd is my uncle.'

All vestige of colour left Millicent's face. She opened and closed her mouth then lowered her head.

Laura reached across for her hand. 'Lass, when I dwelled beneath his roof it was one of the worst times of my life. He . . . He's depraved, but I think you've learned that for yourself, ain't yer?' she murmured, ignoring Bridget's distressed moan. 'Why did you insist on staying there? Why would you want to, knowing—'

'I don't know what you're talking about.' Millicent stood abruptly. 'I'll not stop here to listen to this. I'm off.'

'Millicent, stop, please—!' But Bridget's plea was cut short by the slamming of the door. Laura patted her shoulder in reassurance then raced outside in pursuit of her niece.

This needed airing. She'd get the answers she sought, even if she had to drag them from the girl by force. She couldn't leave it like this, *wouldn't* leave her in such danger. Millicent had to reveal the truth or her ordeal would never know an end. Hadn't she learned that herself the hard way?

'Wait, lass.'

She shook Laura's hand from her shoulder savagely. 'Leave me be!'

'I'm sorry, but I can't do that. I *need* to know—'

'Why? You tell me that. What has anything got to do with thee, anyroad?'

'I'll tell thee why: because I couldn't live with myself, knowing you're suffering . . . *that*. That my uncle's getting away with it again. I couldn't, for I know how it feels.' She nodded. 'Aye, he did the same to me.'

Like a pricked balloon losing its air, the girl visibly deflated. She dragged out a huge sigh. 'I didn't, *couldn't* . . . couldn't speak of it to anyone. I . . . I don't know what to do,' she finished on a whimper.

Laura bit back tears at the torment exuding from her that she recognised only too well. 'Eeh, lass. Why do you stay?'

'I've no choice. None.'

'But of *course* you do. Walk out right now, leave and never return—'

'And he'll make sure my aunt suffers for it.' She nodded wildly. 'He will, he's vowed to, and I believe him. He's the divil!'

So that was his game. That was why this poor girl stayed. It wasn't through choice; she was there against her will. Ambrose was forcing her arm with terrible threats. Bastard: he was nothing else. How she loathed him.

'I wish I'd never left the boarding house,' Millicent continued, eyes squeezed shut. 'That's where I were dwelling with my sister, a boarding house in Salford, had for years, ever since our parents died. We were doing all right. Then my sister wed and moved out and I were alone, and shortly after I grew sick. Aunt Bridget looked after me.'

Laura nodded, recalling the day she and Daniel had hoodwinked Ambrose into believing his yard was on fire so as to gain access to his house and check on Bridget's welfare. The Irishwoman had arrived back saying she'd been visiting her niece who had been taken ill. 'So what happened? How did you finish up in my uncle's clutches?'

'Aunt Bridget found it difficult getting up to Salford to see me. She asked her master if he'd allow her an hour or two off each day after she'd seen to her duties, just until I were well, and he suggested I stop with them so she could keep a proper eye to me. She were made to fetch me to the house to meet him. When I arrived, he managed to get me on my own and told me I were to inform my aunt that I wanted to stay. That I weren't to take no for an answer. Otherwise, he'd make my life and hers besides a living nightmare.

'I were too shocked and afraid to go against him. I did as he said. Aunt Bridget didn't want it, I could tell, but she'd no choice in t' matter. He'd spoken, and that were all there was to it. When later she got me alone and I backed up what he'd said and pleaded with her to agree, she had no choice but to give in.'

Closing her eyes, Laura shook her head. 'Why can't she see him for what he is and get as far from him as she can?'

'I reckon it's more a case of she won't see, you know? God alone knows why, but she loves him.'

How, after all the maid had learned? Her level of devotion was staggering. Could love really be as blind as that? Or was there more to this than met the eye? Were other factors such as fear or sheer denial at play here? Laura was beginning to think so. Nevertheless: 'To put you in his reach, though . . . She knows what he's a taste for.'

'I'd suspected she might be aware.' Millicent nodded sadly. 'She does her utmost to keep a watchful eye over me.'

'Yet it ain't enough, is it? For my uncle will find a way regardless. He allus does.'

'Aye.'

Seeing the girl's shiver of revulsion, fresh fury coursed through Laura. Now, she knew all her good intentions of leaving the past where it was, of allowing Ambrose to ruin his life all by himself, had been but naivety on her part. She did want revenge still, had all along.

She'd been foolish to think she could bury her feelings. He couldn't continue getting away with his disgusting ways. He had to pay. And by God, she'd make sure she was the one to see he did.

'You have to tell Bridget—'

'She can't ever find out!' Millicent was aghast. 'Knowing she'd played a part in putting me in that position . . . it would kill her. Or *he'd* be the one to finish her off, should she confront him. Nay, nay. I'll get us out of this, for you see, I've a plan. A good 'un, aye. One that'll not take me long to put into action. Not now, with my promotion—' She broke off and a poppy-red hue crept up her neck to stain her face. 'That's why I were a reet bitch with thee when tha started at the mill. That's why I resented thee stealing what I saw – what I *needed* – to be my job.

'A better position means more brass. And brass is the ticket out of his lair. Earning extra, I could afford to find fresh and decent lodgings, to be free of him, and I'd take Aunt Bridget with me. That's what I were focused on, and still am. And aye, I were glad of it at first when you got caught in the mule,' she admitted. 'Saw it as a sure thing that I'd take your place. I did, an' all. But it didn't take long for the guilt to set in, and by . . . I were terrible sorry. I felt awful to think I'd wished thee such ill will and could be happy about it when it were granted. But I were desperate, and desperation makes you act queerly. It *makes* you do wicked things. I am sorry, Laura. I am.'

'I understand, lass. I do, really. I've done things I'm not proud of when in the grip of despair and fear.' She shook her head to scatter the memories. 'As for your plan . . . though a good idea it might be . . . who's to say Bridget will agree to leave with thee?'

'I'll make her see sense. I will, honest. I'll concoct summat believable. I'll beg on my *knees* if I must. Please, Laura. Please don't tell her. Let me do it my way. Let me try.'

'And in the meantime? What will you do whilst you're busy saving? Put up with it, with his wicked ways?'

Sucking in air, Millicent nodded bravely. 'Aye. It *is* only watching, after all. He don't touch. I can . . .' She took another deep breath then continued with conviction, 'I can handle it a while longer.'

'Lass, this is madness. Why don't we go back in there and tell your aunt everything and see what happens? Take a chance. *Try.* It's gorra be better than suffering my uncle's attentions, surely? Bridget mightn't take it so bad. It might just all work out for the best. Youse could leave his house this very day, dwell with me till you get on your feet—'

But the girl was adamant. She shook her head determinedly. 'She mustn't know, Laura. Not ever. You can't say owt. Don't make me regret telling thee my secret.'

Sighing in defeat, Laura nodded, though it went against every fibre of her. 'All right, lass. But I want you to believe me when I promise thee he'll get what's coming to him. When and how, I'm yet to figure out, but it'll happen.'

This wasn't just her problem any more. It wasn't only herself affected. And who was to say even Millicent would be the last? No, she wouldn't be, not if he had his way. His insatiable lust guaranteed that there would be more victims to follow. He needed stopping once and for all.

There would be no mistakes. She'd learned from her errors with the Cannocks. With Ambrose, she'd wreak vengeance the right way, the clever way, as she'd first decided was best.

She'd go into it with her eyes open and her head clear. Control was key. She wouldn't be blinded by anger like before. And if she could help it, she'd recruit no one's help in her fight this time around.

'Is everything all right?' the Irishwoman asked fretfully when they returned to the house.

Laura glanced to Millicent then nodded. 'Aye, Bridget. Aye, it is.'

At least it would be.

Chapter 25

OVER THE COMING weeks, Laura threw herself fully into the business. It offered her the distraction she needed, now more than ever before; she shuddered to think what she'd do without it.

She hadn't yet given Edwin an answer. He'd called to her house twice since putting forward his proposition but each time she'd pretended not to be present. Still, she wasn't entirely sure what her answer should be. Loath to hurt him with an outright refusal and too mixed up to know if she'd ever be in a position to accept, she'd taken to avoiding him; she hated herself for her cowardice. Of course, she was fond of him, but marriage? So much had changed since her arrival here. She'd been so adamant back then that she'd never wed again, and then Nathan had come along . . . She hadn't made a mistake with him, not in the long run, had she? Who was to say that giving Edwin a chance wouldn't yield similar satisfactory results? Would becoming his wife be so bad? And yet . . . The conflicting thoughts nagged at her continually.

Then there was young Millicent Figg and her uncle. Laura agonised in silence, imagining day and night – particularly the nights – what she was suffering alone in that house. Could the girl endure it until a solution presented itself? Would Ambrose stick to not touching her? He'd put his hands on *her*, after all, had crushed her with his weight and grabbed her between the legs during that last encounter before she'd left for Ebenezer Court, hadn't he? Would he up his depraved game and begin the same with Bridget's niece?

Yet what could Laura do? Millicent had begged from her her solemn vow that she'd do nothing for now. She couldn't go back on her promise. To do so would be to lose the trust Millicent had put in her completely. She couldn't risk that, couldn't be seen to let her down as well.

The baby steadily growing in her womb was another frequent cause for concern – albeit, Laura suspected, a stress she was making for herself unnecessarily. Though the sickness was, thankfully, abating with each passing day, it also brought her closer to meeting the new person she and Nathan had created; the thought of motherhood both excited and terrified her in equal measures. Would she prove good enough? Would it be healthy, survive? And on, and on.

As for Daniel . . . Daniel had taken a piece of her heart that she'd never get back. With well-meaning pressure from Joyce and Bee, a date for his and Lizzie's wedding had been set: the fifth day of September. Laura just prayed she'd be too large with child by then to attend. It had taken everything he had to see her married to another – she, on the other hand, hadn't the strength for that, she was certain. More than anything else, her crippling guilt towards Lizzie was by far the worst thing. That poor, sweet lass deserved so much better than her for a friend. How she'd cope afterwards, living side by side in the court with the newly-wed couple, she refused to dwell upon.

The women's hard work paid off and, towards the end of the next month, they were in a position to pay back Daniel the money he'd loaned them in setting up. Though initially he was reluctant to accept it, insisting they hold it off a while longer and to pool it back into the business, that he was in no rush for it just yet, Laura and even Lizzie had been adamant. Recognising their desire to feel independent and understanding their need to see they were making a success of things, he relented. That he was proud of what they had accomplished so far was clear to see. The sense of achievement was immense.

''Ere, taste that, tell me what you think.'

Pausing in her task of washing up the mixing bowls, Laura took the small square of cake from Lizzie and popped it into her mouth.

It was a bright but chilly mid-April day and the two women were, as usual, in her kitchen, working on their products. Only today's cake was proving a more difficult task than either had encountered so far in their new career. Getting this right was important, could add a whole new direction to their business and profits, and they were determined to see it happen.

Sighing in pleasure, she closed her eyes. 'Eeh, lass, it's heaven.'

'Aye? You're sure the flavouring's not too overbearing? Now be honest.'

'Nay, you've got it just right with this batch. It's delicious, it is, really.'

Lizzie blew hair from her hot brow and laughed in relief. 'Thank the good Lord for that. I were worried for a while there that we'd have to turn the order down.'

'I had every faith in thee, as ever.'

'Right, then. Let's get started.' Grinning, Lizzie sprang

from her seat with fresh purpose. 'Pass us one of them bowls across, love, and I'll get another mix on t' go for the first tier.'

After sampling their wares from the market, an impressed trader's wife with the shillings to spare had approached them yesterday to ask if they did outside catering – Laura and Lizzie hadn't known what she meant at first, and the woman had gone on to explain. Her son was soon to be married and she wanted to surprise the couple and guests alike with a unique wedding cake in the style of that designed for the Prince and Princess of Wales, which had been the talk of the empire a decade earlier.

She'd seen the creation in a newspaper at the time and had never forgotten it – would it be beyond the women's capabilities? she'd wanted to know. Was it possible they could pull off a replica, albeit on a more modest scale – from her descriptions? Of course, without the royal price tag and at a fraction of the cost? she'd hastened to add.

After a private discussion, an elated Laura and Lizzie had agreed to take on the order, certain they could find spare time to fit it around their usual bakes. Arriving home from Smithfield's, they had got started right away. After numerous attempts, during which they had stressed and fretted they had bitten off more than they could chew, trial and error had paid off – they were finally on the right track. Now, their excitement had returned and, with renewed vigour, they got back to work.

When, days later, the customer came to collect it from the stall, her mouth fell open in surprised delight. For several minutes, she circled it in silence, taking in every detail. Then she gazed from Laura to Lizzie in gratitude and there were clear tears in her eyes.

'You've more than exceeded my expectations. Such talent! If not the empire, it will be the talk of the district, I'm sure. Thank you, truly.'

She wasn't far wrong – it was, in a word, stunning. The whole court had gathered around to marvel at it this morning upon its completion – the women had toiled throughout the night to get it finished. Laura and Lizzie, bursting with happiness, had accepted their neighbours' praise with exhausted smiles. It had been a hard slog but worth it, they both agreed.

Of course, it was significantly smaller than the five-foot wonder presented to the royal couple. And theirs was more simplistic in design as, without a visual representation of the original, they had had to guess at its intricacy. Nonetheless, the three-tiered creation, elaborately iced and decorated and festooned with delicately shaded roses and orange blossom, was a work of art, and they were inordinately proud of it and themselves.

'If I never see another wedding cake, it'll be too soon,' Lizzie announced with a chuckle as they watched the thrilled woman leave.

Smothering a yawn, Laura nodded agreement. 'Well, besides your own, that is.'

'Hm.' Lizzie shrugged. 'Nay, I don't think so. I don't think I'll bother.'

'Oh. I see, well . . . you know best, I'm sure,' said Laura awkwardly, not quite knowing how to respond to this and her friend's dismissive air. 'Everything *is* all right, ain't it, lass?' she hazarded to ask after some seconds.

Staring off with a faraway look, Lizzie nodded slowly. 'Aye. Everything's just fine.' Then, as she was wont to do of late whenever anyone mentioned her upcoming wedding, she swiftly changed the subject. 'So, how did we do in t' end, brass-wise, love?'

Laura wondered if she should attempt again to press the matter but decided against it. It really was none of her business and, besides, if Lizzie wanted to talk about it with her, she'd have done so by now. 'We've made a clear profit, aye. Not much of one, I grant you, but this could be just the beginning. Hopefully, if we get more orders like the last on top of what we're already fetching in on t' regular cakes . . . the money will soon start rolling in.'

'You reckon?'

'I do.'

'Eeh, who'd have thought it? We've come a long way from scrawling letters in t' centre of simple sponges, ain't we?'

Laura laughed softly. 'Aye.'

'Thinking on it, mebbe we should have asked her for her son and future daughter-in-law's initials – we could have included them. Carved them around the edging, like, aye. Would have been a nice touch, that. Aye, well, summat to think about next time, eh?'

But Laura had stopped listening. Gasping for breath, she staggered back in sudden realisation. 'My good God . . .'

'What is it, love?' Lizzie rushed to put an arm around her shaking form. 'Is summat wrong? The babby . . . ?'

'Nay. The babby's fine. I'm fine, I . . . I'm sorry. I have to go.'

'Go? But love, what—'

'I'm sorry,' Laura repeated, wrapping her shawl around herself. Without another word, she picked up her skirts and hurried away.

How had she not made the connection before?

Having set off at a run the moment the train hissed

into Bolton station and having hardly stopped for breath since, Laura was weak-kneed with exhaustion when Breightmet eventually appeared on the horizon. Sucking in air, she slowed her pace, but her gaze remained fixed on the strip of green hills straight ahead.

Her dreams. Adam and Amos's whisperings. A.C. and L.T. A.C. and L.T. Over and over . . .

It now made perfect sense.

It was almost as if they had been trying to warn her, to guide her . . . Of course, Father wasn't aware of the money's existence in life; did a soul develop an all-knowing sense in death? Had to. As for Adam . . . He'd wanted to help her find it, too, must have. Was this his way of saying sorry – compensation, almost – for all he'd put her through? Would it *really* be there?

She purposefully skirted Red Lane, the quarry and Dotty's and all that went with it, and headed towards Breightmet Fold, where she and Adam had dwelled throughout their marriage.

The small farmer's field adjoining the cluster of homesteads where stood their former cottage looked exactly as it always had. She peered out towards its border and the clump of aged trees. Then she was running again, knew she'd solved the mystery, *knew* she was right, had to be.

Then there they were.

A smitten couple's initials from long ago. Before they were wed and the future promised her the world. Before he revealed his true self and everything changed. A.C. and L.T. engraved in the trunk of a broadleaf tree.

They used to go walking around here, her and Adam. They would picnic, just the two of them, would sit beneath the boughs' canopy, laugh and kiss, discuss their hopes and their wishes for the rest of their lives

330

together. The day she'd accepted his proposal, he'd scrawled the letters in the bark with a small knife from his pocket, cementing their union in nature's hold for ever. They stood out clearly still, as though they had been put there only yesterday.

Laura traced her fingers over them. She thought of all that had been and all that had gone wrong and shed a tear. Then she stooped and scanned the tree's base.

She found it in seconds. A tin wedged in a hollow, concealed from the unsuspecting eye by tall grasses. She eased it out of its wooden refuge, put it under her shawl and walked away.

Arriving back in Manchester, Laura headed straight for home. She climbed the stairs and made for the small chest by the window, where she hid the metal box under the folds of clean bedding in a drawer. Then she set off back to the market.

'Love! Eeh, I were that worried.' Lizzie hurried from around the stall to greet her. 'What became of thee? Why did tha rush off so earlier? You sure it ain't the babby? Nowt's wrong?'

'Nowt's wrong,' Laura assured her with a quiet smile. 'I came over a bit poorly sick is all. Fresh air and a lie-down have set me right again.'

'Tha should have stopped put at the court,' her friend chided. 'I'd have managed here.'

'No need, lass. I'm all right, now.'

'Well, if you're sure . . . there's a customer over there wants serving . . . if you'll see to her whilst I tidy up the stock . . . ?'

That night, as Ebenezer Court slept, Laura lay in bed staring at the chest's shadowy outline through the darkness. Finally, as the first fingers of new daylight were touching the sky, she rose and padded across the room.

After retracing her steps, she lit the stub of candle on the side table. Then, sitting cross-legged, she opened the tin and tipped its contents on to the counterpane in front of her.

Ten minutes later, she slipped the find back into the drawer with shaking hands.

Thoughts frozen, mind numb, she returned to bed.

Chapter 26

'I JUST CAN'T believe it. I can't.'

'And why ever not? Didn't I say there would be more orders?' Smiling, Laura passed Lizzie's filled cup across and trained the teapot on her own.

'You did, aye, but . . . Eeh, love. I can't believe it,' her friend said again in wonder, and they both laughed.

A guest at the wedding of the trader's wife's son for whom they had made the royal replica bake had approached them earlier to ask if they would create one similar for her soon-to-be-married daughter. If she was happy with the product, she'd be sure to use them again for another daughter's birthday cake, she'd promised. Things were moving swiftly – business was definitely on the up. Lizzie could hardly contain herself.

'I'll fetch in our Mary to help us this time, shall I?' she suggested now. 'It fair killed us last time trying to do it all ourselfs – what d'you think?'

Laura agreed. 'That's a good idea, aye. We could make it a regular thing, if your sister stands up to muster.'

'Eeh, us taking on staff.' Lizzie chuckled in awe of their success. 'We're going places, us, love. We are that. In fact, I've been pondering . . . Nay, forget it.'

'Go on,' Laura urged, warmed by Lizzie's growing ambition. You'd never have believed she was the same woman who had been too terrified not so long ago to even contemplate giving their venture a try. 'What had you in mind?'

'Well . . . A shop. A proper one, like.'

'Our own confectioner's?'

Lizzie nodded then pulled a face. 'It's a daft idea, in't it?'

'Nay,' said Laura quietly. 'Nay, it's not.'

'Only you see premises to let all t' time and, well, if business keeps up the way it is . . .'

'And my kitchen's hardly roomy, is it? And if we were to take on Mary . . .'

'It'd be more cramped still,' Lizzie finished for her, her enthusiasm mounting. 'Happen, in time, if we saved really hard, we could see about renting summat. Just think of it, all that space. And we could set out everything in t' window all nice, like. That would get the cakes noticed better, draw in more sales. We could take on extra orders on t' side, as we are now, mebbe even employ a couple more hands besides my sister when things really pick up.' She stopped for breath and grinned. Then: 'Even Frank reckons it's a sound idea.'

That the market trader's name had cropped up didn't surprise Laura – every conversation you had with Lizzie of late she'd inadvertently fit his name into it somehow. Had Lizzie's fondness of him grown into something deeper? she mused, as she'd frequently found herself doing of late. But she adored her fiancé, didn't she, had since being a young lass? Besides, as with Daniel, Lizzie would never go back on her word, whatever happened, was too decent a person, Laura was certain.

''Ere, one day, we might even *own* our very own confectioner's,' her friend continued. 'Mebbe a string of them all over Manchester . . . Fancy that.' Rolling her eyes, she let out a guffaw. 'Aye, in our ruddy dreams, eh, love!'

Laura laughed along, though, inside, she was secretly trembling with excitement. That her friend had had the idea, too! But no, what was she thinking? She'd talked herself out of it, had she not? Throughout all those sleepless nights and right into the mornings, she'd told herself she couldn't touch that haul. It wasn't hers to spend. But oh, imagine . . .

No. It could never be. Yet what *was* she to do with it? It couldn't stay buried up in her bedroom for ever. Why had she even fetched it here? She should have left the tin and all it represented where it was. Every cursed thing that had gone wrong in her life stemmed from that money. It was tainted, evil. She wanted no part in it; not now, not ever. No good could possibly come from it.

She was still agonising over what to do later as she walked the few yards to Joyce's house for dinner. If she was honest, she'd have preferred to stay at home with her troubled thoughts, but her mother-in-law had been insistent – it was her way of making sure that Laura got a proper meal inside her; she was convinced she wasn't eating right, what with her working every hour God sent – and she hadn't the heart to turn Joyce down.

As the three of them tucked into rabbit pie Laura tried her best to make small talk with mother and son, but it was useless; she couldn't turn her mind to anything but Lizzie's words and the money sitting in the drawer across the way. By the time the meal was finished and Joyce left to go and fill the kettle at the pump for a last cup of tea, Laura was at her wits' end; she turned to Daniel, saying in a rush, 'I need to speak with thee, lad. Will you come to mine after when it's quiet?'

'What's afoot?'

'Please, not here. I must see thee alone.'

Hearing his mother returning, he nodded, frowning, and Laura breathed a sigh of relief. God willing, Daniel would know what to do.

She was sitting darning by her own fire later, though with only half her mind on the task, when the tapping came at the door. Flinging the sock she'd been mending into her sewing bag, she rushed to open it.

'Hello, lass.'

'Oh. It's thee.' Her face fell. No amount of trying could bring the semblance of a smile to her lips.

'Can I come in?'

'Well, now's not really a good time . . .'

'Please, Laura.'

Inwardly wincing at the hurt lurking behind his eyes, she nodded. Holding the door wide, she let Edwin Howarth inside.

'Tea?'

He shook his head.

'Please, sit down,' she said after a long silence, and he pulled out a chair at the table. She did likewise then trained her eyes on her clasped hands in her lap.

'I've called a few times since . . . but ain't been able to catch thee in.'

'Sorry,' she murmured.

'I know it ain't proper to drop by so late in t' evening, only I figured I'd have more luck this way.' He shifted uncomfortably in his seat. 'We need to talk, lass.'

'Aye.'

'Have you given thought to my offer?'

She'd done barely anything else. She nodded.

'And?'

'I don't know.'

336

His swallow was audible. He blew out air loudly. 'Well, least it's not an outright nay.'

'I need more time, Edwin.'

'How much more?'

'I don't know, I just . . .' She lifted her eyes to his with a sigh. 'I don't love thee. And if you were to be honest, you don't love me neither, not really. It's companionship you seek and, if I *were* to agree to marry thee, it'd be for the same reason. It works for some couples, aye, I'm sure, but I've come to realise it's not for me. I can't live like that, I can't, for it's not enough. If ever I wed again, it must be for love. D'you see?'

'Aye,' he admitted dully after some moments. 'I understand.'

'I'm so sorry, Edwin.'

'Ay, now. Eeh, come here.' He put his arms around her and held her close. 'Don't you dwell on it no more, you hear? It were but a silly owd man's wishful dreaming is all.'

'You really don't hate me?'

'Nay, nay!'

'But I've messed thee about summat rotten, and for so long, I have, I—'

'And now you're being honest and have had the decency to put me from my misery. I blame thee not. It were a selfish thing I did, putting thee in such a situation as that.'

'We can still be friends?' she asked, savouring the comforting feel of the fatherly embrace, so very much like Amos's.

'You just try and stop me.'

'Eeh, Edwin.'

Soon afterwards, standing on the step waving the coal merchant off, she spotted Daniel leaving his house.

She let him in and, after closing the door, turned to see him rooted in the centre of the kitchen, his face a picture of misery. She walked towards him and he watched her from beneath hooded lids, his shoulders hunched as though in dread of what was to come.

'That was Edwin Howarth just now.'

The man in front of her didn't respond.

'He wanted an answer to his proposal. I . . . I turned him down.'

'Laura . . .' Daniel closed his eyes. 'You'll never know what this means to me. Lass, I can't, I must . . .'

She tried to resist, but her soul cried out for him just as ardently – going against all she'd sworn must never be, she let herself be swept up in his strong arms.

He rained kisses on to her neck then pressed his cheek to hers. 'I'm not a weak man, but by God. The struggle to keep my hands off thee . . . it's unbearable.'

'Lad, oh lad . . .'

'The night . . . let me stay. Let me love thee. Say aye. Please.'

One little word. That's all it would take to have what she'd dreamed about, yearned for with every inch of her, for so very long. *One word.*

'Lass . . .'

'And what of the morrow?' she forced herself to whisper. 'You'll leave, shall have to. You don't belong to me, Daniel. You're promised to Lizzie. Nowt can or will change that. Were I to take thee in my bed . . . I'd not have the strength to let thee go. I'd not have the *strength* to live with my sin of betrayal against *her*, the dearest friend I've ever known. We can't. It can never be.'

'But . . . the coal merchant. I thought—'

'I said nay to Edwin for me, Daniel, not you. For I can't wed unless for love, not again.' She nodded when

338

he frowned quizzically. 'Aye, that's right. I didn't love Nathan in t' beginning. Glory be to God, I grew to, but what if I hadn't? What then, if he'd lived and discovered the truth? That's no basis for a sound marriage, is it? I could never put another – put *myself* – through that again.'

'Like me with Lizzie?' He covered his face. 'Why haven't I your backbone? Why can't I be honest with her, call the whole thing off, *be* with *thee*?' Slowly, he lowered his hands. 'I'm going to do it.'

'Do what?'

'Tell Lizzie how I really feel.'

'But . . . you can't. You've a duty, will break her heart, you said so yourself— Daniel, wait!' she cried as he brushed past her and strode from the house. '*Lad!*'

He paused outside Mrs O'Brien's. Turning towards a frantic Laura, who had followed him across the cobbles, he nodded, and she sagged in relief, believing he'd seen sense. Then: 'I must.'

To her horror, she could only watch as, lifting his arm, he rapped purposefully at the family's door.

'Can I speak with Lizzie?'

'Oh, er . . . 'Tis rather late, lad—'

'Please, Bee. It's important.'

The Irishwoman frowned slightly. Then she nodded and stepped aside.

Having followed him in, Laura scanned the kitchen's sea of occupants – spotting Lizzie, she made a beeline for her, skirting past Daniel before he could reach her first. 'Lass . . .'

'What's all this in aid of?' Lizzie looked from one to the other. 'Has summat happened?'

Daniel nodded. 'Aye. You see, it's like this—'

'The shop!' Laura burst out in her desperation, cutting

him off. 'I, I have the brass, lass. I've enough to buy sum-mat outright, I do, and, and me and Daniel couldn't wait to tell thee the good news.' She turned her head to plead at him with her eyes. 'Ain't that right, lad?'

'I . . .' He stared back in stunned confusion.

'Come next door, lass, will thee, and I'll explain,' she told an equally stupefied Lizzie.

The girl and Daniel followed her wordlessly to num-ber five. Inside, Laura set the kettle to boil then sat facing them at the table. She took a deep breath to steady her racing heart, though it did nothing to quieten the lambasting of herself in her head. What had she *done*? However, she'd had no choice, none. She couldn't have let Daniel blurt a confession, shatter Lizzie's heart. She'd plucked at the first thing to come to her mind: that blasted money. There was no going back on her declaration now. She had to tell them.

'Love? Lad?' Lizzie pressed finally, flicking her eyes at them in turn. 'Will one of youse please tell me what in heaven is going on?'

Folding his arms, Daniel raised an eyebrow to Laura in agreement.

She drew in another deep breath and began. She explained about her dreams, of Adam and her father's whisperings of the initials. How Lizzie's passing remark about their latest cake last week had sparked a long-forgotten memory, a possible clue to the mystery of the missing brass, that on impulse she'd journeyed to Bol-ton to find out if she was right.

'You mean you've really found it, the loot them brothers were searching for?' asked Lizzie in wonderment.

Laura nodded. 'Three hundred and fourteen pounds, eight shillings and sixpence.'

'Wha—?' her friend croaked.

'Aye. So there you have it. We'll start looking around for premises next week, if you'd like?'

'If I'd . . . ? Oh, love!' She leapt up, tears spilling, and threw her arms around Laura's neck. 'I'd like nowt more. Nowt at all!'

Gripping on to her friend, Laura hid her face in her shoulder and closed her eyes in despair.

When a still-dazed Lizzie had finished her tea and left for home, Laura put her head on her arms resting on the table and burst into bitter tears. 'See now what you've made me do?' she cried to Daniel.

His voice was low with disbelief. 'You went there alone? Are you insane? Owt could have happened to you, the child. What if Dotty Cannock had seen thee?'

'It didn't. She didn't.'

'Why didn't you *tell* me?'

'I tried to earlier, was desperate for advice. But Edwin turned up, then . . . Why did you do it? Why did you threaten to tell her? And now, to halt your confession, I've gone and promised her summat I can't provide. You've forced my hand in this, you! Just what am I going to do?'

Thrown by her distress, he came to kneel in front of her, his face wreathed in concern. 'What is it? What's wrong? Were what you told Lizzie an untruth?'

'Oh nay. I have the funds, all right.'

'Then I don't understand—'

'I'll not touch it, lad, can't! It's dirty money, that's what. So much destruction has been wreaked for that haul. I don't know why on earth I took it, weren't thinking straight. I want no part of it, nay never!'

'Laura, Laura.' Daniel lifted her up to force her to look at him. 'Listen to me. All that's happened was wrought by the greed of man. The money itself ain't

341

played a part in any of it, it's not. The Cannocks owe thee this. Nay, hear me out,' he told her when she made to argue. 'What that trio put you through. All you suffered at their hands. Then there's the child. Yours and Nathan's.'

She lifted her eyes to his with a frown. 'What about it?'

'They've left that innocent babe in yon belly fatherless. Does it not deserve summat back? Take the brass and use it wisely, make a success of your life, for its sake as well as your own. Call it compensation for the child.'

'No amount could ever be enough! Anyroad, however you dress it up, it's still *wrong*. It ain't the Cannocks' money *or* mine, is it? They stole it, remember?'

'But there's no way of ever knowing who it belonged to or where it came from. The brothers were vague. They mentioned only that their target was miles away. They could have lifted it from anywhere; a different county, even.'

'It's still not right, lad. I feel awful just thinking about taking it.' A thought occurred and she nodded slowly. 'Perhaps I could hand it in to the police. They'd surely be able to trace the owners—'

'Don't talk daft, Laura. It would raise too many questions. You'd have to give them at least some details to work on, and what d'you think would happen? You want to chance them linking the money – linking *thee* – to the Cannocks' deaths, do you? Nay. It's too risky. You've the babby to think of.'

For an age, Laura was silent. Finally, she raised her gaze to meet his.

'Well?'

'All right. All right.'

'You'll use it?'

'I ain't got much choice, have I? Besides, I can't very

well let Lizzie down, now. Mind, if I do agree to this, I need two promises from thee. The first is you must put from your mind telling Lizzie what you almost did earlier. Promise me, lad,' she pressed when he sighed. 'You've made your bed; you can never breathe the truth to her, it'd break her heart.'

His tone was flat with sadness. 'Aye.'

'As for the second thing.' She nodded decisively. 'Before I touch a single farthing of that brass, I need *you* to take a little trip to Breightmet, too . . .'

Chapter 27

HAVING TAKEN A day off from the market, Laura and Lizzie had spent the morning and most of the afternoon trawling Manchester's streets. So far, their search for premises had yielded little success. Either the location wasn't right or the asking price was ridiculously high – the latter issue due more in part to the fact they were women, Laura suspected. One look at them, mere females with no head for business, and most owners immediately thought to try their hand at overcharging them.

'Swindlers, the lot,' Lizzie announced dully as they walked away from yet another landlord who had tried his luck. 'I don't reckon we'll ever find owt, love.'

A despondent Laura reluctantly nodded agreement. 'It makes me so angry that they'll not take us seriously. Ain't our brass as good as anyone else's?'

Our brass. Except it wasn't, was it? She'd stolen it, just as surely as the Cannocks had in the beginning. The thought niggled, but Laura pushed it away with a frown. What was done was done; there was no going back on her decision now. Her vow to Lizzie, that they would realise their dream after all, was more important than mere conscience.

'I bet, had Daniel accompanied us, we'd not be

having such a rotten result,' Lizzie pointed out, and again Laura was wont to concur. 'Actually, love, speaking of Daniel . . .'

'Aye?'

Lizzie glanced sideways at her then shook her head. 'Nay, forget it.'

'Lass? If there's summat tha wants to tell me . . . ?' Laura urged gently, though inside she'd turned into a quailing mess. Her friend knew. She'd overheard her and Daniel through the wall when they had discussed their feelings for one another in Laura's kitchen, that's what this was. Dear God, what was she to say, do? *Lass, I'm that sorry . . .*

'Well, it's just that . . . I, I don't think—'

An almighty bellow pierced the still air, cutting Lizzie's speech short – the women turned in confusion in the direction from which it had come.

'What on earth was that?' gasped Laura, grateful beyond words for the distraction – as was Lizzie, she was quick to notice, if her friend's flush of relief was anything to go by. However, she was obliged to ask, 'Sorry, tha were saying?'

'Nowt, love. It's nowt, honest— Eeh!' Lizzie added on a squeak when the beast-like shout rang out again. 'What *is* that racket?'

'I don't know but, by, it's enough to waken the dead in their graves.'

Their curiosity getting the better of them, they set off at a trot to investigate.

'Mother of God . . .'

It had been six months since she'd seen him last, since she'd sought him out to inform him of her father's passing. The sight of him now conjured up every ounce of her old hatred and more.

'Is that . . . ?'

Choking on a cry, Laura nodded. 'Bridget and Millicent! The swine, I'll *kill* him!'

'Love, nay, you mustn't!' Lizzie said as she made to dash into the fray. 'The babby, remember?'

Though Laura halted, knew she was right, she couldn't contain a growl of frustration. 'But . . . I can't just stand here and do nowt! My uncle will murder the pair if summat's not done, and fast!'

Lizzie bit her lip, then: 'Wait here,' she instructed, before crossing the street.

Ambrose Todd paused in his brutal action of raining blows on to the two women sprawled on the flagstones at his feet to snarl at Lizzie's approach. 'You keep your stinking nose out, whore, else you'll get some of the same,' he slurred with drink-fuelled menace, brandishing a mammoth fist. 'You've seen nowt.'

'I've seen enough, you bullying owd sod, yer!' Lizzie yelled, taking another hesitant step forward. 'Just you leave them be.'

'Ay aye, or what, for that sounds very much like a threat to me?'

Lizzie silently stood her ground and, after a long moment, Ambrose muttered a curse with a dismissive sweep of his arm.

'Oh, I'm bored of this, anyroad. Shift, you snivelling pair of bitches, get out of my way.'

Aunt and niece scrambled from his path and he stalked past, lumbering off in the direction of home.

The moment he'd disappeared Laura rushed to assist the women. Millicent cried harder upon seeing her; Bridget, though dry-eyed, was ashen and shaking uncontrollably.

'Eeh, loves. What has that wicked divil *done* to youse?'

she asked brokenly, helping the Irishwoman to stand whilst Lizzie aided Millicent. 'Are you badly injured?'

'No, no,' Bridget murmured, reaching up to touch a tender spot on her cheek and wincing. 'Nothing's broken, colleen. 'Tis all a misunderstanding, aye—'

'That was no misunderstanding, Bridget. He was pummelling the life out of the pair of youse, for God's sake!' Laura snapped, incensed at her uncle's evilness and his maid's blind loyalty *still*. 'What occurred, at all?'

'An employee from the yard came to the house to fetch Aunt Bridget,' Millicent explained between snatches of sobs. 'He said as how the master had arrived at work roaring drunk and that no one could get sense from him or get him to go home to sleep it off. I'd not let her go alone, and the two of us went to collect him. He left with us quietly enough but, midway, he turned nasty and struck Aunt Bridget. She fell, and I threw myself over her, to shield her, like. His fists were determined to find her, even if he had to get through me to do it, and oh, he'd not stop, Laura. He'd just not stop, just kept punching and punching and punching . . .'

'All right, lass. It's all right.' Laura was trembling with pent-up fury. She put a supportive arm around the distraught girl's shoulders and made to lead her and her aunt towards Ebenezer Court, but the latter pulled back. 'Nay . . . Bridget, you cannot be serious . . . ?'

'I must return, colleen. He'll have a blue fit if I don't. We'll . . . we'll be all right, now. He'll be away to his bed shortly and—'

'Oh, must we, Aunt Bridget?' Millicent's thin face was a picture of misery. 'Can't we go back with Laura and Lizzie, just forra little while at least?'

But the Irishwoman shook her head: 'Best not, love.

Sure, don't fret so. There shan't be any further trouble the day.'

Laura and Lizzie could only watch on helplessly as the two of them bade them a quiet goodbye and sloped off down the street.

'You think they'll be all right, love?' asked Lizzie worriedly.

Laura wiped away angry tears with the back of her hand. 'I don't know. Lord, I hate him so *much* I can taste it.'

Yet what could she do? She couldn't very well storm round there and confront her uncle, could she? She had the child to think about. Nor could she drag his maid and her niece from that hell pit and to the safety of her house with brute force. Bridget just couldn't, or wouldn't, *see*. And Millicent would never leave her aunt with him. There was no way to help, none. That wasn't to say it made the truth any less painful or frustrating.

She'd been in regular touch with them both since Millicent had revealed Ambrose's abuse, had been to meet them every Sunday at church, desperate to know how they were faring. He might have ordered his maid not to seek her out but couldn't control them crossing paths at the Lord's house. Nor did he himself step foot there so he would never know. Bridget, however, was still wary, albeit she did her best to hide it. Though she always greeted Laura with the same enthusiasm, it was clear the strain was getting to her lately: her eyes had lost a little of their usual sparkle and a sadness now lurked behind her smile.

Brave young Millicent had revealed to Laura that her uncle was still paying her unwanted attention but that he hadn't upped his depravity and gone so far as touching. Yet. She insisted she was coping but said that

348

Ambrose's increasing rages were worsening – likely owing to his financial stresses, Laura surmised – and that he was drinking heavily. For how much longer they all could carry on like this, she didn't know. Something would have to give, and soon.

She and Lizzie had begun making their way home when the premises facing her uncle's business suddenly caught her eye; Laura slowed, eyes thoughtful. Motioning to Lizzie to follow, she made her way across.

It was a greengrocer's. A *vacant* greengrocer's. Boasting a double-fronted window and with a house above, it was in a prime position.

A very prime position indeed, Laura thought to herself, glancing to the coal yard. Her mouth hardened. She nodded once.

'Eeh, love.' Lizzie bit her lip uncertainly. 'Is tha sure . . . ?'

'More than I've ever been of owt in my life,' she breathed, eyes like steel.

Laura made enquiries first thing the following morning.

This time, she was prepared – she took Daniel along. As she'd suspected, it proved a much more successful outcome owing to his presence.

The property, they learned, was to be sold by private contract. The owner was relocating abroad and desired a smooth and speedy sale. After taking a thorough look around the place, she and Lizzie sat down to discuss matters.

'It's norra bad price he's asking. The condition and fixtures are sound. It shouldn't take too long or be too much work to convert it into a confectioner's. A few ovens and a new sink in the area out back that will be the kitchen, shelving space in the main room to display

349

the cakes . . . I think that'd do us just fine for now. As for the four rooms upstairs, well, they're ready to move into right away. So, lass? Are you happy for us to go ahead?'

Lizzie laughed in rapturous joy – she'd fallen completely in love with the shop the moment they stepped inside. Then her radiant smile wavered and she released a small sigh. 'Love, about its location . . . Are you absolutely certain you're not for regretting it? Your uncle—'

'Shall be sick with rage and envy and disbelief . . . And I'm going to enjoy every damn minute of it,' Laura told her with quiet passion. 'But it's not just about revenge, lass. It's our dream, remember, becoming a reality. It *is* perfect. Better than owt else we've looked at. It's like . . .' She took her friend's hands and squeezed them and her voice was thick. 'It's like it's meant to be, you know?'

'Aye.' Lizzie's own eyes were bright with deep emotion. 'Oh, Laura, we're really doing it?'

'We really are.'

'Eeh, love!'

'Right, then. Let's go and tell them we've made our decision, shall we?'

Daniel called on Laura that evening and she told him of the news. She explained that she was going to ask Edwin Howarth to look over the legalities and terms of the contract before they signed anything; to her relief, Daniel showed no sign of displeasure at this, instead was quick to agree.

'I trust his expertise,' she told him. 'He has a good head for business, after all.'

'He'll be willing to offer advice, though, d'you think, after . . . ?'

Laura looked away. However much she told herself she'd made the right choice in turning the marriage proposal down, she couldn't help but feel a stab of guilt to think on it. 'Aye. He said he'd like us to stay friends, and I'm glad of that. If he reckons all looks well and good . . . then we'll go ahead and the shop will be ours.' She shook her head. 'Can tha believe it, though, lad? I still have to pinch myself this is even happening.'

'He ain't going to like it, Laura.'

'Ambrose Todd? Aye, I know.' A devil's smile crept across her features when Daniel grinned. 'I can't wait to see his face when he finds out.'

'It's your chance to get back at him once and for all. And what a way you're going to get to do it. Success: it's the best type of revenge, aye.'

'This *is* for Lizzie, though, an' all. It's the least I owe her,' she added in a whisper, not daring to look at him, lest he spied the longing she still and always would harbour for him. 'I can't wait to buy her all the equipment she needs. Proper stuff, mind, from the best stores, that she's allus hankered for – for years, I'm guessing. She's going to be so happy.'

'And you?'

His question threw her. She frowned. 'What about me?'

'Will you be happy, Laura? I mean, *really* happy?'

She swallowed hard and looked away. ''Course I will.'

Continuing quietly, he counted on his fingers as he spoke: 'Aye, you're soon to make Lizzie's dream reality. And today, you mentioned it's your wish that them rooms above the shop are to be for Bridget and her niece, with jobs downstairs thrown in. That if they've a safe dwelling of their own and secure positions, they'll be able to free themselves of that swine's clutches.'

'Lad?'

'You even asked me a few weeks ago to trek to Breightmet, insisted I post some of that brass through Dotty Cannock's door, that you'd not touch a penny else,' he went on, tapping a third finger. 'You felt sorry for her, after everything, couldn't help it. I can just picture her now, cackling with glee at the discovery, not that she deserves it.'

'What's your point?'

'My point is, when will you do summat for thee? Just once.'

'But I need nowt, have everything—'

'*Every*thing?' he insisted, eyes creasing.

Tears stung. She blinked rapidly. 'Daniel . . . please don't.'

'You know, don't you, now and always, you've only ever to say the word and I . . .' He dropped his head then, on a painful sigh, rose to his feet. Stooping, he pressed the most tenderest of kisses to her brow. '*Carpe diem*,' he whispered, before turning and leaving the house.

'But it can never be ours to seize,' Laura mouthed to the closed door.

Chapter 28

AMBROSE PAID THE shop across the way little notice. As was usual, he was barely ever at his yard and, when he was, he was either the worse for drink or too consumed with his own problems to focus on anything else. This suited Laura. Out of sight, she'd watch his comings and goings from the confectioner's window, a grim smile at her mouth.

The day he'd launched his barbaric attack upon Bridget and Millicent she'd been too consumed with horror and fury to pay his appearance heed; now, however, she was seeing him properly and she was shocked by the change. He was tired-looking and dishevelled, smaller somehow, his shoulders stooped under the clear weight of his crippling worries.

Nor had he finished reaping what he'd sown.

Oh no, not by a long chalk. And she knew not a shred of remorse.

As Laura's belly grew, so, too, did the improvements inside the shop, and the conversion was fast approaching completion. And still, she was managing quite well to slip in and out each day to check on the progress unseen; her uncle hadn't the slightest inkling. Even Bridget and Millicent were unaware of her new venture – and its locality. Though she saw them at church, she remained tight-lipped. The least they knew for now, for their own sakes, the better.

By June, they were ready to begin trading. The opening day dawned lead grey with a slight drizzle that showed no sign of abating, but nothing could have dulled their mood. Laura, in particular, glowed with quiet exultancy. The real storm was yet to come and she was ready for it.

At the appointed hour, she and Lizzie crossed the shop floor. Pausing, they gave one another a quick hug. A deep breath, then they turned the small sign to 'Open', threw back the door and stepped outside.

The court's residents were there waiting, every one. They let out a cheer, kissed and embraced the women in turn and offered their congratulations and best wishes for their future success. Then Lizzie led them all inside to show them around and treat them to tea and cake, and Laura was left alone.

Standing in the centre of her doorway, arms folded, she fixed her gaze on the coal yard and her uncle's imminent departure. His drunken tirade, as he screamed instructions and threats to his long-suffering workforce, spilled over to her across the street. Then there he was. He swung through the gates and, before turning for home, flicked his eyes up with a cursory glance in her direction. Then he looked again. And again. His jaw dropped. He juddered to a standstill.

'Lovely morning, ain't it, Uncle Ambrose?'

'You . . .' His gaze took in the fresh new premises behind her. '*You*?'

She smiled.

'Never. *Never!* How?'

The two men whose approach she'd had one eye on from the start reached the yard. Whatever was written on the paper they handed to Ambrose had the power to strip the colour from his face and turn his bones to liquid; he staggered as though he'd collapse. Laura threw him another smile, turned and re-entered her shop.

'My source was right?' asked Edwin when he arrived a short while later. 'The creditors came?'

Laura nodded. 'They came.'

'And?'

'It happened just as you said it would. They issued my uncle with a notice to vacate the premises. His yard's been repossessed.'

'What we discussed . . .'

'Aye.'

'You're still in agreement, lass?'

'I am.'

'Right, then.' He nodded. 'I'll start making enquiries.'

'Edwin?' Laura called when the coal merchant, having turned to leave, reached the door. 'Thank you,' she whispered. 'For everything.'

He gave her a soft wink. 'What are friends for?'

'So what d'you say, then, love? Should we give Widow Jessop's idea a try, see what the customers think?'

Eyes thoughtful, Laura bobbed her head slowly. 'Aye. Aye, it's a gradely idea.'

'I think so. Frank agrees, too. It'll mean setting up a new display for her creations, but I reckon there's room in t' corner over there for the time being. Frank said he'd lend us a hand should we need it.'

Frank Higson. They saw almost as much of him now as they had when they ran the stall next to his on the market. He was forever popping by the shop for one cake or another, or just to chat – Laura had joked to Lizzie that they would have to start charging him rent soon if he kept it up. Blushing, her friend had been quick to change the subject.

'Widow Jessop reckons that bite-size fancies would be best,' Lizzie continued. 'They'll appear more appetising. Besides, kiddies will find smaller pieces more manageable.'

'Aye. We'll talk over the plans with her at the court later.'

'Eeh, look at us, branching out again!' Lizzie laughed, and Laura chuckled along.

Her friend was right. The business, and their confidence in it, was going from strength to strength.

As well as their usual bakes, along with new recipes that Lizzie had practised and soon perfected, they were taking on increasingly more specialist orders. Unique cakes, personally designed for various celebrations, contributed largely to their profits and the women had taken on Mary O'Brien full time to help with demand. Joyce was also at hand if they got too busy. And now, the old herb woman had proposed a new notion: to disguise her bitterest medicines in a much more palatable cake form, which would appeal greatly to youngsters and others with delicate tastes. It was fresh thinking, innovative, and Laura was sure it could do well.

'There he is again,' Mary announced wearily as the time approached noon, jerking her head outside. 'He's getting worse, he is.'

Lizzie went to stand beside her sister at the window, and Laura followed. Through narrowed eyes, she watched the pathetic figure of her uncle gazing forlornly through the padlocked gates of his lost yard.

'Auction day this afternoon, ain't it?' Mary spoke again. 'I wonder who the buyer will be?'

After shooting Lizzie a look, Laura shrugged. 'Who knows, lass?'

''Ere, see, he's crying. See him scrubbing at his tears? He'll not accept it's gone, will he?'

'Come on, you, back to the kitchen and your duties,' Lizzie intervened, ushering her sister away.

Alone, Laura nodded. 'Oh, he'll accept it,' she murmured to herself. 'He will, very shortly. Make no mistake about that.'

By the time Daniel arrived at the shop Ambrose was slumped on the ground outside the yard with his back against the gates. Swigging from a bottle of spirits, he was in a world all of his own, staring into space.

Having sent Mary home, the three of them now sat in tense silence awaiting Edwin. When finally the door opened and the kindly coal merchant stepped inside, they rose as one.

'Well?' asked Laura in a whisper.

Edwin nodded.

'Oh, my . . .' She had to lean against the counter for support. 'Thank you, God. *Thank* you.'

'Ready, lass?' he asked when she'd regained her composure.

'More than I've ever been for anything in my life.'

Ambrose glared at Laura, lip curled, as she crossed the cobbles towards him. 'What the hell do *you* want?'

Either side of her were Daniel and Edwin, whilst Lizzie took up the rear, and she drew strength from their unwavering support. She halted before her uncle. 'I have summat for thee.'

'Huh! I want nowt from a gutter whore like thee, nowt!'

'Oh, you'll want to see this, believe me.' She waved the papers under his nose.

'And what the bugger's that when it's at home?' he asked, squinting at the print.

Laura stooped until their faces were level. Her gaze was cool, measured, her words concise. 'These are the deeds to your coal yard.'

His eyes slowly bulged. 'Liar,' he breathed.

'I'm afraid not, uncle dearest.'

'Nay. 'Tain't possible. Where you found the money for that half-shit shop of yourn, I'm yet to figure out – probably earned it lying on your back, I'll bet. But the yard? You'd have more chance of finding rocking horse shit than the brass for that! You could never afford it, you couldn't!'

'Aye, you're right there. I couldn't, not alone.' She nodded agreement. 'But I could with Edwin Howarth as a partner.'

'Joint ownership,' Edwin confirmed, tapping the deeds. 'Now, if you don't mind, Mr Todd, we'd like thee to shift from our premises. This here's now private property and, if you show your face again, we'll have thee arrested for trespassing.'

'You bombastic owd bastard,' Ambrose whispered incredulously. 'You're as deranged as she is. This is my yard, d'you hear? Mine! I'll break every head here if youse don't get out of my face!'

'Move it, old man,' Daniel growled, his patience spent. 'The only skull getting smashed in shall be yours if you don't get gone right now and take your drunken arse home.'

Pure murder turned Ambrose's face to puce. Then he threw back his head and laughed. 'You reckon so, d'you, young pup? Well, come on, then. Let's see what you've got.' He dragged himself to his knees then staggered up to his full height.

Daniel was shaking with rage – worried that fists were about to start flying, Laura stepped forward. 'Just go *home*, Uncle Ambrose. It's over, d'you hear? It's ov—' The last word died in her throat on a strangled scream when he struck out suddenly, catching her in the stomach with his beefy fist.

The group erupted.

As Daniel and Edwin launched themselves at Ambrose, Lizzie hauled a dazed Laura away towards the safety of the confectioner's.

'Lass . . . The child, lass, he . . .'

'Sshhh. Oh, love.' Lizzie was beside herself. 'You're going to be just fine, you are. Don't fret, don't fret!'

'Bridget? Bridget, it is thee,' Laura croaked, holding out a hand to the woman and girl standing frozen in shock in the distance.

'My aunt insisted we go looking for the master, for he ain't graced home all day,' Millicent babbled, running towards them. Her face was bone white. 'Laura . . . we saw. We saw what he did. The babby, Laura. What about the babby!'

'Go and fetch the doctor.' Lizzie's voice was firm. She sent Millicent on her way with a shove. 'Go, hurry up!'

Inside the shop, Laura allowed her friend to guide her to a chair behind the counter.

'Have you any pain, love?'

'Nay.'

'Is there any movement at all?'

'Nay.'

'Oh 'eck.'

'Why did I do it, Lizzie?'

'Do it? Do what? This is his doing – his! *He* hit out at thee, love—'

'Why did I seek revenge? Why didn't I learn from

what's gone afore?' Laura spoke quietly. She felt weight-less, far away from here, suspended in shock. 'I knew it solved nowt, but I went ahead with it anyway. I bought the yard from under him to get my own back, but he's bested me again. This is *his* final act of revenge. He's murdered my child.'

'You mustn't talk so, for the babby will be just fine, you'll see—'

'Edwin helped me in more ways than one. After look-ing over that contract for the shop for us he happened to mention its closeness to my uncle's failing business, and I broke down. I told him everything, all that my uncle had done, was still doing with poor Millicent. He was enraged. It was he who put the idea to me about buying the yard, said he'd go halves with the cost, and I leapt at the chance.'

'I know, love, I know. But you mustn't dwell—'

'When the yard went to auction, Edwin said he'd do whatever it took to be the highest bidder, and he was. He did it, did it for me. He even asked around weeks ago to find out exactly when the creditors would come to collect their debt from Ambrose. The opening day of our shop . . . it was no accident. I planned that day 'spe-cially, wanted to see him broken, wanted him to see *me* beginning a new venture just as his business went under. It worked. It all went perfectly, just as it should. But that wasn't enough. I needed more, to finish him completely. I took his yard and now he's made me pay for it. The child . . . The *child* . . .'

'Laura, love, please try and save your strength. The doctor will be here very soon.'

'I have to see him one last time. I must. I have things to say, Lizzie.'

Her friend was horrified. 'Nay, you must stay put and wait for the doctor!'

360

'Please. I must speak them. My uncle has to hear.'

Seeing she wouldn't be dissuaded, Lizzie relented with a sigh. 'All right, love. Give me your arm. That's it, lean on me for support.'

Outside, the skirmish was still ongoing – spotting the women emerge from the confectioner's, Daniel yelled across: 'For God's sake, get her out of here, Lizzie!'

'I tried, but she'll not listen, lad!'

'Lift him up.' Laura had halted in the centre of the road a short distance from where the men were scrabbling in the gutter. 'Daniel, Edwin . . . I must speak with him.'

Though they frowned, they did as she bid. Grabbing Ambrose's head, they turned his bloodied face, twisted with evil, towards her. Grunting like a stuck pig, he bucked and thrashed with all his might, but his energy was flagging, and the other men's strength was too much to fight off alone. Finally, he sagged, but his eyes as they bore into hers held a world of pure black hatred.

'Uncle Ambrose.'

'Bitch! You're nobbut a troublesome, devilish little—'

'Keep a civil tongue in your head,' Daniel snapped, shaking him hard.

'You'll hear me out, Uncle Ambrose,' Laura repeated calmly. 'It's over, now. Do you understand? Even should the child . . . even should the child not survive what you just did—'

'Now that, I didn't mean to do,' he blustered, squirming beneath her stare. 'You, you got in the way and—'

'You're a liar. You meant it, all right. But here's the thing: I just don't care any more. Not about the feud, not about the past, not about you. You once said you'd ruin me, and I warned you to be careful I didn't ruin

361

you first. I succeeded not with that. You did it all by yourself, for a fool and his money are soon parted.

'I swore I'd make your life hell. I swore I'd take everything from you, as you did to me. It was your time to suffer. But I have lost in that quest as well as you – I lost my peace of mind, for I allowed hate into my heart. Now, it's finished. I'm on the up and you're on the way down, that much is true. The tables have turned. It was my fight and I'm the victor, but the revenge doesn't taste sweet. For it never ends, does it, if you continue to stoke the flames of bitterness? Well, *I* am putting this fire out. From today, I refuse to waste another second of my life on Ambrose Todd.'

Complete silence followed her speech. Ambrose stared at her for an age. Then he broke contact and lowered his head. Laura breathed easier.

'Wait. I want to say something.'

All eyes turned to see Bridget making her way across. She paused in front of a shocked-looking Ambrose and a single tear rolled down her cheek. In a cracked voice, she addressed him as she'd never done before.

'I can't be as forgiving as your niece, here. I detest you for all you've put me through. I loved ye, sir. I would have waited until the end of time for you, but you used the fact to your own advantage and in the most despicable way. You've belittled me, assaulted me, stripped away my self-respect. You played with my heart and you broke it. Worse of all, you hurt my Millicent. Aye, ye did, I know it,' she told him with a nod when his face flushed brick red. 'I always feared you'd go too far and I'd have to walk away. Now, I feel only relief that it's here. You, sir, are on your own. I put my curse on ye, and I hope it catches up with you before you meet the fires of hell.'

'Figg. You can't leave me. You *need* me. *Figg!*'

'My name is Bridget,' she said over her shoulder, before turning once more and disappearing inside Laura's shop.

'It's over, let him go,' Laura told the men. Then she, too, crossed the road without a backward glance.

'He's gone,' Edwin announced, entering the confectioner's moments later. Then Daniel appeared behind him. And Laura knew, she just knew . . .

He made his way across the floor and paused in front of her. 'Laura.'

Lad . . .

'The child?'

'I don't . . . I don't know.' She motioned to Millicent, standing with her aunt. 'The lass has been for the doctor. He's on his way.'

Biting back tears, Daniel nodded. Tentatively, he placed his hands on her stomach and stroked the neat globe. 'Fight,' he whispered. 'You must fight, little one, you must— 'Ere!' He swivelled his gaze to Laura. 'Was that . . . ?'

'Aye,' she choked, laughing through a sob of overwhelming relief. 'It kicked, Daniel. It kicked.'

'Oh, my love.'

'Oh, lad.'

He rose and wrapped her in his arms, and Laura lost herself in his embrace.

Then someone cleared their throat.

Drawing back and glancing around at the uncomfortable faces, Laura felt the changed atmosphere, the realisation, seep into her soul. *My God.* She shut her eyes, not daring to look. 'Lizzie . . . Lass . . . I . . .'

The slamming of the shop door shattered the air.

'She's gone.'

No.

'Daniel!' Laura cried.

Face pale, he opened and closed his mouth, his guilt absolute.

'Lad, what have we *done*?'

Chapter 29

'I'LL, ERM, I'LL take Bridget and Millicent along to mine, give youse chance to sort . . . Aye, well.' Edwin coughed awkwardly. 'Come along with me, lasses. Let's get a cup of tea and some grub inside you, eh? I've a leek pie in t' oven I made fresh this morn.'

The Irishwoman's voice, low with surprise, followed them out: 'You cook? You're a rare breed indeed, so. Sure, fancy me being waited on for once . . .'

'Bridget seems to have a thing for coal merchants, don't she? It's just a pity she wasted so long on the wrong one,' Daniel said. Yet one look at Laura's distraught expression and his false smile slipped from his face.

'You think this is the time for jokes?'

''Course not, I was just trying to . . . 'Course not,' he repeated on a sigh. He ran a hand through his hair. 'What the hell are we going to do, Laura?'

'I don't know. Actually, yes, I do.' She snatched her shawl from behind the counter. 'We look for her. We find her and we front this out. We, we were just lost in the moment, we'll explain that to her, aye, and—'

'And you'd be lying.'

Laura and Daniel whipped round to see Lizzie

365

standing in the doorway. Frank Higson was by her side. Most surprising of all, she was smiling.

'You love each other,' she added, nodding.

'Lizzie, lass—' began Daniel, but she stopped him.

'It's all right. I think I've allus known. Least I knew you loved Laura. I just needed to see it without doubt, with my own two eyes, that she felt the same. Now I have.' She turned to Laura with that same smile. 'When he took you in his arms, love, the look in your eyes . . . I'm right? You do share his feelings?'

Laura swallowed several times. Then: 'Aye.'

'Right. So why don't we sit and talk this through, the four of us, like adults. Civilised, like. For I've some things I'd like to get off my chest an' all.'

'You're really not angry, lass?' asked Laura when they were seated around the table in the back room.

'Nay, love, I'm not. I'm relieved.' Lizzie looked at Frank, and it was like the sun had come out behind her eyes. 'So many nights I've lay awake, knowing I loved this man right here, fearing there would never be a way for me to be with him. I dreaded us wedding,' she continued, turning to Daniel, 'but I hadn't the courage to break things off. You see, you're not the man for me. I don't love thee, never have, not really. Oh, I thought I did, aye, forra long time. But it were nobbut a young girl's infatuation, a crush, if you like. What I have with Frank . . .' Her sigh was one of sheer contentment. 'That's real. He's everything to me.'

'I don't know what to say,' said Daniel, shaking his head. 'Thank you, lass. Thank you.'

'No need for that, lad. A body can't help who it falls for. Just do me one favour.' Reaching across, Lizzie took both their hands. 'Love each other, always. Be happy. ''Specially you,' she told Laura softly. 'You've had more than your fair share of sadness, but let the day mark an end to all what's passed.'

'Oh, lass.' Laura threw her arms around her neck. 'I don't deserve you.'

'Aye, you do. It's me what's lucky to have our friendship. You've done so much for me, and I don't just mean the shop. I've grown in myself since knowing thee. You showed me I can do anything, follow any dream, if I'm brave enough. Ta, love. Now it's time you did the same. Save, go abroad, *wed*, and to hell with what anyone might say.'

When the new couple rose to leave Daniel held out a hand to Frank, who shook it warmly. 'Look after her, for she's one in a million.'

He cast Lizzie a besotted smile. 'Have no fear of that, lad, I will.'

Alone, Laura and Daniel stood facing each other with tears in their eyes.

'Joyce will give us her blessing, won't she?'

'Mam will want her family's happiness, same as Bee O'Brien. Lizzie and Frank, me and thee . . . and this little one.' He kissed his fingertips and touched them to her stomach. 'There's a brand-new future ready and waiting, for all of us.'

A stir of guilt filtered through her joy. 'Us . . . It's not a betrayal to Nathan, is it, lad?'

'Nay, lass, nay. My brother loved us both. And we'll never stop loving him. Nowt will ever change that. Come here.'

Daniel opened his arms and she walked into them.

'We've been through so much together.'

'Aye.'

'I've suppressed my feelings for thee, ached for thee for so long . . . I, I just . . .'

367

'Lass?'

'I'm afraid it's all going to be taken away from me, as it allus is. I'm . . . I'm afraid to love.'

Smiling, he took her wet face in his hands and pressed his lips to hers in a feathery kiss. '*Carpe diem,*' he murmured.

And Laura did.

A SHILLING FOR A WIFE

Emma Hornby

Sally Swann thought life couldn't get much worse. Then a single coin changed hands.

A dismal cottage in the heart of Bolton, Lancashire, has been Sally's prison since Joseph Goden 'bought' her from the workhouse as his wife. A drunkard and bully, Joseph rules her with a rod of iron, using fists and threats to keep her in check.

When Sally gives birth, however, she knows she must do anything to save her child from her husband's clutches. She manages to escape and, taking her baby, flees for the belching chimneys of Manchester, in search of her only relative.

But with the threat of discovery by Joseph, who will stop at nothing to find her, Sally must fight with every ounce of strength she has to protect herself and her son, and finally be with the man who truly loves her. For a fresh start comes with a price . . .

Available in paperback and ebook now . . .

MANCHESTER MOLL

Emma Hornby

Moll thought she could keep her family safe . . .

Eighteen-year-old Moll Chambers works her fingers to the bone doing all she can to support her family. With an ailing father and a wayward mother, Moll is the only one who can look after her siblings, Bo and Sissy.

But Manchester is an increasingly dangerous place to live, overrun with a ferocious rivalry between gangs of so-called 'scuttlers': young men and women bent on a life of violence and crime. And they have her brother in their sights. Soon even Moll can't protect Bo from the lure of the criminal underworld.

Then the scuttlers looked her way.

When she herself falls for the leader of a rival gang, Moll's choices place her and Bo firmly on opposite sides of the city's turf war.

With her loyalties now torn in two and tragedy lurking round every corner, will Moll be able to rise above the conflict and protect those she loves the most? Or will stepping out with a scuttler spell ruin for them all . . .?

Available in paperback and ebook now . . .

THE ORPHANS OF ARDWICK

Emma Hornby

After a cold, hard winter on the streets, three orphans are about to give up hope when an unexpected turn of events brings them to the doorstep of Bracken House.

Taken in by the firm but kind-hearted cook, the young friends can hardly believe their luck. But behind Bracken House's impressive façade lies a household steeped in troubles and mystery, with residents above and below stairs battling their own demons and dark secrets.

Not everyone is happy with the new arrivals, and soon the orphans' safety is in danger. If they want to stay in the first home any of them have known for years, they must unravel the past and bring hope to the future. Will they succeed? Or will they come to regret ever leaving the mean slum streets they once called home?

Available in paperback and ebook now . . .

A MOTHER'S DILEMMA

Emma Hornby

Minnie Maddox cares deeply for mothers and their babies – she makes a living by taking in unwanted babies and finding them good adoptive homes – and is delighted for her neighbour when she finally becomes a mother after decades of trying. But when the baby dies of natural causes while under her roof, and knowing her neighbour will be devastated, Minnie swaps it with one of the infants in her care.

Now seventeen, Jewel Nightingale knows nothing of her true origins. But, assaulted by her hateful cousin and making the dreadful discovery that she is pregnant, she faces a desperate dilemma. Fleeing her job as a domestic maid, she follows an advertisement to a house in Bolton's dark slums, where a woman promises to help her when the child is born. Little does Jewel know that there's a terrible price to pay . . .

Can she keep herself – and her baby – safe? And what will happen when Jewel discovers the truth about where she came from?

Available in paperback and ebook now . . .